RIPE FOR REVENGE

It's never too late for a new career

To my good friends Chris &
Anne.
(I will see you same place, same
time, same table, same pub)
(For you know what!

By Paul Sak.

Paul Anthony Saker

This is to all the dirtbags out there (you know who you are) who deserve worse than you get.

ACKNOWLEDGEMENTS

Thanks to my wife Carmel for fixing all the stumblings and bumblings in this book and to both her and her sister Glynis for keeping me inspired.

CONTENTS

BREAKING NEWS:

Jackie Ruthers, the notorious casino boss, was found dead in his apartment this morning. He was found by his cleaning lady Anne Vickers shortly after she arrived at his Belgravia flat. Initial reports indicate that he died of a massive coronary. Paramedics were called to attend to the cleaner who, owing to her advanced years, was very distressed by the event. Police do not suspect foul play at this time.

CHAPTER 1

Jim looked up as Harry entered the pub and beckoned him over to the pint waiting for him. Harry sighed as he let himself slide gratefully into his chair. He lifted his beer and silently sent a "Cheers" to his old friend. They both closed their eyes as they each savoured their brew. It was passing with flying colours.

Jim and Harry had been at school together. Sixty years and some had passed since then, but they still found the same things as funny as they did when they were running around the playground dressed in shorts.

Harry put out his hand and gave a dog that had been brought in by its owner a good scruffing behind his neck.

"Hello boy, yeah, you enjoy that, eh?" The dog wagged its entire body in grateful contentment. "Did you hear about those bastards who were running that dog fighting club down in Croydon? They stole dogs from everywhere so they could be used as practice fodder for their own fighting animals."

Jim shook his head. "Fined and let out to do it all over again no doubt. There should be some system by means of which scum like that get shredded. They are no use to society." Both men took a long, thoughtful sip at their beers.

"Should be a special branch of the forces that deals with rat shit like that, outside of the normal ineffective corridors of law. Jeez, I've made my jaw ache, I was clenching my teeth so tight."

"Calm down Jim, you'll give yourself a coronary before you've finished that drink. That would be a right travesty of justice right there."

They both laughed. "Are you well Jim?"

"Why, are you getting scared I might fade away? No chance, I've got bugger all to do but keep fit. My body's in better shape now than it has ever been. I think if I snuffed it, they would have to beat to death the other bits of me that would still be doing sit ups, lunges and God knows what else. It's a waste Harry, I'm like a bloody Ferrari forced to drive forever in a twenty-mile-per-hour zone."

"Yeah, I know what you mean, like a racehorse put out to grass way too early. Once you're over sixty-five, you're expected to start dribbling down your shirt, pissing your pants and talking to people who aren't there. It's funny, but so many of my mates in the army have turned out like that. It's almost like all the fire came out of them when they were in action and there's nothing left anymore."

"But you liked your time in the army Harry, didn't you? Or should I call you Captain?"

"I did, it was a good life, always a roof over your head and a steady job. And fun too, if you didn't wind up with a bullet up your arse."

"Do you miss it, Harry?"

"I miss the buzz. Ready for another Jim?"

"Yeah, bugger it, me parking my arse off here is not stopping anything from getting done. I'm surplus to requirements. You know about Mervyn, eh? They say the poor guy's only got six months left and the last two of those will be spent looking at the ceiling. I saw him the other day, and do you know what scares me the most? He doesn't look sick. Even now, he still looks as fit as a fiddle! We should get him along next time Harry. Poor sod might as well enjoy what time he's got left."

"Yeah, let's do that."

That evening, Jim sat watching the news. He was like a moth to a flame. He hated what he was watching but needed to know what was going on, or, more often than not, what was going wrong. The beers consumed with Harry earlier swirled around like a tempest inside his head along with the wrath stirred up by the information pumped out by the TV. People in power, especially those in possession of that toxic combination of arrogance and stupidity, seemed to hold court in every sector of the world.

Then there was the sector of society Jim classified as "oxygen thieves". Those who were taken to dragging their knuckles on the ground whilst breathing through their mouths, those in possession of room temperature

IQs. It was to this sector of society that his venom was to be unleashed as the news item covered the story.

The pressure inside his emotional boiler was approaching danger level again. He needed to operate the pressure valve – a stern letter to the papers was required. Very few were actually printed, as they tended to incite every kind of wrath known to God upon his targets. His recommendations for correcting the offenders would have made Vlad the Impaler blush. Nevertheless, one would have to be despatched with haste to maintain his sanity. He reached across, opened his laptop and began to type:

I am appalled by the disgraceful scenes in our parks and gardens this weekend. The rubbish discarded by the crowds of revellers is beyond belief. Do these people have no sense of decency at all? Where were they brought up? Did their parents and mentors fail to point out that living up to one's crotch in rubbish is not something we should aspire to? They should be forced to their knees with their hands tied behind them and made to pick up every piece of their rubbish with their mouths before they leave.

He hit the full stop with such vengeance that he thought he may have damaged his keyboard. He sucked in his breath between clenched teeth and reread his letter.

He began pounding again… *And then for good measure they should be made to lick the paths clean until their stinking tongues look like shredded liver. Only in this way will this subhuman slime be less inclined to litter in the future.*

His hand hovered over the keyboard as he heard the doorbell ring. He glanced at his watch. "Who the hell is this, at this time of night?!"

He groaned himself out of his chair and shuffled off to open the door. The elderly lady from No.12 across the road stood there smiling in the rain.

"Hello Doris, what can I do for you?"

"I was wondering if I might ask a favour." She looked up meekly at the downpour.

Jim sighed, "Come in Doris."

"Thank you Jim. It is Jim i'nit?"

"Yeah, the last time I looked. Sit yourself down Doris, do you want a cup of tea?"

"Ooh, yeah, that would be luverly."

Jim went into the kitchen and made a quick cup of tea, bashing the teabag to speed things along. Upon his return, he saw, to his irritation, that Doris was sitting in his chair reading his rant to the newspapers on his laptop. He walked over and closed it in front of her.

"There, do you want some sugar?"

"Nah, I'm sweet enough dearie."

Jim allowed himself a perfunctory smile. "So, how can I help you Doris?"

"Well, I was wondering if you might be able to feed me cat, Archie."

"Feed him? I don't understand."

"Just for a few nights, I've gotta pop out."

"I've never had a cat, do they eat like dogs?"

"'E won't be no problem, 'e's as good as gold me Archie. I'll leave the food out an' everyfink."

He watched as Doris slugged back her tea.

"Mm, that's a nice cuppa that Jim. 'Ere's me phone number in case yer need it. I'll let you know when I'm back."

She stood up to go and rummaged in her handbag. "And 'ere's a spare set a keys for ya. 'E likes 'is supper at abaat five and 'is brekkie at abaat eight. Toodaloo."

Jim took the keys offered to him and followed her to the door. She stepped out and turned around.

"Thanks ever so, Jim, yer very kind. Nice things will 'appen to you, mark my words."

Jim watched as she crossed the road to her house. "I hope so Doris, I do hope so," he sighed.

He went back inside and slumped down in his chair – his again, at last. He looked at Doris's empty teacup. She had moved in about a year ago after her husband had died. Their old house was too big for her apparently. When she moved in, he went and introduced himself, and now and again they would see each other in the street and pass the time of day. It was hardly a close friendship. He wondered why he of all people had been chosen to look after the cat. Was he the only friend she had? The thought made him suddenly sad, and he thought that maybe he should have offered her a biscuit as well. He looked at the number she had given him and dialled it.

"'Allo, Doris speakin'."

"Er, hello Doris, it's Jim, I just wanted to say that your cat will be OK with me."

"Thank you, Jim, I know 'e will."

"Er, yeah, have a good evening, goodbye."

He sighed, looked back at his laptop screen, gritted his teeth once more and signed his letter, "Angry from Wimbledon". It was despatched thus to the editor and, as an afterthought, to Harry as well.

CHAPTER 2

Mervyn stared at the WhatsApp message from Harry. They wanted to get together with him for a drink. He knew he'd go but was dreading it. The outpouring of sympathy or even worse the avoidance of the subject. Everybody desperately trying not to mention his impending death. He knew they meant well but he couldn't come to terms with it himself and was not sure how he would behave in company.

That same morning, Jim was also battling to come to terms with his situation. He had been invited to join the daily coffee gathering at a café in town by another elderly neighbour, Tom.

"It's really nice Jim, people of our age get together to have a good ole natter about stuff, and the pastries are lovely," Tom had told him.

Jim arrived at the allotted café and saw Tom wink at him encouragingly as they sat down. Jim grinned weakly.

A minute later, another soul toddled in and sat down with them. "Sorry, I'm a couple of minutes late today," he said patting his knees. "Who's this then?" he wanted to know, looking straight at Jim.

"This is my neighbour, Jim. I told him about what we have going here, and he couldn't wait to see for himself."

Jim squeezed another grin out, hoping it didn't look too much like a grimace. He realised he had failed as the man turned his head to one side.

"Ooh, I know that look. The ol' joints seizing up a bit? I suffer from lumbago, had it fer years."

The man turned to Jim's neighbour. "What about your septic boil Tom? How's that coming along?"

Then began a detailed description of carbuncle squeezing, lancing and gore. Jim let his mind wander, giving it a good push into any direction other than the conversation he was party to. He was grateful that the new visitor had mentioned that his neighbour's name was Tom. Disturbingly, Jim could not recall ever knowing the man's name; maybe Alzheimer's was not as far away as he thought.

His attention was drawn to the arrival of another man at the table. As the new man sat down, he was reminded by Tom that he was six and three quarters of a minute late. To Jim's horror, it was not long before the new arrival's ailments were up for discussion as well. He had apparently succumbed to senile warts. His friends were at pains to ensure that Jim had all the details. He assumed, quite rightly, that little else was discussed by his friends over their daily coffee and pastries.

By the time said pastry had arrived, they were into the details of how he had tried to pick the warts off, but it had apparently not worked out well.

Jim had had enough; he stood up suddenly, leaving his pastry uneaten, and startling his companions as he did so. "Er, um, I'm sorry, I just remembered, I need to be somewhere." He waited anxiously for some complaint or chastisement but received only knowledgeable nods from the others.

"Yeah, it 'appens, eh? My little Emma reckons I should wear nappies."

"You know, I thought it was Tuesday all mornin'."

"It is Tuesday," Jim pointed out, and instantly regretted it.

"Yeah, see, that's what I mean!"

The others all began to speak at once about how Tuesdays were never good days, but Jim had escaped through the coffee shop door and was enjoying the icy air, cleansing the memory of the past ten minutes of his life.

He decided not to catch the bus but to walk home. He needed to be away from his fellow humans for a while. He let his thoughts march on. What did most of his fellow humans do for the common good? Sure, there were good people out there, but the majority of the human race was seemingly hellbent on destroying the place. Forests burning, weather spinning out of control, famine, contagions, all manner of things that Mother Nature was trying to correct. The problem always came back to same thing – there were too many humans. The only thing they ever did successfully was breed. The poorer they were, the more children would be spawned. He let himself shrug – what could he do about it? He had never spawned anything. Not for want of trying, he reminded himself.

His thoughts went back to Trudy, his late wife. They had met at university. He, the engineering student, a practical pragmatist; she, the ethereal philosophy student. They hardly agreed on anything in the real world, but within the magical garden of their relationship, they were the perfect match. Their graduation ceremony was combined with their marriage and although children were denied them, they filled the vacuum adequately with dogs of all sizes and temperaments. After Trudy died, the last two dogs followed her within the year. He had been wifeless and dogless for almost two years now.

As he looked up, he saw a plastic bag and paper cup get tossed out of a passing car. He walked over and picked them up and placed them in a bin. A little further along, he noticed that the car had stopped, and the driver had gone into a house. As he approached the car, he became aware of his keys in his pocket. The thought came to him in an instant and shocked him badly. The mere thought of doing something wrong was abhorrent to him. But with each step, the rapture of the act became more and more intoxicating. He felt dizzy with exhilaration as the keys gouged a furrow in the paintwork from the back to the front of the car as he passed. Looking straight ahead, he kept going at the same steady pace and turned the corner homewards, pocketing his keys as he did so.

His heart was racing badly. But what was so much more alarming was the absolute thrill that was coursing through him. He searched for fear, guilt or shame but found only deep enduring satisfaction.

CHAPTER 3

When it came time to feed the cat, Jim went into Doris's house with some trepidation.

"Hey, puddie, puddie."

He looked around the kitchen and saw the cat food next to a bowl. He scooped it out and placed it on the floor.

"Here puddie, puddie."

Jim had the intense feeling of being watched. He became aware of a cat looking at him from around the corner of a cupboard. He couldn't make out if the cat was wearing a curious expression or a furious scowl. He assumed it was probably the latter.

"Look, puddie, I don't want me to be here anymore than you do, but your mum's away and you, being devoid of an opposable thumb, are not in a position to open any packages yourself. So if I were you, I wouldn't be too picky."

The cat held its ground behind the cupboard, whilst it considered the situation.

"Well, there it is, take it or leave it, I'm off."

CHAPTER 4

The following day, Jim searched through the letters to the editor. He assumed that the letter had been binned like the rest of his tirades. Nevertheless, he persisted and on the third day he was amazed to see a letter addressed to "Angry from Wimbledon".

The letter was entitled "Angry from Wimbledon, time to get Serious". Jim read the letter slowly, with a sense of wonder…

Angry from Wimbledon is right, how much longer do we have to endure the rubbish in the parks? Where can decent people now go for a pleasant walk? Why do we have to overlook the rubbish and the rubbish that put it there? Surely there is another way, a better way forwards?

It was signed *Disgusted from Skegness.* Jim frowned and shook his head. His letter must have been printed after all!

He went to the shed where all the old newspapers were stacked awaiting a firelighter and other duties called upon in the normal course of life. He selected the ones following the date of his own letter. He scanned the letters page, nothing. He searched every other page, nothing. He checked the dates to see if he had missed one, they were all there.

He scratched his chin – there must be another paper or publication where his letter had been printed, but why then did the reply arrive in this paper? Was it coincidence? It was bloody infuriating, that's what it was. He wouldn't get any rest until he got to the bottom of it. He thought about sending an email but suspected that the receiver would be jobbed only with the task of vetting suitable letters for publication and not with solving mysteries. The only way to not get fobbed off was to speak to someone. He checked the number and dialled.

He heard a voice answer his call: "Wimbledon Warrior, how can I help you?"

"Hello I need to talk to someone about a letter I wrote that wasn't published."

"I'm sorry sir, it really is at the editor's discretion which letters get published."

"Yeah, I know, but somebody replied to that letter, how can that happen?"

"I'm sorry sir, I don't understand?"

"No, neither do I, that is why I am calling."

"I'm sorry?"

"I know you're sorry, you've told me three times already."

"I'm sorry sir, I'm just trying to help."

"That's four times."

"I'm sorry?

"Five."

"Sorry?"

"Six. I can keep this up all day – believe me, I have way more time than you do."

"I'm sorry sir, is this a prank call or a joke of some kind? There are other people waiting on the line, I really must help them now, I'm afraid."

"Seven. Please put me through to your editor, or put me on hold whilst you talk to your other callers, I don't mind."

"Please hold."

"Thank you for not being sorry agai…" Jim heard pan pipe music straining down the line. Before the first phrase was complete, a recorded voice came on the line: "*We are experiencing high call volumes, please don't hang up, your call is important to us.*"

After the third irritating circuit, Jim mumbled, "Important is it? Right, I'm phoning about an enormous gunfight taking place in the high street, there are at least five hundred people dead, maybe you should send a reporter down there."

"Rawlings, deputy editor, you say there are dead people?"

Jim coughed. "Oh hello, no, no gunfight. I just hate pan pipes."

"Sorry?"

"Oh no, not you as well. Listen, somebody replied to a letter I sent you that you didn't publish. How can that happen?"

There was a pause on the line. "I don't know, I will look into it."

"You will, will you?"

"Could I have your name please."

It's, er, Angr… er Jim Spoonwall, spoon as in runcible, wall as in the Great one of China."

"Thank you Mr Spoonwall, we will take note of your enquiry."

Jim put down the phone and looked at it. "Take note my arse."

He looked out of the window and thought back to the car keying incident. Try as he did, he couldn't find any shadow of regret, just a warm feeling.

He was still enjoying his warm feeling when the phone rang, making him start. "Hello?"

"Mr Spoonwall?"

"Yes, who is this?"

"I'm Disgusted from Skegness."

Jim paused. "How did you get my number?"

"That would be telling. Did you like my reply?"

"What I would like, is to know how you found my letter in the first place and how you know my name?"

"Let's just say, for the time being, that it found me. Did you mean what you said in your letter?"

Jim was suddenly cautious. Was this some kind of witch hunt to track down people prone to violence?

"Look, what I said in the letter should not be taken out of context. I would never take matters into my own hands, do anything unlawful." Jim felt the keys in his pocket and his pulse began to race, had somebody fingered him? "Who are you?"

"Just a concerned citizen like yourself. I don't blame you for being careful, there are so many scam artists around. I can assure you I am not one of them. Look, why don't we meet and have a chat, just compare notes so to speak. Somewhere nice and public, I'm sure you're on your guard. I would be."

Jim remained silent, he was trying to think.

"Look, tell you what, I'll leave it up to you. If you fancy talking to someone who thinks that the justice system has lost its way, give me a ring. You have my number on the phone now. If not, fine, you'll never hear from me again. Goodbye Jim."

Jim stared at the phone, scared that it might burst into life again, but it remained respectfully silent. He glanced through the window, half expecting the police to come screaming up and break down his door, but the street remained quiet.

CHAPTER 5

It was a bright Saturday morning. Early spring had arrived by express delivery and London was bathed in a healing swathe of sunlight that melted away the gloom of March. Jim felt a spring in his step. Despite the odd events of the previous days, culminating in the weird phone call from Disgusted of Skegness, he had slept like a baby.

He was on his way to the pub to meet up with Harry and Mervyn. Normally he would have dreaded it, but for some reason he could not fathom, he felt confident and in control and was actually looking forward to seeing his ailing companion.

As he stepped up to the bar, he saw Mervyn give him an apologetic wave from behind his pint at a table in the corner. Grabbing his own pint, he marched briskly over to his friend.

"Hello Mervyn. I'm not going to ask how you are, I know all about that, so let's just say cheers."

Mervyn smiled and took a long slug. "Thanks, I'd rather not go on about it. Nothing I can do about it is there?"

"There isn't Mervyn. But you can do something with the time you have left."

"What do you mean?"

"Well, most of us have to hang on to our savings, worry about our health, try to eat the right things that usually taste like boiled grass and fucking cardboard and all that bollocks. You don't have to do any of that, do you? You can go do whatever you bloody well like. If you want to eat lobster every day and pack away six bars of chocolate to round it off, who gives a shit? You can stop buying the cheap crap wine that you can afford and buy something you love instead. You can cram in all the things you were too scared of, or too stingy to do before."

"I can see you've been giving this some serious thought, Jim."

"Actually, I haven't. It just occurred to me as I was walking towards you. I didn't see a man condemned to death. I saw a man unchained by life. It was quite a revelation actually. Come to think of it, I've had quite a few of those in the last couple of days."

"Really, like what?"

Jim paused. Maybe he should shut up before dropping himself in the shit. He made his decision, and told Mervyn about his key incident. When he got to the bit about actually gouging the guy's car, Mervyn's eyes opened wide with shock. Jim thought he had gone too far, but then Mervyn let his head roll back and laughed out loud.

"Oh Jim, that is brilliant! Serves the bastard right."

"And you know what Merv? I don't feel one iota of guilt, just this everlasting warmth inside. I can't describe it. It's like something out there is patting me on the back and saying 'Well done'."

"Well, you guys seem to be having a good time!"

They both looked up to see Harry smiling down at them with three new pints in his hand.

"I'm assuming you still drink Doom Bar?"

"I do, but Merv here might be moving on to something more exclusive soon."

Harry gave Jim a disapproving look. "Well thanks for reminding us Jim, that's nice of you."

Jim shook his head. "No, you silly tit, I was telling Merv here that he doesn't have to do anything he doesn't want to anymore, he can go wild."

Harry looked at Mervyn. "How are your kids Merv?"

"Buggered if I know, haven't heard from them in years. Just waiting to get their hands on my house, probably."

"Sell it Merv. Fuck 'em, sell it and spend it. As I said, nothing to lose."

Harry looked down as another dog walked past their table with its owner in tow.

"I see those dog fight bastards from Croydon got a fine and one got three months."

"Yep, gives him time to do some networking with people of similar interests, whilst being provided with free board and lodging courtesy of the British taxpayer. He must be pissing himself laughing." Jim looked over to Mervyn "What you staring at Merv? Judging from your expression, I could have sworn Liz Hurley just wandered in topless."

"I'm just thinking about what you said."

"Get that image out of your thoughts Merv, you'll do yourself a mischief."

"No, you arse, I'm thinking about, you know, doing a bit of what you fancy does you good."

"You're too old for her, you silly old sod."

"Bloody hell Harry, does your mind ever get out of your pants? I'm talking about doing something with my last few months."

They all fell silent as they became immersed in their thoughts. Jim's thoughts went back to Disgusted from Skegness. What was that all about? He told them the story. The consensus was that leaving the situation like a dangling participle was the worst thing he could do.

Jim knew they were right, it would drive him mad. He hated if-only wishes way more than bad mistakes.

And so it was that when they parted company that night, Jim agreed to contact Disgusted from Skegness, see where it led and report back in two days' time. Same place, same table.

CHAPTER 6

Jim punched in Disgusted's number on his phone.

"Hello Jim, what a pleasant surprise. So you've decided to see how deep the rabbit hole goes have you?"

"What?"

"The Matrix when… never mind. Shall we meet? Maybe over lunch?"

"Er, what do you want from me?"

"Nothing, it's what you want from me that matters."

"I don't understand, I don't want anything from you, I don't even know who you are."

"True. But if we meet, that would all change, wouldn't it?"

"What is it you think I'm looking for?"

"Meaning Jim, that's what you crave. A reason to wake up early in the morning, a reason to work a little later in the evening. And in so doing, leave your mark on this world."

"Wait a minute, what does this all cost?"

"Only the time that you are willing to give. Remember, you phoned me. You can still walk away if you wish, it's your call."

Jim looked at his phone (*No "if onlys"… ever*). "OK, you've got me. Where and when?"

CHAPTER 7

Jim walked up to the OXO building on the Thames South Bank. He had seen the restaurant from the river but had never tried it out until now. As he made his way out of the lift and stepped into the foyer, he saw a grey-haired man, about his own age, coming towards him. The man had his hand out. "Mr Jim Spoonwall I presume?" They shook hands and the man showed Jim to a table overlooking the river.

The man looked at him with his head to one side and smiled. "You are not what I expected."

"Who did you expect, King Kong?"

"Jim, I think we are going to get along famously. Jeremy Grant, alias Disgusted of Skegness, pleased to meet you."

"What's Skegness like these days? Last time I was there it reeked of disappointment."

"I would imagine it still does. I've never been there, not sure where Skegness is to be honest. I made it up on the spur of the moment after reading your letter."

"Oh."

"I'm sorry, I've disappointed you. Let's order something to drink. I will try not to disappoint you again."

"Good. So what is this all about?"

"Would I be right in assuming that you are currently frustrated by the careless attitude of certain members of society and the lack of any meaningful consequence for their actions?"

Jim heard alarm bells going off. Somehow, he had been rumbled, someone had spotted him gouging the car. "Look, I'm sorry, I don't know what got into me. I'll pay for the respray."

"I haven't the faintest idea what you are talking about Jim. Can we move on?"

"Er, yeah, suppose so." Jim shifted awkwardly in his chair.

"Let's say, hypothetically, that I could offer you an opportunity to enact the type of punishment you recommended in your letter to those litter louts. What would you say?"

"I would say that it would be breaking the law and I would have nothing to do with it."

"Pity, because that is exactly what I am offering. An opportunity to right some wrongs, to do what our so-called justice system is too impotent to do itself. As you so rightly point out, it is against the law, but that same law allows criminals and lowlifes to propagate under its protection. Have you ever tried getting any police station to take an interest in following up on a case of somebody littering? Probably not, but mete out some corrective punishment to them and see how the law jumps to their defence. Am I making sense?"

"More than you could ever imagine actually. What form does this opportunity take?"

"It takes the form of like-minded people having bonded together to create an organisation that undertakes certain operations. These operations clean up the world when the so-called authorities are incapable or unwilling to do so themselves."

"Like a bunch of vigilantes?"

"Yes, but without the crudeness and lack of discretion. The organisation has some backing. For some of our members, field work is a little rich for the blood so they contribute financially. After all, we all want the same thing at the end of the day – peace and decency from our fellow humans. The authorities don't have the flexibility, we do."

"Are you lot some sort of covert government organisation like that film, um, *Kingsman*?"

"Ha, we'd like to think so, but we are not quite as bona fide, I'm afraid."

"So, what do you do, meet every Thursday for a cup of tea and finger some litter lout to beat up with your walking sticks?"

"Essentially, yes. We identify targets and develop suitable remedies."

"Looks like you have it sussed. Why do you need the likes of me?"

"We need to swell the ranks, get in new blood."

"Let's say that I was interested, hypothetically of course, what happens next?"

"Well, we go through the targets on the file and single one out that you would feel comfortable dealing with. Then you go into action."

"What, all alone, no back-up or training?"

"Not unless it's necessary."

"So have you got this list on you or what?"

"No, I would prefer to start with one on your list, presuming you have one."

"I do, the PM is at the top and then most of his cabinet just below that."

"Hah, yes, but maybe we should start with a project that is a little less challenging."

"Let me give it some thought."

"You do that Jim. And now, let's decide on what to eat – I hear the oysters are great if you like that sort of thing."

By the end of the meal, Jim had been accepted into the new order as a neophyte, ready to take on his first mission, sort of.

CHAPTER 8

Jim set to with vigour to identify some targets but found the task extremely challenging. The people he hated were all untouchable. The touchable ones in his life, he didn't hate.

As he pondered his predicament, he heard a noise outside. He peeped through the curtains and saw two scruffy looking characters working their way down the road, pointing at the roofs of the houses. He watched as one scurried down the alleyway of a neighbour's house with a ladder whilst his mate knocked on the door. Jim knew immediately what they were doing, his neighbour had told him about it. One would distract the owner whilst the other loosened some tiles on the roof; they would then charge the home owner to fix it.

"Bastards!" he thought to himself. He was about to do what he had done before and stand in his front garden, thus foiling their attempt to duck down his alleyway. But emboldened by his new vigilante status, he decided to sneak out quietly down the alleyway and hide behind the wheelie bin. As an afterthought, he brought along his ten-pound hammer, for reasons he had yet to work out.

Crouching down was more difficult than he had expected. He heard and felt his knees cracking with the effort. He tried desperately to keep his wheezing to a minimum as he heard the ladder man come down the alleyway, set his ladder against Jim's wall and climb up to reach the roof tiles.

With a barely muffled groan, Jim tried to get to his feet, but his knees were having none of it.

"Bugger," he mumbled and made his way in an undignified crawl towards the ladder, clonking the ten-pound hammer alongside him as he went. He eventually arrived at the ladder and hooked the hammer head over the step. With another barely muffled groan, he started to lift himself up. Unfortunately for both Jim and the man at the top of the ladder, he only managed to pull himself halfway up before his weight shifted the ladder shaft and sent it and its occupant toppling over into the street.

There was a sickening thud as the man hit the road. Jim heard the accomplice's receding footfalls as he ran off. Jim's breath was now rasping.

He stared at the fallen man who crawled out into the road on all fours, and was promptly run over by a Waitrose home delivery truck.

Having quietly retreated into his house, Jim placed the ten-pound hammer back into the broom cupboard and opened the front door.

The driver of the delivery truck was on his mobile as Jim walked out. "He just crawled out from behind the car, I didn't see him," he was saying to someone on the phone.

By the time the police arrived, the driver had been given a cup of tea by one of Jim's neighbours. Between them all, they recovered the fallen ladder and worked out that the man had been trying to remove tiles when he had fallen off his ladder, and then crawled out in front of the truck.

"It wasn't the driver's fault," Jim told the officer. "The sneaky bugger must have been in the alleyway there, up to no good, when he fell off his ladder."

"Serves him right. They ripped old Sheila off earlier this afternoon. It's a disgrace what they do. Is he dead?" said the divorcee from No.18.

"I would imagine so," said Sid from No.22. "The wheel's gone over is 'ead, made a bit of a mess of it."

"OK everybody, please move back and let the ambulance crew do their job," said the policeman as the ambulance reversed up to the body. "Please all go back to your houses now."

The officer turned to Jim. "You didn't happen to see his accomplice by any chance sir?"

Jim shook his head. "No, I just heard a noise when the truck driver jammed his brakes on, so I came out to see what was going on. Do you know who they are officer?"

"There have been reports of two guys pulling the loose tiles stunt in the area."

"Anything else I can do officer? Would you like a cup of tea?"

"No thanks, sir, I would just go back to your house, remember to lock your door and try to forget all this. Oh, just one thing. Could I please have your name for the record?"

Jim gave the officer his name and address.

"Thanks officer, it's all been a bit of a shock, I'll take your advice. Goodnight."

"Goodnight, sir."

Jim closed his front door and slid the lock into place. He turned and held his hands out in front of him. They were steady as a rock. That, in itself, was an unsettling thing. What was going on? From car gouging to murder in less than a week. Admittedly, he'd had no intention of murdering the guy, although toppling him from a two-storey roof was hardly likely to be harmless.

He poured himself a stiff scotch with brown sugar and flopped onto his couch just as the doorbell rang. He cursed and went to the door, expecting to find the police constable there. Instead, he found Doris looking up at him.

CHAPTER 9

Mervyn looked at his watch. He'd only been in the waiting room for five minutes but it seemed like half a lifetime. He jolted at the thought and started punching numbers into the calculator on his phone. He had so far spent 0.002% of his remaining life waiting for a flu jab. Jim's words came back to him – use your time wisely, go wild. The nurse came over to a couple who Mervyn assumed were in front of him in the queue. The old lady was sitting in the surgery's wheelchair, her partner was settled into an ordinary chair next to her.

The nurse smiled. "Do you need that wheelchair at the moment my dear?"

The old lady twitched. "No, I'm not a cripple you know."

"Would you be able to sit somewhere else? We have somebody who needs the wheelchair."

"So long as it's got wheels on it. I have to have wheels."

The old lady looked around and spotted an office chair in the corner with small caster wheels.

"There, bring me that one."

"Are you sure, my darling? It might be a bit unstable."

"Yes, it's got wheels on it!"

The exchange was made, and the nurse left with the wheelchair.

"I'm not putting up with a chair with no wheels," she pointed out to her nodding partner.

The nurse returned with a concerned expression. "You can go home you know. Doctor has already seen you."

"What?"

"THE DOCTOR HAS SEEN YOU. You can go home."

"We can't, we need a taxi."

"OK, do you want me to call you a cab?"

"No, we need a taxi to get us home."

The nurse picked up her phone. "Hello, yes, I have a couple who need a lift home. This is St Simon's Hospital." With the phone still at her ear, she looked across at the old lady. "What's your address love?"

"What?"

"Where do you live?"

The old lady turned to her partner. "Tell her where we live."

"What?"

"Tell her where we live."

"Why?"

"She needs to know."

"Who's she?"

"She's the doctor."

"She should know where we live."

"Tell her where we live."

"It's number twenty-four…"

"No it isn't, we don't live at number twenty-four."

The nurse spoke into her phone again. "We won't be a minute."

"Where is it then?"

"Where's what?"

"Our house."

"You should know."

"It's number twenty-four…"

Mervyn could stand no more. He stood up and, as he walked past the nurse, he whispered, "You deserve a medal," before walking through the door.

"Saint's preserve us," he mumbled. "Please take me out before I get like that." It was at that moment that he realised his prayer would most likely be answered. He did a little skip and strutted off down the road. He would have to speak to Jim again – he needed a plan.

CHAPTER 10

Jim looked down at Doris as she stood at his door. "Hello Doris, are you OK?"

"I'm fine Jim, I was worried about you!"

"Why?"

"Well, it was very brave of you, what you did. Knocking that 'orrible man off yer roof."

"You saw me?! Do you want to come in Doris?"

"No, I don't want to be a nuisance. I just wanted to see if you're OK to feed me Archie again, and to say well done."

"Does anybody else know?"

"No, just me. Don't worry, mum's the word," she said, tapping her nose. "I'm not stupid Jim. If you need an alibi, I'm up for it. What did you tell the fuzz?"

"I told them that I heard the van's brakes and came out to see what was going on."

"Fair enough, I was inside your house as well, just dropping the keys off so you can feed me cat whilst I'm away this weekend. Don't volunteer that information, only use it if they come back asking more questions. I'll do the same. Chances are they won't bovver. The food is kept in the larder next to the fridge. One packet, twice a day, don't forget. I'm leaving Saturday morning and will be back Sunday night. Goodnight Jim."

Jim watched as Doris trotted across the road, and slowly closed his front door.

CHAPTER 11

Jim slouched back into his couch and reached for his whisky. The sugar had dissolved nicely, and the liquid had a nice liqueur smell about it. He was just about to take a slug when the phone rang.

"For fuck's sake, what now?"

He recognised Mervyn's voice on the phone. "Hi Jim, I just had to talk to you a bit about what you were saying about me seizing the day, Carpe Diem and all that."

"Wait a minute Merv, I'm just gonna get my drink… Right, fire away."

"Well, today I had a bit of a road to Damascus moment – you were absolutely right. The problem is that I'm not sure how to get started, I need some advice."

"Now?"

"Is there a problem?"

Jim thought to himself: *Yeah Merv, remember the car gouging? Well I thought I'd notch my act up a bit, so I just killed someone for touching my roof tiles. The granny from over the road who caught me in the act is blackmailing me. If I don't feed her bloody cat, she's going to rat on me. Do you think I should rub her out as well?* But he just sighed and said, "No Merv, it's fine. What do you want to know?"

"Well, where to start really. What should I do differently?"

"You are already doing things differently Mervyn. You phoned me. It's always us that must phone you, remember? Don't force it, let it come naturally. If it's anything like my experience, you'll be caught up in the whirlwind quickly enough."

"What should I do next?"

Jim closed his eyes. "Think of someone who is really hateful and work out how to kill them."

"Er, really? And then what?"

"Carry out your plan. Goodnight, Mervyn."

CHAPTER 12

Jim had read somewhere that serial killers needed to advertise their exploits. He realised that the urge to talk about the ladder toppling was becoming all consuming. The only other person who knew was away for the weekend, leaving her cat to be fed twice a day.

"Shit, must feed the bloody cat!" After a frantic search, he found the keys on the mantelpiece and walked across to No.12.

As he wandered into the kitchen, the cat sauntered up to him with an expectant meow. "Hello, um, whatsyername, I see you've pondered your options." He tried to remember where she said the cat food was. Something about the fridge? He opened the fridge door. All he could see that a cat might like were some chicken fillets.

He took one out and presented it to the cat. After some sniffing, the cat looked up at him with a Garfield expression indicating disapproval. "Bloody hell, do I have to cook it, is that it?" Jim put the chicken on to boil and sat down. He looked at the cat, the cat looked at him.

"I killed someone yesterday you know. I didn't mean to, at least I don't think I meant to. I can't help thinking that it was OK. I don't seem to be able to conjure up any remorse. That's wrong, isn't it?"

The cat continued listening, keeping an open mind.

Jim frowned. "Your mum saw me do it. She's putting the squeeze on me, that's why I'm here feeding you again, you know."

Jim stood up and took the chicken off the boil and proceeded to chop it up on a plate he had found. "I also met a man from a secret organisation that bumps baddies off. I'm not sure how that works really." He blew over the chicken pieces to cool them.

"Do you think I'm a bad person?" The cat weighed up the evidence, made its decision and came over and rubbed itself against Jim's legs. Jim nodded as he placed the plate in front of his new confidant. "Thanks, I hoped you'd understand, I needed to know that it was OK."

He watched the cat munch contentedly until it was finished. Then he picked up the plate, washed it and left after wishing the cat a pleasant day. He promised to return later.

Instead of going straight back to his house, he made a detour to the corner shop and bought a pack of cat treats.

CHAPTER 13

Jeremy Grant saw the SMS from Jim Spoonwall. *One down, next to follow as and when the opportunity presents itself.*

Jeremy raised his eyebrows. "Wow, Mr Spoonwall doesn't hang around." In all likelihood, that was a record. From initial contact to first task completion in less than twenty-four hours.

He cast his mind back to his other recruits – some had yet to get to first base. He experienced a mild thrill. It was a feeling he had less and less these days.

Back in the day, as operative DQ29 in the secret service, those thrills were a regular occurrence. "Taking out the trash," as he used to call it, was an encompassing and thoroughly rewarding job. He was highly prized by his superiors as a man who could be relied on to shorten unwanted lives.

So many years ago now. His retirement had lasted two months. He had tried to get a job with the regional daily newspaper as a reporter, using his service in the forces as a recommendation to specialise in conflict. He eventually landed the job of janitor. He held sway over the litter bins and dusters. The most dangerous weapon he was allowed to operate was the vacuum cleaner.

One evening, he was doing his rounds and came upon an after-hours meeting. Two reporters were discussing the new female sub-editor. One reporter was telling the other how he had managed to get her into bed the previous night. Jeremy nodded to them as he tipped their bin contents into his bag, fully expecting them to wait until he left, but to his astonishment, they just carried on with their story, completely ignoring him in the process.

As the days wore on, he became more and more aware of how invisible he had become. Back in the day, he would have been ecstatic, but now he found it depressing how his advanced years had reduced him to such a level of irrelevance in everybody's lives that he could no longer be seen or recalled.

He sat in his house pondering his discovery and how valuable it would have been to him as an operative. He recalled his trainer telling him that every situation had opportunity, you just needed to shift your viewpoint sometimes to see it. That was when it clicked. All old people were invisible. The grey-haired shufflers who everybody moved rapidly past in life, never noticing their presence. What a precious aptitude that was, if only it could be used to advantage in some way.

Over the next few weeks, he tested his theory out, at first by just watching the reaction, or rather lack of reaction, to his presence.

One day, Jeremy watched as a short, arrogant reporter called Will, with little regard for personal hygiene, cornered one of the secretaries in the copy room. She was young and naïve, and politely tried to get past him, but he persisted in pushing himself against her. Eventually, another reporter came in and she made her escape. Jeremy listened whilst Will told the other reporter how she had come on to him and was begging for it.

That night, Jeremy's mind went into overdrive. He was like a man possessed, a man with a mission. The following evening, he accessed Will's computer and set up the links and history records he had prepared. He then accessed another machine, sent off an anonymous note to the Chief Editor, emptied the litter bin and moved on.

He decided to stay on the next morning. Whilst he vacuumed the carpet, he moved over to where he could watch the Chief Editor access her machine. He watched her body language and knew when she had found the mail. She picked up the phone and made a call. A little later the IT technician arrived and, together, they went to Will's machine.

"It's password protected, we'll have to wait until he gets in. Ah, here he is now," said the technician.

The Chief Editor turned towards Will. "Hi, just routine, could you log into your machine please."

"Why, what's going on?"

"Nothing, just log in."

Will did as he was asked and stood back.

"Can you please show us what you last accessed through the web?"

"Now listen, what's going on here?"

The Editor nodded to the technician, and he tapped on Will's keyboard, bringing up a string of files accessed over the past week.

"Why you doing this?" Will wanted to know.

The technician opened a file. Jeremy looked away as he gathered his rubbish bag and took it into the corridor.

He heard the shout as the child porn site he had planted appeared on the screen. He never saw Will again. But Jeremy was on his way to a satisfying and highly successful new career.

CHAPTER 14

Harry and Mervyn both looked up eagerly as Jim came into the pub. Sitting at the same table as the other day, they listened to the feedback that Jim had to offer about his meeting with Jeremy.

"He's about seventy maybe, and keeps himself in good shape. Very sharp twinkling eyes that look deep into your soul when he talks to you."

"So, what are you supposed to do now Jim? Have you got a project or something?"

"No, of course not Harry, I don't want to do anything shifty."

"I do." It was the first time Mervyn had said anything; they both turned and looked at him.

Jim was trying to catch Mervyn's eye, but Mervyn was gazing at the ceiling. "Shut up Mervyn," Jim was saying under his breath.

"You want to do something shifty?"

Mervyn caught Jim's look. "No Harry, just joking."

Harry stood up. "Sorry guys I'm on a short chain tonight, it's the wife's bridge night and I'm the cook."

"You're a good man Harry."

"I know Mervyn, remember to tell Sheila that when next you see her."

Jim watched Harry leave. "Bloody hell Mervyn, I thought you were going to drop me in the shit there."

"Sorry about that, I didn't think it was that serious."

"What, me telling you to go bump someone off?"

"Nah, I know you were joking, but it did get me thinking. Maybe I could do something for the common good. If it was a bit risky, so much the better really. I don't have a lot to lose."

"Look Mervyn, I'm not really the one to give any advice, I'm sort of feeling my way around. I'm not sure we should force the pace."

"Alright for you to say, but forcing the pace is exactly what I want to do."

"Do you believe in fate, Merv? I think I do, sort of. Let's give it a day and see what happens."

"OK Jim, fate has one day, twenty-four hours, starting from now. Then, if nothing comes up, I'm going hunting."

Jim rolled his eyes. "Whatever pickles your fish, Merv."

As he walked back to his house, Mervyn was especially watchful for wrongs to be righted. A man had stopped to let his dog have a poo. Mervyn slowed down and watched the scene but, to his disappointment, the man whipped out a plastic bag and skilfully plucked up each turd, leaving no trace on the pavement.

A couple of kids with hoodies were standing chatting at the corner, but scowl at them as he did, they just looked up and turned away. It wasn't going to be easy.

When he reached the door of his home, he had one last look up and down his street and confirmed that all was well. He sighed dejectedly and stepped inside. He made himself a cocoa and considered his options. If he was going to hit the streets, he would need to be armed; some means of defence and attack would be needed.

He went to his shed and rummaged around for likely weapons with which to arm himself. He came back into the house with his primary selection of items and laid them out on the kitchen table for consideration. There was a monkey wrench, a peening hammer, one large screwdriver, a garden fork and a pickaxe handle. He picked each one up in turn and considered their merits. The monkey wrench was rusty, the peening hammer's head was loose, and the pickaxe handle was just too damned heavy. That left the screwdriver and the garden fork. He picked each one up in turn and tried out a few stabbing motions.

After another sip of his cocoa, which had now gone a bit cold, he concluded that the pair would work well in combination – the garden fork for long range and the screwdriver for close scuffles.

He made himself another cocoa, emboldened and encouraged by a new sense of purpose. He tried to remember the film with Charles Swansong, or whatever his name was, where he went around beating up lowlifes, what was it called again? Dead Fish, Dread Dish, Head Mist? He had a make-do weapon in the film, made from an old sock with coins in it. Within five minutes, Mervyn had found a sock with only one small hole in it and enough change to pay for one hour of parking.

"Bugger," he mumbled as he swung the sock with a knot in to prevent the pitiful amount of small change from leaking out. He returned to his cocoa, dejected, only to find that it had gone cold again.

He turned his attention to the fork and screwdriver, trying each one out with a few more stabbing motions. He began to doubt that the fork would penetrate anything, its pointed ends having been worn down by decades of gardening. A little later that evening, after ordering a grinding machine online, he fell into a well-earned, peaceful sleep.

CHAPTER 15

Jim realised he was looking forward to feeding the cat at No.12 and was a little sad that Doris would be taking over again that evening. The cat had shown understanding and given good advice when Jim had needed it. The cat was also very supportive of his new role.

"I'm a bit worried about Mervyn," he explained to the cat that afternoon whilst the chicken was boiling. "I feel responsible too. He might get into real trouble or maybe, even worse, get into no trouble at all and just fall into a deep depression. What do you think I should do?"

The cat gazed at Jim whilst it mulled over the problem and then rolled onto its side and stretched out purposefully.

Jim nodded. "You're right of course, let things stretch out a bit and run their course, anything I do now will just make things worse. It really is a comfort to have you around to bounce things off, I'm going to miss our little chats."

The cat rubbed itself up against Jim's legs again. "Thanks, you too."

Later that evening, Doris came over to collect her keys and thank Jim.

"No, thank you! Your cat and I had a lovely time, it really is a very clever cat that."

"Look Jim, I 'ope you won't mind but I need to go into 'ospital for a day and night to 'ave me goitre worked on. It's bin givin' me a bit of jip recently."

Jim winced at the thought of having a goitre worked on. He wasn't sure what a goitre really was but he was in no hurry to find out. "Must I look after your cat again?"

"Ahh Jim, would ya mind?"

"Of course not, Doris, it's a pleasure."

That evening, Doris watched as her cat sniffed disapprovingly at the cat food she had squeezed out of the pouch. It looked up at her with reproachful eyes and ate less than half of what was offered.

CHAPTER 16

Across the road, Jim was settling down to some research. He was gathering as much information as he could about the dog fight gang in Croydon. The more information he gathered, the tighter he clenched his jaw. This lot really were a nasty bunch. Unfortunately, the information was sketchy. If he was going to have any impact, he would have to get closer to the detail, but how? Maybe Mr Disgusted of Skegness would have some ideas.

"Hello Jim, nice to hear from you. You've been busy so it seems."

"Well, yes. I didn't expect him to get squashed under the…"

"Whoa, Jim. No details please, especially not over the phone."

"Oh, right, sorry. I am looking into another, er, project that I would dearly like to, um, influence, sort of thing."

"What do you need from me Jim?"

"I need some info on…"

"Good, let's meet. Is tomorrow lunchtime good for you?"

"Yeah, where?"

"I'll let you know later today, OK?"

"Er, yeah, fine."

When Jim received the new location – the restaurant at the top of the Tate Modern – he was initially peeved as it meant another tube journey and a bit of a walk. His knee was still giving him problems from when he crouched down in the alley. Nevertheless, the excursion would afford him a chance to wander around the gallery itself which never disappointed, provided his knee behaved. He decided to take his walking stick just in case.

Fortunately, his knee did behave, and he arrived uncharacteristically five minutes late for his lunch date with Jeremy after becoming absorbed in one of the rolling films on display. He saw Jeremy at a table by the window looking over the Thames and walked up with an apologetic smile.

"So sorry, Jeremy, lost track of time in the gallery there."

"No apology necessary Jim, time in a gallery is always time well spent."

"It is very nice of you to spare me some time. I hope I'm not wasting it, but I'm not sure how to proceed."

The waitress arrived and they ordered their drinks. Jim waited until she had left before continuing.

"Have you read anything about that dog fighting ring in Croydon?"

"Yes, they were fined and let back on the streets if I recall correctly, I think one received a light prison sentence."

"Yeah, that's them. They got off with a slap on the wrist. That is not right, people like that should be removed from society and made to pay heavily and continually until their… Sorry, getting a bit carried away." Jim unclenched his teeth and took a couple of deep breaths.

"Another apology not required Jim. Continue."

"Well, I was thinking that maybe our, well my, attention should be focused on correcting that situation, but I don't know how to get going."

"Well, let's start with their names and addresses, that won't be too much trouble. We should also be able to get details of the operation they ran. Previous convictions and that sort of thing will be needed to understand the type of people you are dealing with, and a general profile of their characters. Once you have that, you can start formulating a strategy. Normally, the next move would be a bit of reconnaissance to nail down their routines but let's get the basics to you to start with and see where that gets you, shall we?"

"How are you going to get all that?"

"That is my problem, not yours Jim. The less you know about me, the better really. It works both ways. The old need-to-know rule is very prevalent in our field of endeavour, not everybody in society sees things from our point of view. Whilst we have some sympathisers out there who are willing to see squirrels when our operations bear fruit, we are better off working in the shadows."

"I thought you might want to know about what happened the other day?"

"I don't *need* to know Jim. Nevertheless, if you feel the need to share, and many of us do, that's fine, I'm your father confessor."

"No, I suppose I'm OK for the moment. I have someone I confide in who is completely trustworthy and, like you, gives very good advice."

"Just be careful with whom you share your secrets, Jim."

"I am, Jeremy, I am."

CHAPTER 17

Mervyn sat up, wide awake. *Death Wish*, that was the film he'd been thinking of. He pulled on some pants, tucked his feet into his slippers which were warm from the radiator and trotted down to the TV. After a bit of fiddling and cursing he was ready to watch the film starring Charles Bronson on Netflix. He paused it, made himself a cocoa and shook some biscuits onto a plate. Armed with that and a notepad and pencil, he settled down to do some serious research.

Mervyn sat back as the final credits began to roll. He looked down at his notes and brushed away the biscuit crumbs. He had only written one line: "Hit the streets."

He bit his lower lip in deep thought. He could well roam the streets for years and never find anyone who deserved having their stomach torn to shreds with a garden fork. It was a problem. How could he find those deserving of a miserable and acutely painful death? Then there was the matter of degree. What should be meted out to someone who steals an exhaust? Does that deserve a fork in the thigh maybe? And what about someone who picks on those less fortunate? Maybe a stab in the eye with the screwdriver?

He realised to his frustration that a schedule of precedent was required before any just punishment could be handed out. He wondered if there were any law texts that could assist. After some serious thought, he concluded that a conversion table was needed. The law would provide general guidance as to the prison time that would be given for a defined crime. All he needed to do was convert prison time into applications rendered by a garden fork and/or screwdriver. He set to his new task with vigour.

He was pondering whether the difference between a five-month and six-month sentence warranted an additional random stab from the garden fork or merely a well-aimed prod from the screwdriver when another problem started to loom. By the time he had reached a life sentence, he would be required to stab to a degree that would result in the victim's body resembling one that had gone through a blender. Furthermore, the conversion table was taking on the complexity of a railway timetable on steroids. He could hardly be expected, having observed some misdemeanour, to request a few moments to run his finger down his list to ensure fair punishment, even if the lighting was quite good, and likely it would not be.

"Bugger," he mumbled, and returned reluctantly to square one.

Jim saw the call from Mervyn and checked his watch – twenty-four hours to the second. He shook his head. "Hi Merv."

"Twenty-four hours is up, and nothing has happened. I was prepared to go hunting but there are some administrative problems. I thought maybe you could help."

"Administrative problems?"

"Oh yeah, loads of them, they're going to slow me down you know."

"I'm sure they are. What are you talking about Merv?"

"You know, my new mission in life."

"Your new mission is being slowed down by administrative problems already?"

"Yeah, I knew you'd understand."

"Yeah, it's as clear as a bell. Do you want a beer Merv?"

"That would be nice."

"OK, give me half an hour."

Jim sighed, pulled on his coat and, picking up his walking stick, wandered off to the bus stop.

He climbed on and went upstairs, hoping to get a front seat, but they were occupied so he settled in behind the stairwell.

At the second stop, two teenage boys in hoodies came up the stairs, shouting to one another as they did so.

"Yeah I don' give a fuck, I'm gonna bust his head."

"Whilst you do that I'll shag 'is bird."

"Yeah, then I'll 'ave a go, ha ha."

At the following stop, a black schoolboy in uniform come up the stairs and sat behind Jim.

The hoodies started up again.

"Look what's escaped from der zoo."

"Oi, does that black come off if you wash?"

The other one laughed. "'E wouldn't know, bloody wog!"

At the following stop, Jim saw the black student walk past and go down the stairs.

"Oi, wait up, we wanna come too."

Jim heard the two hoodies running towards the stairwell. As they got there, he put out his walking stick just above the top step. They both tripped headfirst down the stairs. The first one's head smashed against the handrail, crushing his nose with a sickening crack. The second tried to regain his balance as his arm slipped into the handrail and broke as the rest of his bodyweight pulled against it.

Someone at the bottom screamed as the two boys lay in the stairwell moaning. Jim stepped over the first one and pretended to help whilst pushing one boy's body further down, thus causing his fractured bone to tear through his skin. A scream came out of his mouth amidst sobs.

"These lads need medical assistance," shouted Jim. "Someone call an ambulance."

Everybody else on the bus kept their distance, so Jim looked at the one with the broken nose and slowly stood on his face as he stepped down onto the lower level.

"I'm sorry everybody," said the bus driver, now standing outside. "Can you please catch the bus coming up behind. We are going to have to wait, the ambulance is on its way."

Jim stepped off with the rest of the passengers. He looked up and down the street but couldn't see the black lad.

With one stop to go, he decided to leave the scene and, enjoying the evening air, hummed a little tune as he walked to the pub.

CHAPTER 18

By the time he arrived at the pub, Jim was in very high spirits. Mervyn waved him over to his table where a pint was waiting.

"How you Jim?"

"Never better Merv, and you?"

"Fine, I must say you look pretty fit. Been working out or something?"

"You could say that. So, what's all these admin problems Merv?"

Jim listened as Mervyn explained his issues of matching crime and punishment. To Mervyn's surprise Jim suddenly burst into song:

"My object all sublime,

I shall achieve in time,

To let the punishment fit the crime,

The punishment fit the crime."

The last two lines had Mervyn join in as well. "Gilbert and Sullivan, *Mikado* isn't it?"

"Buggered if I know Mervyn, fine voice you've got there."

"Used to be in the hospital choir Jim, back in the day."

"Do you miss it Merv?"

"What, being chief pharmacist? Good God no, hateful bloody job. Enjoyed the choir though."

They took thoughtful sips.

"Maybe you're going at it all wrong Merv. Not that I know what the fuck I'm up to most of the time. But maybe you need to find one target. That then gives you time to work out what to do with them and you get to do it on your terms, sort of thing."

"Hmm, who do I hate? Bloody hell Jim, there's so many! And that's just the ones that come to mind immediately. Trouble is that most of them are world leaders and politicians."

Jim laughed. "Yeah, I know. I had the same problem."

"Maybe we could team up. Have you got any people lined up Jim?"

"I might have but I think it's probably better if we work alone. I don't know. Let me ask my mentor."

"Yeah, do that. Tell him your prospective partner is in a bit of a hurry and doesn't really care if he gets caught."

CHAPTER 19

Jim heard the doorbell. When he opened the door, he saw a biker with his visor pulled down covering his face. In his hand was a large envelope which he held out to Jim.

"From Jeremy," the biker explained with a crackle in his voice that suggested he was in the latter part of his life. The biker turned and limped his way back to his bike.

"Thank you!" Jim called out but received no response.

Jim closed the door and tipped the contents of the package onto the lounge table.

His eyes opened wide with delight, then surprise and finally fear. The notes were incredibly detailed. The transcripts of the court proceedings were there, along with police interviews, profiles of those involved, photographs – just about everything Jim could imagine he might need, and some things he would never have dreamt of. Even their medical records were attached. Jim chewed his thumbnail nervously. "How the hell did Jeremy get access to all this, and so quickly too?"

He started to fear that he was in over his head, a bit like a little boy who wanted to be a train driver suddenly being given access to the footplate of the Mallard, shown the throttle, and told to give it stick. There was an enormous amount to go through. He would need to sift through and summarise, make logical links. Probably set up some project schedule, God forbid. He was an electrical engineer for fuck's sake, he needed somebody who loved analysis and schedules and all that shit. Somebody who made lists and … Mervyn!

He grabbed his phone and dialled Jeremy.

"Hello Jim, did you get the stuff I sent you?"

"Yes, thanks Jeremy. I must say it's way more, er, better than I expected."

"We aim to please Jim. I haven't gone through it myself. If you want me to peruse it at all, please let me know. Now, how can I help you today?"

"Well, I was wondering if I could maybe bring in a partner, so to speak. A likeminded individual who has certain skills that I think I am going to need."

"You have carte blanche to do whatever you want Jim. I just oil the wheels and try to give sound advice. There are no rules, nobody would follow them even if there were. Especially at our age. What we endeavour to achieve goes beyond any rules in any case. I trust your instincts. I suggest you do the same."

"Do you want to know anything about him, meet him maybe?"

"No, you've already told me more than I need to know."

"What?"

"You have a partner, and he is male. Leave it at that. Anything else Jim?"

"No, I think that's it for now. Need to get going through all the stuff you sent. How the hell did… no, sorry, never mind. Bye Jeremy."

"All the best Jim."

He immediately dialled Mervyn.

"Hey Merv, you're in!"

"Yes Jim, I am – where did you expect me to be, having tea with the Queen?"

"No, you silly arse, you're in on my project. We are going to be working as a team, we are going to set up a cell, an operation centre."

"Ah, that is good news because I've been trying to sharpen my fork with this grinder that I got from Amazon and it's taking forever. It will be good to take a break from that."

"What? Are you alright Mervyn? I'm talking about you being on a *Project*. You know, righting some wrongs?"

"I know Jim, you don't have to repeat yourself, my short-term memory isn't buggered you know."

Jim was starting to have second thoughts already.

"Whatever, look, I think maybe you should pop over and I'll explain it all."

"I can come over now if you want."

In little over an hour, Mervyn arrived at Jim's place. Jim led Mervyn into his lounge where he had laid out all the printed sheets. Jim held out his hands. "Check this lot."

Mervyn cupped his hand round his ear. "Sorry Jim, you'll have to speak up, I don't have my hearing aid in."

Jim rolled his eyes. "CHECK THIS LOT."

"No need to shout, I'm not deaf. Whoa – that's a lot of stuff. What are we into here?"

"It's about that dog fighting ring."

"Oh, a dog biting thing, right."

"There's a big pile of sheets to sort out."

"That's the problem with dogs, isn't it?"

"What?"

"There's always big piles of shit to clear up. I had a collie once…"

"Good. I've separated them into two parts, the court and the Croydon files."

"Who did?"

"I did."

"That's bad news, I hear they're painful. How did you catch them?"

"Catch what for fuck's sake?"

"Chronic piles."

"CROYDON FILES, Mervyn, the files on the actual operation in Croydon. Maybe you should go back and get your ear trumpet or whatever, you really are as deaf as a bloody post!"

"Oh right, so what do you want me to do?"

"Start with that pile there. Who knows, maybe at the end, we can perhaps get the dogs a home."

"Bloody hell, how are they involved? I thought they were good guys?"

"I'm sorry?"

"The Battersea Dog's Home, I always thought they were good guys."

"I said perhaps get the dogs… Mervyn, just shut up and read those." He slapped the heap down in front of him and went off to start with the court proceedings files.

After a while he saw Mervyn starting to separate papers and draw up some flow diagrams. "Good," thought Jim. "Mervyn's in his element at last."

CHAPTER 20

By the following day, thanks to Mervyn's natural analytical skills, Jim's lounge had been transformed into an operations room. An evidence board had been erected and faces had been stuck up with lines connecting them logically.

They stood back and admired their work. It all looked rather professional. The faces of seven male Caucasian individuals stared back at them from the board.

"They're a rough looking bunch of buggers aren't they Jim?"

Jim nodded vaguely. "How the hell are two old doddery farts going to nail this lot?" he wondered.

Mervyn had summarised the main facts onto a plain white door that they had found in Jim's shed.

Seven main operatives

Fighting ring set up at a rented warehouse in 127 Maglin Street

Meetings every Friday night 20:00 to 24:00

Crowd size +/- 100 persons by invitation only

Bouncer security at door

All transactions cash based

Bookies present to take bets

Bar facilities provided

Dog rating and trials usually Wednesdays. 18:00 to 24:00

Operations seemingly ceased since police raid one month ago

Dogs destroyed

Jim sighed. "They got the last bit the wrong way round, shouldn't have been the humans that got destroyed."

Mervyn walked up to the seven photos. "We could try and nail each one in turn, or maybe wait until we have the whole rats' nest together."

"What makes you think they will get together again?"

Mervyn looked down at the piece of paper he had in his hand. "Look at this, one witness reckoned that the takings were in excess of a hundred thousand pound a fight."

Jim whistled. "That's a lot of cash!"

Mervyn looked over at the seven faces staring back at him. "In one way, it might be to our advantage. Those bastards are not going to give up on that sort of income. They are going to start up again."

"The one who was given three months, the leader, won't they wait until he is out?"

Mervyn shuffled through the papers. "He admitted to being the leader." Mervyn looked from the photo, back to his records, went to another stack of papers. "Hmm, funny that, he's also the youngest and… if I remember, there was something… Yeah, here it is. He only moved into the area a couple of months previously. Used to live in Coventry, was involved in some gang war stuff up there."

"I thought the dog fighting had been going on way longer than that."

"So did I Jim, the rental of the warehouse was taken out, er, let me see, over a year ago. Now where was the… yeah, here it is, dogs started disappearing at about the same time."

"Maybe he took over from somebody else?"

"Possibly, or maybe he was paid off to take the fall, so the operation could start up again."

"Surely the cops would have checked up on all that."

"From what I can see, there was considerable pressure from the local community to find the ringleader and put him away. Maybe a confession was just too convenient to turn down."

"So how does this help us Merv?"

"Well, if you were the real leader and still free, what would you do?"

"Er, probably let things calm down a bit and then get together with my team and start up again. Maybe organise an online meeting to go through the logistics, get another warehouse somewhere, make a fighting ring thingy and get some fighting dogs, then send out the invites and off we go."

"Shit."

"What?"

"My bloody hearing aids are running out of power again. I was listening to music on them all morning."

"I didn't know you could do that. Look let's have a bit of a break. Maybe I need to talk to that Jeremy guy again, he seems to be on top of things. Let's sleep on it, I'll give you a call tomorrow. I've got to go and feed the neighbour's cat now anyway."

Jim walked out with Mervyn and went over to No.12.

The cat was waiting for him in the passageway. "Hey Archie, how's things?" They walked into the kitchen and Jim sat down as the cat hopped onto the other chair.

"I've had a bit of a weird day. We are trying to stop some really nasty bastards from hurting animals. Look, it's dogs they are hurting but I'm sure you understand that's wrong, eh?"

The cat gave Jim a wide-eyed look. "Yeah, sorry, it's just that you lot and dogs sometimes don't get on, I should have realised you are bigger than that. I've brought in a partner, he hasn't got long to live but is a really good analytical type, so long as his bloody hearing things are working."

The cat jumped off the chair and stood looking up at the fridge. "I've bought some more chicken, I'll put it on. I was rambling, wasn't I? You're right as usual, I need to concentrate on the job at hand."

CHAPTER 21

Mervyn's mind was raking over the facts that he had been sifting through. How were they going to bring them down? Unless more information came in from Jim's contact, there seemed to be no other way than tracking their movements. They would need loads of people to do that. It would be useful if they knew who the leader was, then they would only have to follow him around. He took a piece of paper and wrote down *Identify leader.* They would then need to set up a method of watching him somehow. He had no idea of how to do that, so he wrote down *How do we put a tail on him?*

That was enough for now. They needed to get past those things before going any further. He looked at the time. Way too early to go to sleep; he needed those documents of Jim's.

As if by divine intervention, he saw an SMS from Jim. *Hi Merv, I've scanned and emailed that stuff from Jeremy. Have a good evening and remember to charge your hearing aid.*

He went to his computer and opened up the files. Then, with a cup of cocoa and some extra-thick chocolate biscuits, he set to with a will.

He started off with their names: John Gough, Arnold Smith, Peter Jenkins, Joseph James, Bob Cherry, Arthur Dunn and the guy in chookie, Dave Duncannon.

He immediately crossed off the one in prison and John Gough, Arthur Dunn and Joseph James, concluding that gang leaders would never have names like that. That left him with Bob Cherry and Peter Jenkins. He was certain it was Bob Cherry but just to make sure, he checked if they owned cars. Cherry had a brand new Jag and Jenkins had a six-year-old Subaru.

"Gotcha!" shouted Mervyn, slapping his hands on his thighs. "No boss is going to drive a bloody Subaru, whatever that is." He went and made himself another cocoa and, remembering Jim's advice about living it up, added a generous slug of rum. It had been a good evening's work so far.

He sent off an SMS to Jim: *Bob Cherry is our man. That is the bastard we put a tail on,* then settled down to the details of how one puts a tail on somebody.

Firstly, a car would be necessary so that there would be warmth, shelter, comfy seats and room to carry things. Secondly, a camera with a zoom lens would be needed so that they could remember what they'd been looking at. Then there were the backup essentials as Mervyn called them: warm drinks, cold drinks, pork pies, pens, scotch eggs, pencils, assorted pastries, notebook, pencil sharpener, biscuits, serviettes, binoculars, spare camera batteries, map of public toilets in area, spare cash and a car vacuum cleaner.

The "methodology of the tail", as Mervyn put it, was outlined succinctly in four clear steps. Wait outside suspect's house, follow suspect when suspect appears, note where suspect goes, don't get caught following suspect.

Mervyn sat back and read through his notes. After adding mustard and salt to the backup essentials, he leaned back in his chair, satisfied. "My work here is done. Let the games begin." And with another rum-charged cocoa in hand, he despatched himself off to bed.

CHAPTER 22

Jim read the notes that Mervyn had sent him. He shook his head. "We are so fucked," he sighed.

He read the footnote informing him that Mervyn would gather the essentials and drive across to pick him up for the "*stake-out*".

A little later, he received an SMS: *At Waitrose, please indicate preference of pie (Gala or Melton Mowbray) and pastry (custard yum, cherry ripple delight or apple custard fold).* Jim typed in his preferences whilst trying to pretend he wasn't a bit miffed about not being given a choice of biscuits.

Half an hour later, Jim's doorbell rang. Jim blinked with shock as he opened the door to see somebody wearing a fur hat, dark glasses, face mask and turtleneck sweater pulled up to his chin.

"Why are you dressed like that, Merv? You look like a bloody Ninja Turtle."

"Discretion Jim, can't be too discreet considering the task at hand."

"Am I supposed to 'suit up' as well!? This might take a while, you'd better come inside Mervyn, you want a cup of tea?"

"You wouldn't happen to have any cocoa would you Jim?"

"Help yourself, I'm going to select one of the many disguises I have hanging up in my cupboard for when I need to go into deep cover."

Jim rummaged around haplessly. Apart from a pair of Mickey Mouse ears his nephew had brought round and forgotten, there was little to choose from. Eventually, he settled on a deer stalker hat that he hated and a pair of horn-rimmed glasses that he should wear, but seldom did.

"This is as good as it gets Mervyn. Are you ready?"

Mervyn looked over at Jim and nodded approvingly. "Let's get this stake-out under way. I've established that the subject is approximately six clicks south of our current location, which means we should be in position by zero seven hundred hours."

Jim sighed. "OK, squadron leader, I have your six, let's Foxtrot Uniform Charlie Kilo Oscar Foxtrot Foxtrot."

Mervyn trundled through the morning traffic in a manner that set Jim's nerves on edge. Normally he took no notice of Mervyn's driving style, which could best be described as a random mixture of apologetic caution interspersed with devil-may-care abandon, neither of which was applied to suit the prevailing traffic conditions. But this time, he was painfully aware that they would, in all likelihood, be called upon to follow a suspect who drove in a normal way.

"Here's our stake-out location," said Mervyn as he turned into a cul-de-sac. "Look, there's the Jag," he pointed out excitedly. They drove down to the end of the road, having discovered that there were no places to park. Mervyn then proceeded to turn the car around. After more than twenty shifts backwards and forwards, they were facing the right direction.

"We can't stop here Mervyn, we're blocking the turning area."

"I don't know what else to do. I could…" Mervyn's voice froze as he gripped Jim's arm.

"What?" Jim followed Mervyn's gaze.

Bob Cherry was walking across the road to his car. To their horror they realised that his car was pointed in their direction.

"Shit Merv, he is going to want to turn here, we are blocking his path. Quick! Drive down the road past him, GO!"

Mervyn started the car and stalled it. He panicked, started it again and, after revving it into the red zone, dropped the clutch. The rear wheels squealed as the poor car shot forwards with a sickening lurch. They were rapidly approaching Cherry's car and could see him watching their approach with an incredulous look on his face. Mervyn, still in a total state of panic, had his foot hard down on the throttle as the car screamed into the red zone again in first gear. As they were about to pass Cherry's car, Mervyn, now beyond panic, slid down in his seat to hide, thus losing sight of where he was going.

Through terror-struck eyes, Jim could see the approaching road junction. "Brake! For fuck's sake BRAKE!" Mervyn did as he was told, launching the pork pie, pastries and thermos flask into the back of Jim's head. The car came to a stalled halt halfway into the main road. Cars began hooting as they manoeuvred around them.

Mervyn's head wobbled around, taking in the scene. "Where are we?"

"In the middle of a bloody nightmare I hope – for fuck's sake, reverse back out of the traffic." Mervyn did as he was told and reversed into the front of Bob Cherry's car.

CHAPTER 23

Mervyn looked in his rear-view mirror and watched Cherry get out of his car and check his front grill before walking up to Mervyn's window. He tapped on the roof loudly. Mervyn opened his window. Cherry peered in.

"Are you fucking mental?"

Mervyn started nodding uncontrollably whilst letting out a sob.

Cherry looked over at Jim. "Oi! You! Sherlock Holmes, what's your fucking problem?"

Jim shook his head. "Nothing Mr Cherry, we are very sorry, we will pay for any damage." Jim felt his heart ponder a cardiac arrest as he realised he had blurted out Cherry's name.

"You're fucking right you're gonna pay, you doddery old sods." He went back to look at his car again but stopped and returned to the window. "Hey, how do you know my name?"

Mervyn was hyperventilating and incapable of speech. Jim closed his eyes and felt a bead of sweat run off his nose. He heard words coming out of his mouth. "You're famous… sir, down at the dog pen umm thing, we, er, love betting on dogs tearing each other apart. Love it, don't we Merv? Can't get enough of it."

Cherry looked down at Mervyn. "Hey, wheezy. You like dogs do yer?"

Mervyn looked up at Cherry. "Yes… er, sir, um, love the blood and gore, and bits flying off everywhere, it makes us very, um, happy." Mervyn let out a whimper and returned to hyperventilation.

Cherry frowned and went to have a look at his car.

"We are dead… it's all over… Even I thought… I had… longer… than this," Mervyn managed between desperate gasps for air.

Cherry returned and leaned down to the window again.

"You're a couple of lucky old fucks, I can't see any damage." He stood up and looked up and down the street. "We've had a few administration problems and have had to relocate. We will be letting all our customers know the new location in due course. Do we 'ave your numbers?"

Jim looked at Mervyn; the man was close to self-induced asphyxia. He closed his eyes and read out his number. Cherry punched it into his phone and dialled it. Jim's phone rang.

Cherry smiled. "Good, just checking you ain't full of shit." He glanced down at Jim's lap. "Nice pork pie you've got there. Off you go boys, 'ave a nice day."

He walked slowly back to his car.

Jim shook Mervyn's leg. "Mervyn, Mervyn, concentrate now. Start the car, for fuck's sake, remember to put it in first gear, and slowly move off around the corner so he can get out." Before Mervyn had opened his eyes, Cherry had reversed back and gone round them and turned into the main road without a backward glance.

"OK Mervyn, look, he's gone, we need to go too. We've pushed our luck further than I would have imagined possible. We need to get far away RIGHT NOW!" Mervyn opened his eyes with a start and, in a trance-like state, started the car and drove slowly onto the other road. He continued for a short distance and then pulled off into a Sainsbury's car park and stopped the car.

"I can't drive, look at my hands, look at my body, the whole lot is shaking. Now my legs have started too."

"OK Merv, take a breather. Do you want a spot of coffee?"

"No, I need something a bit stronger."

"Like?"

"A cocoa and rum would be nice."

"A cocoa and rum, are you fucking serious?"

Mervyn nodded his head.

Jim glanced over to the Sainsbury's shop. "OK, just wait here, I won't be long."

Jim returned with a carrier bag and a hot chocolate in a sealed cup to find Mervyn sitting on his bonnet.

"Ah, Jim, needed some fresh air, feel a bit better now."

Jim put the cup on the bonnet and poured in a good slug of rum from the bottle he had purchased. "There you go Merv, get that down you." Jim looked down at the bottle and took the thermos flask of coffee out and decided to have a slug himself. The liquid stung beautifully as it coursed its fiery way down his throat. Mervyn held his cocoa out for another tot.

"Not such a bad idea Merv. This rum goes well with coffee."

They were onto their fourth rum when they heard a voice behind them. They turned to see a police constable standing there. He pointed to the rum bottle on the bonnet.

"I'm sorry sir, you are not permitted to consume liquor here. May I enquire how much you've had and whether you intend to drive this vehicle?"

"You're right cluntstable," slurred Mervyn. "Probably had too much."

"Please, leave your car here and take public transport home sir."

"OK constable, will do, thank you for understanding," said Jim, taking Mervyn's keys and locking the car after taking the pork pie and pastries and putting them into the carrier bag. "Come on Merv, let's get out of here."

CHAPTER 24

Mervyn had woken early the following day. His dreams had been dominated by visions of rabid dogs chasing pork pies around the inside of his car, whilst Bob Cherry stood outside rocking it violently. He wasn't sure he had the inner strength to see the project through. He thought back on how he had borne up in action and couldn't help concluding that he was a natural coward. "A Goddam yellow belly," as General Patton had so succinctly put it in the film. He might be a liability if they were under fire.

He aired his concerns later at Jim's place. "I was a quivering wreck, Jim. The fact that I didn't soil myself was solely due to an empty bladder and an empty bowel."

Jim smiled and put his hand on Mervyn's shoulder. "I was no better my old friend. It was only because I was in the car that my grovelling didn't involve licking his boots. But look on the bright side, our performance certainly raised no alarms in Mr Cherry's head. We certainly got the non-aggression bit down pat."

Mervyn chuckled. "Yeah, we did, didn't we? What a sneaky pair of old buggers we are. What do we do now?"

"I guess we wait until Mr Cherry tells us when they are getting together."

"And then?"

"We go along."

"And do what? I don't know about you Jim, but I don't think I can watch dogs ripping into each other."

"Hmm, we need a plan."

"What we need is a combat-type of person, a sort of military action man who goes in and sorts them out."

"I wonder if Harry would be interested? Captain Harry Johnson – he said he missed the buzz. Maybe we can give him some buzz."

"I'm not sure his wife would release him from cooking duties on bridge nights Jim, but it's worth making a few discreet enquiries."

Jim picked up the phone and dialled Harry. "Hi, Harry, you remember we were talking about those bastards running the dog fighting thing in Croydon?"

"Er, hello Jim, yes, I'm fine, thanks for asking, hope you're well too. Yeah, I remember."

"Well, if I gave you the chance to take them out, would you be interested?"

There was a pause at the other end of the line. "OK, what's this all about… really?"

"Fancy a drink this afternoon?"

"Darn right."

"Two Bells then. Usual place. I'm bringing Mervyn along."

Mervyn looked at Jim. "Well, that was nice and subtle Jim, I can't imagine what indiscretion looks like in your world."

Harry said nothing whilst Mervyn and Jim regaled their adventures of the last couple of days.

"We decided that we are both a bit jelly-legged when things go down to the wire, that's when we thought of you. A military man with a lust for glory and all that."

"You're pulling my plonker, eh? Very funny guys, I must say you've got one hell of an imagination. Who made this up anyway?"

Mervyn shook his head. "It's all true Harry, do you think I'd make up a story like that to make myself look like a right prat? Remember, my clock's ticking down. I need to do this, however useless at it I might be."

Harry looked from one to the other. "Bloody hell, you really are serious. Have you any idea how dangerous this could be?"

Mervyn shrugged. "It's not the danger that scares us as much as the probable cowardice that it will generate in both of us. We just might not be very effective when the chips are down. That's where you come in. A military man of action. Been in the field of fire. Knows how to handle himself."

Harry bit his lower lip, only too aware of the stories and half stories he had made up about his time in Iraq, Afghanistan and even the Falklands to entertain his old friends. Maybe he'd overdone it a bit, maybe this was the time to tell them that he was in the catering corps. His biggest fright was when he burnt the souffle of a visiting General. The worst battle he had been involved in was when the spuds had not been delivered and he had to keep the troops happy with three days of couscous. He scanned his list of merits to bring to the table and came up with… none. He nodded and felt his stomach churn as he heard himself say, "Sounds like fun, nothing like a bit of action again. When do we get started?"

CHAPTER 25

Bob Cherry strode around the warehouse. "So, if we, like, took this place for our enterprise, are we gonna 'ave the landlords sticking their noses in to see 'ow we're doing and stuff?"

The agent shook his head. "No sir, what you do is your affair, my clients are very discreet, very hands off."

"OK, we'll take it. No money transfers and that bollocks, we'll be paying cash. I'm gonna give it to you personally, I don't want any other blokes poking their noses in, get it?"

"Er, yes sir, will I be coming here to collect it?"

"No, you fucking won't. One of my lot will drop it at your office after hours, when all yer tarts 'ave fucked off home. Yeah?"

"Very well Mr Cherry, if I can just ask you to sign a lease agreement…"

"No paperwork, you'll get yer money. Take it or leave it."

"I just need to confirm that that is in order with my client."

"Yeah, you do that. I'll have a look around."

The agent spoke quickly on the phone and came over to Cherry, who was discussing something with his two accomplices. "My client is in agreement, provided the money is deposited up front for the full period of the lease, plus one month's deposit."

Cherry sneered as he addressed his two friends. "You 'ear that, the bastards don't trust me. They're obviously smarter than I thought. Yeah, tell your wanker of a client he's got a deal. I'll bring the dosh over tonight. Goodbye, you just left."

Cherry watched as the agent headed through the door. "Right Pete, you fuck off and get the bricks and stuff. Arnie, you make sure the rest of the lads get their arses over 'ere as soon as Pete's dumped all the stuff. I want this wall done by tomorrow."

The following day saw a wall built in the middle of the warehouse to form a circle. To one side, a long bar was constructed and topped with a kitchen top.

Cherry walked around, inspecting the work. "Yeah, that'll do. John, when's the fridges arriving?"

"Tomorra, Bob."

"Right, weekend after next is our first fight. John, you make sure we've got the dogs ready. I'll send out the invites. Time to get rich lads."

CHAPTER 26

Harry sat in his chair watching the news in a distracted fashion. Somebody had had their conviction for multiple rape charges overturned due to certain evidence having been gathered without proper procedures being followed.

He was only half following the story. He hadn't been able to concentrate on anything other than the meeting with Jim and Mervyn. What was he going to do? They had him down as Captain America and Rambo rolled into one. He knew the longer he went along with things, the more difficult it would become to extricate himself. But there was something else that was bothering him to a far greater degree. He could feel a deep-down, very unfamiliar thrill that wouldn't go away. It was like something that had been hidden away in a cupboard for most of his life. The door had opened, and it wanted to come out.

Harry's wife Sheila came in and watched the news. "Look at that, another piece of rubbish getting off on a technicality."

He was about to reply when the phone rang; seeing it was Jim, he braced himself and answered.

"Hi Jim, how's things?"

"I received the invites for Mervyn and me for the dog fight on Saturday after next. We each have an entry code as they call it, which we declare at the door. Mervyn and I have decided you can choose which one of us you wish to replace."

Harry's heart jumped into his mouth. "Look Jim, I think it's time we have a serious meeting."

Mervyn was very relieved when he heard that Harry had called for a strategy meeting. "That's good Jim, Harry is taking control of the ground ops. I was hoping that would happen."

They all arrived at Jim's place that evening, kitted out with various drinks and snacks. Mervyn pulled out a menu from the local pizza takeaway with a suggestion that they get a home delivery. They all arranged themselves a drink and sat around Jim's dining room table.

"Thanks for coming over, Harry. I hope Sheila didn't mind."

"No Jim, she's off at one of her bridge sessions."

Mervyn took out his copy of Jeremy's notes and looked at Harry. "Right Harry, we're all yours. How are we going to do this?"

"I was rather hoping you were going to tell me."

Everybody looked at everybody else.

Jim looked down at the table. "We have caught up with the car wheel, haven't we?"

"Maybe we need to talk to your Kevin mate again," said Mervyn.

"Kevin?"

"Sorry, er, not Kevin, Nigel."

"Who the hell is Nigel?"

"Your mentor, the one who gave us this." Mervyn tapped his pile of papers.

"God help us, we are so fucked. His name is Jeremy."

"Oh yeah, that's it, difficult name to remember."

"Can I ask what the overall objective of this project is?" said Harry quietly.

Jim and Mervyn looked at each other.

"Well, um, I think, well Jim and I think, that we need to stop them from doing dog fighting and all that sort of thing."

"So can I presume that you want them to stop forever?"

Mervyn nodded enthusiastically. "Yes Harry, forever is good."

"And should I presume that you would like to send a message to all would-be dog fighters that they should desist?"

Mervyn nodded again, swallowing a large digestive he had popped in. "Mmmm. Yes, that too, a big message."

"How?"

"What? Well, we were sort of hoping you could step up and flesh that bit out Harry."

"Hmmm, I presume the boring option of reporting them to the police has been discounted?"

Jim and Mervyn both nodded enthusiastically. "Been done, didn't work Harry."

Harry stood up and walked over to the large white door brought in by Jim and Mervyn earlier that week and picked up a board marker. He thought for a while and then began to write:

Options

1) *Strongly worded letter to dog fighters.*
2) *Going in and having a word.*
3) *Forming a protest outside site of dog fight.*
4) *Passing by in car and hurling insults.*
5) *Passing by in car and hurling objects.*
6) *Physical damage to dog fighting site.*
7) *Mild physical damage to dog fighters.*
8) *Moderate damage to dog fighters.*
9) *Heavy damage to dog fighters.*
10) *Kill the lot of them.*

Harry stepped back to admire his list. "You will notice that the severity increases as we go down, as does the risk I suppose."

Jim examined the list thoughtfully. "I think the risk sort of peaks in the middle somewhere. Where we really piss them off, but fail to neutralise them, if you see what I mean."

Mervyn nodded. "Mmm, maybe we should put ratings for effectiveness of purpose and risk to ourselves and see where that gets us."

After some deliberation, they were left staring at the following:

Options	*Personal Risk*	*Effectiveness*
11) Strongly worded letter to dog fighters.	*1*	*0*
12) Going in and having a word.	*6*	*0*
13) Forming a protest outside site of dog fight	*3*	*2*
14) Passing by in car hurling insults.	*1*	*0*
15) Passing by in car hurling objects.	*2*	*2*
16) Physical damage to dog fighting site.	*5*	*4*
17) Mild physical damage to dog fighters.	*8*	*5*
18) Moderate damage to dog fighters.	*8*	*6*
19) Heavy damage to dog fighters.	*9*	*7*
20) Kill the lot of them.	*5*	*10*

"So, what now?" Jim wanted to know.

"We take the effectiveness score and take off the risk score and the biggest number is the one we go for," said Mervyn cheerily.

After a bit of mumbling and a couple of whistles, they considered the result… *Kill the lot of them* was the clear winner.

"Right, now we have that out of the way, all we have to do is work out the best way of bumping them off," said Harry, clearly warming to the task.

"Make another list Harry, they work well."

"Yes, they do rather Mervyn, don't they? Right let's see."

With much energy and enthusiasm, a new list appeared:

1) Shoot (Pistol, rifle, arrows, poison dart)
2) Bludgeon (Clubs, socks full of coins, pickaxe handle, anything that comes to hand)
3) Stab (Knife, garden fork, screwdriver, Samurai sword (courtesy of Harry))
4) Gas (Poisonous, explosive, smothering)
5) Burn (Petrol, wood, flame thrower, melted tar, napalm)
6) Bomb (Make our own, gunpowder, dynamite, C4, grenade)
7) Drug overdose (Cocaine, heroin, tik, sleeping pills)
8) Poison (Chemical, natural)
9) Biological (Anthrax, smallpox, virus, bacteria, Novichok)

"That's a good base to start from. Let's shorten the list a bit, some of this stuff is tricky to apply."

"Tricky?"

"Yeah Mervyn, I mean, if we decide bludgeoning with a coin-loaded sock is the way to go, who is going to actually apply said sock to the enemies' heads? Are we, for instance, going to suddenly rise up, socks in hand and be able to crush all the heads effectively without getting beaten to death in the process?"

"Hmmm, see what you mean. We are probably not equipped for melee. Hand-to-hand fighting is probably going to end badly."

Jim pointed at the seven faces glaring down at them from the board. "I think looking at that lot, it's a bloody near certainty, not to mention the fact that we wouldn't be able to stop our knees folding underneath us from fright before we even pulled our socks out of our pockets."

"Hmm, folding knees is a distinct possibility judging from our recent encounter with just one of them."

"Let's extract all the scenarios where our knees could be a problem and get rid of all those things involving exotics."

"Exotics Jim?"

"Yes Mervyn, I'm maybe not the most observant person on the planet but I didn't see Novichok, C4 or grenades on special at Morrisons recently. I've also noted a severe shortage of anthrax, pistols, napalm and dynamite or am I just looking in the wrong aisle?"

The list rapidly condensed to:

Shoot (poison dart)

Gas (explosive)

Burn (petrol)

Poison (chemical, natural)

The three conspirators frowned at the board in deep thought. Mervyn slipped in another digestive, Jim took a long slug of his beer. Following further deliberation, poison darts were removed after Mervyn pointed out that a hiccup could cause one to be swallowed. Gas and petrol held the distinct risk of lighting oneself up in the process and were deemed imprudent.

They all nodded sagely at the remaining solution on the board… Poison.

Jim turned to Mervyn. "I think we need a pharmacist or toxicologist for the next round. Mervyn, the stage is yours." Mervyn stood up and with a confident swagger went to the board. He wiped it clean and turned to his audience of two. Unfortunately for everybody, whenever Mervyn was offered the stage, he felt obliged to make a speech.

"Gentlemen, the task before us is a grave one indeed. We have many things to consider in making a sound judgement and must leave no stone unturned to ensure a favourable outcome. I need not remind you that an error at this stage…"

"You're right Mervyn, you need not remind us, so don't. What do we poison those bastards with? From my point of view, it must be a very painful and unpleasant way to die, much aligned to the death they inflict on their dogs." A general nod of approval met Jim's assessment.

Mervyn put his hand to his chin. "Hmm, that does narrow the list somewhat. It might be useful if its action was delayed somewhat so that we could be long gone by the time they start writhing in agony so to speak."

"Good thinking Mervyn, nicely out of the way, I like that."

Mervyn looked up at the ceiling; the other two took sips of their beers, watching him. "Destroying angels," breathed Mervyn reverently.

Jim and Harry looked at each other. "Is that what we are to be called or are you asking for divine help over there Mervyn?"

"No, you arse. That is what we use, destroying angels."

'Oh good, I didn't know we had those at our disposal, we could have dispensed with all this other bullshit and just pulled in the angel gang to sort things out. Why didn't I think of it earlier, it's all so obvious to me now. Do we go to church to summon them, or does a quick prayer usually do the trick?"

"Fungi."

"Same to you."

"They're mushrooms, or rather toadstools. Very nasty ones too. Start working between eight and twenty-four hours after you've ingested them. Then you start throwing up and crapping yourself. But then, and this is the good bit, you recover, or think you do, whilst all the time it's turning your liver and kidneys into mush."

"Where do we find them Merv?"

"Edges of woods if I recall correctly. I'll have to Google it a bit."

"You know Mervyn, I rather like that. Destroying Angels, that's what we will be known as."

Jim put his head in his hands. "Bloody hell Harry, I've heard it all now. You can call yourself the Yogi Bear Club if you like but please just leave me out of those collectives. Has anybody got any ideas about how we convince those arseholes over there to gorge themselves on toadstools?"

"Good question Jim, that's the next part of our project. Just before we start, pass me that menu; let's order our pizzas, they'll take a while to deliver."

Everybody looked down at the choices.

"I like mushrooms on my pizza normally but all this talk of livers turning to mush has put me off a bit."

"I know what you mean Harry… Hang on a minute, there's an idea – maybe we could doctor their pizzas a bit, or maybe a lot."

"What makes you think they're going to order pizzas Mervyn?"

"Mistaken delivery, you don't really think they're going to bin them, do you? I have a pizza oven in the garden, hasn't been used for years. It'll be fun."

"Yeah, cooking up toxic pizzas, can't wait."

CHAPTER 27

The next couple of days saw Harry reading up on how to make pizzas, whilst Mervyn and Jim went for long walks in the forests looking for anti-social fungi. Mervyn had researched how to identify destroying angels and they had managed to discover seven separate patches where the fungi were happily flourishing. As an extra precaution, Mervyn had diligently researched antidotes for the toxin within the toadstools should any of them accidentally eat some.

"It's a bit like making an atomic bomb," Mervyn told them enthusiastically. "There's always a danger of fallout so to speak."

They sat at the pub table, all leaning conspiratorially towards each other.

The plan as to how they were to deliver the pizzas was still very vague. In an attempt to apply the minds at their disposal, Harry had conjured up another list. He handed a copy out to Mervyn and Jim. "Just rate your first and second choices, here's a pencil."

The list read thus:

1) Knock on door with pizzas, feign wrong delivery.

2) Knock on door with pizzas, leave them on doorstep and run.

3) Bring them along and pass them round.

4) Knock on door and pretend to be giving free pizzas as a promotion for new pizza house opening in area.

5) Forget pizzas and boil down mushrooms into a soup, put soup in their beers, coffee or whatever they are drinking on the night.

Harry collected the lists and looked at the results.

Jim spoke in a hushed tone. "Well, we seem to have all gone for the gutless option number 2 which suits me fine. The way I see it, this has the highest chance of success because it demands very little courage from any of us."

Mervyn nodded towards Harry. "Hey Jim, you and I might be cowards but remember Harry here is someone to be reckoned with."

"Yeah, sorry Harry, no offence meant."

Harry pushed his chest out a little. "Huh, don't be silly, nothing wrong with going with the gut… er, safest option, that's good tactical logic."

"I think it would be a good idea to dress up a bit Harry, so you look like a pizza delivery man."

"Me, why do you think I should be the delivery man?"

"Logic Harry, you're the military dude with all the field training and stuff, and this Bob Cherry bloke has seen Mervyn and me."

Harry looked at Mervyn and Jim in turn. "You mean I have to take the pizzas myself to this place?"

Mervyn smiled encouragingly. "Of course, Harry, you didn't think we would go and steal your thunder, did you? You get all the glory, get that taste of operation in the field, you know, all that stuff you said you missed."

"Oh, um, yeah right, wow can't wait. This is going to be awesome. I suppose."

CHAPTER 28

As the weekend of the dog fight approached, work had intensified on the detail. The toadstools would only be picked at the last moment to ensure freshness, but they all helped with the pizza making and had practised for several days to get the fire in the pizza oven just right.

"After this is over, I don't ever want to see another bloody pizza. At least we only have to eat our successes now. I had gut ache all night from that other one. If I didn't know better, I would have sworn someone popped some of those bloody toadstools in it."

"Sorry Jim, the dough was still raw, and I put in ten times too much yeast, decimal point problem. Won't happen again."

"I bloody hope not Harry, I've still got a fermentation going on inside my guts."

"These ones are pretty good. I like this one with anchovies. Apparently, our toadstools taste quite nice as well."

"How's the branding going Mervyn?"

"Fine, I have knocked up a little Italian-looking frog as our logo, we are calling ourselves Pizza Monty Carlo. I have printed the labels that will go on the boxes. I've taken the precaution of buying another Pay As You Go phone, like the crooks do in *Line of Duty*, in case someone wants to phone our head office to check up on something. After the job is done, we dump the phone in the canal. I've found a straw hat which Harry can wear, and I've printed out a hat band with the frog on it."

"Half a mo, Mervyn, I thought I was doing a dump and run? Why do I need to dress up like a gondolier?"

"Belt and braces, Harry, belt and braces. What happens if somebody opens the door before you've had time to bend down? You know how your back gives you jip. You might have to go through with the 'delivery for Mr Johnson' routine."

"What the fuck is that?"

Mervyn picked up one of the pizza boxes and struck a pose. "Evening sir, pizza delivery for Mr Johnson. No sir, this is the address I was given. You can phone them if you like but I have to leave them at this address, those are my orders."

"You mean I might have to talk to them?"

"Yes, exciting isn't it, Harry? I know you can't wait. Just remember, no heroics on the night, we don't want to alarm them."

"No heroics, yeah right, I'll have to try and remember that."

"Tomorrow, we'll have a drive past the warehouse, just to make sure we know where to go. We've been told things start at eight o' clock, so if we go one hour earlier, we will be sure to find them there setting stuff up. If any of you think of any snags that might occur, write them down and send them to us all so we can mull them over."

CHAPTER 29

Mervyn watched as snag warnings began to appear on his phone, mostly in the small hours of the morning.

Car won't start.

Traffic jam makes pizzas go cold.

I'm too old to pass as a pizza delivery man.

Toadstools have gone.

Do we have enough cheese?

They might want me to eat some pizza to prove it's ok.

How do you make a frog look Italian?

What if they tell me to come inside whilst they eat their pizzas and don't let me leave?

How are we sticking the labels to the boxes?

What if he punches me on the nose when I ring the bell?

At their final planning meeting, contingency plans were designed for each hazard thus:

'Car won't start' – Go by bus.

'Traffic jam makes pizzas go cold' – Everyone eats cold pizza.

'I'm too old to pass as a pizza delivery man' – No you're not.

'Toadstools have gone' – Look for more, quickly.

'Do we have enough cheese?' – Yes

'They might want me to eat some pizza to prove it's ok' – They probably won't.

'How do you make a frog look Italian? – Put a string of onions round its neck.

'What if they get suspicious and pull me inside whilst they eat their pizzas and don't let me leave?' – When did you ever invite a delivery man in?

'How are we sticking the labels to the boxes?' – Pritt

'What if he punches me on the nose when I ring the bell? – Duck

"I must say, I'm a little unsure of a couple of these contingencies, Mervyn."

"Me too," said Harry, a little too quickly.

"Which ones bother you, Jim?"

"Well, this one here, Italians don't have strings of onions round their necks, it's the French that do that."

"Shit, you're right, I'd better change that. What else?"

"The cheese, are you really sure we have enough?"

"Hmm, OK, let's buy some more, we can never be too careful. Anything else?"

"No, everything else is tickety-boo, wouldn't you say Harry?"

"Er, well, I was just a bit…"

"It's toadstool picking time gentlemen!" Mervyn passed out pairs of rubber gloves to them all.

"When you've picked them, make sure you don't touch your mouth or anything, can't take any risks."

"Talking of risks, I was wondering about this delivery I'm supposed to make…"

"No worries there Harry, the pizzas will be sealed in their boxes, you won't need to touch them. Let's go."

They bundled into Mervyn's car and watched anxiously as he kept both eyes on the map on his lap and paid very little attention to the afternoon traffic.

"I marked the toadstool locations off on my map," he explained, whilst holding the map in the air with both hands so that everybody could see.

"Mervyn, hold onto the bloody steering wheel and lower the map, we can't see out the windscreen."

"Eh? Don't worry, got my knees steadying it. You see here and here is where we found the biggest crops."

"Right, give me that bloody map, I'll direct you."

"Are you sure Jim? I can manage perfectly well you know."

"I'm absolutely certain. Right, turn left at the lights. No LEFT, LEFT, THAT WAY."

"You said right turn."

"No, I bloody didn't. I said, Right, turn left."

"Well, what is that supposed to mean?"

"Just carry straight on until we get to a T-junction, then turn RIGHT, OK? That way."

"I'm not stupid, I know which way is left and right. Oh, here's a T-junction, where do I go now?"

"RIGHT!" said Jim and Harry in unison.

"I think only one of you should direct me, otherwise it's going to get confusing."

"I very much doubt it could get more confusing than it already is Mervyn. Right, we're coming up to your first toadstool stash on our left, just pull in here, Mervyn. HERE, HERE… now you've passed it."

"Oh, why didn't you say so? No worries, I'll do a U-turn, here we go."

Mervyn swerved the car round in a sickening arc to the sound of squealing tyres and angry car horns.

"Right, there we are lads, see I told you we'd get here safe and sound."

No sooner had the car come to a halt than Harry and Jim opened their doors and jumped out, breathing the fresh evening air in grateful gulps as they did so.

Harry looked across at Jim. "Delivering the pizzas to the dog ring will be a piece of piss after this. Do you think we could get a bus back?"

Equipped with gloves and plastic bags, the three marched off to the edge of the woods.

"Keep your heads down, don't want to be recognised."

"Who by Mervyn? All the CCTVs hanging in the branches put there by the Woodland Trust?"

"Can't be too cautious. There they are, they look nice and fresh, don't they?"

The three of them stood staring at the mushroom patch for some time.

"They look so… harmless."

"Yeah, just like my first wife," chuckled Harry. "What do we do? Pull them up with their roots or what?"

With a flourish, Mervyn produced three pairs of scissors. "Snip 'em off into the bag, try not to fiddle with them too much."

Amidst several groans and grunts, the three set to cutting off the little fungi. Jim lost his balance once and fell on top of them, spoiling some of the crop, but eventually three well-filled bags were taken gingerly back to the car.

"What do we say, if we are asked what we are doing?"

"Got that covered Harry," said Mervyn confidently. "School project."

"To achieve what exactly?"

"Don't over-analyse, Jim. Right, put the bags into the black plastic bag in the boot along with your gloves, and off we go."

"I thought I might have a bit of a stroll, catch the bus back."

"Oh, sorry Harry, no bus routes out here, climb in."

CHAPTER 30

"You won't forget my bridge night this Sunday, eh?"

"No Sheila, got it noted."

Harry was watching the news in a distracted fashion. He wasn't sure he could go through with this delivery thing. Apart from the chance that they would rumble him, he was about to commit pre-meditated murder. He felt a trickle of cold sweat roll down his back. He shivered.

Sheila looked at him. "I don't blame you dear, it's terrible, made me shiver too when I first heard about it."

"What?"

She nodded towards the TV. "That rapist bloke, Tom Blunt, who got off scot-free. Was burnt alive in his car. There was an old lady there who tried to save him, Emily Nolan, bless her, but she couldn't do anything, how could she? I suppose he had it coming, if I have to be honest. Funny how life works out, eh?"

CHAPTER 31

Detective Inspector Ash Kamau tapped the report. "That's the second piece of lowlife to have come to an untimely end in as many weeks. Maybe there is such a thing as poetic justice after all."

"Pardon Boss?"

"No, nothing Ella. Just do me a favour and pull out that docket on Jackie Ruthers, the gangster dude who died last week."

CHAPTER 32

It was 'P-Day' as Mervyn had labelled it. They all met at Mervyn's place at two in the afternoon. The labelled pizza boxes were stacked in one corner of the dining room awaiting their deadly cargo. Mervyn had brought in extra wood and reported enthusiastically that the wind was from the east, so the fumes from the toadstools cooking wouldn't pose a problem.

"Hey, wait a minute Merv, you said nothing about toadstool fumes."

"Oh, didn't I? We need to be a bit careful, some toadstool fumes are really quite nasty apparently, not sure about ours but best to err on the safe side I always say."

"Why am I not feeling a huge wave of relief. Where are they?" Jim sighed.

"I put the black bag and everything in the fridge."

Mervyn walked over to a large sheet of paper held by Prestik against the kitchen wall. "Here is our countdown to 'P-hour', where Harry gets to deliver the package. I've worked the times back, based upon the time study I did when we were practising our pizzas. You can see that we need to light our pizza oven here and then start the pizza dough prep round about then. I've put in a one-hour contingency for unforeseen delays."

"Very nice Mervyn, I like it. Very thorough."

"Thank you, Jim. Shall we begin?"

Things started off a little panicky until Mervyn remembered where he had put the matches, but after that, each member performed their tasks smoothly enough. It had been decided that the toadstools would be cooked separately in a frying pan and added to the pizzas at the end. Mervyn, aware of the proximity they would be in to the fumes, had provided his grandmother's copper bedpan which sported a good long handle, thus keeping them away from the bubbling fungi.

When it eventually came time to cook the toadstools, all utilised facemasks, and spent a good amount of time mincing around as they were cut and placed into the bed pan. They were soon sizzling away nicely as the three kept their distance with wide eyes fixed on the toxic concoction.

With half an hour to spare, the pizzas had been slid into their boxes and sealed ready for their final journey.

All three conspirators watched the boxes as they stood piled up, unable to take their eyes off them for too long.

Mervyn disappeared for a moment before returning with an overall and straw hat complete with frog-emblazoned hat band.

"OK Harry, this is the bit you've been waiting for – time to suit up!"

CHAPTER 33

The boxes containing their precious cargo were placed gently into the boot of the car in an insulated box to keep them warm, after being wrapped in another black plastic bin liner and sealed. Everybody climbed into the car and opened the windows in case the pizza fumes made their way into the cab.

"Right, here we go," said Mervyn as he turned the key.

An ominous silence prompted Mervyn to turn the key again. He pumped the clutch a few times, pulled on the handbrake and then let it off again… nothing.

"I think the battery is flat, it looks like I left the lights on last night."

"Well, I suppose that's it then. We'll just have to call it off. Damn, I was really looking forward to a bit of action."

"I know you were Harry. Maybe we should catch a bus?"

"Which bus do we need to catch Merv?"

"Er, sorry Jim, I didn't research that bit."

"Well that's helpful. And it's on an industrial estate so we'd have to walk over a bloody mile from the bus stop, assuming we knew which bus to catch, which we don't."

"There has to be another way, Jim."

"Well, I'm all bloody ears Merv."

"Maybe this is fate's way of telling us we were in the wrong."

"What are you on about Harry? This is fate's way of telling us that Mervyn is a bloody dickhead."

"I'm sorry guys, maybe we can bump start the car. You get out and push."

"For fuck's sake Merv, I'm too old for this shit."

"I reckon we should call it…"

"Shut up Harry and push!"

The initial heaving and groaning had no effect. "Mervyn, have you got the handbrake on?"

"Oops sorry, right, here we go."

The car lumbered down the road at about half mile a century, accompanied by much wheezing and groaning.

Suddenly, Mervyn dropped the clutch, bringing the car to a dead halt and causing Harry and Jim to thump their heads against the rear window.

"Mervyn, what the fuck are you doing? We need to get some speed up first."

"I was worried that that was the fastest we were going to go."

"I think you might be right. This is ridiculous, we…" Jim's voice froze as a flood of flashing blue lights bathed the car.

The police car pulled in front of them and stopped.

"Oh shit Jim, they're onto us. We're all going to rot in jail. I knew we should have called it off!"

"What are you talking about Harry? Just keep bloody quiet!"

The policeman stepped out of his car, putting on his cap as he did so. "In a spot of bother gentlemen?" He looked straight at Harry.

Harry stared at the man, then at Jim and then back at the policeman. "We're doing nothing officer, just going for a… um."

The police officer walked over to Mervyn, who was slowly and painfully getting out of his car. "Flat battery sir?"

"Yes officer, I'm sorry."

"No need, have you got a set of jump leads? Mine won't reach your battery but together we might get you going."

"Yes officer, I do." Mervyn shuffled around to the back of the car and opened the boot. All three froze at the sight of the black plastic bag with its ominous contents.

The policeman leaned forwards into the boot. "Mmm, nice smell, what's that you've got?"

"No, don't sniff it in! I, er, I mean it's just our pizzas and you shouldn't smell them too much because um, er, it er…"

"It will make you hungry officer," interjected Jim in a panicked falsetto. "That would be very unfair of us."

"Ha, not willing to share your tasty morsels?" The policeman smiled. "Just joking gentlemen. I'll connect up my jump leads, you connect yours to your battery and we should have you on your way in no time."

Mervyn's hands were shaking so much by this time that he could hardly open the bonnet.

Between the three of them they managed to connect the leads as the policeman revved his car into action and nodded at Mervyn to start his car. As he did so, the car leapt forwards, closer to the police car. He pulled the gear stick out of gear and then panicked again, grinding the gears for good measure. Eventually, to all three men's amazement, the car's engine leapt into life.

The policeman stepped out and disconnected all the leads, closing the bonnets of both cars. "There we go, don't stall the car, you'll need to keep it revving for a while to give the battery a bit of charge."

"Thank you, officer, I don't know how to repay you for your kindness, thank you, thank you."

"A slice of that pizza would be nice."

"Aaah, no, not possible because it's, er, umm…"

"We've eaten it all, all gone it is, inside us, all of it, inside us, harmlessly being digested, nothing wrong with it… at all…"

"Just joking gentlemen, have a good evening."

"You too officer, thank you," Jim offered in falsetto again.

They watched the police car drive off.

"I wonder if he's going to call that in?"

"Yes Harry! 'Helped three doddery old farts deliver enough poison to kill a small town.' Come on, let's get out of here."

Intensely aware that stalling the car would render them stranded once again, Mervyn elected to stay in first gear. The car's engine screamed its way along for the rest of the journey. As they approached the warehouse, they saw several cars parked outside along with the Jaguar Mervyn had connected with previously.

"Over there Mervyn, park in the shadow and turn your bloody lights out." Mervyn did as he was told but kept the engine running. Harry's heart was pounding so loudly he could hardly hear what anybody else was saying. He fingered his straw hat nervously, leaving sweat marks on its rim.

"Well Harry, it's over to you, action stations, Geronimo, or whatever you squaddies say."

Harry closed his eyes tightly, trying to steady his nerves. He repeated the words in his head: "Pizza delivery for Mr Johnson, sorry sir, my orders are that I have to deliver them here, 117 Belfore Park, you can phone head office if you wish, the number is on the box."

"Guys, what happens if…"

"Don't worry Harry, you'll know what to do!"

Jim stepped out to the back of the car and very gingerly lifted the plastic bag onto the ground. He lifted out the warm pizza boxes and handed them to Harry. He straightened Harry's hat and stepped back. "There, you look just like a pizza guy. Go get 'em. Or rather, go give 'em Harry, it's your moment."

Harry turned and without a word started towards the warehouse. He was beyond fear, he couldn't believe that his legs were still working. Every step brought him closer to his death. He was sure it would be painful. He would probably be fed alive to the dogs as a special opening night bonus attraction. He could only hope that the bastards would be tucking into his pizzas as they watched him being torn to shreds.

Suddenly, he was at the door. The entrance was bathed in a sickly yellow light shining gloomily from a rusty lamp above the door. He could hear barking coming from a large van parked someway off to his left. A button was illuminated with an orange light; balancing the pizzas on one hand, he saw his finger push the button. A buzzer sounded somewhere inside the warehouse. With a groan, he started to get down on one knee to place the pizzas on the stoop, but his hopes were crushed as he heard a voice from behind the closed door.

"Who the fuck is this?"

Harry heard his voice coming from a long distance away. "Pizza delivery for Mr Johnson." He got to his feet with the pizzas, grimacing as he did so.

"No Mr Johnson 'ere, fuck off."

"I have to deliver these to 117 Belfore Park."

The door opened slightly. "Who the fuck are you?"

"I'm Harry Johns… er, the pizza man, er, delivery Johnson, Belfore 117."

The man turned and shouted, "Hey Boss, did you order pizzas?" The man looked Harry up and down, saying nothing.

Eventually, another man appeared behind the first one. "What's your problem?"

Harry closed his eyes. "Pizza delivery, Mr Belfore 117 Johnson Park."

"What? Didn't order none."

"Pizza Mr Johnson, 117 Belfore Park. Sorry sir, sorry sir, my… my… my… orders are I have to deliver them here, 117, Belfore Park, you can phone head number if you wish, the office is on the box."

The new man looked at the boxes.

"What are they?"

"Pizzas sir."

"I know that you dumb fuck, what's on 'em?"

"Er, um toad, er, toa.., toasted mushrooms and, er, cheese and other things, tasty things, very tasty… sir."

"You can leave 'em but I ain't paying you fuck all."

"Prepaid sir, already paid all the money, all of it, paid, every last penny of it, nothing else to pay."

"Take 'em John. What the fuck. Oi, you, tell your 'ead office that if they come sniffing round 'ere for any money, they'll get fucking duffed."

"Yes sir, will do, thank you very much sir, very kind of you."

"Go on then, fuck off."

"Yes sir."

Harry turned and walked away. Feeling their eyes burning into his back, he had to keep telling his legs not to break into a seventy-year-old sprint. He heard a voice say, "What a burk," followed by a loud bang, which he initially thought was a gun shot, but then thankfully realised was the door slamming shut. He held his breath and turned around, expecting to see them following him with pipe wrenches in their hands, but the courtyard was empty and silent, except for the sound in the distance of the dogs barking from within the van.

CHAPTER 34

Mervyn had kept the engine running and positioned the car facing the exit, ready for a quick getaway should it be required. As he saw Harry walking back towards them, he let out a little whoop.

"He's done it Jim, he's done it. Look at it him strolling back without a care in the world, I wouldn't be surprised if he's whistling a little song."

Harry saw his two friends smiling at him from the car. He felt like crying. He didn't think he would ever see them again, convinced as he was, that parts of his anatomy would by now be digesting within some dog's stomach. The thought made him slightly dizzy. He paused and looked back towards the warehouse to hide his expression of bewilderment and nausea.

"Look at him, he's savouring the moment. He's checking that all's well. I would have been running for the car long ago, what a professional, eh, Jim?"

"He's the man, there's no doubt."

With trembling hands, Harry opened the rear car door and fell into the back seat, exhausted beyond measure. Sparing no time, Mervyn roared off through the entrance and proceeded back home.

"Well done, Harry, that was seriously impressive. What did they say? Did you see them?" Jim turned round to see why Harry was not answering. The man was fast asleep. "Will you look at that Mervyn, he's having a little nap. Nerves of steel, unbelievable."

Back at the house, Harry sat with a large scotch in his hand, trying to work out if the terror of the last hour was real or just a horrific nightmare. He looked at his friends' smiling faces and managed to compose his thoughts. "Yeah, straightforward really, just fed them the line that we had practised."

"Amazing."

"Of course, I had to ad lib a bit. They were very suspicious and were giving me a bit of lip, but I just kept my calm and relied on their innate greed. Summed them up pretty quickly, you know, part of my training."

"Well Jim and I would have been stuttering and stammering if we had to say anything other than our lines. Well done, Harry, here's to you, our very own action man."

CHAPTER 35

Bob Cherry awoke with a bit of a headache. The evening had raked in just over eighty thousand pounds. Not bad for a first night. The crowd was down on normal though; he would follow up on the no-shows later. The pizzas had been a big success, a couple had been left over but were set upon by the rest of the crowd. Pity they had mushrooms all over them, he hated mushrooms, bloody typical that they'd all be covered in the damned things.

He stacked the notes into bundles and dialled his right-hand man. The phone just rang out; he left a message: "Are you at the warehouse yet?"

About five minutes later a text message came back: *No, feeling like shit.*

"Whose fault is that piss cat?" *Get your arse down there with the rest and clean up.*

The phone rang. "Boss, I'm really not feeling good."

"Who gives a fuck? You telling me a hangover stops you working?"

"I can't get off the crapper, it's coming out both ends, I shat myself too."

"Bollocks, wear a nappy and get down there!" He hung up. "Fucking wanker." He punched in another number. "Arnie, yeah, it's Bob here. Don't wait for Pete, the bastard's whingeing he's ill…"

"I've got the shits boss, puked all over myself. I think we ate something funny."

"You too?! Fucking useless bunch of wimps, can't handle a couple of pints. What's going on here?"

He phoned three others with no answer. "Fuck you all. Do I have to do everything my fucking self."

CHAPTER 36

Humphrey Bright leaned against the toilet seat. He had been heaving up nothing but bile for the last two hours. It wasn't fair, he should be celebrating with his mates. He had bet heavily on a dog at the dog fight the day before and had made a few bob. He thought back – maybe he'd caught something off somebody at the dog ring, or maybe it was that slice of pizza he had scoffed. It wasn't as if he could complain or report them for serving up dodgy food. It wasn't fair. Another fit of heaving struck him.

CHAPTER 37

Jim left Mervyn's place and went straight round to No.12 where the cat was waiting for him in the hallway.

"Hello Archie, old buddy. Have I got news for you!" They walked into the kitchen and the cat settled down on the chair as Jim regaled the goings-on of the previous night. "Harry was amazing, a real stalwart. With him on the gang, we make a really solid fighting unit."

The cat cocked its head sideways whilst giving a long look into Jim's soul.

"What, don't you believe me? He was really solid."

The cat continued its look.

"Hmm, well, I beg to differ. If you meet him, you'll change your mind. Your mum is away to the hospital again, I hope everything is going OK. Do you think she is alright?" At first, Jim thought the cat was about to produce a hair ball but the longer he watched the more he was convinced that the cat was laughing.

"Well, I'm not sure what I said was funny, but I'll trust your opinion that she is fine. I hope boiled chicken is still OK. I must remember to check with your mum about that. I'm not too sure when she is due back, she just said it would take a few days."

CHAPTER 38

Detective Inspector Ash Kamau looked down as a file flopped on his desk.

"Thought you might be interested in this Ash, based on what you were saying the other day about lowlifes getting some unlucky breaks. Here's another, just came in from Wandsworth."

Ash opened the docket. There was a photo of a man lying flat on his face on a pavement, a large gash across the back of his head and a brick close by. The man had been declared dead at the scene.

According to the witness, the man had fallen to the ground after the brick "fell from the sky" and hit him on the head. Upon investigation, the brick appeared to have become dislodged from an awning in the roof directly above where the man had fallen.

The witness, Gladys Ingrams, an elderly homeless lady, was sleeping close by, and was convinced that the whole building was about to come down on her. An inspection showed that the rest of the brickwork was in good condition, but by that time the homeless lady had taken her belongings and moved on.

He turned to the profile of the deceased, James Buckworth. Sure enough, the man had form. He had recently been remanded in custody pending an investigation into child molestation. He was released after the principal witness had disappeared.

Kamau frowned and retrieved two other files. Was there a connection or was natural justice taking its course? All three deaths were apparently accidental, but all had a slightly bizarre element about them. Massive sudden heart attack with no previous history of heart problems, burnt alive in a car and now a head crushed by a falling brick. Should he even be concerning himself with shadows when there were so many other tangible crimes to be solved? Was he looking for something that just wasn't there? He gathered all three files together and put them in his bottom drawer.

CHAPTER 39

Bob Cherry walked up and down in front of his gang. "Are you girls all better after your hangovers? What a bunch of pricks you lot are. Oh, I was feeling so poorly Bob. Oh, me guts was sore. Bloody wimps all of you."

"It wasn't the booze boss, it was sunnink we ate."

"Really, you know what I think? I think you're a bunch of lazy cunts who decided to come up with this load of bullshit to cover your arses. That's what I think."

"Bollocks! It was that bloody pizza."

Cherry walked over to the man and shouted in his face. "Did you say bollocks to me, you arrogant chunk of shit?" He headbutted the man, sending him flying backwards. As the man fell, Cherry proceeded to kick him in the head with his steel toe-capped boots until the man was silent and still.

"Anybody else got an opinion? Thought not. Gutless fuckers."

Cherry went over to the man on the floor, now slowly trying to get up. He aimed another kick to his head. "Get this piece of shit out of here, we've got work to do. I want everything shipshape for another show in four days' time, got it?"

The men went about the task of tidying the place and washing the arena. They put the torn carcasses of two dogs into black plastic bags and began sweeping up the blood-soaked sawdust from the ring.

"I don't know about you Arthur, but I still feel a bit crook."

"Shhh, don't let Bob 'ear or you'll wind up like Arnie over there. I must say I've felt better meself."

"I reckon it were them pizzas, we all ate 'em and we all feel shit."

"Bob's alright though, 'ow'd that 'appen?"

"He didn't eat any did he?"

"Didn't 'e? I didn't notice."

"Yeah, said he didn't like mushrooms or sunnink."

"You don't think 'e sort of laced 'em do you Joe?"

"Dunno Arthur, but I intend to find out."

CHAPTER 40

Mervyn stared at Jim with a concerned look.

"What do we do now Jim?"

"Well, I'm going to enjoy this pint and maybe have a scotch egg."

"No, I mean about the dog gang."

"Oh them, well, first we pay them a visit to see if they've mended their ways."

"Why do we have to do that?!"

"I'm joking Harry, we do absolutely nothing, nada."

"Hopefully, nature will take its course. Let's keep our eyes peeled for anything in the papers."

"You haven't told your wife anything Harry, have you?"

"Nothing passes my lips about an operation, Merv. We take our secrets to the grave, resisting torture methods was part of my basic training."

"Really, Harry, were you in special ops? I thought you were in the regular army – no wonder you are so cool under fire."

"Can't talk about it Merv. You wouldn't believe it if I did."

"I don't know about you guys but I'm quite keen to get on with another project. Twiddling my thumbs is going to drive me nuts."

"Got something in mind Merv?"

"Not off the top of my head Jim, maybe we should scan the newspapers and see what scum floats to the surface. I'm feeling way more confident that we can take them on now that Harry is part of the team."

"Yeah, I guess you must be itching for some more action, eh Harry?"

"Of course, yeah, sure, wow, bring it on. But maybe we should cool it for a while, just to let the trail go dead sort of thing."

"Don't see anything wrong with a bit of background research. Let's formulate our plans, then we can release you into the fray again when we're ready – don't want you getting bored eh?"

"Er, yeah, just to give you a heads up, the wife has been nagging to get away. I might have to take a few days off, you know, keep her quiet. Don't want to raise her suspicions."

"No of course Harry, don't worry. With any luck when you come back, Jim and I will have the next operation already planned for you. That would be good, eh?"

"Yeah, thanks Merv that would be, er, unbelievable."

That evening, Mervyn and Jim scanned every local and national newspaper for likely targets.

Meanwhile, over supper, Harry decided to bring up the subject of a vacation.

"Sheila, you know how you were saying we should get away?"

"Was I? I don't remember that."

"Yeah, you know, get away for a few days, you'd like that, eh?"

"Would I? Why?"

"Well, you know. I think you need a nice break."

"What makes you say that? Have I been crabby lately or something?"

"No of course not, but it would be a good idea, eh?"

"I wouldn't mind going to Paris."

"Hmm, problem is, we'd only be able to afford a couple of days there."

"How long were you thinking?"

"Oooh, a couple of weeks at least, maybe more."

"How do we afford that long Harry? It isn't growing on trees, is it?"

"I thought we might dust off the tent and maybe go camping somewhere nice like Eastbourne or Margate."

"The tent?! You mean that mouldy thing in the shed that hasn't seen the light of day since our honeymoon? Very funny."

"Just needs airing a bit."

"Airing! It needs beating to death first."

"Come on Sheila. It would be like the old days. Get that old romance back into our lives."

"In the old days Harry, we were able to bend over and get up again without needing to call the paramedics. You don't seriously expect me to crawl around on my hands and knees inside that smelly old tent, do you?"

Harry sighed. The brick wall he was up against was not showing any doorway, not even a locked one.

"Well, where do you want to go then?"

"I want to go to Paris."

CHAPTER 41

Bob Cherry thumped his fist on the desk. His whole gang had gone down sick again. Three were in hospital. Somebody was taking him for a bloody fool. He had reluctantly realised that there was something wrong. They weren't all just a lazy bunch of bastards. He made his mind up and drove to the hospital.

"Mr Arnold Smith is in Ward 7, sir."

"Thanks luv." He walked down the corridor, trying not to breathe too deeply. He hated hospitals. "Fuck you Arnie. Sick bastard making me come into this shit hole," he mumbled through clenched teeth.

He stood at the ward entrance scanning the beds' occupants. The sister walked up to him. "Can I help you?"

"Yeah, I'm looking for Arnold Smith."

"Do you know Mr Smith sir?"

"Yeah, he's a mate."

"Do you know what might be wrong with him?"

"I thought that was your job."

"We are trying to ascertain the cause. He has ingested a poison of some kind."

"Like what?"

"He has all the symptoms of fungal poisoning, toadstools of some kind."

Bob's mind raced. "Has he said anything?"

"He's pretty delirious but the staff nurse thought he said something about pizzas. You wouldn't happen to know where he bought his pizzas would you?"

"No, haven't a clue." Bob turned and walked out of the ward.

The sister called after him, "Don't you want to see your friend?"

Bob sat in his car tapping his steering wheel as he thought, "Those fucking pizzas."

He started the car and roared off. When he arrived at the warehouse he drove around to the back and parked his car. He could see the black plastic bags piled into the skip. He switched the torch of his mobile phone on and started opening each plastic bag. Eventually he found the thing he was looking for. He ripped the lid off the pizza box and took it with him back to his car. Sitting inside he dialled the number on the box.

Mervyn heard the phone ring. He couldn't make out why it had a different ring tone. He saw his own phone lying silent on the mantlepiece. Following the sound, he arrived at his jacket hanging against the door. Without thinking, he picked the phone out of his pocket and answered.

"Hello."

"Is this Pizza Monty Carlo?"

Mervyn shrieked.

"Hello, hello. Answer me you fucking bastards. I'm gonna kill the fucking lot of yer!"

In a flat panic, Mervyn took the phone and dropped it inside the electric kettle, turning it on as he did so. He stood and watched as it bubbled away, trying to get that horrible voice out of his head. *I'm gonna kill the fucking lot of yer.*

A little later Harry and Jim were in Mervyn's kitchen, listening to Mervyn's quivering voice outlining his phone call.

"For fuck's sake Merv, you were supposed to dump the bloody thing in the canal, remember? The canal, not your bloody pocket!"

"I know, but after all the excitement, I forgot."

"Why the hell did you answer it?"

"I don't know, I just wanted to be helpful, it might have been important."

"Well, I suppose it was, eh? Did you answer with your name?"

"I can't remember."

"Bloody hell Mervyn, they might be on their way round right now. What do we do Harry?"

Harry was staring at Mervyn. "What? We get the hell out of, er, we evacuate Mervyn from here and he must go with you Jim, and I must run, er, I will make a tactical retreat." And with that, Harry shot out of the front door leaving it open as he left.

"He's probably right Mervyn. What did you do with the phone?"

"Boiled it."

"I beg your pardon?"

"I boiled it in the kettle."

Jim turned to look where Mervyn was pointing. He got up and lifted the kettle lid. "Does that inactivate it? Did Harry give you that tip?"

"I don't know, it was the first thing that came into my head."

Jim shrugged as he spooned the phone out with a ladle. "Better take it with us and crush it or something, it still seems to be lighting up."

Jim nudged the phone under the cold water tap; as he did so, it rang again. They both stared at it, and then, as if possessed by some uncontrollable desire, Jim watched as his hand picked the phone up and answered it. "Hello, Pizza Monty Carlo here."

"What, who is this? I'm coming for you bastards!"

"Yeah, you and whose army? You're a dead man walking… Fucker!" Jim then switched the phone off and dropped it.

"What did you do that for?"

Jim stared into the distance. "I haven't the faintest idea Merv, but hell, it felt good."

They both shot off in Mervyn's car, whilst Jim tried to open the back of the phone. "I can't get the back off Merv, drive to the canal."

They arrived at the bridge and looked around. "All clear Jim."

Jim opened the window and tossed the phone over the wall. "Right Merv, round to my place."

CHAPTER 42

Bob Cherry stared at his phone; his hand was shaking badly. It was no accident – they were gunning for him and proud of it. He tried to remember what the delivery bloke looked like… Man, medium build, medium height, medium looks, medium everything.

What had the delivery man said? Just waffle, bland, medium waffle. He had nothing. Vehicle – no sign. No CCTV, he'd made sure of that himself. "Fuck, fuck, fuck," he snarled. Who wanted him out of commission? Not him, but his operation! Who stood to gain from his dog operation going tits up? Who had the balls to answer the phone and brag about the hit?

The thought arrived lit up in neon lights. The Lambeth outfit, the only other London dog ring South of the Thames. "Eric Crabbs, you slimy chunk of shit, I'm gonna fucking do you!" He bit his thumb nail. He had to think. Had to keep his cool. Not raise any alarms. Pretend to act dumb. He knew where Crabbs ran his operation, a fancy wooden barn. He'd been there a while ago to see if he could pick up any tips. He remembered when Crabbs had spotted him in the crowd.

"Well, if isn't Mr Bob bloody Cherry. Spying on us are ya? The little snot nose wanna see how the big men do it? 'Ave a good look son, that crappy Croydon outfit of yours won't last a fucking month."

But it had, it had lasted a good six months and was dragging punters from Lambeth in the process.

"Crabbs, you are so fucking dead!"

He was about to call some of his crew when he remembered that they were all out of action. He could have been too. He had to act quickly. They probably hadn't rumbled that he was OK, unless some of his own bunch had ratted. They were mostly faithful, maybe he was a bit hasty with Arnie, but the bastard had pissed him off. Best to go it alone – he didn't know who to trust anymore.

"Dead man walking" – what did that mean? Maybe the poison was in him too, maybe it wasn't the mushrooms. He might not have much time. No time, had to act fast, think, think, think.

He went into his loft; he might need a shooter. There was an empty petrol can in the corner. A thought came into his head. When did they have their fights? He checked the date. It was today – the third of every month. "Bloody hell," he cursed. He might not have another chance.

He made up his mind, pocketed the Beretta 9mm pistol and grabbed the petrol can. He cut a piece of hose off in the garden and went to his car. He syphoned the fuel from the Jag into the can until it was full. He couldn't risk being seen on a garage CCTV filling up a petrol can, people didn't do that often anymore. He wiped the can off and put it in the boot of the car, along with the rag he had wiped it with. He climbed in and drove calmly through the evening traffic.

The barn was lit up brightly. It had a cowboy look about it. Several cars were parked outside. He parked his car alongside them and strolled off to the barn with his gun tucked inside his belt.

He walked to the back and checked the doors gently. They were all locked. He looked around and found several planks which he propped up against the doors to prevent them from opening. He then strolled round to the front door; after trying it gently, he saw that it was also locked.

He turned and retraced his steps to the car. He glanced around for any CCTVs and confirmed that their absence was in line with his own planning at his warehouse.

Taking the petrol can out with the rag, he casually wandered over to the front door and gently started pouring half the petrol in and under the door, making sure that the rag was well soaked and halfway under the door as well. He bent down and lit the rag. The petrol fumes caught and singed his hair. He stood up rapidly and ran round to the back door. Somebody was shouting and trying to open it, but the planks he had in place were doing their temporary job. He poured the rest of the can under that door and, listening to the shouts inside, lit the puddle. There was a woof as the petrol ignited rapidly inside.

The thumping on the door ceased. He was about to leave but decided to stay and listen to the screams as the flames began engulfing the building and pouring out from every window. He briefly saw the unmistakable face of Crabbs at one of the windows before the fire wrapped around him and pulled him back inside.

"Burn fucker burn, that dead man certainly ain't walking." Cherry smiled and threw the can against the burning door. "There's my calling card. Bye bye."

He climbed into his car and calmly drove away. He saw the lights of the fire engines approaching in the distance. He glanced back at the barn just as the roof caved in, sending sparks high into the sky. He shared the view with the driver who was carrying the dogs, now parked up with nowhere to go.

CHAPTER 43

The fire was reported in the papers the following day. 'Tragic loss of life at private club, only one survivor' the headlines read. The names had been withheld pending contact with the families.

DI Ash Kamau read the initial reports that had come in. Arson was suspected, a petrol can had been found at the site and the fire had been started at both doors. The occupants were trapped inside and there were signs that the back door had been jammed by planks. The report went on to say that the club had been closed down for illegal gambling but had been allowed to open again two months later after the investigation was dropped due to lack of evidence.

Kamau glanced across to his assistant PC. "Ella, see what you can dig up about the gambling story on this place for me."

On his way home on the tube, Ash flicked through the evening newspaper. His eye caught a story about a local hospital having to deal with several cases of poisoning. The hospital was advising anybody with sudden violent nausea to report immediately to their doctors. The symptoms resembled those experienced when toadstools were consumed. It was unclear why they were not able to establish the source.

That evening, Harry pushed his mushroom omelette around his plate. "Sheila, did you hear there are some mushrooms doing the rounds that are poisonous?"

"Yes, my friend Sue, you remember, the nurse, was telling me that they have about ten of the victims there at the moment. She thinks some of them might not pull through. Really bad it is. And you know what's funny? None of them can say how they got it. A couple have mentioned pizzas apparently, but they seem to be going in and out of consciousness. It's worrying that they can't find the source."

"I think I'll have a cheese sandwich if you don't mind."

"Hmm, I think I'll join you."

The following day, Ash saw that the morning paper carried a story of how four people had died the previous night of mushroom poisoning.

'TOADSTOOLS IN PIZZAS, EXPERTS BAFFLED' ran the headline. Several more were in a critical condition, and there seemed to be no leads on where the pizzas had come from.

The deceased were identified as John Gough, Peter Jenkins and Arthur Dunn, all Croydon residents. Authorities were appealing to anybody who could shed light on the source of the toadstools to come forwards.

Ella walked over holding a file. "Ash, you know that club that burnt down? There was a suspected dog fighting ring operating there, but the investigating officers bungled the search authority, and the case was closed."

Dog fighting? Something was nagging him, what was it? He shrugged and put the file along with the others in his bottom drawer.

CHAPTER 44

It seemed prudent to both Jim and Mervyn that Mervyn should lay low for a while at Jim's place. Unfortunately, they had left in such a hurry, he had taken nothing to sustain him.

"I'll have to go back Jim. I can get pills and stuff from the chemist, even a shirt or two and trousers are no problem, but I need my underpants."

"Your underpants?"

"Yeah, they're special material, to stop me coming out in a rash."

"You know Mervyn, as life goes on, I start to learn how many snags I've managed to avoid. I suppose I should be more grateful. Going back to your place is a bit of a risk. Not all of those buggers are dead and that one who called sounded quite healthy and dangerous."

"I've weighed up the risks Jim, and ordinary underpants are a no-go."

"OK, we'd better go round sooner rather than later I suppose."

"No Jim, this is something I have to do alone, I can't expect you to risk your life, you're not an action man – if it got nasty, you'd be out on a limb."

"OK, but you're not going alone. Harry would love to ride shotgun, I'm sure."

Mervyn brightened up. "Yeah, it would be nice to have someone to cover my back, he'd love it."

Jim phoned Harry.

"I'm sorry Jim, could you say that again?"

"Mervyn needs you to protect him whilst he picks up some underpants from his house."

"Why?"

"They're special underpants he…"

"No, why me?"

"We need somebody conversant with bodyguard techniques. Do you have a weapon, Harry?"

Harry shut his eyes and cursed silently. He had eventually agreed to the Paris option with his wife, but due to the cost, he needed to hold it as a trump card for ducking out of something really nasty that Jim and Mervyn volunteered him for. A card to be pulled only when danger really threatened. Now it looked as if he was going to have to waste it on an underpants rescue mission. He vacillated momentarily, and then made up his mind.

"Paris."

"I'm sorry Harry, what was that?"

"Paris, me and the missus are off to Paris."

"Oh, that's nice. When?"

"Er, very soon, no time you see, sorry, got to go, will talk when we're back."

"It won't take… Oh, he's gone. Did you know Harry and his wife were off to Paris?"

"No, he never mentioned it."

"Oh well Merv, it's back to the two musketeers. I can at least sit in the car and honk the horn if anything dodgy happens."

Mervyn bit his lower lip. "Thanks Jim, you don't have to do this, but it would be nice to have back up."

"Come on Mervyn, let's do it now before we both talk me out it."

The house looked watchful as they approached. They drove past once at Jim's insistence, just to recce the target, then turned at the bottom of the road and parked a little way down from where Mervyn lived.

"Right, this is it." Mervyn groaned as he lifted himself from the car.

"I've left the keys Jim, if there are any shots, just drive away."

Jim watched as Mervyn toddled towards his house. As he went inside, Jim continually scanned the road. He looked at his watch, almost ten minutes had passed. "How many bloody underpants can one man need?"

A car started coming slowly down the road. All he could see were the headlights in the side mirror.

It looked like a Jaguar and was crawling along stealthily. Jim's heart started to race. The sweat started to pour off him. He was going to be shredded, tortured, water boarded, hung, drawn and quartered. And then the Mini went past with an old man at the wheel.

As he turned the corner, Jim saw Mervyn struggling towards him with two huge suitcases. "Thank God!" said Jim reverently and meant it.

"I decided to get everything I might need Jim." The two wrestled the suitcases into the boot and high-tailed it back to Jim's place.

On the other side of town, Harry was having a far less successful time.

"Harry, are you insane? It's half past six. I've started cooking supper."

"Yes, I know Sheila, but I wanted to give you a surprise."

"You have. Maybe next time, try and make it a pleasant one."

"Come on Sheila, you're the one who wanted to go to Paris."

"But tonight? Right now? The train leaves at twelve tomorrow! Are you planning for us to sit on the platform all night?"

Harry hung his head and sighed. "You're right, of course, I just wanted to…"

He picked up the phone. "Hi Jim, I'm coming round, let's do this."

"No worries Harry, all sorted, we've done it."

Harry put the phone down gently. He looked at his shaking hands. "Coward," he said gently.

CHAPTER 45

Ash Kamau looked up as his assistant put a piece of paper on his desk. "Sir, those names you asked me to run, they were some of the alleged Croydon dog fighting ring that got let off."

"I thought they sounded familiar, thanks Ella. Get hold of the hospitals in the area, I want to know the names of all cases of poisoning that have come in. And get the file on the gambling joint that burnt down too please." Ash tapped his pencil against his mouth, pulled out all the files in the lower drawer and laid them out on his desk.

What was going on? Was it just a coincidence? Five incidents, each one involving some form of lowlife getting taken out. In each case, said lowlife had slipped through the net previously. All, apart from the torching of the club, had been treated as accidental. The two incidents relating to the dog fighting organised crime groups sounded for all the world like gang wars and reprisals.

Ash privately judged gang wars as natural attrition but was careful to keep his opinions to himself. He also had a sneaky feeling that some vigilante activity was involved. He soon learnt that yet another victim had succumbed to the poison, leaving only Bob Cherry and Arnold Smith from the original dog ring alive. The latter was also in hospital. Maybe it was time to have a chat before it was too late.

The sister of the ward led Ash to the bedside of Arnold Smith. "Mr Smith is a little weak, Inspector, I'm not sure he will be able to help you much."

"Thank you, Sister, we are just trying to ascertain the cause, we need to ensure that the source is contained."

Smith opened one eye as he heard his name called. Ash was shocked to see that the man's face was bruised and one eye was completely swollen. He turned to the sister. "Did the poisoning do that to his face?!"

"No, the bruising is on several parts of his body. He has either had a bad fall, or more likely been in a fight Inspector."

"Hmm." Ash turned to the man lying in the bed as the nurse left them alone. "Hi Arnie. I am Detective Inspector Ash Kamau. Do you want to tell me why you are here?"

Smith watched the Inspector for some time before replying. "A mate brought me."

"Did your mate beat you up before dropping you off?"

"Fell over."

"Really." Kamau looked around the ward and leaned forwards closer to Smith. "Listen to me Arnie. The poison has already killed your mates, chances are you won't make it either. Now is your chance to get even, you've got little to lose."

"He'll kill me."

"From where I'm standing, he already has."

"He didn't believe us – the pizzas we got at the warehouse, that's what made us crook."

"Why didn't he believe you, Arnie?"

"He didn't eat any. I reckon he knew."

"Of course he knew, he's played you for a right bunch of arseholes, hasn't he?"

"Then when I tell him, he loses his shit and smacks me up. The lousy bastard, why would he do that? We did well good at the dog fight."

"I know, Arnie. He told us about it. He took twice what he told you."

"Bob told yer?!"

"Of course he did, why do think I'm here? Bob has told us all about how you poisoned everybody and tried to beat him up but he had to defend himself. You're in a lot of shit my mate."

"Cherry's lying, he told us we were all wimps cos we felt shit, I didn't lay a hand on him, he just put the boot in. Look, I'm not feeling good, can you get the nurse?"

"Sure mate."

Ash called the nurse and dialled in to arrange a twenty-four-hour guard on Smith. "The poor bastard has got enough to contend with without having this Bob Cherry bloke paying him a visit," he thought.

CHAPTER 46

The rescue of Mervyn's underpants had put both Mervyn and Jim in a good frame of mind. Another dangerous mission had been brought to a successful conclusion. They were going from strength to strength, so it seemed, and there was no problem too challenging. Or at least that was the conclusion they came to after finishing four bottles of Rioja and a bake-in-the-oven camembert.

Harry phoned the following morning, but Jim postponed his proposed visit until the following day. At first, Jim was concerned that he and Mervyn may have fallen foul of the toadstool fumes, but after giving the situation some detailed analysis, they realised that the camembert was to blame.

The daunting task of identifying their next quest was upon them.

"I haven't found anything about anybody slimy getting away with things. We seem to be running low on head feed in that department."

"Sorry Jim?"

"You know, head feed, supply."

"Hmm, maybe we should look further down the line. You know, try and influence the situation earlier in the life cycle. A prevention is better than cure sort of thing."

"I'd be no good lecturing at borstals, I think I might wind up trying to strangle the little pricks."

"But it would be sort of rewarding if we could steer some potential scumbags from an inevitable life of crime."

"Really Mervyn, what do you suggest, hanging round street corners and handing out brochures, starting a youth club in Haringey?"

"Well, no, I was thinking more in the line of scaring the louts off the streets."

"Ah, now that sounds a little more rewarding. Do we prod them into submission with our walking sticks, or bore them to death regaling what the average pensioner does with his day?"

"You know Jim, you can be very cynical sometimes."

"I'm sorry Merv, you're right, what's your plan?"

Mervyn outlined his original plan involving screwdrivers and garden forks.

"It all sounds a bit medieval Mervyn. A bunch of crusty old citizens armed with torches and pitchforks roaming the neighbourhood. Maybe we should round up Doris and her mates and re-introduce the Granny Gangs in an attempt to paint the incentive as gender-neutral."

"There you go again. I was looking at the local crime reports that the police send out. Most of them are either bicycle or exhaust theft. My neighbours had their bicycle grabbed last week."

"I still have my bicycle, doubt if the wheels still turn though."

"Those penny farthings fetch a fortune now Jim."

"Very funny Merv. Maybe we could use mine as bait. Wait, I've got an idea."

Jim retired to his shed the following day and, after a combination of rummaging and distant recall of his days as an electrical engineer, gave rise to a creation that made him swell with pride. He showed it to Mervyn and Harry.

"What the hell is that, Jim? It looks like something they used in Victorian times to cure epilepsy."

"You're getting warm Harry. I present to you, gentleman, the Educator. This device will assist with educating the wayward back to a life of decency and self-worth."

"How does it work Jim?"

"Well, you attach the Educator to an article that is not to be stolen. Then, when the wayward, with misguided intent, try to steal said article, it will explain to them that they need to make a lifestyle adjustment."

"Sounds very sophisticated Jim."

"I'd like to think so Mervyn. I was thinking maybe we could try this out at your place. You said that you'd had a spate of bicycle thefts over there; maybe we could use my old bike as bait and see if the Educator can make a positive change to some poor wretch's life."

"Sounds very noble."

"It does, doesn't it Harry? We should probably set up the device under the cover of darkness, as we are still unsure of how safe Mervyn's place is."

That evening, Mervyn, Jim and a nervous but resolute Harry, determined to turn over a new leaf, positioned the bike in Mervyn's front garden, suitably chained it to the wooden fence, and installed the Educator. Mervyn, with a sudden touch of genius, redirected his front security camera to centre on the bike, making sure he could see it on his mobile before they all left.

"I have set it to ping my phone if it detects any motion," Mervyn explained with obvious pride as they settled down in Jim's lounge for a beer.

"How was Paris, Harry?"

"Eh? Oh, ahem, yes well, we changed our minds at the last minute."

"Oh, why was that?"

"Ah, you know, women."

"Not for some time Harry. It's been, er, hell, almost twenty years since Leandra walked out on me now, with those two toxic children of hers."

"Didn't you ever fancy having kids of your own Merv?"

"Yeah, up until the day she introduced me to those two little swines. They were undoubtedly the most effective birth control devices that ever existed. I must say that Leandra and what she spawned deserve one another wholeheartedly. Never a day goes past that I don't offer up a prayer of thanks that they have each other in their lives every day."

"You're a heartless man Merv, maybe… what's that?"

Mervyn moved over to his phone and picked it up. "Someone's leaning over my fence."

They gathered round and watched as a person, face hidden by a peaked cap and hoody, slowly opened the garden gate. He produced a bolt cropper and reached out to grab the bike. As he did so, the individual appeared to engage in some sort of break dance. Still holding the bike, he began jerking his body to and fro for some time before throwing himself to the ground. As he did so, a bolt of lightning followed him from the bike and danced around his crotch area momentarily before fizzling out. The individual didn't seem to show any inclination to get up again.

"What the hell was that?"

"Er, that was the Educator applying its, um, education."

"Bloody hell Jim, what did it do?"

"Well, it applied a few volts to his body."

"How many is a few?"

"Don't really know, I didn't count the turns on the transformer but judging from his reaction, there seem to have been a few more than I had anticipated."

"I think he shares your opinion. We can't leave that thing there. I think it might be illegal."

"Are we talking about the guy or the device?"

"Come on, let's get there quick."

As they drove over to Mervyn's place, Jim watched the security camera footage on his phone. Just before they arrived, he saw the individual lift himself onto his hands and knees and crawl out through the gate.

"He's out on the pavement, lost sight of him."

As they turned the corner, Harry caught sight of the figure stumbling down the middle of the road away from the house.

"Right, let's get the bike in the house and the Educator in the boot. I'll disconnect it."

"Bloody hell Jim, do you think he's OK?"

"Well, let's hope he had an enlightening evening."

"More like an evening of lightning."

CHAPTER 47

The nurse looked down at Crabbs, lying on his back, covered in bandages from head to toe.

"He's very lucky to be alive. It's a miracle that anybody could have survived that fire. He's going to need plastic surgery on his face, he can't speak or communicate, but apart from some third degree burns on his body, he's comfortable, all things considered. Are you family?"

"No, just a mate. Can't he communicate at all?" said Bob Cherry quietly as he looked down at the bandaged face of Eric Crabbs.

The nurse looked sadly at Crabbs and shook her head. "Right, I'll leave you two alone. He probably won't make a sound. It will be very painful for him to do so."

"Painful, eh? Right, I'll remember that."

Cherry looked down at the call button, not far from Crabbs' hand.

"Let's just move that away, shall we? There, that's a lot better."

Cherry looked around the ward. He and Crabbs were alone.

"Hello Crabbs. How ya doing there?"

He watched as Crabbs' eyes focused and recognised his visitor. Crabbs' hand began shifting slightly looking for his button.

"Aaah, you lost something? That's a shame. I thought we'd have a little chat."

"Yoo gaa awaa yoo astar."

"Sorry, you'll have to speak up, I can't make out what ya on about, is that Russian?"

"Aaa gonna ge yoo yoo faaaaaa."

"Ooh, that sounds sore. Let's see how ya doing."

Cherry took Crabbs head and twisted it. Crabbs let out a gurgle of agony.

"Oh, sorry mate, I didn't mean to hurt ya. I'm just a bit curious why you poisoned my lot?"

Crabbs stared at Cherry, breathing heavily.

"Did ya think we was too stupid to know it was you, you chunk of shit? You weren't supposed to live. But actually, I prefer you like this. It's more fun. Here, let me help ya get nice and comfy."

Cherry wrenched the man's head around again as another gurgle emanated from Crabbs' mouth.

"There ya go. They think ya gonna survive, but you won't. And the pain that ya just felt is gonna be like fun up against what's coming. Ah look, here comes nursey. Let's get ya button back."

Crabbs' eyes moved rapidly between the nurse and Cherry.

Cherry turned to the nurse sadly.

"He's like a bruvver to me. He's always looked after me, now I'm gonna look after him. Sorry my mate, but I gotta go."

The sister looked at Crabbs' eyes darting around. "Don't worry Mr Crabbs, I'm sure your friend will be back soon, won't you sir?"

"Yeah, absolutely, I'll pop in again tomorrow."

CHAPTER 48

Jim decided it was time to give Jeremy a call. In the cold light of day, uninhibited by a filter of Rioja-induced optimism, he was beginning to suspect they might be teetering on the brink of some badly misjudged calamities.

"Hello Jim, I thought I might be hearing from you. I see there has been an unfortunate run of bad luck bestowed upon the little bunch of individuals you were interested in."

"Yeah, we, er, they seem to have been very unlucky. Still, never mind, eh?"

"That's the spirit Jim, always look on the bright side. What can I help you with today?"

"Well, we've been keen to get on with a new, er, project, and we've had a bit of success with an invention of mine, but I'm worried that we are pushing our luck a bit, so to speak."

"Right, nothing wrong with a little prudence Jim."

"We are also a bit thin on the ground with targets, victims, subhuman scum or whatever the technical term is."

"Let's just call them projects for now. I think this is something we should discuss face to face Jim. Are you up for that?"

"Yes, certainly, should I bring my gang… er, partners along?"

"I think we should keep numbers to a minimum at the moment Jim. If we're not careful, we might have to start renting out conference centres to handle the swelling in the ranks of the likeminded."

"Ha, we should be so lucky."

"You'd be surprised Jim. OK, same drill as before, I will let you know where and when, if that's OK with you?"

"Yep, fine."

Jim smiled when he saw the venue suggested by Jeremy. The Wolseley on Piccadilly – another place he had always meant to try out.

Jim arrived a little early but found Jeremy at the table waiting for him, nonetheless.

"I hope you don't mind Jim, but I took the liberty of ordering some champagne to celebrate a job well done. I have to admit that I was very impressed with the manner in which you applied yourselves. Taking out two outfits with such efficiency was truly a master stroke."

"Two?"

"Ahh, you see, you inadvertently left one bereaved member of the first OCG with the impression that he had been hit upon by the second. You triggered a nice little feud that is still raging, and with a little fanning, could well spread to other OCGs as well. There is nothing so satisfying as a chain reaction of self-induced eradication of slime."

"Oh, I didn't realise that. I wish we could claim the credit."

"You can and must Jim. Without the application of your skills, those two outfits would be operating with impunity. There seems to be a reluctance on behalf of the authorities to bring them to book for some reason."

"Hmm, so where to now for us?"

"The sky is the limit Jim, but let's not run away with ourselves. If I may be so bold, there was probably an element of beginner's luck involved as well."

"Bloody great truck load of it. If I look back now, there were so many things that could have gone so horribly wrong, it doesn't bear thinking about."

"Well onwards and upwards – here's to you and your team. Cheers!"

They both took long slugs of their champagne and flicked through the menu.

"I had the scallops last time, raw on ice. Delicious if you like that sort of thing Jim."

"Hmm, never had them, not sure."

"Go on Jim, give them a try. If you hate them, order something else, I'll finish them off for you."

"OK, hell, why not? Crazy to miss out on something, especially at my stage of life."

"Absolutely. You mentioned some invention of yours on the phone. I'm intrigued."

"It's just a transformer really. I re-engineered it not to trip when it applies its surge of current to greedy fingers. Just keeps on delivering a nice high voltage."

"You say you've had some success."

Jim regaled the story of his bicycle used as bait.

"How did you know it wouldn't be lethal?"

"I didn't – didn't know if it would work at all actually."

"You need to give some thought to having corpses littering your own property."

"Yeah, you see, that's what I mean. We're a combination of headstrong with stumbly bumbly, and I'm not sure they work too well together."

"I would suggest you give some more thought to your invention. Maybe make it portable and obviously not traceable. Has promise though."

"Do you really think so?"

"Yes, I do Jim, maybe as a backroom task for in between projects."

"Hmm, that's an idea. But we haven't found any other shit bags, that's our main problem."

"Ahh, now that I can definitely help with. The list is very long, not surprisingly. There is no shortage of shit bags, as you call them, roaming around without the inconvenience of convictions attached to their person. Remember, I recommend that the individuals you select have qualities that you personally find especially repugnant. That always guarantees maximum satisfaction. It would help if you gave me a short list of repugnant qualities to work with."

"Hmm, OK. Can I get back to you on that?"

"Of course you can, Jim. Here come your scallops, let's see what you think."

CHAPTER 49

Ash Kamau flicked through the file on Bob Cherry. He had form, unsurprisingly, but what was remarkable was the way in which he seemed to avoid having much stick to him. He was greasier than a bacon pan. It was as if he had a guardian angel. It wasn't the justice system per se that seemed to be at fault, but time and time again, the evidence against him seemed to be either badly prepared or missing when it came time to go to trial.

There definitely seemed to be a possibility that the angel in question had worn a blue uniform at some point in their career. Ash shook his head, nothing was more disgusting in his book than cops on the take. It defiled everything he had ever worked for.

He had come to the UK with his parents from Kenya back in the sixties. When Ash was barely ten years old, his father was killed in an industrial accident. A lorry load of railings had fallen on him and, despite there being clear negligence on behalf of the contractors, a team of slick lawyers denied the widow and her son any compensation.

Throughout his teenage life, his memory of justice denied lay festering like a sore within him. Unlike many who turned against society under such stress, Ash was determined to work with society to make a difference. He had joined the police force at the age of 18, part of the less than one percent of its black members. To think that his colour wouldn't make a difference would have been naïve. His colour meant that promotion was always going to be hard earned, and that superiors, way less qualified than he, would guide his career. Nevertheless, he was good at his job, having been commended once for outstanding bravery when saving two children from their armed, drug-crazed stepfather.

His methods and attitudes were "old school" apparently. His seniors, often almost half his age, had told him that he had to move with the times, that the copper on the beat and strong-arm tactics in the interview room were things of the past. Technology, performance and respecting the criminal's rights were the new masters and he needed to adjust.

He had nodded and made an undertaking to move along. But privately, he had no intention of changing his attitude towards his job or his superiors. In his opinion, crime had been shown to pay and it was the namby-pamby way in which the force was bound to act that had brought that about. The rules and regulations favoured the perpetrator every step of the way. You virtually had to be on your knees to get any of them to co-operate with your enquiries. Most of them were surrounded by so many lawyers, the likes of which the prosecution could never afford, that one barely had a chance to say hello before they were screaming police brutality.

He suspected that the only reason he had not been asked to retire was because of his skin colour. The force did not want to be seen to be racist in any way. It was bullshit of course, but he went along with it. His Kenyan lineage had produced little enough favours in his lifetime, he might as well grab what little he could from it. They had put him onto "special projects" which basically meant any scraps that nobody else wanted to bother with. He suspected that it might also include any incidents that somebody in the force would like to be overlooked.

People like Cherry should have been jailed and the cell door lock pissed upon. The revelation by Arnold Smith that Cherry had poisoned everybody made no sense. But it was interesting to note that Cherry, for whatever reason, had kept clear of any poison. Cherry was seemingly the only one of the Croydon bunch healthy enough to deliver a vendetta to the Lambeth crowd. There was only one survivor of the Lambeth crowd, now laid up in hospital. A visit to him would be timely.

An hour later, Ash stood at the entrance to the ward. The nurse walked up to him with a smile.

"Hello sir, can I help you?"

"Yes, I've come to visit Eric Crabbs," he said, showing her his ID.

She turned and pointed to the bed in which Crabbs lay, staring at the ceiling.

"How is he doing?"

"He cannot communicate too well but shows every sign of a full recovery."

As he approached the bed, he saw Crabbs' eyes dart towards him.

Ash pulled up a chair and sat down beside the bed.

"Hello Crabbs, I'm Detective Inspector Ash Kamau. Anything you say will be kept between us and possibly won't be used in a court of law, do I make myself clear?"

Crabbs continued to fix his gaze on Kamau.

"The nurse there tells me you are not too good with the communication, so I am going to ask you some simple questions. One blink for yes, two blinks for no, OK?" Ash watched as Crabbs blinked three times in succession and reached for his button. His button was carefully moved out of reach for the second time in as many days.

Ash leaned closer to Crabbs. "OK, you chunk of shit. Let me put this a little more clearly for you. Your chances of getting out of here alive are between nothing and fuck all. I am your only lifeline. Your mates are greasy spots on the ground and your enemies are going to tear your balls off and feed them to you. You know it, I know it. The difference is you care, I don't give a fuck. You've got ten seconds to become co-operative after which, I'm out of here." Ash looked around the ward, humming to himself as he did so.

Crabbs turned his hand into a painful thumbs up.

"Good, first question, do you know who did this to you?"

One blink.

"Good, now we are getting somewhere."

"Was it Humphrey Littleton?"

Two blinks.

"I see you're in no mood for a little light humour. Let me see, who could it be, umm, Bob Cherry?"

One blink.

"Well I never, I must be psychic, eh? Do you know why he did it?"

One blink.

"Does he think you poisoned his lot?"

One blink.

"Suppose you want to get back at him, eh?"

Long stare.

"Hmm, would you like a guard placed outside your ward?"

Long stare followed by a slow single blink.

"Hmm, we're going to run out of coppers at this rate. You had better be grateful. Goodbye." Ash got up and went to find the nurse.

"Excuse me nurse, has Mr Crabbs had any visitors since he was brought in?"

"Just one, he explained to me that he was a very good friend of Mr Crabbs and would be personally looking after him. He said he would visit every day actually."

"Has he? Visited every day that is?"

"Well, I'm not sure, not while I've been on duty."

Ash pulled out his phone and brought up a picture of Cherry. "Is that the man who came to visit?"

"Yes, that's him. Mr Crabbs was very agitated when he left. His friend told him he would be back soon. I wonder what happened?"

Ash gave the nurse his card. "If you see this man again, just phone me – any time, night or day."

"Oh, OK Inspector."

CHAPTER 50

Harry looked down at his beer. "So, what did Jeremy have to say Jim?"

"He wants us to make a shortlist of people we would prefer not to share this planet with."

"I'd say you've got a bit of an oxymoron there. That list isn't going to be very short at all."

"Well Merv, it's more a list of groupings really, sort of categories of human slime that we three personally would like to eliminate."

"Oh, OK, that's quite a nice thing to do over a beer. Can I start?"

"Go for it Merv, I'll take notes."

"Well, anyone who hurts animals shouldn't really be allowed to hang around, should they?"

"Hang around?"

"Yeah, you know, draw breath."

"Right." Jim wrote *Deny air to animal harmers* in his notes. "That's a good start."

"That includes poaching too."

"Right."

"Those creeps that fiddle with kids should be done away with as well."

"Yup, they aren't needed." *Do away with kiddy fiddlers*

"And those pricks with hoodies who go around picking on people, they need buggering up."

"OK." *Bugger up hoodies* "What if they don't have hoods? Or what if it's a perfectly normal person wearing a hoodie?"

"Yeah, good point, umm, and thugs I suppose."

"Right." *And thugs*

"OK, well done Merv, you got anything to add Harry?"

"What about those bastards who get to the front of a long queue and only then start to think about what they want to order? I wouldn't mind crushing their heads in for them."

"Might be a bit extreme there Harry. But let's put it down." *Crush heads of dithery queuers*

"And those sods who start counting out the exact amount in small change after they get the bill at a supermarket queue?"

"Shit, yeah, that drives me bloody nuts." *Supermarket queue change counters*

"And those arses who block the aisles, slowly pushing their trolley along whilst their fat heads go backwards and forwards like bloody windscreen wipers, they should all die."

"Yep, good point." *Slow aisle blockers deserve death* "Whoa, that's coming along nicely. Let's get another round."

They all settled back with a fresh pint whilst Jim read out the list, nodding to each other after every item.

"Hmm, maybe we're being a bit flippant."

"How so Merv?"

"Well, that one about thugs, what defines a thug?"

"An individual who beats somebody up?"

"Hmm, what if the person deserves being beaten up."

"I see where you're going. What do you suggest? Maybe we should leave that one out."

"No, I just think it needs greater refinement, something like… Any person or persons who behaves, in the view of the observer, in a way that displays a thuggish tendency based upon personal observations or reports upon which the observer can reliably depend."

"OK, that seems to cover it. Let me get that down."

"Maybe we need to expand the other ones in a similar vein?"

"Example Harry?"

Harry tightened his lips in concentration. "Any behaviour that pisses the observer off in a way that causes the pissed off-ee to require the death or serious malfunction of the pissed off-er."

"Very succinct Harry, you've obviously done this before. Right, let me get this off to Jeremy and see what he comes back with."

"What did he say he would give us Jim?"

"Now what did he call it? I think it was a sort of technical term, umm, ah, that was it, he will send us a list of shit bags."

CHAPTER 51

Ash Kamau had had due cause to wheel in Bob Cherry for a chat. He had the confirmation that Cherry was running the dog ring from Arnold Smith and he was sure that it was Cherry who had lit the barn with Crabbs & Co. inside. Cherry was slippery, he was not famous for being careless, and the fact that he had shown no signs of going to ground most probably meant he had something or somebody covering his arse.

Cherry was probably more danger to his own kind than he was to the general public and their pets at the moment. With any luck, he might take out some of the trash without the force having to lift a finger. "Natural attrition," Ash mumbled under his breath as he closed the file. "Let's see what pans out."

At that same moment, Bob Cherry turned into the corridor leading to Crabbs' ward. It was time to pay his dear old friend another visit. He had been savouring the moment all day, so the sight of the police constable standing guard outside the ward's entrance made him swear out loud. "You fucking piece of shit," he ground out under his breath. "Gone crawling to the cops for protection, have you? I can guess exactly what your stinking mouth has been blabbing about."

Cherry continued walking past the policeman, glancing into the ward and catching a glimpse of Crabbs clutching his button press in his hand. "You're gonna be desperately looking for your button when I get to you, you fucker." He walked out of the hospital, got into his car and reached into the cubby hole for his other phone. He heard the voice on the other end.

"Yes?"

"I need your copper on guard duty outside St Matthews Ward 9 to disappear for an hour. Let me know when."

CHAPTER 52

Jim was back in his shed. Inspired by Jeremy's directives to make the Educator a little more portable, he had set himself a challenge. He read up on taser technology and revised some basic physics. After several shopping trips, he had his new Educator ready for field trials. He called Mervyn into the garden to witness the first test.

"Are you sure it's safe Jim?"

"That's a bit like asking the guy who pushed the button on the first atom bomb if it's safe isn't it Merv? Safe isn't really its function."

Mervyn's gaze moved to a vaguely humanoid structure in the middle of the lawn. It was made mainly of wood bound with bits of wire and had what looked like pieces of meat layered upon it, wrapped loosely in muslin cloth. "What's that Jim?"

"Aha, that's my pupil. He represents the one who needs to be educated. I have tried to make him as realistic as I possibly can."

"It looks like a pile of cloth-covered sausages."

"Quite so, I have gone to the trouble of layering the wooden skeleton with nice slices of stewing steak to represent muscular tissue."

"Bloody expensive experiment Jim."

"Not at all, the wood is just bits and pieces I had in the shed and the stewing steak we can eat when we're finished."

"I think I might become a vegan more quickly than I expected." Mervyn turned to look at Jim, but he had disappeared into his shed.

As Mervyn watched the shed door, a metre-long bar began to appear, followed by Jim clad in a device that resembled a World War II flame thrower. A backpack hung around Jim's shoulders and a large cable connected it to the long bar. "Here we are Merv, the Educator Mark II."

"What's the difference Jim?"

"Ahh, well you see Merv, this one is portable, no need to plug it in except to charge it up. It should be a bit more directional too if I've done my calcs correctly."

All the time Jim was talking, Mervyn watched the business end of the device swaying around towards him with malevolent intent. "Could you aim that bit somewhere else Jim, it's making me a tad anxious."

"Perfectly safe Merv, I haven't activated the capacitor."

"Hmm, I'm still thinking about the atom bomb comparison."

"Right, let's see, you stand there Merv, I'll just set the pulse to *Stun*."

Mervyn stepped back several metres. "Sounds like Star Trek, Jim. Are you sure you should be holding it?"

"Perfectly safe Merv. Right, here we go."

There was a whirring noise followed by a blinding flash and a loud bang.

Mervyn, blinded by the flash, stood rooted to the spot, whilst a smell of electrical discharge was slowly replaced by a smell of burnt meat. With his ears still ringing, he blinked towards the outline of Jim, seemingly riveted to the spot. As his sight began to return, he followed Jim's gaze.

The pupil was in flames, its clothing now dripping with the fat which was melting and catching alight as it ran from its arms. As they both watched, the pupil's head fell off and rolled slowly towards them, burning merrily as it came.

"I think I'm going to be sick," said Mervyn, unable to take his eyes away from the burning head.

Jim lowered the bar with trembling hands. "I don't think we'll be able to eat that meat, Merv."

"Well, that's one small glimmer of light in an otherwise ghastly experience. If that was what a *Stun* looks like, I can't even begin to imagine what horrific scenes *Terminate* is going to conjure up."

"Hmm, I'm going to have to make a few adjustments. But all in all, a good start. With a bit of luck, we should be able to take it to the frontline this weekend. Look, it's ready to go again, that's encouraging, eh?"

"I can hardly contain myself Jim. If you don't mind, I'm going to have to go and sit down for a while. I've come over a bit faint."

"Yeah, I know what you mean Merv, it's exciting eh?"

CHAPTER 53

Jim had meant to clean up the list of people not required on Earth, but due to a dithery finger, coupled with a shortfall of due care and attention, the list pinged off to Jeremy in its raw state, thus:

Deny air to animal harmers

Do away with kiddy fiddlers

Bugger up hoodies and thugs

Crush heads of dithery queuers

Supermarket queue change counters

Slow aisle blockers deserve death

Jim phoned Jeremy as soon as his panicky finger stopped pushing the Undo button with no effect.

"Hello Jim, I see you have just sent me your list."

"Yeah, I, er, it's a bit raw, I meant to clean it up a bit."

"No worries, Jim, let us see what we have here. OK, so animal cruelty is top of your list, no shortage of qualifiers there. I presume kiddy fiddlers are paedophiles and the like, plenty of them around. Hoodies and thugs, again, I presume that you are referring to their behaviour and not their choice of apparel, that is a long list indeed. Hmm, the queue offenders and aisle blockers are going to be a little tricky, the current legislation does not single them out, unfortunately. You might be a bit out on your own there."

"Yeah, we are a bit new to this, I suppose we should have left some of that..."

"Not at all Jim, it is not your fault that the irritating behaviour of others has yet to be brought to book. Why, animal cruelty and paedophilia were widely accepted in times gone past, we civilise very slowly. How's your project progressing?"

"Oh yeah, I've made some progress on the Educator. It's now portable and it works nice and quickly, but it overcooked the target, so we weren't able to eat it, unfortunately. But I reckon it's just a couple of tweaks away from a working prototype."

"Very encouraging… I think. Anyway, this list. I will whittle down a couple of likely projects from each category that can be accessed in your immediate area and send them off to you with a profile on each, OK?"

CHAPTER 54

Ash stared out of his office window. He had missed something. Something wasn't fitting together with the other bits of the puzzle. Cherry setting light to Crabbs' outfit with them all trapped inside fitted the profile – brutal, easy and effective. Poisoning Cherry's gang with toadstools just didn't sit right.

The mushrooms used, destroying angels, *amanita virosa*, were not growing on everybody's doorstep and were relatively difficult to identify accurately. He just couldn't imagine Crabbs' bunch mincing around the forests with straw baskets harvesting toadstools. They were hardly likely to be part of any pusher's menu either, as they had no hallucinogenic properties. And then, this pizza story, what was all that about? Had they really eaten pizzas with toadstools on them?

It was time to do some rummaging. He could organise a forensic team but knowing the procedure, that would take endless time and paperwork. He was probably already too late. He took a pair of rubber gloves and some plastic bags, checked the location of Cherry's warehouse and set off.

As he drove around the back of the warehouse, he gave a sigh of relief. The waste had not been collected. He saw several bags torn open and their contents strewn about. Foxes maybe. He doubted that they would have touched any toadstool-infested food. Pulling on a mask and the rubber gloves, he soon spotted the sad remains of two dogs in two torn black bin liners. At last he found what he was looking for, a couple of pizza boxes, which he photographed and placed into a large plastic bag. One pizza box had some spilled content within it, and he placed that carefully into another bag.

Once back at the station, he despatched the boxes for analysis to the lab and went about searching for the pizza company. Unsurprisingly, he drew a blank. He brought the image of the pizza logo up onto his screen. He shook his head. He just couldn't see Crabbs and his bunch of knuckle draggers sitting around a screen with some desktop publishing system designing a logo.

It was time to test out his hypothesis and pay Crabbs another visit.

As he walked to the ward, he immediately became aware of the police guard's absence. "Shit!" He quickened his pace. Inside, Crabbs had been elevated slightly but other than that he looked the same.

Crabbs' eyes followed Ash's approach. "Hello Mr Crabbs, trust you are doing well?"

"Guard gaan," struggled Crabbs.

"Yes, so I see, when?"

"Naa."

"Hmm, don't worry, it's just routine," Ash lied. "I see you are able to talk a little." Crabbs closed his eyes.

"We had such a nice chat last time Mr Crabbs. Remember, I'm the one who's keeping you healthy." Crabbs kept his eyes closed.

"Can you tell me how you poisoned them?"

"Ooo?"

"Bob Cherry's gang."

"Didn't."

"Now, now Mr Crabbs, remember our little arrangement. I walk and my guard goes with me if you become uncooperative, remember?"

Crabbs opened his eyes and painfully turned towards Ash. "Ahh… din… do… it."

"Who did then?"

"Dun… fuckin'… know." Crabbs suddenly gazed at the ward door.

Ash followed Crabbs' gaze and saw Bob Cherry staring at the two of them from the ward entrance.

CHAPTER 55

Harry, Mervyn and Jim sat looking at the list of names that had arrived by bike courier from Jeremy.

"I wonder why he didn't just email them to you."

"Not secure enough I suppose Harry. I see he's given us three of each category."

They pawed through the notes. "What a bunch of human garbage!"

"You're right Merv, none of this shit should be roaming the streets."

"How do we choose?"

"Let's start at the top with this bastard who's been torturing cats in the neighbourhood. What a fucking psycho! I'm going for him."

"Hmm, it says he's been identified twice and was found with cat blood on his clothing, but the judge let him off with a warning. Can you believe that?"

"OK, shall we go for him first?"

They all agreed and immediately fell about the task – or, more accurately, stumbled about how they were going to take him on and take him out.

"Maybe we could deliver a Chinese takeaway this time with mushrooms in it."

"OK Merv, let's write that one down."

"I wouldn't mind trying out my Educator on him."

At the mention of Jim's Educator, Mervyn had a dizzy moment of nausea before regaining his composure. "Well Jim, maybe when it's a little less er, unstable. But write it down."

"Hmm, I see he lives in a block of flats near Clapham. We can't just knock on his door and fry him."

"Maybe we could lure him into attempting to hurt a cat somewhere and then pounce on him."

"A possibility Harry."

"Wait, I've got just the thing!"

"Yeah Merv, what's that?"

"It's a Sylvester cat suit that my ex-wife bought for a stupid fancy dress party."

"Yeah, help me out a bit here Mervyn, I'm not seeing the plot."

"Well, it would have to be pretty dark, but one of us could dress up and lure him with pathetic mews and then when he gets drawn in, we nail him."

"It would have to be bloody pitch black for him to fall for a cat the size of a bear looking like Sylvester, but fuck it, let's get all the ideas down first."

"Maybe something like a stuffed toy that looks like a cat, we could maybe drag it around to look like a cat."

"I think maybe we are getting a bit ahead of ourselves. This bloke might never go out – we need to find out about his regular routine."

"You're right Harry, that training of yours coming to the fore again. We are going to have to put a tail on him, like we did, well nearly did, with that Cherry bloke."

"Oh no, not that again."

"This bloke is different Merv, he isn't in a gang, he is a pathetic little shit, remember that. He doesn't have a car, so we can tail him on foot."

"Speak for yourself, he's thirty-four. When he runs for the bus, where does that leave us old farts?"

"Let's see if Jeremy can give us any more details on this bloke. Derrick Dunston. Sounds like a prick, doesn't he?"

CHAPTER 56

Jim was a little crestfallen when the next meeting with Jeremy was at a McDonald's. He took out the notes they had made and looked sideways at the menu on offer.

"You seem a little uneasy Jim."

"I'm not sure what you are going to recommend today, Jeremy."

"Life is full of challenges Jim, this is surely one of them in this place. I'm having something out of a tin. We are here because routines are by nature predictable. Our enemy is predictability. That is why I love working with operatives such as yourselves. What do you have for me today?"

"Well, actually it's more of a cry for help. We are not sure of how to track down this guy, er, Derrick Dunston."

"Ahh, Dunston, I thought you might set your sights on him. He is, fortunately for us, very predictable. Spends his time stacking shelves in the supermarket during the day, has no friends, lives alone and spends a good amount of time in the evening with ladies of the night. He takes the same route to work and back each day. I have his route laid out for you in the envelope here."

"Oh thanks, that's nice. We were thinking that maybe…"

Jeremy held his hand up. "Only tell me what you have to Jim."

CHAPTER 57

The three sat in Jim's living room sifting through Jeremy's papers. The route that Derrick Dunston took was full of promise as far as Mervyn was concerned. The man always made his way through the park on his way back from work. "No doubt scouting for victims, sick bastard. I seem to remember, let me check, yes, two cats' remains were found in the park. We must nail this chunk of excrement double quick Jim, before he does it again."

"When was the last time they found a cat Merv?"

"About a month ago apparently. What are we going to do?"

"I think laying a trap is the way to go. Lure the bastard off the beaten path into the undergrowth and fry him right there."

"A sort of ambush? I'll bow to your judgement Harry."

"Yeah, something like that."

"What do we use for bait? Remember my Sylvester suit."

"How the fuck is that going to work Merv? This bloke is obviously a raving ratbag, but Sylvester cavorting around going meow or whatever you intend to do is going to send him off screaming."

"We need a convincing lure, something that is domestic cat size preferably."

"We could pull it along with my fishing line."

"Good idea Merv. Right, anybody got anything that could pass as a cat?"

Everybody shook their heads.

"Wait a mo. Maybe I do have something." Jim got to his feet. "I need to get into the loft."

They followed Jim upstairs and watched as, accompanied by much cursing and one pinched finger, he manoeuvred the ladder into place and ascended into the loft.

"What's going on up there Jim?"

"Well, there's a surfing contest going on in the corner there and just across the way, they are lining up for a guess my weight competition. What the fuck do you think is going on up here Mervyn, I'm trying to find a cat!"

Mervyn turned to Harry. "He's very touchy these days, isn't he?"

"You'd be touchy too if you had to sort through eight inches of dust and cobwebs. I haven't been up here in years. Ah, here it is."

Mervyn watched as a cloud of dust and fluff came floating down from the trapdoor followed by a larger amount of solid muck which landed at their feet. Jim came back down the steps puffing and wheezing. "I hope I don't have to go back up there for a good while."

Harry kicked the fuzzy heap lying on the floor. "What is it, Jim?"

"Let's dust it off, shall we?"

Mervyn and Harry exchanged glances whilst Jim carefully lifted the thing and carried it at arm's length into the garden. Everybody stood back whilst Jim proceeded to apply a broom to the heap; slowly, it began to take form – four legs, furry body, large flat tail and a beak.

"There, what do you think?" said Jim triumphantly.

"I'd say that you've just brushed off a duck-billed platypus Jim."

"Right, it's stuffed you know."

"I'm not surprised after living in that shit hole of a loft of yours."

"Well, what do you think?"

"Where the hell did you get it?"

"My Aunt Tilda always had it on her mantlepiece. When she died, nobody else wanted it, so I took it."

"Yeah, not every day you get the chance to pick up a platypus on the cheap I bet. How does this improve our lives?"

"That is our lure."

"A duck-billed platypus in Clapham?"

"It's a definite step closer than the dancing Sylvester."

"Thank you, Harry. Look at it this way, if he does spot its identity, which I doubt, he'll still want to follow it."

"You know Merv, Jim has a point there – if I saw a platypus in a park, I think I'd follow it!"

"OK, in the absence of anything more convincing, I suppose it's worth a go. I'll get my fishing gear and, in the meantime Jim, maybe you could drill a little hole in its beak so I can tie it on."

"Do I have to? I don't want to mess it up Merv."

"Yeah, I must admit it has had an exemplary life so far. I'll get my fishing gear, you drill the hole."

CHAPTER 58

By the time Ash had got to his feet, Cherry had gone. He went to the corridor and looked in both directions. No sign of him. He went back to Crabbs, now in a high state of alert.

"Where's da fukin' guard?"

"Don't worry, Crabbs, that's why I'm here, whilst the guard stepped away." Ash had to think fast. He had no idea where the guard had gone or why he had left his post. He could see that his story was not having any calming effect on Crabbs either.

"Ah demand protection."

Ash leaned closer to Crabbs. "Listen, you puddle of piss, the only demands around here are going to come from me, got it? Why does Cherry want you so badly?"

"He thinks we did 'im but we didn't."

"Who did then?"

"You're da coppa, you figure it aat."

"OK, this is what I figure. You deserve to die and if Cherry wants to do that for me, so much the better. Why should the taxpayers in this country keep a piece of crap like you alive, fed and watered? That copper out there has got way better things to do than hang about here. I need to have a reason not to walk away Crabbs. So far, I'm battling to find one."

"What you want?"

"I want you to sing like a fucking canary. I want you to go on record and finger every other rotten operation that you know about – names, dates, places, you know what I want."

"I'd be a dead man."

"No, Crabbs, that's wishful thinking, you are already a dead man. What I'm talking about is raising you from your grave. Remember what I've already told you. I don't give a fuck either way. You give me what I want, or your useless life comes to an end. Either way, I go away happy."

Crabbs closed his eyes.

"Right, time to go, I need to catch the shops. I was going to say see you soon, but I doubt that I will."

"Wait."

CHAPTER 59

The park was peaceful in the dapple of afternoon sunlight that sprinkled through the trees. Three elderly men made their way leisurely along the path.

"It's nice here, eh?"

"Yeah, as long as you're not a cat I guess."

Harry stopped and turned. "This Dunston bloke will almost certainly go out through that gate over there to get to his flat. He might take any of these three paths to get there, or he might even walk across the grass, being the prick that he is. Anyway, our best chance of intercepting him will be over there where all the paths converge and go between that thick clump of bushes."

They looked over towards where Harry was pointing. "Looks like a good place to hide in there too."

They looked around carefully to see if they were being watched, then one by one, they casually ducked into the bushes.

"I haven't done this since I was a kid."

"What's that Harry?"

"Well, you know, duck around in the bushes, making sure the Parkies can't see you."

"Parkies?"

"Yeah, you know, the Park Keepers. Miserable old bastards, they were always trying to catch us."

"What for?"

"We used to bomb them with mud balls."

"What's that thing over there Jim?"

Mervyn was pointing towards a large metal box in amongst the bushes with tubes coming out of its side, surrounded by a fence.

"It's a substation of some kind."

On the side it had a sign, *Danger of death. Keep out.*

"What goes on in there Jim?"

"Transforms voltage from high to low or the other way round. A bit like that Educator thing of mine, but way more powerful."

"Oh. Have you done any more meat frying with that thing?"

"I'm giving it another trial when we get back, want to watch?"

"No, even my morbid curiosity doesn't stretch that far. If you don't mind, I'll stay inside this time."

"Well, I've seen all I need to, we can't be seen from the path or from the flats. I'd say we have our stake-out and ambush location gentlemen."

"Yep Harry, I reckon this is perfect. Have you drilled a hole in the beak yet Jim?"

"I have Merv, a very small one."

"Fine, so it's over to the weapons technology department to perfect our prototype." They both looked at Jim.

"You're right, let's get back, hang some steaks up and get frying."

CHAPTER 60

Cherry watched from his car as Crabbs was lifted on the gurney into the ambulance. Two police car escorts waited to join the convoy.

Under his breath he smirked, "I can only imagine the number of bastards you fingered to get that VIP treatment Crabbs. That's fine, I'll just have to let the lads know that Crabbs is a nark. And every copper who gives them a visit from now on is courtesy of him. That's one job I don't have to worry about anymore. Bye bye Crabbs." He reached into his cubby hole and pulled out his other mobile phone. He dialled the only number.

"Yes?"

"Crabbs is going on holiday."

"I know."

"Where is nice this time of year?"

"I'll send you a peg."

CHAPTER 61

Mervyn watched as Jim pulled three large steaks from the fridge and sprinkled them with salt and pepper.

"Why do you have to risk buggering those up again with your zapper Jim? It seems such a waste."

"Aah, Merv, I need to make sure that the potential difference is sufficient to cause the damage we need without setting the neighbourhood alight. Short of testing it out on an actual body, this meat is still the next best thing."

"Are we going to have to salt and pepper Dunston before we zap him?"

"No, you twit, this time I think I've got it right. Confidence, Merv, very important in this line of work."

Mervyn remained in his armchair as he watched Jim step out into the garden with his steaks on the plate. Several minutes later, there was a whirring sound, followed by a prolonged flash and crackle. Despite himself, Merv rose from the chair with a sigh and shuffled into the garden.

Jim was standing with a look of smug satisfaction on his face. The now familiar form of the target had three medium to rare steaks hanging from its framework. "We have ourselves a lift-off Merv. No flames, just enough heat and voltage to terminate the target – and, as an added bonus, three nicely done steaks."

"Not to mention a head still attached to its body. Well done Jim, I never doubted you. Shall I tell Harry his steak's ready?"

"Yes, indeed and tell him to crack that champers in the fridge, this deserves a celebration."

The three munched contentedly on their steaks. "Mmm, I have to say Jim, this lightning broiled steak is really nice, very juicy too."

"Thank you, Harry. When we are done eating, I must let you have a go with the Educator."

"Oh, why is that?"

"Well, obviously, you're our point man, you know, Top Gun and all that. You need to familiarise yourself with the equipment before you go onto the frontline, eh?"

"Are you telling me I'm going it alone in the park bushes?"

"No, of course not, Jim and I will be there to do our bit."

"Oh, and what is that exactly Merv?"

"Well, I'll be operating the lure."

"Eh?"

"The bait Harry, the platypus attached to my rod and line. I have lured many fish in my time you know, quite looking forward to landing a Dunston."

"Oh, and Jim?"

"Technical back-up Harry. We all have our part to play."

"So, tell me again how this is going to work, I seem to have missed something."

"Well, we all go into the park and settle down in the bushes alongside the substation."

"What does settle down mean? Lean against a holly bush?"

"Hmm, good point Harry, we need some chairs."

"And cushions."

"OK."

"And a flask of coffee."

"And tea and biscuits. And maybe take a book along as well."

"It's going to be dark Mervyn."

"I could take my Kindle."

"That's a great idea – your face lit up like a low glowing moon as it lurks in the undergrowth. No Mervyn, no Kindle."

"I'll take my phone and listen to music on my hearing aid then."

"For fuck's sake Mervyn, this is an ambush, pre-meditated murder. Not an afternoon on Brighton beach. We need to be focused and alert at all times when we are in position."

"OK, you're right. But we can still take some tea and biscuits, eh?"

"Of course, while we're about it, let's set a nice table with a tablecloth, some cucumber sandwiches and a pastry or two, shall we?"

"Now you're just being silly. Carry on, Jim."

"OK, we settle down and await our target. Oh no, wait, we first position the platypus in the bushes on the other side of the path and lay out the fishing line. Then we settle down."

"When we see Dunston approaching, we activate the platypus and reel it in, in a convincing manner."

"That's where my skills come in Harry."

"Very impressive Merv. Carry on Jim."

"Well, we'll probably enhance the illusion with suitable audible back-up."

"Oh yeah, what's that?"

"A few miaows to make it convincing."

"Can I have an example?"

Mervyn crouched forwards. "Miaow, miaow, miaow."

"That sounds just like an old fart with an Eastenders accent saying miaow."

"Let's hear your cat then."

"That will sound like an old fart with a North Kent accent saying miaow."

"You're right, what do we do then?"

"I'll download some cat sounds on my phone, and we can play them through my remote speaker."

"OK, so the platypus is getting dragged across the path and the speaker is belting out cat sounds, then what?"

"Well, Dunston will not be able to resist following the platypus, especially when I give it a bit of a spurt – works every time with trout. As he comes through the bushes, you step forwards with Jim's machine and zap him."

"Is that it?"

"Yeah, pretty much. What else were you expecting Harry?"

"Well, let's see. How do we know when Dunston is approaching?"

"Hmm, we'll need a look-out. You'll be manning the Educator, Merv will be operating the platypus, so that will have to be me, good point."

"And how do we recognise him?"

"We have this photo of him, see here."

They huddled around the picture.

"I don't know about you, but he looks like every other bugger to me.

There must be thousands of blokes who look like him."

"Hmm, it's going to be tricky, especially in low light."

"We are going to have to do a recce. Spot him a couple of times, until we can be sure – we don't want to fry some guy who might want to comfort a lost cat."

"Or a lost platypus."

"Right Harry, let's get you familiar with the latest in weaponry."

CHAPTER 62

The sun was low in the sky when they arrived at the park. Mervyn started towards the bushes.

"Where are you going Mervyn? We need to be in the open to start with if we're to have any chance of seeing him clearly. You and Harry go and sit on the bench. I'll sit further up on that one over there. After you spot him going past, stand up, so that I can watch him from a distance and get to know him." A few people passed by, a couple walking their dogs, one pensioner in a motorised wheelchair, a couple of kids kicking a ball.

Then they all saw him at once. It was not his looks, it was his demeanour. He walked like a reptile, his head slowly moving from one side to the other. As he passed them, Mervyn and Harry stood up. You could see them both checking their pictures of him. They glanced over towards Jim. He continued to watch the approaching man, with revulsion. He then stood up and walked towards his friends, passing Dunston as he did so.

"That's him Jim."

"Certainly is, no doubt about it. What a creepy bastard." Jim felt himself shiver. "Can't wait to rid the planet of that thing!"

"Look Jim, if you want to operate the Educator, that's fine with me. You know it better than me."

"Nah, Harry, that's very nice of you but we need a cool head and a steady hand, and that's you my old buddy, that's you."

Later that evening, Harry sat eating supper with his wife. A cool head and a steady hand. A dizzy head and uncontrolled St Vitus dance were more likely. He was a liability, he put the mission at risk. He had to come clean, however humiliating it would be.

His wife's voice came floating into his conscience. Some police raid had occurred some doors down from her office that morning. She described how they had sealed off the road and run around with guns and bulletproof vests whilst they smashed in the front door. There were no shots fired, just a long line of handcuffed people being led away in police vans.

"That's nice dear. Sorry, I have to make a call." He stood up and went into the lounge.

"Hi, Jim, it's me Harry. Look. I've been giving some thought to our upcoming operation and I…"

"I knew you would Harry. I said to Mervyn, I bet old Harry's going through the operation, applying his combat trained eye to the detail. You really are an asset, without you on our team, old Merv and I would be lost. It really has done him the world of good, you know. Given him a purpose and everything in the closing part of his life. We owe that all to you Harry. You and your cast iron nerve are what is keeping old Merv going, you know that eh?"

"Er… Oh, good, umm."

"So where are we going wrong Harry? Put us old stumbly bumbly buggers back on track."

"Well, actually, it seems OK, I think. Not too many things need changing, very few probably. I haven't really given it much… er… I'll get back to you."

Jim looked at the phone.

"What did Harry want, Jim?"

"I actually haven't the faintest idea Merv."

CHAPTER 63

The witness protection Ash had managed to organise for Crabbs had fallen into place like clockwork. He had made the request that morning, and an hour later the witness protection team had taken over and spirited Crabbs away. Ash didn't know where they had taken him, neither did he care. What he had cared about was whether the information Crabbs had given him held any credibility.

Only after the first raid had produced encouraging results did Ash start to relax. Twelve taken into custody after a drug bust, plus stock with a street value of around four million pounds. Not a bad morning's work. It was amazing what could be achieved when the correct incentives were offered.

The chief had been very impressed and had congratulated Ash on a job well done, as had most of the staff at the station.

He was amazed that so many people knew who he was. Nobody had attempted to find out exactly how Ash had managed to get Crabbs to be so cooperative. He knew that he would have to complete a report on his interview with Crabbs at the hospital but felt that a little vagueness about the exact dialogue would probably be prudent. The official line would be that Crabbs feared for his life after surviving the fire and sought witness protection in exchange for all the dirt he could conjure up. Not inaccurate, just the path followed to get there was somewhat different.

Ash's thoughts moved to Cherry. What was that bastard doing at the hospital at exactly the time the guard went missing? The guard said that somebody had called him and said that Ash had needed him at the reception immediately. Whoever it was knew that Ash had put the guard there in the first place, information that could only have come from within. Ash had to admit that Cherry's appearance and rapid departure had almost certainly been the final nudge that Crabbs needed to make him cooperate, but he knew that he would have to be careful whom he confided in. The station was as leaky as a sieve.

He needed a breather from the whole Crabbs-Cherry thing. He had delivered the information Crabbs had provided to the flying squad, and by all accounts, several more raids were imminent. He just hoped the leak wouldn't screw things up. He leaned down and pulled out his "Project File" as he called it. The collection of seemingly unconnected deaths of various scumbags. He took the contents and spread them across his desk.

- Jackie Ruthers, the casino boss and gangster, suffered a sudden heart attack, found by the cleaner lady.
- The rapist Tom Blunt who had burnt to death in his car and the old pensioner passing by. She had been commended for well-meant but ill-advised bravery in trying to save him.
- The child molester James Buckworth, killed by a loose brick falling from a window. The homeless witness, Gladys Ingrams, had made a big thing about the building being unsafe and how she had to move on.
- The bizarre poisoning of all the Croydon dog fighting ring, leaving only Bob Cherry, Arnold Smith and the dude in prison, Dave Duncannon.

The burning down of Crabbs' place was delightfully normal, having all the hallmarks of a fairly run-of-the-mill OCG murder by arson. The thought occurred to him that it only looked normal against the other four cases. On its own it would be quite unusual. He pondered that thought and then let it go.

Was he chasing shadows? He hated dangling uncertainties.

Reluctantly, his mind came back to Crabbs. Why did Cherry not finish off Crabbs when he first visited him? Was he interrupted? Why even talk to the man? He was obviously hellbent on trying to kill him, you don't set a place like that alight and expect anyone to survive. Why not just finish him off there and then while he had the chance? If Ash hadn't been there that day, Crabbs would have been history.

CHAPTER 64

Mervyn was practising different retrieval rates across Jim's carpet as he wound the platypus towards him with his rod and reel.

"How long do you need to practise with that Mervyn? You've been at it for almost an hour now."

"Well Jim, I researched, and a platypus can move at twenty-two miles per hour through the water. Isn't that amazing?"

"Mind boggling Mervyn."

"On land they move slower with a shuffle. So that's what I'm trying to simulate with my retrieval."

"Mervyn, that's great, I'm sure you're getting the platypus shuffle down to a T, but when are you going to start making it look like a cat?"

"Oh damn, you're right, it's supposed to look like a cat. I'd better start again."

"I was thinking, we should get going sooner rather than later. When do you think you'll be ready?"

"Give me the rest of the day Jim, tomorrow maybe."

Jim phoned Harry.

"Tomorrow! Why so soon Jim?"

"Why not Harry? Mervyn said he'll have his cat dragging perfected by then. Tempus fugit Harry."

"Oh God, alright."

"I thought you'd be pleased to get into action again Harry. Is there some reason we should hold off?"

"Yes, I'm a coward. I'm shitting myself about this sodding operation, I've hardly slept a bloody wink and when I do, I wake up in a cold sweat dreaming about your fucking killing machine," thought Harry. He let out a groan. "No, tally ho, Geronimo, hi-ho fucking Silver, let's get it over with, then I can bloody relax."

"OK Merv. We're on for tomorrow. Harry wants to get it done, he said he's so excited about it he can't relax."

"It must be nice to be like Harry, eh, Jim? I have to be honest, most of my retrieval techniques have involved me trying to stop my hands shaking so badly that I drop the bloody thing."

"Yeah, Merv, I keep trying to focus on what that Dunstable bloke looks like, I'm so bloody worried I'll finger the wrong bloke."

"I never thought of that. That would be terrible. Now I have that fear to deal with as well."

The following morning was cold and rainy. Mervyn looked out of the window. "We'd better take our brollies Jim."

"Yeah, I'm a bit worried about the Educator. If it gets wet, it might short across the insulators."

"Is that bad Jim?"

"It would mean that the operator would get fried instead of the target maybe."

"Oh, well that's cheery. Should we let Harry know, or should we just make sure we stand well back when he lets rip?"

"What?!"

"I'm joking Jim, a little witticism to brighten up the day."

"Thanks Merv, what would I do without you? I'd better tell Harry that if the rain persists, we might have to make a plan."

Harry listened to Jim's news. Initially, he couldn't work out whether he was relieved or not, but by the time Jim had finished explaining why it might be risky, Harry was close to cardiac arrest.

"You mean to tell me that thing of yours can backfire!?"

"Well, not if it's dry… probably."

"Probably what? It will? It won't? What are you saying?"

"I think maybe you should wear rubber shoes, just in case."

"So, a pair of wellies is going to save me from certain death is it?"

"Can never be too careful Harry – health and safety you know."

"So apart from bringing a pair of wellies, is there anything else you have maybe forgotten to tell me? Should I wear a wetsuit and goggles maybe? Get a Michelin man suit? Come in dangling from a fucking helicopter?"

"No, that's it, Harry, ha ha, I love the way you inject a little laugh into things. Oh look, it's stopped raining and the sun's come out, let's keep our fingers crossed, eh?"

Harry spent the rest of the day praying for rain and cursing the bright sun that burnt down, uninhibited by a single cloud in the sky. He picked out his wellies from the shed, scooped out the cobwebs and creatures that had taken up residence there for the past decade, and made his way to Jim's place.

Mervyn was ready with his wicker picnic basket, fishing rod and reel, and the platypus wrapped in newspaper. Jim had his remote speaker fully charged with thirty minutes of cat sounds ready to play on his phone. The Educator was wrapped in a large tent bag with a pair of binoculars. Three camp chairs were folded and ready to go.

"I think I'm going to take an extra jersey just in case it gets a bit nippy."

"Hmm, good idea. Better take the brollies as well, just in case."

"So, if it starts pouring, we are still going ahead are we?"

"You know Merv, Harry has got a point. The rain could screw things up."

"Yeah, he's right, a soaked platypus-cat ploughing through the mud isn't going to be very convincing no matter what speed I pull it at."

"Yeah, and my remote speaker might not work so well if it's wet."

"Not to mention the bloody lightning device I have to hold short circuiting through my body."

"Oh, no, that's OK Harry, with rubber boots you'll probably be fine, but these other issues are showstoppers. Well, we'll just have to hope for fine weather won't we. Let's go."

They hefted their equipment into Mervyn's car. Except for the Educator, which wouldn't fit in the boot and had to be placed on Harry's lap in the back. "This thing can't suddenly switch itself on, can it?"

"I doubt it Harry, the isolator switch will in all probability stop that happening."

"How reassuring!"

As they were about to move off, Mervyn turned to his passengers. "What day is it today?"

"Thursday."

"No, it's Friday isn't it?"

"If it's Saturday, Dunston won't be there, will he?"

"Hang on, let me look. It's Wednesday, we should be fine. Let's go."

CHAPTER 65

They looked out across to the gate of the park. "Right, here we are. The light is fading. I think we should split up and rendezvous by the substation. I'll carry the platypus, the fishing tackle and the refreshments. Harry, you've got the machine. Jim, can you carry the three chairs? We mustn't look like we are anything but three separate old men going about their evening recreation."

"Isn't it going to look a bit funny me wandering around with three chairs?"

"Hmm, well, if anyone asks, you like three so you can stretch out a bit. Now remember, act naturally."

At that, Mervyn gathered his stuff and, with a loud tuneless whistle, set off with a gait that looked like he was doing a soft shoe shuffle.

"What's he walking like that for?"

"Harry, I haven't the faintest idea. Come on, let's get behind the bushes before somebody spots us trying to look nonchalant."

The chairs were set out and, within seconds, Mervyn dived into his picnic hamper and pulled out a pork pie.

"Shouldn't we be checking that everything is ready before we start our four-course lunch and wine pairing?"

Mervyn sighed and put his pie reluctantly back into the hamper. "I'm really quite peckish."

"Here Harry, let me help you with the Educator. Merv, best you tackle up, then get the platypus in place across the path when the coast is clear."

Mervyn gently unwrapped the platypus and threaded the fish line through the little hole in its beak. Then he stroked its fur back into place and kissed it on the head.

"Did I just see you kiss that platypus?"

"It's for good luck Jim, I always kiss my trout lures, works every time."

"Well, I suppose every little bit helps. Are you ready with the machine Harry?"

"As ready as I will ever be I suppose."

"Right, I'm going to set up my observation post over there. I reckon we have about half an hour's wait maybe. I'll tell you when I see him coming and I'll switch the speaker on."

"I think we should only make natural sounds, so as not to alarm anybody."

"What the fuck are natural sounds Mervyn?"

"Well let's see, he's coming could be an owl hoot, keep quiet a crow, start winding a seagull, and, er, shoot him a duck."

"OK, so keep quiet is an owl, what sort of owl?"

"No Harry, keep quiet is a crow, sort of a squawk."

"What's an owl mean then Merv?"

"An owl's a…"

"Fucking bad idea. If we can't get it right now, I can only imagine what it's going to be like when the pressure's on. Seagulls, ducks and bloody pelicans, no, it's not going to happen. Hand signals OK?"

"Like what Jim? We need to practise."

"No, we bloody don't."

"What's 'he's coming'?"

"Thumbs up obviously."

"I don't think that's obvious at all, thumbs up might mean start winding."

"Thumbs up will never mean start winding, start winding is this." Jim made a winding motion with one hand. "Keep quiet is this." Jim put his finger to his mouth.

"OK, that one's obvious, I'll give you that. What about shoot him? That could be thumbs up too!"

"Never. Finger pulling trigger, like this."

"You could be scratching yourself. What if I'm not looking?"

"I'll do a *psst* to get your attention."

"Talking of psst, I need the toilet."

"Well Harry there's plenty of bushes."

"No Jim, I need to sit down."

"You have to be kidding me – you need a crap, now!"

"No, I can't pee standing up, I have to sit down."

"Well squat or sit on a branch."

"No, that won't work."

"I don't suppose you brought along a potty in your picnic hamper did you Mervyn. No? What is this world coming to? I can't believe it. This can't be happening, not now."

"There must be a public toilet here in the park, I won't be long."

They watched Harry walk off along the path in search of a toilet.

"Bloody hell Mervyn, we might wind up doing this alone, he might be there shaking the last drips off for half an hour. Come on, let's put out the platypus."

Jim checked his watch. "Still about fifteen minutes to go Merv."

"Plenty of time for that pork pie now Jim, do you want a wedge?"

"No thanks Merv, not just yet." Jim took up his position, moving his head around to get the best view of the path. "Whoa, somebody's coming Merv." Jim looked through his binoculars. "Bloody hell, I can't see a thing."

"You've got the lens caps on Jim."

"Oh, yeah, I knew that. Er, it's an old lady with a dog."

They watched in silence as she approached. When she drew alongside the bushes that Jim and Mervyn were skulking in, they heard the old lady's voice. "Come Benny. No, come. No leave that alone."

Mervyn looked down at his rod – the line had gone taut. Without thinking, he grabbed the rod and started reeling in the line. There was a scream and a growl. "No Benny, leave it, horrible thing, come, now!" Her footsteps could be heard receding as she hurried away with her dog in tow.

Jim and Mervyn looked down at the platypus – one of its legs was half hanging off. "I'm sorry Jim, I shouldn't have struck so hard."

"Not to worry, Merv. Actually, it being maimed might help its allure to that sicko Dungheap or whatever his name is." There was a sound of somebody crunching towards them through the bushes; instinctively, Jim grabbed the Educator and aimed it in the direction of the approaching noise.

"Ah, that's better. Whoa Jim, put that bloody thing down!"

"Oh, it's you Harry, bloody hell, you gave me a fright there."

"Not half as big a fright as I had looking down the barrel of that sodding contraption of yours. So, anything to report?"

"We just had a big bite." Jim held up the injured platypus with its leg swinging loosely. "We'll explain later, let me get back to the observation post."

As Jim started to move, he saw Dunston's unmistakable gait as the man entered the park. "For fuck's sake Merv, get the bloody platypus out there, he's coming!"

Mervyn stumbled out across the path and placed the platypus reverently on the ground. Then, he picked it up again to give it another kiss.

"Come on Mervyn, hurry up, what the fuck are you doing with that thing out there," Jim whispered.

Mervyn shuffled back, breathing heavily. "Did he see me?"

"No, I don't think so. He seems to be looking at the ground most of the time. Right, let me switch on the speaker." The speaker made a loud whoop as it announced its awoken state. "Shit, I forgot it did that." Jim looked out at the approaching Dunston, still loping his way, unalarmed, towards them.

All three could hear nothing but their own hearts thumping inside them. Harry looked at his shaking hands, wet with sweat. He wondered if his wet hands would enable the current to jump through his body instead of his target's; he closed his eyes and prayed incoherently. Mervyn held his rod and reel so tightly that the rod tip began quivering.

Jim looked down at his phone. As he fumbled to open the cat sounds track, the phone slipped out of his fingers into the undergrowth at his feet. He let out a whimper as he fell to his knees to retrieve it.

Glancing up, he saw Dunston no more than fifteen metres from their position. He looked at Merv and gave the start winding signal with his hands. He pushed the play button on his phone. A long wailing mating call of a cat came forth.

Dunston stopped and looked up. The pathetic shape of a platypus with a broken leg began making its hesitant journey across the path in front of him. For a moment he did nothing, then a sick grin, followed by a girlish giggle, came forth from his mouth.

He started walking steadily towards the platypus, making an attempt to cut off its escape. Jim signalled to Mervyn to wind faster. Mervyn duly picked up his pace and saw the platypus entering the bushes from the path.

In hot pursuit came Dunston. Suddenly, he was in the clearing next to the substation. Before he could say anything, a whining sound started, followed by a blinding flash as Harry initiated the Educator, fully believing it was his last moment on earth.

To everybody's amazement, the electric shock caused Dunston to fly into the air and fall backwards over the railings of the substation. Beyond horror, Harry continued to press the trigger, pointing the Educator towards Dunston's body as he did so. Electricity pulsed around the railings, the substation and the jerking body of Dunston for an eternity. Eventually, the Educator's battery ran flat and cut off the current. Everybody stared at the smoking medium-to-well-done body of Dunston, now inside the railings and flopped against the substation.

After an age, Jim gently took the Educator away from Harry and laid it back in its case. As if in a dream, each of them gathered their equipment and, after a quick glance up and down the path, split up and made their way silently back to the car.

They all sat in the car as it started to rain. "I think I need a moment, guys, my legs are shaking again, I can't drive."

"With all due respect, Mervyn, I think maybe we should get out of here while we can. I'm not sure what that looked like, but I wouldn't be surprised if some public-minded citizen from the flats has contacted the authorities."

"Harry's right Merv. Do you want me to drive?"

At the thought of somebody else driving his car, especially somebody who didn't have a licence, Mervyn jumped into action, turned the key and hesitantly they made their way back to Jim's house.

Harry stood in Jim's lounge "Would it be alright if I stayed the night, Jim?"

CHAPTER 66

Ash flipped through the incident reports from the previous day. His eye caught the report of a death by electrocution in a local park. Apparently, some idiot had climbed over the fence of a substation and electrocuted himself. He was about to move on but decided to check the deceased's identity. Derrick Dunston, a local resident, recently accused of animal cruelty and let off with a warning, no previous convictions. There it was again – somebody slightly slimy, let out onto the streets, meets a sticky end.

He looked for witnesses, but apart from a pensioner at the nearby flats seeing some flashes around the substation and calling it in, nothing. What would somebody be doing inside a substation fence in the first place? Ash shook his head. Too many coincidences, too many weird accidental deaths.

He decided to pay the park a visit. A tape had been put around the area and he could see two municipal workers in yellow jackets talking to one another on the path.

"Morning gentleman." Ash held up his ID. "Can you tell me what happened here?"

One of the men indicated back towards the bushes. "Morning sir. Bloke bought it back there. They've just taken his body away. Right mess he was. Burn marks all over from the shock." The man looked over his shoulder at Ash as he walked towards the substation. "We reckon he must have hopped over the fence here, cos there was a bit of jeans torn off on the spike."

Ash looked at the substation. "Are there bare wires on that thing that he touched?"

"Well, there's the funny thing. We was both wondering how he got electrocuted. Cos even inside the fence, there ain't no live components exposed that we can see."

"Really, no signs of him tampering with it or that type of thing?"

"Nuffink. We've shut down power to ensure it's safe, but everything looks normal, except for the burn marks on the station, the fence and the poor geezer himself. He was a right mess."

"Do you think he was electrocuted?"

"Yeah. I'm not a doctor but them burn marks all over him was just like electrocution stuff."

"Hmm, do you mind if I have a look around?"

"Yeah, help yourself mate. The gate's open if you wanna go inside and have a butchers."

"Thanks."

Ash stood back and looked at the scene. The ground immediately surrounding the substation, both in and out of the fence, had been churned up by the feet of the power people and those who had taken the body away. It had been raining the night before, around the time that the flashes had been reported.

As Ash looked around, he saw a wrapping lying in the leaves. He pulled on a rubber glove and picked it up. It was from a Waitrose pork pie and the use by date was for that day. He slipped the wrapping into an evidence bag and continued looking around. He was about to go when something caught his eye. He bent down and picked it up gently. Turning it around, it looked like a furry duck's webbed foot. He took another bag and placed the foot carefully inside. After a further search revealed nothing new, he returned to the path where the two men in their yellow suits were standing.

"Thanks gents, do you know who was first on the scene here?"

"Yeah, we was. We go off shift soon."

"You don't happen to know if anybody possibly had something to eat in there lately, do you?"

"What, in there? You gotta be joking, the sight of that geezer done to a crisp was enough to churn your guts."

"Right, thank you gentlemen."

"Right you are sir."

CHAPTER 67

Ash watched as the forensic lab technician held up the little furry webbed paw. "Where did you get this?"

"Down in the bushes, next to where that person was electrocuted in the park, why?"

"Just give me a mo."

Ash watched as the technician accessed her computer and brought up several pictures, glancing between them and the little paw. "Look, I'll need to confirm it but I'm almost sure that this paw belongs to a platypus."

"I didn't know you got those here."

The technician laughed. "You don't, they are extinct in most parts of the world; eastern Australia and Tasmania are the only places where they still occur."

"Shit, he was a long way from home!"

"And some! Let me get back to you on this, OK?"

CHAPTER 68

Jim awoke suddenly, he looked around the bedroom blinking his eyes. The events of the previous night came back to him in waves. The sight of Dunston, dancing around as Harry fired the Educator, Mervyn standing to one side with a fishing rod in his hands. Then the weird flight of Dunston backwards as he seemingly sailed over the fence and the eerie sounds of cats wailing away as all this took place.

"Bloody hell, did I dream all that?" he thought, already knowing that it was factually engraved into his brain. He went downstairs and found Mervyn sitting at the kitchen table with a cocoa. "Did you sleep alright Merv?"

"Right through Jim, and you?"

"Amazingly yes. Pre-meditated murder seems to be the perfect remedy for insomnia, who would have thought?"

"Do you think we're murderers, Jim? Is what we are doing wrong?"

"I'm not sure of the fine print and technicalities Mervyn, I guess we'll only know for sure when we get to the pearly gates. But from where I'm standing, I reckon we just lightened the load on human decency by getting rid of that bastard."

"I think so too." Harry was standing at the doorway in a dressing gown borrowed from Jim.

"Hi Harry, did you get any sleep on the couch?"

"Out like a light. Haven't slept that well in an age. My bladder was about to pop."

"I just had a thought – what if it was the wrong bloke? I'm sure it wasn't, but we didn't actually confirm his identity."

"True Mervyn, but I doubt whether he would have calmly shown us his national insurance card so we could ensure that he was the right one to fry."

"No, I suppose not, but I think we must remain mindful of our responsibilities – we have a reputation to uphold."

"A reputation. I've never thought of it in that way. A reputable enterprise. Satisfaction guaranteed. Slimeball extermination. Do you have some human trash that needs taking out? Call us, we'll make your day by blowing them away."

"Do you think we have covered our tracks well enough Jim? We didn't really perform a tactical retreat. It was more like a run for cover."

"We brought everything back Merv." Jim looked across at the equipment piled in the corner. "Educator, check, rod and reel, check, speaker, picnic hamper, three chairs and last but not least, our furry friend." Jim held up the platypus.

Harry held out his hands. "Let me have a look there Jim." Harry turned the platypus over. "His foot's gone."

"What!? Let me see! Shit, you're right, it must have dropped off after that bloody dog had a go at it."

"If they find it, they could trace it right back to us Jim."

"Right Merv. I can see it now. 'Bloody hell! Look, it's a platypus paw. Only one person has a platypus north of the equator – put a cordon round Jim Spoonwall's house immediately and bring the bastard in.'"

"Hmm, nevertheless, we should get rid of it, don't you think?"

"I… I think he looked after us actually, he played his part, and I for one intend to show my gratitude," said Jim, taking the platypus back and stroking its muddy fur as he did so. "Right. Let's have some breakfast and then let's see if our escapades made the morning papers."

CHAPTER 69

Ash flicked through the forensic report. The pork pie had been purchased and presumably consumed on the day in question. He wondered if he should ask for a post-mortem on the stomach contents of Dunston, but then what would that prove either way? If he hadn't eaten it, they were no closer to anything conclusive. They could hardly round up everybody who had bought a Waitrose pork pie and even if they did it, what then?

He then turned to the cause of death. Electrocution, there seemed to be no doubt about that, the burns confirmed it. The report went on to say that the burns were on the main parts of the body and feet. No burns were found on the hands or fingers, which was unusual. The burns on the feet confirmed that he was standing when he was electrocuted. No exposed electrical circuitry was found. That was the thing that made no sense. It was almost as if the substation was an innocent bystander. Was it maybe lightning? It was raining at the time.

Then there was the webbed paw. It did indeed belong to a platypus. There were traces of alum and borax in the paw which pointed to the creature having been stuffed. It was estimated that the creature had been stuffed for at least thirty years. It hadn't been there very long either, but what did that have to do with anything? He didn't have a clue, literally.

Ash put his head in his hands. What was he getting into? He should just let this one go. He could just imagine the comments if he raised the case's profile too far. "Hey Ash, have you hunted down that three-legged platypus that roasted that guy yet?" "Why not put out an all-points bulletin and get those WANTED signs up. Have you seen this platypus? Armed with duck beak and dangerous, should not be approached." He could hear the cackles of laughter. He chuckled himself, you couldn't blame them actually.

He shut the file and put it in the bottom drawer along with the other deaths.

CHAPTER 70

Jim returned from the local shop with three different newspapers, three Danish pastries and a bottle of fabric cleaner.

"What's in the bottle Jim?"

"Oh, it's just fabric cleaner… for the platypus."

"Really, is he going on display? Is that wise?"

"Mervyn, I know you and he have problems, but I for one know how to treat a faithful friend."

"You didn't by any chance get a couple of side shocks yesterday did you Jim? You know, sort of addled your brain a bit? We should burn it."

"Oh really Mervyn? And who was giving it a bit of tongue there in the bushes? Snogging away, I couldn't tear you apart. But now you've got what you want, you just turn your back, typical."

Harry picked up the first paper and flicked through the pages. "Hey, here we are: *A person was found dead in a park in South West London last night. It is thought that the man was accidentally electrocuted after climbing into the restricted area of an electrical substation. The identity of the deceased is being withheld whilst his next of kin are informed. A spokesman from the Electricity Board stated that substations were inherently safe, and that the public should not be alarmed, provided they adhere to the warning signs. The investigation is ongoing.*" Harry looked up at Jim. "They think it was an accident. We didn't plan for that."

Jim shook his head. "I never gave the substation a thought. It just happened to be there. I was amazed when he flew over the fence."

After a coffee and pastries, Jim went to the next room and phoned Jeremy.

"Ah Jim, congratulations are in order again I see. I have no idea how you engineered this particular project, nor do I wish to know, despite being extremely curious. I must say that you and your team are extremely impressive in your newfound field of endeavours."

"Er, yeah, thank you. But the reason I phoned was because we don't know for sure that we nailed the right man."

"Have no worries on that score Jim. You got your man. It is confirmed that the man was singularly responsible for the agonising deaths of at least fifty souls in the area, probably a lot more."

"Well, that's a relief, we thought we had the right guy, but it's nice to be sure."

"Certainly. I would suggest you all take a well-deserved breather. Let me know when I can be of assistance again."

"Yeah, I think we'll just run our fingers down the list we have and see who else deserves our attention."

"Very well, Jim, happy hunting."

CHAPTER 71

Jim looked at the keys on the shelf. Doris was off again having her goitre attended to for a couple of days. Not that Jim minded, he had grown very close to Archie the cat and was looking forward to telling him all about their latest escapade. Picking up the keys, he took a pack of free-range breast fillets and a tub of Greek yogurt from the fridge.

Archie was in the hallway waiting for him as Jim closed the front door of Doris's house. It struck Jim that, despite Doris's advanced years and dithery demeanour, the house always smelled clean and fresh. So often old people's houses smelt of old people. All his uncles' and aunties' places he was dragged along to visit as a kid had their own particular old person's smell. Aunt Agnes's place had a smell of boiled cabbage, Uncle Joe and Aunt Jean had the smell of sour damp flannels as their signature. Then there was Uncle Ed, who nurtured an odour that could best be described as that of death. He wondered if his house had a smell; suspecting that it probably did, he pondered what sort of smell it might be.

They both walked into the kitchen. Archie hopped onto the stool and settled down to listen to the latest news, whilst Jim slipped the chicken pieces into the pot.

"I think you're going to like this one Archie. We targeted a very nasty individual called Derrick Dunston."

At the mention of Dunston's name Archie curled up his back and let out a hiss.

"Aha, I see this man's reputation is not unknown to you. Then I don't have to tell you what an absolute waste of human cells he is – or was."

Archie stared at Jim intently, waiting for his story.

"We lured him with a stuffed platypus."

Archie cocked his head to one side.

"It's a bit like an aardvark-dog-otter sort of thing, that has a beak and lays eggs."

The cat flopped down onto his stool and rested his head on it.

"No, really, I'll show it to you sometime. Anyway, this Dunston bloke chased it and then Harry took my Educator and electrocuted him, set light to him sort of."

The cat sat up.

"Yep Archie, Dunston is dead, gone. Can't hurt any more of your friends."

Archie jumped down and rubbed himself against Jim's legs, purring as he did so.

"You're welcome my mate. It's good to know that I've done the right thing. I really needed your approval. I suppose I should have got it before we started really, but there you are. Ooh look, your chicken is just about ready, let's have a celebration supper."

Together they enjoyed the meal, Archie with his chicken and Jim with a half jack of whisky he had brought along especially.

CHAPTER 72

Jim, Harry and Mervyn were back in the pub again. Mervyn lifted his beer. "Where shall we three meet again, in thunder, lightning or in rain?"

"Very dramatic Merv, cheers."

"Well, we certainly showed Mr Dunston a thing or two."

"Yeah, he won't make that mistake again."

"I must say that I've been a bit off meat since your machine started its trials, Jim."

"We must cure you of that Merv. Maybe we should have a proper barbeque."

"Good timing, I'd say. Did you hear about that butcher in Dulwich? They found him, or at least his body, frozen solid in his freezer after the long weekend. Locked himself in there somehow. Apparently, there's a rumour going around that they are selling the contents off at half price to the less squeamish."

"Really Harry? I wouldn't mind, as long as the joints I get are not covered in bits of clothing. Imagine, you pull out of the oven what you thought was a pork roll and find that it still has a wrist watch on it."

"Stop it Jim! Let's move on to our next project. What is on the list?"

"I think that this time, when we do our planning, we should look back at all the things that could have gone wrong on the last two escapades and fit in a few more contingencies."

"Like what Harry?"

"Well, for instance, none of us had any idea that the shock Dunston received would send him flying like a dart conveniently over the fence onto the substation, did we? None of us recognised the convenient fact that the substation could be blamed for his demise. That lucky break almost certainly transformed what would have been an obvious assassination, with all the nasty investigations that go with it, into a tragic accident. In other words, we were bloody lucky. Not to mention what ifs, like what if the old lady with the dog had followed the bloody platypus in and found us lurking in the bushes like a bunch of zombies on the prowl."

"We would have explained to her that we were er… conducting an experiment to… er, attract owls."

"No, we fucking wouldn't Merv, you would have carried on winding the platypus to hell and I would have turned the shock machine on and sent her to oblivion."

"Do you really think so Harry?"

"Yes, I bloody do. If we are going to keep on being lucky we had better stop relying on luck."

"But what about the dog fighting ring? You carried that out with precision and ice cool calm."

"OK." Harry sighed. "I need to tell you both something. I wasn't calm, I was shitting myself. I was in such a fucking state by the time they opened the door that I had no idea what I was saying or why. I could have caused all our deaths – and, knowing that lot, they wouldn't have been pleasant ones."

"Rubbish Harry. I'll never forget the way you just took a kip when you got back into the car."

"That wasn't a kip Merv, that was me passing out from terror."

"Bollocks, your training in the forces. That performance under fire…"

"I was a fucking canteen cook Jim. I had knife fights with carrots and onions. I did hand to hand combat with chicken carcasses and surrounded sausages with pastry. The only soldiers I organised were the ones you dip into your boiled eggs. I've been lying to you guys, I'm a natural born coward."

After a bit of a silence, Merv stood up. "I would like to propose a toast to Harry. Probably the bravest man I will ever know."

Jim stood up and raised his glass. "To Harry. For bravery beyond the call of duty."

"Yeah, that's it, take the piss."

"We're not Harry. What you did out there took way more guts. We are both constantly shitting ourselves. I feel so rotten that we sent you into that, you should have told us."

"I meant to, but the moment never seemed quite right. I was too much of a coward to admit that I was a coward."

"You're not, Harry. From now on, we must all be completely honest with each other. As you said, we've dipped quite deeply into the luck bucket recently."

"OK, I think we all need and deserve another beer. When I get back, let's look at our list and do some proper planning."

CHAPTER 73

Ash sat in the canteen nursing a coffee. The nagging feeling that he was missing something would not go away. He wanted to go to the chief and request opening a docket on all "natural" deaths of shady members of society, but he knew he would need far more evidence than he had. He also knew that if he said and did nothing, he would be left alone. Nobody was riding him for results, not anymore. He pondered his situation and came to the conclusion that, under the current circumstances, he couldn't complain. He could at least keep on rummaging undisturbed.

He returned to his desk. A report of a butcher frozen stiff in his own freezer was coming in. He frowned. Another door had been discovered at the back of the freezer in which the butcher had died. Upon further investigation, it had been found to contain contraband abalone with a street value of half a million pounds. In addition, frozen pangolins were found in the freezer, and rhino horn in the basement.

The three hypotheses ran along the lines of:

a) A rival poaching ring being involved,

b) The butcher possibly being taken out by his own people or

c) Accidental death.

Ash had immediately discounted the first two. If it was a hit, there were no signs that the perpetrators were disturbed, in which case, they would not have left behind stock of that value. That left accidental death – or Ash's own theory that somebody was taking out the trash again. He decided a visit to the Dulwich shop was in order.

The shop looked like any other butcher's shop. He wondered how many people had bought their sausages and chops there, completely unaware of the place's dark alter ego. The slabs were clear of meat, only the green plastic mock parsley strips lay in the window to tempt the passer by. He walked into the customer area and flashed his ID to the forensic officer. "Any idea what happened here?"

"He was definitely trying to get out. Broken nails and blood on the inside of the door latch and knob that concur with the wounds on his hands."

"Was the door locked?"

"No, that's the funny thing. These doors don't lock. When we arrived, the door was open. The assistant came in to open up, he found the body inside and phoned the police."

"Fingerprints?"

"Only the assistant's so far and of course, the deceased's."

"Where is the assistant now?"

"He went to the station, they're taking his statement."

"Any CCTV of the entrance?"

"You'll have to ask down at the station."

"Fair enough, thanks." Ash decided to return to Wimbledon. He was out of his territory anyway and would need to discuss his theories in way too much detail if he wanted to dig.

He browsed through the report. The door had shown no obvious signs of having been jammed shut but the deceased had clearly wanted to escape. The assistant, Joe Hatch, had opened up the shop as usual. During his usual morning routine, he had opened the freezer door to find his boss on the floor. The boss, Charlie Kerns, had no form, and had been running the butchery for some eight years since emigrating from South Africa. They had spoken to the butcher's part-time accountant, who had dropped off the business's books two days before at closing time, and was one of the last people to see the butcher alive. The books showed a steady turnover in line with a high street butcher.

Ash stared at the report. Did most butchers have part-time accountants? He would have imagined that they just dumped it all in the laps of an accounting firm. Maybe the accountant was running a second set of books for them. He looked up her name and went over to Ella. "Hi, could you track down this accountant, Nancy Graham, please?"

As he walked back to his desk, the Superintendent walked in. "Er, Ash, can I have a word please?"

The man turned and walked to his office with Ash in tow. "Sit down Ash."

"What's up boss?"

"I've just had Dulwich on the line. What the hell were you doing over there?"

"I was following up a hunch."

"They think you're trampling on their patch. You have to go through the proper channels, bloody hell Ash, you know that."

"Sorry boss, my mistake."

Ash's superior looked at him for a while and shook his head. "Just do it by the book Ash, OK?"

"By the book boss."

"What is this hunch you are following?"

Ash closed his eyes and sucked in his breath. He'd been dreading this moment.

He gave a brief summary of the events, from the death of Jackie Ruthers the casino boss to the death of the butcher in Dulwich.

"So, you are telling me there is this secret society that is responsible for every natural-looking death of a criminal, and the tools of their trade are bricks, toadstools, locking them up in freezers, summoning up lightning and scaring them to death, is that it?"

"It's a theory I am following up." Ash clenched his jaw.

"Apparently there is also a platypus foot involved according to a lab report I saw in passing. You'll pardon me for being nosey, but how does that fit in with the theory Ash? Are they dabbling with the dark arts maybe or do they beat people to death with rare dead animals? I'm fascinated to hear your theory on that one."

"I'm at the early stages of the investigation boss, I…"

"Look Ash, I don't really care, but don't you dare let the press or even the rest of the station get wind of this garbage. Heaven knows we have enough crap to deal with without this lunatic bullshit of yours getting out. OK? Now go."

Ash walked back, fuming.

Ella came over to his desk. "That accountant you were looking for. I'm drawing a bit of a blank. The phone goes to voice mail and the postal address is a PO Box."

"Where does she live?"

"No residential address was given."

Ash closed his eyes and shook his head. Maybe the chief was right, maybe it is all lunatic bullshit.

"If he doesn't care, why should I?"

"Sorry Ash?"

"Nothing, leave it with me Ella."

"Oh, and one other thing Ash. That guy Arnold Smith who you visited in hospital, the one who ate the toadstools, he's off the danger list apparently. Expected to make a full recovery."

CHAPTER 74

"I reckon we should have a look at the paedophile list, what do you think Jim?"

"Yep, that's fine with me. Jeremy only put two names on the list, let's see which one we hate the most."

After two minutes, Harry looked up from the notes they were all studying. "I'm sorry, I can't read any more of this. How can human beings do this to children? This one was only three years old for God's sake."

"I know Harry, it's terrible, this bastard had the parents' trust. They were bringing their kids to him to be cared for. How the hell did this go undiscovered for so many years? *The esteemed founder and benefactor of this wonderful charity*. That's how he was described when he was given a peerage for his life's work."

"*Insufficient evidence* – what a travesty. This detective here discovered home movies of the bastard filming himself in action. Look at the smug smile on the sod when his case was thrown out of court. *A tragic victim of a vicious smear campaign* his lawyer declared."

"It says here in Jeremy's notes that all evidence was found to have gone missing due to an admin error. Since then, he has taken a sabbatical from his charity work."

"Where is he now Mervyn?"

"Er, aah, here we are, lives on his private estate near Gatwick."

"Well gentlemen, I think we can rule out pizza deliveries as a solution, and marching through the gates with Jim's blaster is likely to raise a few eyebrows. In any case, we don't want to leave a trail of traceable modus operandi. This needs a bit more subtlety and lateral thinking."

"You're right Harry."

"Would it be OK if we make this one's death particularly unpleasant?"

"Yes Jim, I think that would be in order."

"OK, let me contact Jeremy right now and see what more he has on this chunk of shit."

"Good morning Jim."

"Morning Jeremy, we rather like, er, actually hate, this Lord Percival Brandford-Smythe."

"A particularly unsavoury piece of work, I thought you might zone in on that one. Are you sure you don't want to give yourself and your team a bit of a breather?"

"No time for breathers Jeremy, we are running against the clock. We'd rather get as much done as possible and too much time might let us start thinking too much. At our age that is dangerous."

"It's your call Jim, as always. I'll pass over what I have. I hope you have a strong stomach. I have unearthed some visual material as well."

"I don't understand why they can't reopen the case if there is new evidence."

"The new evidence will wind up where the other evidence went. Connections in high places Jim. There are others who share the same habits as Brandford-Smythe."

"Can we get to those bastards as well Jeremy?"

"Chewable chunks Jim, chewable chunks. I will not deny you that satisfaction if you seek it. You have my promise."

"Thank you, Jeremy, we won't let you down."

"I know Jim, goodbye."

The material arrived a little later. As Mervyn opened the package, his hands began to shake slightly.

"I feel queasy, it's like opening a bag that you know is full of soft dog shit."

"I know Mervyn. But it's all for a good cause, we owe it to all those kids."

"You're right Jim, let's do it for them."

CHAPTER 75

Sam Weller slammed his phone down after hearing that his Putney operation had just been shut down by a police raid.

"Who the fuck is grassing on us?"

"Bob Cherry reckons he knows."

"Cherry? Since when did he become a source of reliable information?"

"Dunno, want me to find out?"

"Yeah, find out. It won't be cheap, knowing that prick. Give him a bell."

The man did as he was told and dialled Cherry's number.

"Oi Cherry, word's out that you know who the canary is."

"I might do, what's it to you?"

"Mr Weller wants to know."

"Really, nosey bugger ain't he? Maybe we can do a deal."

"Deal?"

"Yeah, you know, help each other out."

"How's that?"

"Well, I give you what you want and you give me something in return."

"I'll ask the boss."

"Wait you dumb fuck, you don't know what I want."

"What is it?"

"I want to make use of Sammy boy's fence, I want in. You know, share and share alike."

"Mr Weller, he wants to know who our fence is."

"Tell him to fuck off."

"Mr Weller says fuck off."

"Let me speak to him."

The man handed the phone over to his boss.

"You can fuck off Cherry. I don't want your greasy goods anywhere near mine."

"Fine, the way the cops are shutting your shit holes down, I'll be able to walk in and clean up anyway. I just thought for old times' sake that we might be able to share."

"How come the cops ain't nailing you, you sneaky cunt?"

"I don't go round bragging about my operation to my mates, do I?"

"Alright, who is it?"

"Na, na, na. It don't work like that. We meet, on our own, and then we have a little whisper in each other's ears."

"You think you can take me?"

"I know I can take you Sammy boy. But why would I bother? Remember, you lot phoned me. I don't give a fuck either way."

CHAPTER 76

Ash stood and looked out of the window at nothing in particular. Maybe he was chasing ghosts, maybe he wasn't. The only way to find out was to dig. He knew deep down that his perseverance would come to the fore. It nearly always caused trouble as well. That damned determination had cost him his marriage. His wife had left him, taking their son with her to go and live in Spain. He missed his son, and, if he was honest with himself, his wife as well. Not that the feeling was reciprocated in any way he could detect.

Unaware that his looks and demeanour, despite his age, still drew the attention of much younger women, he lived the life of a hermit, rarely socialising above that which became necessary from time to time.

Had it all been worth it? On the balance of things, probably not. So many scumbags slipped through the net, not because of their skill but because the system protected them at every turn. Here he was again, hampered not by the criminals but by the system. He had just been crapped out for doing his bloody job.

He walked back to his desk and picked up the note that Ella had left there. He phoned the post office and checked on the PO Box given by the accountant. "Hello, I'm interested in a particular PO Box." Ash read out the address.

"Yes sir, that one is available."

"Oh, right. How long has it been available? I don't want other people's post clogging it up."

"Let me just check sir, about a year now. Can I book it for you?"

"Let me get back to you."

He looked at the file again. "Nancy Graham, you don't exist, do you?" She was the last one to see Charlie Kerns alive and now she had evaporated. He put his hand out to the phone and then hesitated. "Fuck it."

He picked up the phone and dialled Dulwich police station. "Hi, can I have CID please… Hi, I would like to talk to the detective in charge of the butcher shop fatality please… Hi, I'm DI Kamau from Wimbledon. Yeah, that's right, the one who was stomping on your patch. Yeah, the Chief shat all over me. No, that's not why I'm phoning. Can I ask you something please? The freezer door, was there anything that suggested it might have been jammed? Would you? That would be very kind. The forensic report would be perfect, thank you. No, don't worry, I'm in the shit all the time. At my age you get used to it. Cheers."

Ash flicked through the forensic report on his screen. The handle and door inside had blood and tissue matching the deceased. His hands were lacerated from the obvious attempts he was making to open the door. The latch was a simple push rod arrangement from the inside thus ensuring an easy exit. The outside was a pull handle.

A photograph showed all the items picked up from outside the freezer by the forensic team. Two till receipts from a few days ago, a hand brush and pan, a small black piece of plastic, a bulldog clip, two wooden skewers, an empty bucket and several bundles of fluff.

Ash was about to go onto the next page when something struck him. He zoomed in on the picture.

He looked at the photos of the outside door handle again. "I'm willing to bet this was no bloody accident."

CHAPTER 77

"Lord Brandford-Smythe resides at Brandford Manor close to Gatwick Airport. He drives a GT Bentley convertible. He considers himself a socialite and doyen of the arts and is particularly keen on grouse shooting. You just have to hate this bastard more and more, don't you?"

"Sounds like a right burst arsehole, doesn't he? Arrogant, conceited, obviously thinks he's untouchable."

"He might well be. I doubt that he strolls around the park in the evening, and we aren't going to find him hanging around some dodgy club either. Is there anything in those notes about where we can get close to him Mervyn?"

"There's a lot to get through here, mainly about his past, the non-chequered bit anyway. He has staff who work at the manor, a butler and a chauffeur. There's a gardener too. He has dinner parties once a month, and an art appreciation event where up-and-coming artists get to display their talent. There's one coming up in two weeks' time."

"Where's that held?"

"At the manor."

"Hmm, maybe we should get along there."

"I'm Googling it now, let's see what the story is. Umm, here we are. Brandford Art Fess. Blaah blaah, wonderful philanthropist and kiddy fiddler is holding the annual…"

"What?!"

"No, made the kiddy bit up, sorry Jim, just slipped out. The annual art show is open to all neophyte artists. All submissions should be entered by the 23rd. Artwork should be no larger than one metre square, sculptures no more than one metre cubed. Artists are encouraged to work on their pieces at the show and preference will be given to such. Spectators will be by invitation only."

"Bugger, well that's out. I don't know about you two, but I don't get my name on the honours list much."

"Why don't we enter our own stuff?"

"Oh, yeah Merv, silly me, let me just pick out a couple of my own masterpieces."

"They don't have to be good – remember, art comes in many forms."

"It doesn't come in any form I'm capable of."

"You know, maybe Merv has got a point. Our only way in is by doing our own stuff, we would certainly not look suspicious by doing that."

"Are you out of your mind Harry? They would spot us a bloody mile off once they catch sight of the unspeakable crap that we would be capable of."

"Speak for yourself Jim. Anyway, have you seen some of the stuff hanging in the Tate? We just need to talk it up a bit."

"Talk it up a bit? I'd have to shag the Blarney Stone let alone kiss it to acquire the gift of the gab required to talk my stuff up."

"Well, unless anybody else has any ideas, I reckon we should go with this. It's low risk, and if it fails, we have lost nothing. In the meantime, if a better solution presents itself, we just change tack."

"Bugger you Harry, I hate logical arguments that make perfect sense and thus make me do something rotten."

"Maybe it won't be rotten Jim. Maybe it will be a great gift to mankind."

The following day saw the three men wandering around the Tate Modern. Jim stood at a Dali. "You guys think we can knock up something like this do you?"

"Keep moving Jim."

They walked into another room filled with canvases all painted off-white.

"Hang on a minute. Now this is a bit more my style."

"There you go Jim. Now go for the chat-up line."

"Er, OK, this one here shows how we come into life full of er, um, pure innocence. And progress through, er, life as shown by these other ones that show we achieve nothing of any significance only to die once again, er, innocent."

"There you go, brilliant. I'd say you're a natural."

"So Merv, what happens when some smart arse turns up and says it's a load of bloody crap?"

"Who cares Jim, you're not trying to make a career out of it are you? Anyway, if anybody does pull that one, just use the ole 'None so blind as those that will not see' line. I've shut many people up in my life with that line when I didn't have a clue what I was talking about."

"What about you Harry, what do you fancy doing?"

Jim followed Harry's gaze. "Something like this Jim."

They walked over to a collection of wooden sticks entwined in different coloured cotton. They both stood there staring at it. Jim turned round and called Mervyn across. "OK Merv, give us a line about this one."

Mervyn cocked his head to one side and frowned. "Well, um, let me see, I think it obviously underlines the struggle man has, as he constantly tries to make nature bend to his will. It shows us how futile his attempts will always be."

"Bloody hell Merv, that's pretty impressive. I reckon you could make a dog coil seem like a Donatello. Maybe we can pull this off after all."

"That's the spirit Jim. Let's go and get some materials. I need an easel, a canvas and a set of oils I reckon. What about you Harry?"

"Don't know, think I'll have a look around the shed and maybe the loft too. If all else fails I'll tell Sheila she can have a clear out, that usually produces some amazing crap."

"Fine. And you Jim?"

"I think I'll get a sheet of hardboard and throw some paint at it. I've got loads of half empty tins at home."

"Right, I'll apply straightaway. I'm suddenly feeling creative."

CHAPTER 78

"The Super wants to see you, Ash."

Ash turned his head away. "Another crapping out about bloody Dulwich no doubt." He stormed into the Superintendent's office ready to let rip.

The boss had his back to Ash as he looked out of the window. "I've just had some bad news Ash. They got to Crabbs."

Ash stepped back slightly. "What?"

"Crabbs got taken out sometime in the night. The details are still coming in. Double tap to the back of the head, probably with a silencer. Professional hit."

"For fuck's sake, how did they know where to look? Even I didn't know where he was!"

"I don't know, but we obviously have a leak." The boss turned round and looked at Ash.

"I want you to follow it up Ash. There was only a handful of people who knew his location. It has to be one of them. Drop the other bullshit and get onto it. Our whole witness protection programme looks like a whore's handbag at the moment. Look, I know we've had our differences. Frankly, you are a pain in the arse, but you're straight and I know I can trust you. Get to it."

Across town, Bob Cherry received an SMS from Sam Weller: *Our mate Crabbs got unlucky, be nice to my fence.*

CHAPTER 79

Lord Percival strutted into the drawing room. "Right Caruthers, how are the invitations coming along?"

"Well sir, we have most of the local gentry coming along. Lord and Lady Duncannon have declined. We do have the Earl of Deran and possibly John Smithers, and most of the shooting fraternity will be there of course."

"Good, very good indeed. And what of the entries?"

"We have well over fifty so far, plus three more entries that came in today. All three are in their seventies would you believe sir."

"Well, we mustn't be seen to favour the young. Do we know them, Caruthers?"

"No sir, can't say that we do."

"Hmm, very well, carry on."

CHAPTER 80

Jim stood in his garage and inspected the sheet of hardboard he had wrestled from the loft. Apart from a couple of dubious stains in one corner, it looked reasonably presentable. Unlike Mervyn, he was in no mood to splash out any money on his art. It would have to be produced from what could be spared and preferably what would otherwise wind up in the dustbin.

So far, apart from the board, he had found fourteen tins of paint in various states of aging, a wooden stepladder, one very stiff brush and a roller that had been occupied by a colony of earwigs. Energised by waves of creative energy, he propped the board up on the stepladder and proceeded to nail it into place. After some awkward moments, several bent nails and more than a little cursing, the board became fastened to the stepladder in a manner that would, more or less, have to do.

Having little idea of what to do next, he resorted to an eeney, meeney, miney, mo method of selecting the first paint tin. Upon opening the lid, it revealed a whitish paint, streaked with yellow slime and a large thick skin resembling a rice pudding. After prodding around inside the tin for a while with a twig, he managed to break the skin up into curly lumps, interspersed with bits of bark that had become separated from the twig.

Being mindful of the probable mess he was about to make, he stripped to his underpants and removed his glasses. Thus armed, he dipped the roller into the paint pot and proceeded to transfer what didn't land on the floor onto the board. Being somewhat visually impaired after the removal of his glasses, he had failed to notice that along with the paint, the colony of earwigs were also being applied to the board. Once the whole board was covered, he stepped back, picked up his glasses and, without a backward glance, walked back into the house.

By way of contrast, Mervyn, mindful of what would happen to any money he had left upon his rapidly approaching death, had had the time of his life buying a full set of oil paints, brushes and pallet knives, all arranged beautifully in a large mahogany box. This was accompanied by a beechwood easel, scale callipers and a full set of pastels just because.

Mervyn rechristened Jim's study as his 'Studio' and set everything up in there. He leaned forwards in his chair, opened the beautiful lid of the mahogany box and examined the contents. After admiring them for a considerable time, he decided to pick up each tube and read some of their names: French Ultramarine Blue, Burnt Sienna, Veridian (Hue), Cadmium Red Deep (Hue). He unscrewed the tops of the linseed oil and pure turpentine bottles and gave them a sniff, fluffed the brush's bristles with his fingers and gave each palette knife a twang.

With a contended smile he lifted the first canvas onto the easel and adjusted it until it was just right.

He looked at the canvas for some while, then decided to give the turpentine bottle another sniff. He tried the palette for size and glanced at himself in the mirror. He needed a hat.

Harry, frustrated by his failure to find anything vaguely inspiring, had fallen back on his contingency plan. "Sheila, you're not going to throw any more of my stuff away, are you? Please don't, I now have only the essentials left."

Within two hours there was a pile of things stacked up in the alleyway next to the dustbin. He nonchalantly wandered up to the pile and, checking that Sheila had retired safely back to the house, set about the pile like a man possessed. It was a treasure trove, most of it was completely unfamiliar. Here and there were things that he had not seen for years. The discovery of each of these would require a moment of contemplation and reminiscence, and in many cases, a covert mission to return them to their rightful home.

Within an hour, he had gathered up what reluctantly qualified as redundant and placed it carefully in the centre of the garage floor. There were two left ski boots, a large padlock with no key, a broken typewriter, three metres of anchor rope, a cracked water pump, a box full of old spark plugs and a teddy bear with no limbs.

He was especially impressed with the rope. It was nice and thick and chunky. This, he felt, had to somehow be central to his creation, along with the teddy of course. The teddy's severe bodily challenges would have to somehow fit in with the overall theme. The rest of the tableau would no doubt present itself in the fullness of time. Feeling slightly drained after the intense creative concentration that had been called for, he decided to reward himself with a beer.

CHAPTER 81

Initially, Ash was irritated about the new task the Super had dumped on him, but as he started to turn it over in his mind, he realised that it fitted in with his theory. Another scumbag had bitten the dust. The only difference was that this one was far closer to home. Somebody on the force was directly involved. Then again, was that a difference or just another piece in the jigsaw?

He began warming to his task. He could also conduct his other investigation under the auspices of the job his boss had given him. With a bit of ingenuity, he could avoid having to tread so lightly now.

He began by calling for the files on the witness protection programme afforded to Crabbs. He saw with some satisfaction that the files were released to him immediately. The Super had arranged clearance already.

There were only two people involved in witness protection who had the official knowledge of Crabbs' location. He needed to have a chat whilst they were still fresh and fidgety. The first person, Inspector Trudy Danvers, was a 48-year-old single woman with some thirty years' experience in the force. She had entered the witness protection division eight years ago.

Ash watched as she approached the interview room. She had the demeanour of a librarian, precise and studious. He stood up as she entered the room and invited her to make herself comfortable. She sat, unsmiling, and stared at Ash.

"I am recording our interview."

"I understand."

"Do you know how Mr Crabbs' location was leaked?"

"No, I do not."

"How many witnesses do you have on your books currently?"

"I am not at liberty to discuss ongoing programmes."

"Have you ever lost a witness, apart from Crabbs?"

"No."

"Cause of death?"

"Double shot to the back of the head, 9mm parabellum at zero range."

"How do you know that Crabbs didn't make contact with someone?"

"We don't, but we have no evidence that he did. He appeared paranoid about his own safety, not surprisingly, given that he fingered more than twenty illegal operations in the area."

"How do I know that you didn't leak the information?"

"You don't. But I didn't."

"OK, thank you for your time, I'll be in touch."

CHAPTER 82

Harry had warmed to his task in the garage with such enthusiasm that he began to wonder why he hadn't had a go before. The previous day, he had lifted the rope with a string tied to a rafter so that it hung vertically, with about half of its length coiled on the floor. He mixed up a concoction of wood glue diluted with water and applied it liberally to the rope until it was well soaked. He left it overnight and found a delightfully rigid rope that happily stood to attention after the supporting string was cut down the following morning. He carefully slid the padlock down over the rope and let it rest on the floor.

The limbless teddy had its helplessly exposed rectum reamed out to accept the insertion of the rope and, following more lashings of wood glue, was mounted upon the top of the rope. As Harry completed this operation, several globs of glue oozed out of the teddy and ran down the rope giving the whole affair an unsavoury appearance.

Awash with creativity, he placed the typewriter on the floor in front of the rope and the ski boots in front of the typewriter. He radiated the spark plugs around the whole affair. And with the panache that graced only the truly gifted, took the water pump and threw it into the dustbin without so much as a backward glance.

Jim, on the other hand, had only returned to his creation around midday. Mervyn arrived seconds later and stood beside Jim as they both took in the scene before them. The paint had run down the board in places and created a string of stalactites along the bottom of the board. Assisted by the now dried globs of paint skin, the surface had dried to resemble a lunar terrain. But by far the most noticeable and acutely disturbing feature of the artwork was the way in which the earwigs had left trails in the drying paint as they made their desperate meanderings across the surface until their energy, hope and luck ran out. Their remains lay frozen in time, the futile tracks that led them to their deaths left in the paint for all to see.

"I think that might be one of the most depressing things I have ever seen in my life Jim. It is truly extraordinary."

"I had no idea… I didn't mean to kill them. I had forgotten they were even there."

"Well Jim, look at it this way, in death they will be more famous than the rest of their community."

"I wonder what I should do next?"

"Don't touch it Jim, let it dry for another day, then sign it."

"Hmm, how is yours coming on Merv? At least one of our artworks will have the old professional mark about it. Done in oils on canvas and everything."

They went to Mervyn's studio. Mervyn unconsciously pulled on the hat that he had purchased the day before as he went to stand in front of his canvas. Jim walked around to see what Mervyn had created. The canvas appeared to be the colour of canvas all over except for a small '*Mervyn*' painted in the bottom left-hand corner.

"So, what are you going to call it Merv? The Passage of Time? No, I think that's been done. The Destiny Of Man maybe? No, I reckon that's probably been done as well. Bit of a bugger that one."

"Very funny. So far, the only bit that I knew was essential was my signature. I'm still working on the rest of the composition. Oh, who the hell am I kidding? I haven't a clue what to do and even less of a clue how to do it."

"Why don't you paint something in black and white, then blob some red in it somewhere?"

"What?"

"I saw it at the Tate the other day, it looked really good."

"I know. It was. The only difference was that he could paint. I, on the other hand, cannot."

"Rubbish, Merv. It's just that your style is not his style."

"Black and white, you say."

"With a touch of red somewhere. Look, I've got to pop to M&S to pick up our curry for tonight, see what you can come up with whilst I'm away."

Jim returned a little over an hour later. He walked in to see Mervyn sipping a cocoa in the kitchen. "Hi Merv, had any ideas?"

"Ideas? I thought you meant I should finish it before you came back."

"What! You're kidding me, right?"

Mervyn looked up in a dejected manner. "No, I'm afraid I'm not."

"Well let's have a look!" Jim marched into the studio and stood before the canvas. Mervyn came in and stood beside Jim, nervously fiddling with his hat. On the canvas, now painted white, were two black figures painted in stickman style. The one at the back looked grumpy, the one in the foreground had a skirt, a smile and a knife sticking out of her back. A trickle of red was on the knife.

"Before I started, I thought of my previous wife – after that, everything came to me very quickly. It took me less than five minutes I would say."

"It's certainly different…ish. A lot of pent-up anger in there I would say."

"Oh yes, plenty of that. My jaw ached from clenching my teeth so tightly whilst I was painting it."

"The expressions are difficult to interpret. Is she happy to be attacked? Or maybe clueless and stupid? Is he angry or remorseful possibly? It makes you think Merv, and that's what art is all about apparently. I'd say your job is done. What are you going to call it?"

"You really think so? I was thinking of 'Did She Fall Or Was He Pushed?'."

Jim stared at the canvas with his head to one side. "Oh, I like it Mervyn, I really do. Makes you think about it all over again. I see you painted over your signature again. Sign it and leave it. That's two down. I wonder if Harry has conjured anything up."

CHAPTER 83

Ash could not help feeling that the woman he had just interviewed sounded genuine. Either that or she was a very good liar. He had become very adept at sniffing out bullshitters over the years and she did not smell like one of them.

The other person who knew of Crabbs' location was already late by five minutes for his interview. Lateness was one of Ash's pet hates and he had let it show on many occasions when he would have done well to let it go. This was not one of those occasions.

A man in his early thirties walked into the interview room. Ash looked at his watch and said nothing.

The man cocked his head in Ash's direction. "Kamau is it?"

Ash smiled inwardly, it was going to be so easy and pleasant to rev up this arsehole. The man sat down and looked at Ash. "Can we get started? I have a lot to do."

Ash leaned back in his chair and smiled, saying nothing. Eventually the man shifted in his seat. "Is something funny?"

"No, quite the opposite, I would say. That is unless you find the assassination of one of your protected witnesses amusing?"

"Now listen Kamau…"

"No, you listen to me. And it's Detective Inspector by the way. From where I am sitting, and with the evidence I have in front of me, you could be in deep shit. Let's get this straight, I think you are an arrogant little prick. As long as I have that opinion of you, I am going to be biased in my judgement of your innocence. Is that the way you would like to continue?"

"You can't talk to me like that!"

"I just did, arse wipe. If you want to leave, go. I'll just record that you were unprepared to assist with my enquiries."

"I am going to put in an official complaint, this is outrageous."

"Please do, I have the form right here." Ash bent down and pulled a form from his drawer and laid it on the desk. "Interview going well for you so far?"

"Look, I came willingly to assist and did not expect…"

"You were late, and so far have not provided one shred of information, all you have done is waste my time and adopt an arrogant and evasive manner."

"This is… OK, let's calm down, shall we?"

"I'm calm, it's you that seem to be uneasy. I have noted that and have to warn you that it will weigh against you if we have to take your situation to the next level."

"What next level, what do you mean?"

"It's me that's asking the questions. Heard that before?"

"Yes." The man looked down at the desk.

Ash, having satisfied his desire, switched his tone whilst activating the recorder. "Good morning, I am Detective Inspector Kamau. Thank you for coming in to assist us with our enquiries."

CHAPTER 84

Harry agreed to bring his creation around to Jim's place. He had been delightfully vague about what it actually was and seemed somewhat concerned about it being damaged in transit. His concern was heightened when he went to get the centrepiece only to find that he had inadvertently glued the rope to the floor. With the help of a spade, he had been able to eventually separate the rope from the floor and the various parts were duly loaded into some shopping bags. He elected to carry the rope, teddy and padlock components separately.

He had barely climbed onto the bus before he started to have regrets. The main part of his creation had attracted the wonder of a small child until she realised that she was gazing upon a quadriplegic teddy, painfully impaled upon a rope. The child became increasingly distressed despite her mother trying to avert the child's gaze, whilst giving Harry very dirty looks.

By the time the mother and child's stop had mercifully arrived, the child was beyond help.

"Perverts like you should be locked up!" sobbed the woman as she coaxed her broken child away.

"It's disgraceful," said an old lady passenger, scowling at Harry as the bus continued its journey.

Three teenagers climbed on at the next stop. Despite Harry's attempts to hide it, the teddy and rope had drawn their attention. "You see, first he got it legless, then when it was armless, it got buggered!" They leaned back and laughed.

Harry gazed out of the window, begging the bus to reach his stop. He thought of getting off but realised that that would only prolong the agony. It seemed to him that the bus driver had lost interest in the accelerator pedal and developed an undying attraction for the brake. The bus trundled its reluctant way along, slowing down at the sight of anything moving or looking like it might move in the foreseeable future. This agonising lack of progress was accompanied by a suffocating lack of oxygen. Everybody on the bus seemed to be selfishly sucking in more than their fair share of air and leaving nothing for him.

Eventually, after several centuries had passed, Harry's stop arrived. As he proceeded to alight, the bag carrying the spark plugs broke and sent them scattering over the pavement. He bent down to retrieve them, not noticing that the teddy end of the rope was now in line with the bus doors. Unaware of the situation, Harry continued to scratch around for his spark plugs whilst the bus driver tried to close the doors several times upon the unfortunate bear. By the time Harry had retrieved all the spark plugs, the bear had been pummelled into a shape resembling a banana, thus removing the last remnants of appeal that the creature had ever had.

Jim opened the door of his house to see Harry standing there. "Bloody hell Harry, what happened? You look like shit."

"I couldn't even begin to tell you, just help me with this damned thing will you."

Jim took hold of the rope and teddy, giving it a doubtful glance as he took it into Mervyn's studio.

Mervyn came out. "Hi Harry, whoa, what have we got here?"

"It needs a bit of setting up and some adjustments here and there, but first I need a bloody beer. No, make that two."

Harry finished his beers in short shrift. "Right, let me put that bloody thing together so you can all have a laugh."

"Do you need any help, Harry?"

"No Merv, this is something I have to do by myself." He breathed a deep sigh, lifted himself from the chair and marched off with the resolution of a soldier going into battle.

Despite his resolve, the sight of the teddy after its cruel treatment in the bus doors came as a shock. Its thin, pinched face seemed to cry out in anguish to the world. Another deep breath was needed before he could approach any nearer. Then, keeping his eyes away from the teddy's pleading face, he constructed his sculpture. As he put the final spark plug into place, he got to his feet with a huge groan and stepped back. "It is done," he said, with all the gravity that the occasion demanded.

Jim and Mervyn, prompted by Harry's announcement, arrived and stood in awe. After what Jim felt was a respectful silence befitting the moment, he turned to Harry and, in a hushed voice said, "Harry, that is one of the most haunting things I have ever seen. And I mean that in the truest sense of the word. That is going to haunt me for the rest of my life."

"I agree with Jim, it really is very powerful Harry. What frame of mind were you in when you created such a thing? You have a really dark talent there."

"Hmm, the trip here had a lot to do with the final touches. Let's have a look at what you two have come up with."

When the tour of the art collection was complete, they all gathered back in the kitchen. Mervyn made himself a cocoa with a stiff shot of rum. "All of our pieces have very dark themes, don't they? I wonder what that says about us. I didn't start mine with dark thoughts. At least, I don't think I did."

"Me neither, the thing just took on a life or rather death of its own. When is this art show?"

"The day after tomorrow."

"Right, I need to get a base for my thing. Do you have something around Jim?"

"Yeah, I'm sure we can help you there Harry. Do any of us have the faintest idea what to do when we get there?"

"Well, I suppose they will tell us where to display…"

"No, not that Mervyn. What is our aim with regards to Lord bloody Percival The Pervert?"

"I think we have to play that by ear Jim."

"Oh, shit no, not another Wing-It-and-Hope-We-Get-Lucky Plan."

"Well, I'm all ears Harry, but until we get there, we aren't going to know what to do anyway. I suggest we scout out the place and generally try and find out how we can get to the bastard."

"Hmm, I suppose you're right. Any idea how many other people will be there, Mervyn?"

"No, haven't a clue. Let's just ride in like the cavalry and take our chances when they present themselves."

"Well, there we are, a solid plan at last. Now I can sleep easily."

"Oh, Harry, I forgot to ask. What is your sculpture called?"

"An Unfitting End To A Pointless Life."

"I was feeling depressed, now I'm just suicidal."

"Is that a personal comment or an alternative suggestion?"

CHAPTER 85

As Ash turned off the tape recorder, he looked up at his interviewee and smiled. "Thank you for your cooperation."

The man stood up and went to leave, then stopped and turned.

"Yes?" asked Ash

"No, nothing." The man left.

"Have a nice day." Ash called out.

He looked down at his notes. Despite the man being an arsehole of the first rank, he didn't fit the profile of a liar any more than his previous interviewee. Something didn't feel right. He had the itchy feeling that he was looking in the wrong place, as if he was looking for fingerprints in a room scrubbed surgically clean just before he arrived. There was always something a bit mucky about every situation, but with this one, you could eat your food off the surfaces.

He suddenly imagined a person wiping everything down ten steps in front of him in a corridor, just before he arrived. He needed to duck down an alleyway and find some dustbins.

Ash looked up to see the Superintendent walking towards him. "Ah, Ash, made any headway on the Crabbs case?"

"Early days boss, interviewed the two officers on witness protection, look pretty clean."

Ash watched as the Superintendent walked out.

"Keep to the middle lane, the spotlessly clean middle lane that would take us nowhere," thought Ash.

CHAPTER 86

The sun shone brightly across the lawns of Brandford Manor. Mervyn followed the signs showing the way to the Art Festival, driving hesitantly along the driveway, constantly looking left and right.

"Bloody hell Merv, let's get there. My leg's gone to sleep supporting this contraption of Harry's and my trousers are full of paint flakes from my own bloody monstrosity."

"I'm being alert and taking in the lie of the land. We need to be diligent."

"Diligent my arse, you're being ditherent. Put your foot down."

Just as Mervyn found the accelerator, a person appeared in front of them armed with a clipboard and supercilious grin. The car ground to a skiddy, grinding stop.

"Take it easy, it's not Silverstone you know."

"I'm sorry, I was told I was dithering and…"

"What?!" barked the attendant.

"No nothing, we are here for the Art Festival."

The man looked at them disapprovingly." Exhibitors I presume. Names?"

Mervyn gave their names whilst groans and grunts continued from his passengers.

"Follow the signs, you can park up on the left there and steady on that heavy foot of yours."

Mervyn moved off at a snail's pace and parked badly, stalling the car as he did so. "I hate this place already, what a pompous prick. I hope we don't have to deal with that dickhead again."

"I don't care, we've arrived. I have to get out, now!"

With a chorus of moans and whines, Harry's sculpture came hesitantly out of the car door followed by Harry and Jim as they crawled their way into the sunlight. Mervyn looked over at Jim who was bent double with a look of agony on his face.

"I think I might be stuck in this position forever. Whose bloody idea was this anyway?"

"I think it was yours Jim."

Jim straightened himself slowly. "Next time Mervyn, tell me to shove my ideas up my arse please."

The three of them looked around; there were several artists sitting at their easels, working away. Others stood by their work, awkwardly looking about. "Look over there, there's a bit of clear space under that tree, let's set up there. I'll get the chairs out. We'll come back for the priceless art and provisions."

They settled down after Harry had laid out his spark plugs on the baseboard that Jim had found for him. After a bit of swearing, Jim set his board up against the stepladder and slumped into his chair.

Mervyn had spread a chequered tablecloth onto the ground and laid out some pork pies and Scotch eggs. "Cider anybody?"

"Mervyn, I take it all back, you are a prince amongst men." Harry gazed around him. "I suppose we should check out the competition after we've had a bit of a breather, no rush mind."

They munched on their Scotch eggs and watched as a man approached them with a handful of tags. "I have tags here for each of your entries, note the number of your tag and enter your piece's title and your name in the ledger you will find in the marquee over there. I suggest you do it promptly." The man walked off.

"Is it just me, or is there a plethora of snotty bastards in this place?"

"OK, I'll go and do it. What's the name of your thing again Jim?"

"Shit Harry, what was it again? Um, er – bugger, I haven't a clue."

"Mine was 'Did She Fall Or Was He Pushed?'. If anybody asks, I, er, he was pushed, definitely pushed."

"Thanks Merv, I'll bear that in mind."

"Well Jim, decision time."

"Guys, I need some help here, what do you think?"

"How about, 'All Life Has No Meaning'?"

"Whoa, Merv, that's so terrible."

"Well Jim, so is your piece. Not bad you understand, but it has terror in abundance."

"OK Harry, thanks for that. 'All Life Has No Meaning' it is. I think I need another cider, I'm getting slightly depressed."

"You know Jim, in some ways it's quite uplifting – because of our newfound quest, our lives are not meaningless and with any luck neither will our deaths be."

CHAPTER 87

Jim was just finishing his second cider when the public address system crackled to life. "Will all contestants and guests please make their way to the marquee."

"Bugger, I was just starting to enjoy myself."

"Come on Jim, this is probably where we have to become vigilant."

"Yep, vigilant vigilantes, that's what we are."

They sauntered over to the marquee, where guests were being fawned over by the clipboard man and shown to their seats. They could see tag-man waving his hands at the contestants, telling them to go to their own enclosure. Clipboard-man began walking around, telling two young caterers, dressed up in classical Arab servant dress, how to distribute the champagne on a tray amongst the guests, whilst Jim and his friends stood in their allotted enclosure.

"Who does he think he is, Lawrence of Arabia? This is bollocks, I should have brought my chair."

"Don't worry Jim, the more hateful the experience, the sweeter will be the revenge."

The public address system whined into life again as tag-man was seen to take the microphone. "Distinguished guests, please show your appreciation for your host, Lord Percival." A splatter of clapping came from the guests. Jim was pleased to observe a bewildered silence from the contestants.

A skinny, ferret-faced man with long grey sideburns strutted into the marquee, waving his hand as he did so. He took the microphone from tag-man and began to speak. "Thank you, thank you, you're too kind. Welcome to my little event. As you all know, I take a special pride in my love of art, and am pleased to share this passion with you today. I have handpicked the contestants, so you can rest assured that they are all top drawer. I have an eye for talent, and you will certainly see that today. As usual, you will be invited to vote for your favourite piece. You can indicate your choice by placing the appropriate tag number in that box over there. And should you wish to purchase any of the art on display, I'm sure our contestants will be ready to give you a good bargain-priced deal."

"Fuck that. If any of those toffy nosed twats want to buy my work, they are going to have to cough up big time."

"Really Jim? I was willing to pay them to take mine. I'm buggered if I'm going back in the car with that chunk of shit."

"Have a topping day," Lord Percival guffawed into the microphone before handing it back to tag-man.

"Yeah, whatever, you fucking slimy prick. They are so easy to hate, aren't they?"

"Who Jim?"

"Tit face Percival Pervert and his rat-faced crew. Come, let's get back to our possie, my bloody back is killing me." Harry and Mervyn left Jim to return to his seat whilst they wandered around looking at the other art works.

"They are all very well done, aren't they? But I can't help feeling that they are also all a bit samey. Trees and sky and bushes, a bridge or two, sometimes an animal."

"How would I know Mervyn? Maybe they are all supposed to be like that. I only entered the art world a couple of days ago. What I know about it is bloody dangerous."

As they started to walk back, they saw that a small gathering of people had surrounded their place. Standing alongside his work was Jim, looking decidedly flustered. They caught Jim's eye as they approached. "Ah, here come my associates, er, partners, er, umm."

The little group turned around and smiled at Harry and Mervyn as they walked up.

A stout woman walked up to them. "Good morning to you, we were all admiring your work. We were wondering what school you all follow."

"School? I don't…"

"May I Harry?" said Mervyn giving him a sideways wink.

"Be my guest."

"We follow Pessimism madam."

"I can't say I'm familiar with that movement," said the woman as she turned to the rest of her group. "Where did it originate?"

"Well, that's quite the thing. It's loosely associated with expressionism; it was spawned, as many movements are, in a rather organic way. I personally believe that it arose to meet the desperate demands of current society. Several pockets seem to have popped up in different parts of the world –

Afghanistan, Algeria, Bosnia, to name but a few."

"Well I never, how very interesting. How many artists follow your movement over here?"

"Over here in England? Why madam, it is only us three as far as we know."

"Really, we are quite privileged to have you all here then, I must say. Very impressive. We will see you later, I'm sure."

Harry and Jim watched the group move away. "Hey Mervyn, where in hell did you pluck that pile of bullshit from?"

"Just sort of came out, I could see Harry was a bit at sea."

"A bit at sea? I was bloody drowning. I didn't have a clue what she was on about. That was very impressive Merv. So, we are all, er, Pessimists. It's now official, I rather like that."

As other groups came around, Mervyn, and a little later Jim and Harry, started to expound on the Pessimism movement and what their works tried to convey. Jim handed bottles of cider out to his two friends.

"I tell you what, regorging this amount of cod's bollocks is bloody exhausting, but good fun nonetheless. Cheers. Whoa, here comes another bunch."

The last of the bunches had barely left when the public address system burped into life yet again.

"Lord Percival would like to invite all the guests to partake in cocktails at the top of the hour in the marquee."

"Thank the Lord for that. I don't know about you Harry, but I don't think I have ever spouted such a long uninterrupted heap of disconnected drivel in all my life. I hope they don't compare notes because my story was drifting all over the place."

"I honestly can't remember what I said most of the time Jim. You were in top form Mervyn."

"Yes, it was scary actually. About halfway through, I was starting to believe myself."

"Hmm, I see they have all been invited to get pissed with Lord Pervert. No doubt we'll be told presently that we can put our heads under the garden tap if we're thirsty. Come on, let's have another cider."

By the time Jim and his friends had worked their way through the last Gala pork pie with extra jelly, a few of the other contestants were starting to roam.

"Oh shit, here comes one of our artist mates. I'm not sure he will swallow what we have to offer so readily."

"Fuck him, who cares?"

A short, stocky man came up to the three. "Hello there. I must say, you fellows have made quite an impression, or should I say depression, ha ha. The guests were talking about you, um, Pessimists over here quite a bit. Pessimism, very new isn't it?"

"Yeah, well we sort of invented it, we…"

"Shhh, don't let out your secrets. That pack of prats are clueless to a fault, you've hooked them, now reel them in. Don't worry, I won't blow your cover."

"Would you like a cider? I'd offer you some pie, but we've scoffed the lot."

"Thank you very much, don't mind if I do. Let me go and fetch my chair."

He returned with a fold-out chair. "Were you guys here last year?"

"No, it's our first time, we're a bit new to this."

"It's a load of clap trap really, but at least we get to show off our stuff a bit. Oh, sorry, you're not friends of his Lordship are you?"

"Good heavens no, don't know the bast… er, um, his Lordship at all."

"You're right of course, he is a nasty piece of work, he and his two partners in crime. I suppose you met them?"

"The clipboard one and the tags guy? Yes. Not very friendly, are they?"

"His chauffeur and butler, both a pair of sycophantic little shits aren't they?"

"I suppose we shouldn't really cast opinions."

"Don't worry, I'm not alone, just about all these contestants think the same. Those who know him anyway. I sometimes wonder why I prostitute my art in these bloody fairs. There are rumours of a sordid, nasty past you know."

"What, Lord Percival?"

"All three of them. Nothing proven but the rumours don't go away."

"Really?"

"Humph, they're as slippery as their pets are."

"Sorry?"

"His Lordship's really. He has a vivarium in the folly in the woods over there. Selection of snakes and suchlike. They are obviously not very fussy about who they choose as masters. By the way, Terence McGrath's the name."

"Hi, Jim Spoonwall, Mervyn Pearce and Harry Johnson. You really don't like his Lordship, do you?"

"Hmm, I've shot my mouth off a bit, haven't I? Must be the cider. Do you want to see them?"

"Who, Lord Percival?"

"No, God forbid, I'm talking about the snakes. Percival's cretins will be sucking up to the guests and the guests will be sucking up to Percival. We'll have the place to ourselves. Your artwork will be safe here."

"That's a pity. Lead the way."

They followed Terence around the marquee and into the woods behind the manor. A path opened to an attractive Victorian folly. Terence walked straight up to the closed doors and gently opened them. A waft of warm humid air came out to meet them.

The room was lit in a soft blue light and their eyes took some time to become accustomed. As they did, they were treated to a rare sight. Surrounding them were huge glass-fronted cases, with trees and rocks set out in a grassy, mossy base. Each case had a door through which access could be gained. In the largest case, in one corner, a huge snake lay coiled up.

"That's a reticulated python, he's almost six metres long. Could swallow you whole if he felt like it."

"Very cuddly. What's this one over here Terence?"

"Puff adder. Very lazy, but strikes like lightning. Not always considered deadly but its venom makes your flesh rot."

"That must be fun, and this one here?"

"Don't go too close to the glass. That's a black mamba, the most aggressive snake in the world. He doesn't like you or anybody else apart from his female mate. You can see her over there in the corner, I'm not sure but she looks pregnant. Most snakes try to get away from trouble, that boy goes looking for it."

"How do you know all this?"

"I've kept snakes nearly all my life. These days I try to make people understand that snakes are not evil, only humans achieve that status."

"And these…"

"Mozambique spitting cobras, I must say he really does have some potent species in here."

"I say, who the hell are you?"

They turned around to see Lord Percival's skinny shouldered silhouette in the doorway.

CHAPTER 88

It had been a while since Ash had been inside a pub and even longer since he had been in a pub with somebody. He looked across at Ella. They had worked together for a little over two years, and he had always looked at her as Detective Sergeant Ella Thompson, the fact that she was female being mostly irrelevant.

"Are you going to stare at me all evening or are you going to say something?"

Ash shocked himself back from his reverie. "I'm sorry Ella, I was, er, daydreaming."

"You need to step back from the case a bit."

"I wasn't thinking about the case, for the first time in a long time actually."

"Oh? What were your thoughts chewing over then? I could see your cogs grinding."

"It doesn't matter. So, about the case, do you think I'm paranoid about my suspicions?"

Ella looked down with a smile. "OK, let's talk about the case. No, I don't think you are paranoid. There are some odd parallels involved."

"Parallels?"

"Yes, I think so. Look. With the Crabbs case, the dog ring cases and the substation case, we have no witnesses currently, so let's exclude those for the time being. The other cases, the casino boss, the rapist, the child molester and the butcher, all involved women witnesses."

"That's just chance surely?"

"It could be of course, but the odds of that being the case are, let me see…" Ella punched some numbers into her phone. "Sixteen to one. Would you put your life savings on that horse? Now, consider that they are all women over sixty and those odds extend to, let me see, umm, maybe some sixty-four to one. Those are seriously long odds Ash."

"OK, so what's your point?"

"Maybe it's a wood and trees thing. We might be missing something."

"The Super thinks it's my marbles that are missing. I sometimes think he might be right. Maybe older women are more observant than the general populace. Have more time on their hands to look about."

"Possibly, but did you ever consider it might be more than just coincidence?"

"Are you suggesting we have a granny gang out there?"

"I'm not suggesting anything other than the fact that the odds of that occurring are very low, so it is something to consider looking at. The butcher's accountant has evaporated seemingly. Maybe we should try and track down the other women and see where that gets us."

"I need another drink, same again for you Ella?"

As Ash wandered off to the bar, Ella took a notebook from her handbag and wrote down the names of the witnesses they had been talking about: Anne Vickers, Emily Nolan, Gladys Ingrams, Nancy Graham.

Ash returned with the drinks. "Why didn't you mention this before?"

"I really didn't want to waste your time with what might be crackpot theories, but here in the pub, we can kick the can down the street a bit eh?"

"Suits me, kick away. There was a witness to the substation incident. They were in the flats opposite the park and called it in."

"Can you remember who it was?"

"Can't remember the name, it was a pensioner though, I'm pretty sure of that."

"Can I get onto all of these tomorrow Ash and follow up?"

"Absolutely Ella, go for it."

CHAPTER 89

Jim jumped as he heard Lord Percival's voice. Mervyn felt his knees give way slightly, Harry closed his eyes.

Terence stepped rapidly forwards into the light as Lord Percival took a couple of uncertain steps back.

"Ahh, there you are your Lordship, such a privilege as always to see you once again. I couldn't resist showing my friends here your excellent collection. I hope you don't mind me bragging about you. Gentlemen, I present to you the finest herpetologist in the country, Lord Brandford-Smythe." Harry and his two friends stepped into the light, bowing as they came. Mervyn, still somewhat bewildered, did a sort of curtsey.

Lord Percival mumbled something and then turned to Terence with a stern expression. He opened his mouth to say something, but Terence continued with his dialogue. "I myself have a passing knowledge of herpetology, although nothing in comparison to you sir. I must say, all your specimens are superb. The Malayopython reticulatus is by far the most splendid specimen I have ever seen, and the Dendroaspis polylepis… well, say no more. You are truly a doyen sir.

"I know this may sound like a terrible imposition, but I was wondering if I may mention that I am connected to a charity for wayward children and I would love for them to see your fine collection. Of course, I would only ask that a few be accommodated at any one time. I wouldn't want to impose. I know the little ones would be forever in your debt, as would I and the trustees."

Lord Percival's words froze in his mouth as he savoured the thought of wayward children being forever in his debt. Terence and his new companions watched as the shark took the bait, rolled it around in his mouth and then swallowed it whole.

"Well, I could be persuaded to assist. We should all do our bit I suppose."

Terence turned to his companions. "Did I not tell you what a prince among men his Lordship is?"

Terence turned towards Brandford-Smythe and saw how the man's demeanour had changed. The man could sense young flesh becoming available and was virtually salivating at the prospect. "Sir, we have taken up way too much of your valuable time already. Let me just say what a privilege it was to speak to you. Thank you once again for your time, your wonderful art expo and your most generous offer to make our poor children's lives a little brighter."

Bowing and backing away, Terence turned to his friends and said, "Come, let us leave this fine man to continue with his excellent work." They all bowed as they stepped out the door; Mervyn, despite himself, made another half curtsey.

The four men walked back to the art expo. "Bloody hell Terence, you smeared it on terribly thick back there."

"I did, didn't I? Amazing how much of that crap they soak up."

Upon arriving back at their place, Harry looked at his artwork. "I never thought I'd be pleased to see this chunk of shit again."

The four flopped into their chairs. "I would like to grab another cider, but my hands are shaking so much I think I'd throw most of it all over me."

"Thank God for you Terence. You really do have the gift of the gab I must say."

"I'm sorry if I went on a bit."

"No apology needed Terence. So how do you know Lord Percival?"

"Let's just say that he and I have some history and leave it at that shall we?"

"He didn't seem to recognise you."

"He has no idea who I am. I, on the other hand, know exactly who and what he is."

"If you hate the bastard so much, why do you grace him with your presence?"

"Can I beg another cider from you? I promise I'll pay you back."

Terence took a long slug from the bottle and sighed. "Do you know anything about Brandford-Smythe?"

Jim looked at both his friends. They nodded back at him. "We know that he is a creepy little paedophile if that's what you mean. The things that he has done made us sick to the stomach. I'm not sure that you should be putting him in contact with any children."

Terence looked up with surprise. "Can I ask you, if you despise the man as much as I do, why you are here?"

"It looks like we both have the same questions of each other. You first."

"Very well. I haven't told anybody this. And I have no idea why I am about to tell you. Some time ago, another lifetime ago, my late wife and I decided that our nine-year-old son needed special schooling. He was battling at the state school, and through the grape vine, we heard of this charitable institution that specialised in such cases. This institution was run and funded by Brandford-Smythe. He and his hand-selected team ensured that the children in their care received special attention. My late wife and I consciously sent our only son to that bastard… I'm sorry." Terence took his handkerchief out and wiped his eyes.

"We had no idea what was happening. Our son became more and more withdrawn as the term continued. When the vacation arrived, he spent much of his time alone. We went away for a holiday at the coast and his spirits lifted visibly. He asked us not to send him back. We felt that he should at least stick it out for one more term. If that didn't work out, we would then make some other arrangements. The other arrangements carried a price tag of course, way in excess of Smythe's. Money was tight, and I was between jobs. We put our money problems in front of our son's wellbeing and for that I will suffer justifiably for the rest of my life.

"It happened the day before he was due to go back to that damned place. We didn't know that he had left the house. He walked to the bridge and jumped into the river. He couldn't swim.

"The note he left said that he didn't want to do the things he was made to do in the master's bedrooms anymore. He was nine years old! I suppose you know how the evidence and trial was botched and tampered with."

"Terence, I am so sorry. I had no idea. I shouldn't have asked you to…"

"No. I needed to talk about it. I really do need to talk about it, and to do something about it."

"What is it you intend to do?"

Terence looked up at them with red eyes. "Kill the fucking bastard," he sobbed.

CHAPTER 90

"Ash, the only witness I have been able to make contact with is the one who saw the substation flash. He's eighty-two years old and from what he told me, spends most evenings gazing out the window."

"Pretty much what I do."

"Pardon?"

"Nothing, and the rest?"

"Nothing, all ghosts. I've checked the names of every one of the female witnesses, and none of them appear to exist in the real world. Do you want me to work out the odds of that?"

"No. What's this with you and calculating odds Ella, are you a bit of a gambler?"

"Exactly the opposite. I loved stats at school, still do. I suppose it's a bit anal, eh?"

"I find it rather endearing actually."

"Thanks boss, most of my friends think I'm a nerd."

"The addresses and phone numbers of them, all non-existent?"

"Well, the homeless lady who saw the brick fall on Jim Buckworth didn't give an address obviously, but the addresses of Vickers and Nolan don't check out."

"Do we have any visuals on these witnesses?"

"I doubt it but let me see. None of the accidental deaths were covered by CCTV."

"What about the teams that dealt with these cases? Did they not find it strange that they couldn't trace them?"

"In every case I've looked at, they never had to try."

"So, we have four cases of accidental deaths of people out on the streets with form, in every case a woman in her late sixties was involved in some way and in every one of those cases that person's personal details have been false. There could be more Ella, how would we know? These deaths were fairly public but maybe there are a few more floating about. A couple of corpses rotting somewhere."

"Why didn't they scarper before the cops arrived on the scene if they had anything to do with it?"

"The best place to hide is out in the open."

"Maybe, but it carries a risk. Maybe they want to be noticed?"

"They didn't do a very good job of it until now did they? And I'm still feeling a little paranoid about it."

"No, the odds tell a different story, this is not paranoia boss."

"Well, odds or not, we have bugger-all to follow up on. I'm going to have the Chief dancing on my balls again with this inside leak if I don't show some progress there. Do me a favour Ella, keep your ear to the ground with any accidents. If we get there fast, we might be able to grab our aged lady witness before she evaporates."

CHAPTER 91

Terence's utterance had caused a hush. Not from horror, as Terence had assumed, but so they could each ponder their options going forwards.

"I'm sorry, I got carried away there…"

Jim held his hand up. "No, Terence, look, we are…" He glanced at Harry and Mervyn and both were nodding. "…we are not here for the art. As you have surmised, we also share your feelings about his Lordship."

"Has he harmed children you know of as well?"

"No, but if I offered you an opportunity to contribute to his death, how would you feel about that?"

"I don't know what you mean. I think I'd need to be careful what I say."

"I understand your caution, I'd be wary too. But do we really look like undercover cops to you? We are also at risk with what we are about to tell you. I believe in providence, the old 'right place at the right time' thing, and this seems to be one of those occasions. OK, here goes nothing…" Jim closed his eyes. "We are plotting to kill the bastard. We are here to work out how to do it. Now would be a good time to run if you choose to."

"What if I did run and grassed on you?"

"We'd go into dithery, stupid mode, which isn't difficult, it comes quite naturally these days. We'd mumble about killing time and that there is so much of it to kill now our families have deserted us."

Mervyn stood and went into speech mode. "I'd expound upon how, being Pessimists, we have come to understand that we are all being called inexorably by the funeral bell. That neither us nor his Lordship can inevitably avoid the swishing scythe as it cuts its way towards us. The ticking clock of death needs no winding, its pendulum has no care for the deeds of man. We all need to take heed and…"

"Alright Merv, I think you've made your point. So, Terence, do you seriously think anybody here, or anywhere else, would believe you if you told them that we three old farts are actually a death squad?"

"No, I suppose not. What are you going to do?"

"You mean how are we going to kill him? Well, er, we're still working on that bit."

"I might be able to help you there."

"Really?"

"Yes, our little trip into the vivarium just now was not a spur of the moment thing. I have been looking for a way to get in there for some time and showing you around seemed like a plausible excuse. It was only when that bastard surprised us like that, I decided to take a chance. It was nice to see the slimy little shit fall for it. I had originally intended to blame the visit on you being interested in snakes and all that."

"Oh, so we were to be the fall guys, very sneaky. Why did you want to get into his snake pit?"

"I am an amateur herpetologist. I wasn't making that up. A reptiles and amphibian lover, have been since I was a kid. It seemed fortuitous that the man I hate most in this world should have some of the things I love most in this world. Especially when one considers what could happen if you mix the two together, so to speak."

"Eh?"

"I was postulating that maybe he could get done in by one of his own snakes. I wanted to get in there so I could see what was available. If all he had was a grass snake, two slow worms and a bull frog, I would have been up shit creek. As it happens, what he has there is more than adequate to do the job."

"How were you planning to get the two together? I would imagine that fiddling around with those snakes would be a bit risky."

"Deadly. But that's where I have a distinct advantage."

"Oh yeah, you know how to handle them."

"No, I don't care about getting bitten as long as he does too."

CHAPTER 92

Barry Brumpton slammed the file closed on his desk. Another forty illegal immigrants' payments were in the bank. They would be loaded into the container in Lille and transported through the tunnel into Dover. From there, they would eventually be released in a disused trailer park outside East Grinstead. What they did with themselves after that, if they made it that far, was their business.

Unfortunately, the papers and documents they had been promised on their arrival would not materialise. They were hardly likely to turn to the authorities and complain, and if their relatives heard what happened, there would always be another "more honest" operation ready to take the next batch. Taking money off babies was more difficult. He looked at his watch and, as he left, set the timer to measure the calories for his "marathon" home.

His office looked out over the Royal Opera House. He liked his office, it made him feel good. He was an important man, with an important office to suit. He slipped the file into his backpack and took a slug of water before putting the bottle in the backpack as well. Out of the office, left up James Street towards Long Acre, then down the emergency stairs of Covent Garden station. Never the lift, always the steps, all 193 of them, both up in the morning and down in the evening, a good workout. He made sure that he left at the same time each day. The stairs were always empty at that time.

He arrived at the top of the stairs and looked at the sign: "Do not use except in an emergency". He smiled and started jogging down the stairs. About a quarter of the way down he was surprised to see an old lady coming up with a shopping bag.

"Get out of the way you silly old bitch!" he shouted as he continued his journey downwards. Suddenly, he was looking upwards as his feet slid out from under him and his head came down hard on the step. He bumped down several steps before his momentum tipped him over and he tumbled for some four seconds before coming to rest in a heap. The old lady screamed and trotted slowly back down the stairs.

"Help!" she cried weakly. And then, in a flustered way, made her painful ascent up the stairs. When she was halfway up, she heard footsteps coming down. "Quieekly, zer is poor man down zer, I was coming for ze help. He fall." She wheezed as she battled to get her breath.

The guard called to his mate. "Henry, you take her up, I'll go down and see what's happened."

Painfully the old lady got to the top of the stairs. The second guard took her to the ticket office. "You alright darling? Come and take the weight off your feet. When you're ready, try and tell us what happened?"

The guard made her a cup of tea. "There you go love."

"Sank you. It was, er, terrible, ze man came, he come down ze stairs and he swear. He call me beech. Then I 'ear ze scream. I think, maybe I leave him. But what person do that? When I get there, ee was, ow you say, er, crunched up, yes? I don't know what a to do." She started to cry.

"Now, now, you were very brave my darling. Don't you worry, you gonna be alright?"

"I be fine sir."

"Can I just take yer name and address darling, just in case the health and safety blokes wanna know anything?"

"It is Ania Novak, ze address is flat 123, Cramby Road, Wooda Green."

The guard looked up as the ambulance men arrived. "Down the stairs over here. Can I leave you here for a mo darling?"

"Tak, I be OK."

When the guard returned, the old lady had gone.

CHAPTER 93

The four men looked towards the marquee as the now familiar voice of Lord Percival squeaked into the microphone. "My dear guests, I know that you are all enjoying yourselves, but I would like to just give pause to events for a moment to announce the results of the art competition I have arranged for you today. There was one piece of work that gained a very large number of votes and has emerged as a clear winner. But first, let me announce that the person in third place…"

"Whiney little fart, he really does fancy himself doesn't he? You want another cider, Terence?"

"Thank you, Jim. That would be nice."

"Hey, Jim, you came in second place."

"Ha ha, very funny Merv."

"No, listen."

"Yes, Mr James Spoonwall, a new entrant, with his work entitled 'All Life Has No Meaning'."

"And in first place, with 25 votes, it is… Harold Johnson, with his winning sculpture 'An Unfitting End To A Pointless Life'. Would Mr Johnson come up to the front please?"

Terence looked over to Harry, who was rummaging around in Mervyn's picnic basket. "Hey Harry, you won."

"Where is my slab of chocolate Mervyn?"

"Harry, you won, you've been called to the podium."

"What?" Harry looked up and heard the butler's irritating voice next to him.

"Hey, you, his Lordship is calling you. Get up there. Promptly. Now."

"Promptly my arse," mumbled Harry a little too loudly.

"What did you say?" the butler wanted to know.

"Hey, er, I said I'll probably slip on the grass. What do you want me to do?"

"Get up there, you can't keep his Lordship waiting!"

Harry got to his feet and trotted along, following the butler towards the marquee. As he entered, a round of applause rose to greet him. He saw the grimacing death's head of Lord Percival announcing his arrival. "Ah, here he comes now."

It suddenly occurred to Harry, as the butler took the microphone and placed it in his hands, that he was expected to make a speech. "Go ahead, make a gracious reply," snarled the butler.

Harry lifted the microphone to his mouth. A long whine of feedback lashed out of the public address system. He glanced around his audience and spotted the grinning faces of Mervyn, Jim and Terence at the back. He quickly realised that the grins were turning into open laughter. "Yeah that's it, laugh it up you bastards," he thought to himself, as the feedback continued to wail.

The butler returned. "Don't put the thing so close to your mouth! Godammit."

Harry did as he was told. He coughed and heard it crackle out across the estate. "Er, thank you… very much… indeed… very unexpected… in fact I haven't a clue how…" He looked up and saw Mervyn shaking his head. "Er, a clue… er clue how I beat such a fine collection of artwork." He saw Mervyn nodding.

Mervyn talked out of the corner of his mouth towards Jim and Terence. "That's it Harry, say thank you, kiss his Lordship's arse and get out of there."

A voice from the audience asked, "I was wondering if Mr Johnson would be kind enough to explain a little about his work and the nuance that it achieves and how it relates to other work of this kind."

"Now he's fucked," Jim whispered grimly.

Harry stared at the person asking the question whilst trying to desperately understand what she was talking about and then, having failed, moved on to provide an adequate answer. "I'm glad you asked that."

"No, you're not," mumbled Jim.

"Since an early age, I have been er… struggling, er, struggling…"

"And you still fucking are," mumbled Jim.

"Yes, struggling to come to terms with the, er, inner fabric of man's existence within the space time continuum er, thing."

"This is rapidly going to go up or down, there is no sideways now for Harry."

"Are we spatially competent or do we merely represent an impression in the minds of others? My work tries to represent the feeling of doubt we all have about our temporal reality. The empty boots of a soul that no longer has an earthly identity. The typewriter there with the tale of a life untold. The rope that we hope will bring us to enlightenment, but of course never does. We merely get to the top to find our questions unanswered and crushed in a bus's doors."

"Bow and leave Harry. You're ahead."

There was an awed silence as everybody in the room contemplated Harry's answer, especially the bit about the bus doors. Then a slow wave of claps began, eventually filling the marquee.

"Bravo!"

"Brilliant work."

"What a mind."

Harry felt the microphone being removed from his grasp as he was ushered out by the butler through the throng of well-wishers. He was almost close enough to be grabbed by Jim and Mervyn and dragged away when a voice was heard above the clapping.

"And what about the spark plugs Mr Johnson?"

CHAPTER 94

"Did any scumbags meet their maker today, Ella?"

Ash leaned over Ella as she typed on her keyboard.

"Right, where do you want to start boss?"

"Get the names of any and see if they have form, or at least, recent court appearances. We'll start with that."

An hour later, Ash ran his finger down the list. "Bloody hell, just about all of them have done something shifty by the looks of it. Car accident, car accident, heart attack, motor bike accident, fell down the stairs, all DOA. Find out if any of these had an old lady as a witness."

Ash knew that he would have to get back onto the witness protection case with some renewed vigour. Just as the thought mulled around in his head, he heard the Chief's voice behind him.

"Any progress yet Ash?"

"Not much boss, we are going through the detail, but everything seems to pan out."

"Hmm, maybe he made the same mistake as the other one and contacted a friend from his past."

"Can't rule it out sir."

"Stuck in Mile End would be enough to make anyone reach out, I would say. Anyway, carry on Ash, you're doing a fine job."

Ash watched the Superintendent walk away, unsure of whether his last comment was genuine or richly sarcastic.

"Two ladies gave statements Ash, within an hour of each other from what I can make out."

"Right check their addresses; if one has vaporised, get down there Ella."

"Aren't you coming?"

"No, I just want to check something with our friends at witness protection."

Ash picked up the phone and dialled.

He watched as Ella gave him a thumbs up from her computer, grabbed her things and went out the door. "Huh, good, she must have a whiff of a lead," he thought to himself. He heard the voice on the phone.

"Good afternoon, Inspector, how can I help you?"

"How many people knew about the location of the safe house where Crabbs was put up?"

"Only me and the other operative you interviewed."

"Yeah, OK. But after Crabbs was taken out, who knew about it then?"

"Us two and our own forensic team of two."

"OK, but once news of the hit was out, I suppose it was common knowledge."

"No, as I said, only our own people knew."

"But I suppose, after the hit, it didn't matter who knew did it?"

"It matters very much. The whole point of witness protection is secrecy. Our own forensic team are not party to such unnecessary information. They are there to collect evidence, they had no knowledge of who Crabbs was or why he was there."

"Can I ask you if the safe house was in Mile End?"

"You can ask me Inspector but I'm not going to tell you or anybody else."

"OK. Thank you very much."

"You're welcome Inspector."

CHAPTER 95

Jim made a leap to grab Harry's arm and lead him away under the ruse of triumphal comradery before he blew his cover. Unfortunately, the question posed to Harry had caused him to turn and return to the front of the marquee.

Jim closed his eyes. "Oh for fuck's sake, he's drunk with illusions of adequacy. He's beyond help."

The microphone was given back to Harry. He lifted the thing to his mouth to speak as another whine of feedback came through. The pause it gave him was enough to flush every last morsel of waffle he had prepared for his answer down the drain. He was left… with nothing. He needed time, probably lots of it.

"Could you repeat the question?" Harry whimpered, his confidence in shatters, his brow and crotch damp with perspiration.

"Yes, certainly. I was wondering what metaphorical significance one should draw from the ring of spark plugs."

All eyes turned to Harry in anticipation, all except Jim who had his face in his hands. "Oh God, what is he doing? Not now!"

Harry's left hand had nervously meandered off course down the front of his trousers, where he now tried to give himself some relief from the itchiness his damp genitals were suffering from. The act had a soothing effect and he continued to scrub around in a mooning fashion whilst formulating his reply. By the time he began to speak, everybody's attention had been drawn to the mesmerising effect of his rummaging hand.

Unaware of what he was doing, Harry began, "Allow yourselves to imagine the manipulation mankind has to go through in order to achieve satisfaction. Both mentally and physically…"

Harry paused for the thought to sink in. As he did so he followed the gaze of several guests, who now had their eyes firmly fixed upon the grinding motion of his left hand. Suddenly aware of his own actions, he removed his hand from his trousers and waved it damply through the air. The audience followed the path of his hand as if transfixed by it. Harry, now fully aware of what had just transpired, realised with increasing panic that he had maybe five seconds to patch everything back together.

"Er, umm, thus, he er, um, scratches around in the maelstrom of his confusion, symbolised by the juxtaposition of spark plugs removed from their sphere of influence, as they obviously are… er, and um, hopefully illustrated now by the way in which all of you watched me scratching my nuts. Thank you."

A pause of maybe five seconds passed before another wave of applause rippled through the marquee. This time, people approached Harry and shook his hand, although even the left-handed amongst the audience chose to shake his right hand. He was treated to several bravos, but this time he walked sufficiently close to Jim to be grabbed.

"That'll do Harry, that'll do," said Jim as he dragged him away.

CHAPTER 96

Ella arrived at Covent Garden station with memories of her childhood flooding back. Her mum and dad had often taken her to the Christmas market there. She'd stood in wonder outside the opera house, always outside, never seeing what lay inside the beautiful building. She still didn't know what it looked like inside.

The station was relatively quiet, only a small queue awaited the lift. She saw a London Underground official standing by the gates and went over to him, showing her ID.

"Good morning, I'm Detective Sergeant Ella Thompson of Met Police Wimbledon branch. Can I ask you a couple of questions about the fatality the other day?"

Ella could see that the man was on his guard immediately. "Yeah, how can I help you?"

"Could you show me where it happened?"

The official let Ella through the gate. "It was an accident. The bloke was going hell for leather down the stairs."

"We're trying to understand what happened. Were the lifts not working?"

"No, they were working fine, but you know, some people like to work out on the stairs. Bloody idiots, running down and up sometimes. The stairs are there for emergencies, it says so on the sign there. The berk nearly knocked a lady over as she was coming up. She was the one who saw him take a tumble."

"Take a tumble?"

"Yeah, quite a tumble it was too. Broke his neck apparently."

"He was running down?"

"Yeah, the lady said he swore at her to get out of the way."

"And did she?"

"Yeah, she was alright, just a bit shocked poor thing."

"How old was the lady would you say?"

"About sixty, I suppose."

"And she was using the stairway? Why was that?"

"Dunno, I never thought to ask her."

"Was the lady carrying anything?"

"What? Why, I dunno… yeah, she was carrying a bag of shopping I think."

"She was using the stairs and carrying a bag of shopping?"

"Yeah, I dunno, some people are strange I suppose, although she didn't seem batty or anything."

"Can you describe her?"

"Yeah, she was a foreign lady."

"Glasses, hair colour, build?"

"Yeah, sort of medium. Brown hair maybe, you know, foreign. Why do you wanna know about her? She had nuffing to do with it."

"How do you know?"

"Ahh come on, she was a lady. He was a big strapping bloke. In any case, you could see that she did nothing as he passed her."

"How could you see that?"

"On the TV, we could see it there."

"You have it on CCTV?"

"Yeah, it's all there."

"Why didn't you say so before?"

"You didn't ask."

"Can we have a look at the TV clips?"

"Yeah, come into the office over there."

He settled down at the screen and pulled up a chair for Ella.

"Right, I thought I might need it for the H&S blokes, so I saved it in a separate file. Here's the shot from the top. There he goes, stupid bugger, racing down like that, could have knocked her for six. Here she is coming up the stairs, you'll see him go past… there."

The video showed a man going quickly down the stairs and a woman who stepped aside and turned to watch him run past her. As she turned forwards, she shook her head.

"She said that he shouted for her to get out of the way and swore at her.

This shot here shows him coming to a halt in a heap after he fell. You'll see her come down to help him."

The scene showed the man lying head down on the stairs. Then the lady came down and bent over, blocking the view of him. In a while, she could be seen turning and calling as she climbed the stairs again.

"We saw this happen and straightaway went to see what was going on. We heard her calling for help. I took her up to my office whilst me mate went down to the bloke. When he got to him, he looked dead."

"Could we rewind to just before she gets there and rerun it?"

Ella watched carefully as the video ran again. When it was finished, she stood up. "I need a copy of that clip. Can we go to the stairs please? Can you show me where he fell?"

"We know where he wound up, we couldn't see where he actually tripped because one of the cameras was out of order. But I'll show you our best guess."

Ella stepped back up the stairs from the point where the man was found, until she came to the point where he had passed the old lady, then carefully retraced her steps, flashing her torch as she did so on the staircase. About halfway down, something caught her eye; she knelt down and carefully took out a tissue to take a sample of what she had found and placed it in an evidence bag. Upon arriving back up at the top of the stairs, she turned to the London Underground official.

"Have you ever seen this man before, going up and down these stairs?"

"I dunno, maybe, there are a couple of loonies who do it each day. Like I said, a sort of workout or something."

"Can we also have the video run for the time leading up to when he fell, from a few hours before?"

"Yeah, come back to the office. Can I leave you to go through it? I'm supposed to be at the gates."

Ella ran through the video at high speed in reverse from the time the man passed the lady coming up the stairs. Suddenly, she saw something. She stopped and rewound the footage and played it at normal speed. She stared at the screen, picked up her phone and typed a message to Ash: *Bingo*

CHAPTER 97

Harry was escorted by his friends back to where their artwork, or at least some of it, had recently taken on cult status.

"What the fuck was all that about Harry?"

"You surely don't expect me to explain what I just said up there, do you?"

"I would be seriously concerned if you tried actually."

"I need a cider."

"I bet you do."

"Well, I for one think you did a splendid job."

"Thank you Mervyn. I'll take that as a compliment from a master."

"I very much doubt anybody will be tempted to challenge you. It would be a bit like arguing with Stephen Hawking about black holes."

"A bit like arguing with a sponge more likely."

"Whoa Harry, best get your hands onto your bollocks again, here comes one of your groupie lady friends."

"Oh shit no, not again, I'm out of ammo."

"Oh, Mr Johnson, I just have to say how impressed I was by your speech. You have such a connection with the metaphysical, and to be able to express those concepts in three dimensions, as you have done here, is pure genius."

"It is?"

"Oh please, Mr Johnson, you mock me, you naughty man!"

"Take her, she's ready," mumbled Jim.

"I hope I'm not being presumptuous but if you ever consider selling your piece, I would be most interested. Here is my card. Lovely to meet you sir and I do hope we meet again soon."

"Most gracious," Harry looked down at her card. "Er, um, your Ladyship."

"Oh please, call me Rebecca."

As Harry watched her go, a thought entered his exhausted brain. Here was a way of avoiding having to endure another ghastly journey with his creation.

He called after her.

"Er, excuse me, your, er, Rebecca. I was just thinking, if you are serious about wanting that piece of sh.. er, artwork, why not take it with you now?"

"Really? Can it be deconstructed without damage Mr Johnson?"

"Call me Harry, please. Oh, yeah it comes to bits easily enough."

"And would you be willing to reconstruct it in my house?"

"Eh? Well yeah, that's a piece of pi… no problem at all."

"Now, Harry, what type of money are we talking about here?"

"Oh, I was hoping you would do it for free."

"I'm sorry? Oh, you are so funny Harry, I love that in a man. Let's see, if you promise to come to my place and construct it, would, say, fifty interest you?"

"Absolutely, no problem, quite generous actually."

"Not at all, will you take a cheque? It will clear before you pop around."

She wrote out the cheque, tore it off and held it out to Harry. "Now, you won't let me down will you Harry?" she said with a wink. "I'll see you at my car, it's the dark blue Range Rover over there by the old oak."

Harry walked back to his friends.

"Wow, I can't believe it. I've managed to dump that heap of shit off on Lady Rebecca there, and she even gave me a cheque for fifty quid. How's that for luck? I just have to go around to her place to put it together."

"'Put it together' – is that what you call it nowadays? Best be making sure you've got clean underpants on Harry, Lady Rebecca is going to suck you in and blow you out in bubbles me old mate."

"Rubbish Jim, look here, she made it out to me for…"

Harry stared at the cheque. It was made out for fifty thousand pounds.

CHAPTER 98

Ash was waiting for Ella to make an appearance. As soon as she did, he was at her desk. "What have you got?"

Ella took out the memory stick with the CCTV recordings she had copied and plugged it into her laptop. "These are the CCTV shots I got from the station. This guy used to go for a jog type thing up and down the emergency stairs at Covent Garden tube station. I checked each day before, around the same time in the afternoon that he had his fall, and sure enough he is going down the stairs at about the same time every day, give or take a minute or two.

"This is the day he died. See, there is the lady coming up the stairs, and there he goes past her down the stairs. The camera showing the bit where he fell wasn't working, but you can see here, a couple of moments later, the lady stops and turns, hesitates a bit and then starts down the stairs again.

"Here is the guy all crumpled up, and here she comes down and leans over him. You can't see what is going on because she is squarely between him and the camera. A bit later she turns around and you can see her calling out as she comes back up the stairs."

"OK, so far so good."

"Yeah, but look here. I missed it at first. Look at him in slow mo before she gets to him. He's still moving about a bit. Look at him after she walks away – dead still. Now look back at when she leans over him. See there, that little twitch. Check his head position before she gets to him, now look at it."

"Bloody hell, Ella!"

"The autopsy report said that the probable cause of death was a broken neck, caused by the fall. I'm guessing she helped him along a bit."

"Have we got a look at her face?"

"Not really. But wait, there's more. I ran the film back before they both met on the stairs, and guess what? There she is, about seven minutes earlier going down the stairs."

"What the hell was she doing?"

"I searched the area where he probably started his fall and found traces of something on the step. I've sent it off to be analysed. There wasn't much of it, most of it had been wiped up by the looks of it."

"Ella, this is absolutely brilliant!"

"You wanted to know whether we can see her face. We can't, she keeps her head down."

"You think she knows where the cameras are?"

"Certainly, you can't miss them, but if you are coming up the stairs, the chances are you are going to look down at your feet. We can get her probable height and weight, but features, no."

The phone rang and Ella answered it. She lifted her finger to Ash. "OK, yes, I understand, and probably a towel. OK, thank you very much for getting back to me." She hung up.

"That was the lab. It was traces of washing-up liquid. That's what I found on the steps, and fibres, probably from a towel of some kind. That's what she was doing when she went down the stairs before he arrived, putting washing-up liquid on the steps. She knew when he would arrive. Afterwards, when she went down to find him, I would guess she wiped the steps clean with a towel and plonked it in her shopping bag."

"False address, I presume?"

"Yep, that's what set me off in the first place."

"What about descriptions of her from the guards?"

"What a joke! She was a foreign lady, maybe brown hair, medium build, about sixty/seventy."

"Well, that should narrow it down nicely."

CHAPTER 99

Harry placed the component parts of 'An Unfitting End To A Pointless Life' into the back of Rebecca's Range Rover.

"Thank you, Harry. I'll be off now. I'm going to leave the piece in the car to await your arrival. I must say, I am looking forward to the erection of your masterpiece."

Harry choked slightly and stuttered. "It will be my, er, pleasure your, um, Rebecca to see it put up in a place where it will be appreciated. That is, I mean…"

"I know exactly what you mean, Harry, I'm full of anticipation. Goodbye."

Harry watched as she drove away and realised that he was shaking. He desperately hoped that it was from fear and not lust.

"Well Harry, that didn't work out too badly, now did it?"

"I don't know. I hope I'm wrong, but I think she might be coming on to me. I'm a happily married man you know."

"Well, I don't want to be disparaging about your art, but I reckon you might be expected to work off a bit of that fifty grand with some humpy bumpy."

"Bloody hell Jim, you make it sound so sordid."

"I certainly hope so, how would you like me to make it sound, romantic?"

"Can we change the subject please. Has anybody any idea what we do with his Lordship?"

They all fell silent.

"Just before Harry found fame, fortune and fanny, you were expounding the virtues of those snakes in there Terence."

"Yes, well… the puff adder would be happy to lie in the bastard's bed until he climbed in. The problem is that puff adder bites may only rot the flesh rather than kill you. Painful though it is, he would probably survive well enough if he got to hospital.

"The black mamba is a different story altogether, one whack from him and it's curtains unless you can get to hospital very quickly and get the anti-venom. Even then, there is no guarantee. Problem is, the mamba won't want to just laze about and, unless threatened, he might prefer to just bugger off."

"What about that huge sod in the corner?"

"The python? He'll give you a bite, a nice sneaky cuddle and then he'll eat you."

"Eat Percival Pervert?"

"Oh yeah. He'd swallow that skinny little runt with no problem. It would take a while, but he'd get him down."

"So, what do we do? Open the cage doors, throw Percy in and wait for the fun to begin?"

"Possibly, but they might not be in the mood, and he might hurt them."

"Hmm, maybe we should tie him up first."

"We'd need to know when he last had a meal; he'll get peckish after about ten days."

"Lord Percival?"

"No Merv, you arse, he's talking about the snake."

"Does he stay in the place on his own or do Lurch and Fester stay on the premises as well?"

"The butler and chauffeur? They both stay on the premises."

"Maybe we throw the lot in together."

"Now, Jim, remember, we are only here to take out Lord Percival."

"Yeah, you're right Mervyn, I know."

"There is something you should know about those two."

"What's that Terence?"

"They share their preferences. Used to take turns and help to hold the kids down if needed."

"Why does that not come as a shock? Well, I think our quest just became a little more rewarding."

"One thing though Terence, you are not going to be a kamikaze. You must not be at any undue risk. None of us will let that happen."

"Hmm, well obviously I would prefer to see them die without joining them but playing about with snakes is not all sweetness and light."

"There is another thing. I might have won the big prize, but I doubt his Lordship or his ratty sidekicks are going to invite us back any time soon."

"Harry's right, we are all going to stick out like dog's balls on a cat if we're caught wandering around the grounds."

"Maybe not, I might have an in, so to speak. Remember I am supposed to introduce him to some children full of gratitude."

"That's fortuitous, and of course, you will, as per standard practice, need a full team to accompany you and reconnoitre the place prior to the children's arrival!"

"Now listen guys, I can't expect you to take risks on my behalf."

"Whoa, Terence. Since when did you gain a monopoly on delivering pain and death to Percy? You can deliver the coup de grace, but we are going to be there to help you all the way."

"That's really nice of you guys, thank you."

"We are a match made in heaven… hopefully. Anyway, let's get our shit together and get out of here. Terence, here's my address, Mervyn is staying with me at the moment. Let us know when you can pop around, and we will work from there."

CHAPTER 100

Ash put his head in his hands. "I'm not sure where we go from here Ella. Is there any connection between our victims? Some sort of pattern there?"

"Not that I've spotted yet boss. We seem to be dealing with seemingly unconnected victims apart from the fact that they have all wriggled out of punishment despite being undeniably guilty."

"OK, I'm going to have another look at that witness protection case. See if you can get any headway with the CCTV stuff, will you?"

Ash saw the Superintendent go into his office. He walked up and tapped on the door.

"Hi Ash, what is it?"

"Just a small thing sir. You know, just trying to tie up loose ends. Who told you that the safe house was in Mile End?"

"What? I don't know, you did, didn't you?"

"No, I didn't know where it was until you told me. It's not in any of the files I have been given. Everybody I have spoken to has refused to acknowledge or deny it."

"So, what are you saying?"

"Well, if it is as confidential as everybody makes out, who was it who felt it was OK to spread the word so to speak?"

"It must have come past my desk at some time I suppose."

"That would mean that there is some documentation on this case that I am not seeing."

"Yes Ash, I would imagine there is. Now, can you please excuse me, I have some pressing issues to deal with."

"Surely sir, if I am expected to track down the leak, this is relevant, and by inference, so are those documents."

"Yes, yes, maybe they are. I will have a look. Now please, I have to get some stuff ready for the Commissioner."

Ash walked back to his desk.

"Ella, can you please find out where the safe house is, the one where Crabbs was taken out?"

"Sure thing boss. Oh, by the way, I was thinking maybe we should compare these death-by-granny cases to serial killings."

"How do you mean?"

"Well, serial killers are generally random, vain and sensation seeking."

"I wouldn't say that our granny fits that profile at all."

"That's my point. It would follow logically then, that other serial killer traits are also missing. Like working alone, unstable, predatory."

"OK, so where does that leave us?"

"She isn't working alone, she is an operative, trained and proficient. We are dealing with a professional assassin who is carrying out orders."

"A professional assassin. That would explain the lack of evidence. Which reminds me – damn, what an idiot I am, I'm getting old Ella. That butcher death. I was looking through the items collected by the forensic crew around the freezer door. Come look at this."

He flicked through the photographs of the items until he arrived at a piece of black plastic. "Look at this. It's a piece of a cable tie. Now look at the handle of the freezer door, look at how the outside of the handle is polished at one point. I'm guessing that the door latch was fastened with a cable tie, and the killer came back to cut the tie when he or she was sure the butcher was good and dead. The main part of the cable tie is long gone, but a little piece must have come off when they cut it."

"OK boss, so we can assume he was locked up and left to die. The fact that the last person to see him alive was our evaporated accountant lady makes her a prime suspect. Where to now?"

"I wish I bloody knew."

CHAPTER 101

Arnold Smith sat up in his hospital bed. The nurse had told him that one person had visited him whilst he was delirious but had not stayed. The only other visitor had been the cop who told him that Bob Cherry had poisoned him. He also saw that there was a cop outside his ward. He wasn't sure what to make of it all. Was the cop there to prevent Cherry from trying to kill him, or was he just there to stop him from doing a runner?

An old man came around with a trolley full of snacks, magazines and donated books. Smith had no money but took one of the free local papers. He started to flip disinterestedly through it, looking at the pictures. Dog wins prize, local girl gets scholarship to study overseas, a picture of a load of toffee-nosed twats at some prizegiving. He was about to flick to the next page when his eyes fell upon the picture of a man with a microphone in his hand. The caption read: '*Winner of arts festival, Mr Harold Johnson, wows guests with sculpture*'.

He frowned. There was something familiar about him. Arnold sensed that the man should be wearing a hat but couldn't for the life of him think why. After a while, he continued to flick through to the end before dumping the paper in the trash can.

Lunch had arrived. He looked at the plate of macaroni cheese and the bowl of red jelly and custard. Any food was alright, provided that mushrooms or pizza were not on the menu. At the thought of pizzas, he had a sudden flashback to the night the pizza delivery man had arrived with a stupid hat on. It hit him like a sledgehammer. That was the hat that the man in the picture should be wearing. He pushed the food tray away and swung his body off to one side of the bed. The move made him dizzy and nauseous, and he had to take some deep breaths before reaching down and retrieving the magazine from the trash can. He opened it to the page with the picture of the man. It was him, the pizza delivery man, he was sure of it.

"You nearly killed me you bastard," he snarled.

CHAPTER 102

Jim, Mervyn and Harry welcomed Terence into their inner circle. Terence had phoned Jim the day following the competition, anxious to learn more about their operation, and had been invited to pop around.

They had all been careful to remain vague, or "professionally discreet" as Mervyn put it, about their previous escapades, but had assured Terence that they had a one hundred percent success rate. A truth that gave them a good feeling about themselves and, as Mervyn described, "girded their loins as they ventured forth into their next quest". Or, as Harry had unpopularly described it, "dithered forth into the next cloud of confusion".

The whiteboard/kitchen door had been erected again and Harry had started a new list entitled "Scenarios in which Lord Percival could get snakes set upon him". The title was unfortunately a little too long for the board and had to be squeezed in with smaller writing at the end.

"I can't stand it when somebody writes out something like that. Can't you just write it out properly?"

"Mervyn, can you read it? Do you know what it means?"

"Yes Harry, but that's not the point, it's irritating to look at."

"So was our artwork, but you didn't mind that."

"That is a completely different matter. That writing there indicates bad planning and a sloppy attitude to the job."

"I would say that it should feel right at home with everything else we've done so far then."

"Oh, for fuck's sake." Jim got to his feet and took the board marker and eraser from Harry's hands. He rubbed out the title and replaced it with a question mark. "There, is that more in keeping with everybody's sensitivities?"

"What does that mean Jim? It gives us no boundaries within which to work now."

Terence coughed politely. "Do all your strategy sessions pan out like this?"

"Actually, no. You are witnessing a session that's going better than most. Harry, start writing. Mervyn, behave."

There was a general silence as sensitivities were inwardly nursed before Mervyn broke the silence. "We could tie them up and leave them in the vivarium with the snakes."

"Not going to look very accidental, is it? Unless one of us pops in and unties them after they've been munched."

"Why not just push them in and lock the door?"

Terence shook his head. "No guarantee anything would happen, and they might hurt the snakes. By the way, there is no guarantee that they will be attacked when they are tied up either."

"What did you have in mind Terence?"

"I have been basing my plans on being in there with them."

"Well, that's not going to happen, there has to be another way."

"Can we set out some guidelines? Like, is this supposed to look like an accident? Or is it to look like a revenge killing? A message to all would-be perverts that this is what happens to you, sort of thing?"

"Fair question Terence. We seem to have got away with our operations looking accidental up to now."

"There's no bloody maybe Mervyn – everything we do is one accident after another."

"That's not what I meant, I…"

"We know what you meant Mervyn, it's just Harry being testy."

"Look, the accidental death scenario certainly keeps us out of the way of any scrutiny. But it also has an irritating way of not sending a message to other would-be cretins."

"Let's not fool ourselves. The pizza job certainly has one nasty bastard looking for us, judging from his phone call."

"Pizza job?"

"Don't worry about it, Terence. Let's keep to the job at hand gentlemen. Snaking his Lordship and gang."

"Terence, what is the best way of ensuring they get chomped?"

"If the snake feels threatened, and especially if it's unable to escape, it will nearly always strike."

"So, let's say, we have the snake in a sack, and we put his Lordship's head in the sack as well."

"Yeah, that would do it, almost certainly. Although I think his Lordship might resist a bit, don't you?"

"Possibly, depends on what he thinks is in the sack."

Harry wrote *Head in sack with snake* on the board.

"Actually, it could be any part of his body."

Harry changed it to *Bit of body in sack with snake.*

"What about a box or bin or cupboard instead of a sack?"

Harry changed it to *Bit of body in enclosed space with snake.*

"That's great. We could put it in a laundry basket, or a litter bin, or a biscuit barrel."

"Judging from the size of those snakes we saw, it would have to be a fucking big biscuit barrel."

"Hmm, will one snake be able to bite them all?"

"They have enough venom for sure."

"I just don't see how we are going to get them all to open something, and all want to peep inside at the same time."

A silence followed as each took a thoughtful bite of their biscuits.

"We have an in, so to speak, with the children's visit. We should use that to our advantage. Maybe even use that to get in and wipe them out."

"OK Terence, let's put that up."

Children's charity ruse to get in the door was written on the board.

"As the vivarium is the focus of the visit, it would be fitting for us to be in there with them when we have our preparatory discussion. Maybe I could convince his Lordship to let me go in and pick one of the snakes up to show how we could let the kids have a closer look."

"Hmm. You're going down that 'don't mind being bitten path' again Terence."

"No, I wouldn't try my luck with those mambas but the cobra would be OK, so long as I wore face protection. The python too, as long as there are enough of us to stop him getting a grip."

"I don't want to appear a wimp Terence, but I'm fucked if I'm fiddling about with any of that lot. Look, the thought's made me go all goosey. I think it would be nicer if they were in there with the mamba family and we were on the outside looking in."

"If only we had someone on the inside."

"Can't imagine any of us lining up for that one."

"I don't mean the vivarium, I mean the manor."

"Why Terence?"

"Well, I was thinking that maybe we could incapacitate them somehow and then just dump them in the snake pit."

"First we need to get in."

"What are we going to pose as, child traffickers?"

"No, maybe you say you run a charity that is slightly under the radar officially. Concerned individuals forced to operate outside the law, desperately trying to give these poor kids a better life despite the harsh realities imposed upon them by the current draconian laws of the land. That sort of thing. That way, he will be less likely to run to the authorities looking for accreditation, whilst at the same time being able to look like the Samaritan if the need arises. I would say that we purport to only deal with children who have been removed from their families. That way any cumbersome links will be removed as far as he is concerned."

"Bloody hell, if you don't mind me saying Terence, this all sounds like really complicated stuff that could go wrong at any turn.

Mervyn spoke for the first time in ages. "Maybe we tell them we like children too."

CHAPTER 103

Later that day, after Sheila had popped out to get some shopping, Harry took Rebecca's calling card from his pocket. He turned it over and then sniffed it. The action shocked him. He glanced around guiltily and returned the card to his pocket. He would have to get across there at some stage soon, he couldn't drag it out for ever.

For reasons he could not quite explain, he had not told Sheila about his required visit to Rebecca. She would have made light of it, he knew, and that was part of the problem. He did not want it to be a laughing matter, he wanted it to be a dark, sensuous thing, at least in his imagination.

He sighed and, with a slightly trembling hand, dialled her number.

"Hello, Rebecca speaking."

"Er, um hello Rebecca. It's Harry Johnson here, the bloke who did that monstr…"

"Hello Harry, how lovely to hear from you. I was beginning to think you had abandoned me. When can you come over?"

"Well, it's er, really up to you, I can make it whenever it is convenient."

"It's convenient any time Harry, day – or night if you prefer."

"Umm, can I come over now maybe?"

"Of course you can, the sooner the better. I can't wait."

Harry took a shower and, having checked that he had no ear or nose hair showing, brushed his teeth and trimmed his eyebrows. He looked at himself in the mirror. "What are you doing you silly old fart?" he thought. "Well, if I'm going to be taken advantage of, I might as well look as decent as possible," he concluded, as he shook his head and stepped out to his car.

The whole journey went by in a flash. Before he knew it, he was at the gates of an impressively long driveway leading to an unseen house. He pushed the button of the intercom and the gates opened almost immediately, beckoning him in.

He watched as the Georgian house came into view. He saw the Range Rover parked at the front with the teddy's agonised expression peeping out of the back window. It seemed to be telling him to run whilst he could. As he slowed down, he saw Rebecca coming out to greet him. Harry noted how her silk dress, tied with a sash around her waist, emphasised her curvy figure in a way that made him suck his breath in, giving rise to a sudden bout of hiccups. He stepped out of the car and attempted a smile.

"Hell… hic… sorry, I seem to have hic suddenly got hic…"

Rebecca walked up to him and put her hand gently on his chest. "Oh dear, you poor thing. Now close your eyes."

Harry did as he was told, smelling her sultry perfume as he did so.

"WHAAA!" shouted Rebecca and gave him a firm push.

Harry staggered back, his eyes now wide open in terror.

"There you are, hiccups gone. Works every time."

Harry breathed experimentally, trying to slow his pulse rate. She was right, his hiccups had gone. She turned to go inside.

"Come Harry, let's go inside. I want to show you where I want you to erect your masterpiece."

Harry swallowed hard as he watched her backside sway leisurely up the steps into the house; his pulse rate was climbing again. She led him into the lounge, then turned and smiled. "I was thinking that maybe we could do it over there." She pointed vaguely towards a large couch by the window. "The library is too stuffy, I can't see either of us being happy to have it there. Then of course, maybe, just maybe, my bedroom is the best place. What do you think?"

"I er, umm…"

"Oh, you must forgive me, I'm so keen for you to get started, you would probably like a drink first maybe?"

"Ahh, a scotch would help. I mean, would be nice."

"Oh, really? Some people say that alcohol inhibits their performance, stops the juices flowing, if you know what I mean."

"Oh yeah, maybe you're right. What are you having?"

"I was about to make myself a turmeric latte. It relaxes the soul and helps one to move into a more serene state."

"It does?"

"Well, that's what my guru tells me. Do you want to try one? Maybe, if you are in a state of serenity, you will find everything easier, especially on the job."

"On the jo… OK, if you say so."

"Why don't you get it out? I'll just make sure it's open and then we can get going. The sooner we get started the better. I am so excited, I can hardly wait for you to put it up. I've been wanting to see it inside here since the day of the art expo." She turned and left the room.

Harry closed his eyes – the woman was rampant, but he wasn't sure he was going to be able to do anything. Her down-to-earth, no-nonsense approach was bewildering. He unzipped his fly and plunged his hand inside, hoping to give himself a bit of help. When he looked up, he saw Rebecca had returned with two cups of latte and had a strange look on her face.

"Couldn't you get it out of the car? I thought I'd opened it with the remote." Her eyes focused on Harry's hand shifting around in his trousers. "Oh, you're doing that again. Does that help in situations like this as well? I must say, you had us all spellbound at the art festival the other day. Here's your latte, do you want a serviette or something to wipe your hand?"

Harry rapidly removed his hand and nervously wiped it down the side of his trousers. "I'm sorry, I thought you were umm wanting me to… thank you." Harry took the latte with trembling hands.

"Are you alright Harry? I think this latte arrived just in time. I had no idea that putting up your artwork would be so stressful for you."

Harry gulped down his latte as fast as he could. When he had finished, Rebecca took the cup from his hands and gestured towards his open fly. "Do you need to get busy down there again, or can we go to the car now?"

In a little over ten minutes, the teddy was impaled in all its agony on its rope once more, surrounded by spark plugs and fronted by boots and a typewriter in Rebecca's lounge. In all that time, not a word had come from Harry's lips. The ghastly error of judgement he had made was all too much for him to comprehend or deal with.

Rebecca watched on, assuming his silence was a result of the intense creative effort required to recreate the sculpture. Upon its completion, Harry stepped back, breathing heavily with embarrassed exhaustion, his mind a torment of confusion and guilt.

Rebecca put her hand on his shoulder gently. "Oh, Harry, that is even more poignant than I could ever have believed possible. Thank you. Would you like that scotch now?"

Harry, intensely aware of her hand and her perfume, realised with horror that his body was reacting.

"What? Why? No, please. I have to get away from your body."

"I'm sorry?"

"I er have to get… a wave to some… body, yes, that's it, they are leaving and I must wave goodbye, very important."

"Oh, what a pity, I was hoping we could talk more about your work."

"No, sorry… must run fast, go soon before I…"

And with that, Harry ran to his car, blew a kiss to Rebecca and, having regretted it, roared off down the driveway without a backward glance.

CHAPTER 104

Arnold Smith looked over to where the policeman stood. He was feeling way better and had been told by the doctor that he would be able to go home soon. He was just not sure what his position was. He had no desire to make contact with Cherry. The bastard had beaten him up and, according to the copper, tried to poison him as well.

He slid open the drawer beside his bed and pulled out the article he had ripped out of the magazine. The pizza guy looked like an old fart. He must have been paid off by Cherry to deliver the pizzas. He didn't seem like the sort of guy Cherry would hang out with, being an artist and everything. Maybe he was an old-time crook looking for easy work.

Smith made his mind up and took out his phone. "Hello, is that the *Gatwick Gazette*? Yeah, hi, I was wondering if you could let me know how I can contact that bloke who won the arts festival thing the other day."

"We don't have private details sir."

"Oh, that's a pity. I want to buy more of his stuff."

"If you give me your number sir, I could pass it on to somebody who recently acquired some of his work. They might be able to help you."

Smith hung up. He had to be careful. If Cherry and this bloke knew he was on to them, it would be curtains for sure. He bit his lower lip in thought. There were really only three options – go after Cherry and his mate, run for it and hope for the best, or throw his lot in with the cops.

The first option was almost certain death, the second seemed likely to be the best way forwards.

He saw that the cop had moved off momentarily. He made his mind up and set off with a shuffle down the corridor. He had made it about halfway when he was interrupted by a firm hand on his shoulder. He turned to see his police guard with his taser at the ready.

"Where are you going sonny? You weren't gonna leave without saying goodbye, were you?"

Smith thought of stating his rights, calling his lawyer and demanding justice but quickly realised that he had no idea what his rights were, did not know how to call a lawyer and suspected that justice did not weigh heavily in his favour. He thought of making a dash but was unsure how steady his legs were after being bedridden for two weeks and felt less than inclined to have a taser shot into his arse. Option three started to loom large on his rather restricted horizon.

CHAPTER 105

Harry's heart missed a beat when he saw that it was Rebecca phoning him. Did she want to torment him further? Maybe she had come to her senses and realised that fifty grand was a bit much for a rotten teddy being rogered by a rope. Just as well he had not cashed the cheque yet.

He swallowed and answered. "Hello, Harry speaking." His voice came out as a squeak.

"Harry darling, how are you? I have some wonderful news. Your fame is spreading fast. I have another person enchanted with your work."

"Another person?"

"Yes, isn't that nice? I knew I was making a sound investment. My friend at the *Gazette* contacted me. They were cut off unfortunately, but they gave me the person's number. Have you got a pen and paper?"

Harry wrote down the number.

"Now do follow it up, Harry. I secretly suspect that it's his Lordship you know. I'm telling everybody about you, so don't be surprised if a few more come knocking at your door. Anyway, must dash, please pop in when you're out this way. I'll have the lattes waiting. Toodle pip."

His Lordship? Harry tapped his fingers as he looked at the number. He should probably discuss what to do with Jim and the others. "Come on, do something yourself for once, take control," he said to himself. He dialled the number.

Smith picked up the phone. "Allo!"

Harry looked at his phone and flinched. It wasn't the reception he had anticipated.

"Er, good morning. My name is Harry Johnson. I understand you were looking for me."

Smith froze. "What do you want?" He glanced nervously over to where the police guard was positioned.

"I understand you like what I do?"

"I do? Like what?"

Harry decided to come down to earth and tell this poor guy what he had really done. “Look, I’m not going to bullshit you. I just got hold of an old teddy, no arms, no legs, shoved a stiff bit of rope up his arse and had his head slammed in a bus door a few times. That was pretty much it really. I honestly can’t see what all the fuss is about. But I guess if people are willing to pay me to do it, why should I complain? Do you want something like that maybe?”

Smith’s hands began to shake. He didn’t know who Teddy was but he certainly didn’t want his head slammed in any bus doors let alone things up his arse. He would have to be careful. This guy was a sicko.

“Er, no.”

“Oh, I need to do a special job do I?” Harry smiled and closed his eyes and let his imagination rip. “Need to keep it on spec, I suppose, so I guess unimaginable pain and disfigurement are needed, probably with terribly horrific visual effects thrown in for good measure. Am I getting warm?”

“I don’t want any trouble Mr Johnson, I’m sorry.”

“No trouble at all. I get quite a kick out of it. Can’t wait to get started actually. Can I suggest that I show you the sort of thing I’m talking about, just a little taste, and we can see how you feel about it?”

“That won’t be necessary sir.”

“Oh, OK. I’ll just let rip and see where it gets us. Sort of go all the way. It’s a bit risky because it might just be a mess, maybe it won’t be as dreadful as people have come to expect. That would be awful, I don’t want to disappoint. I suppose I have a reputation to uphold, value for money and all that.”

Smith moved closer to the toilet; he thought he might have to be sick. “Please sir, don’t do anything.”

“Oh…, well OK. I have to admit I’m a little bit disappointed, I was really starting to look forward to another project. Oh well, if you ever change your mind, you know what to do.”

“Yes, sir, I know. I promise I’ll be no more trouble sir, ever.”

Harry heard the phone go dead. “Bugger, I must be losing my touch,” he thought to himself.

CHAPTER 106

"Hey Ash, the constable on duty at the hospital just phoned. He said that Arnie Smith was trying to do a runner."

"Really? That's interesting. Time to get down and have a word with Mr Smith."

Smith recognised the burly black cop as he walked into the ward. He was going to have to make some decisions quickly about what to say and what not to say. Whatever he did say was going to carve out his path going forwards.

The phone call from Johnson had unnerved him badly. The man was so calm and confident, no swearing or shouting, just cold threats confidently delivered. Cherry was obviously the one paying Johnson. They had him in their sights, of that there was no doubt. The nearness of the guard was probably the only thing that had saved him from an unimaginably agonising death. As each hour went past, he realised that there were very few viable choices left for him. Running, he now realised, was a very bad idea. Not only did it expose him to the horrors of Johnson, who seemed to be very adept at finding him, but it would also turn the only protective element he had into a hostile one as well.

The most depressing thing about all of it was that if he just turned himself over to the cops, a prison sentence awaited him. Once incarcerated, he had no illusions about how long he would last before Johnson's skills were applied in there.

Smith was sitting in a chair next to his bed. Ash came over, sat on the bed and looked at Smith. Smith looked at the floor in front of him.

"Went for a bit of a runner, did we Arnie?"

Smith said nothing.

"You have a bit of a death wish don't you Smith? Either that, or you're even more fucking stupid than I gave you credit for. I seem to be saying this a lot recently, but everybody seems to make the mistake that I give a fuck. I don't, especially about lowlifes like you. There's a bit of a trend going around at the moment. Rat shit like you seem to be getting themselves bumped off all over the place. I don't know why and frankly I don't care either. But I would rather like to know who is doing it."

"What's in it for me?"

"Oh well, saints preserve us, it can speak. What's in it for you? Let's see – er, a life possibly?"

"They are already out to get me. What difference can you make?"

"Hmm, probably none. But maybe, just maybe, you blabbing might cause us to get to them before they get to you. I agree it's still not a rock-solid certainty. The only certainty is that if we don't get to them first, your balls will be fed to you nice and raw and then things will go downhill from there. You know it, I know it."

Smith turned and opened his drawer and pulled out the *Gazette* article.

"This is the bloke you're after. Cherry paid him to wipe us out. He's the one who brought those fucking pizzas. He got hold of me on the phone and told me how he loves hurting people and ripping them up. Told me I was next. He's a fucking psycho!"

Ash took the piece of paper and looked at the caption. He screwed up his eyes and then looked at Smith.

"A local artist. This bloke looks about eighty. This is the bloke who has you all shitting your pants is it? What does he do, bore people to death with his paintings? Rip into you all with his zimmer frame?"

"I recognised him as the pizza delivery man, then he spoke to me on the phone and described how he likes to pull arms off people and everything."

"And this is our man is it Smith?"

"That's him and Cherry."

CHAPTER 107

Ash went over to Ella and dropped the newspaper article on her desk.

"There you go, that's our man." She looked up at Ash after briefly looking at the article. "Yeah, I know."

Ella shrugged. "Maybe he's got mob connections."

"Yeah, maybe. Doesn't really have that Al Capone look though, does he?"

"Neither did Escobar. Do you want me to follow up?"

"Yeah, please Ella."

Harry was contemplating his newfound artistic career when the doorbell rang. He heard his wife open the door and talk to somebody.

"Harry, there's a Detective Sergeant Thompson at the door. She said it was something to do with you at the art expo."

"Ah, the price of fame Sheila, let her in, let her in."

Harry went up to Ella. "Hello Sergeant, Rebecca sent you I suppose?"

"No sir, we traced you from the *Gazette* article."

"Oh, I see. Please, call me Harry."

"We are just carrying out some routine enquiries. By all accounts you are an amateur artist, is that correct?"

"Yep, that's me."

"Do you know an Arnold Smith?"

"No, I don't think so, does he also do stuff like mine?"

"He says that you phoned him the other day."

"Oh, that guy, yeah, I didn't know his name. I was told he wanted me to do one of my specials."

"Specials?"

"Yeah, like the other one, but after I'd explained what I did, he sort of changed his mind. It was quite strange come to think of it."

It suddenly dawned on Harry what all this was about. The other guy was trying to steal his ideas. The bastard. "Can I ask you something Sergeant? This Arnold Lane is a bit of a devious character, isn't he?"

"It's Smith. What makes you say that, sir?"

"Sorry Detective Sergeant Smith. I bet he does this all the time. Thieving bastard. Like a bloody parasite. It's unbelievable, isn't it? Every rock you turn over reveals some lowlife who wants to ride off somebody else. You've got him down at the station, have you? Chunk of bloody shit, they make me sick to the stomach. Well, I hope you fix him good."

"Can I take it that you don't like Arnold Smith."

"Who's that? Sorry, you mean Arnold Lane? Do you like him, Detective Sergeant Smith? I mean surely you don't have sympathy for scum like that. I'm really glad you have the bastard in chains down there. I am too trusting by far."

"It's Sergeant Thompson sir."

"Really, is that his real name? So, he is in the police force as well? My God, no wonder you guys want to nail him. What a disgrace!"

"No Arnold Smith is not in the police force."

"Oh, why is he a sergeant then? Oh, sorry, Lane's in the army, you must forgive me, I'm jumping to conclusions again. It's old age you know."

"No sir, he's not a sergeant at all and his name is Arnold Smith."

"No, his name is Arnold Lane."

"How do you know that sir?"

"I didn't until you just told me, Detective Sergeant Smith. I'd never heard his name before you walked through the door."

"The name is Detective Sergeant Thompson sir."

"You told me it was Smith. I'm sorry but you're confusing his name with somebody else now I think, or does the bastard have loads of different names?"

"My name is Detective Sergeant Thompson, his name is Arnold Smith."

"I wouldn't be too sure of that Sergeant, not after what you've just told me!"

"Do you know him sir?"

"No, I don't."

"Would you like to cause him harm?"

"Yes, of course I would. It's only natural, so would you. These people get away with murder, don't they? Well, anyway, it's good to see that you've got him. Thanks for that. How did you know that he and I had spoken?"

"He told us."

"Ah, admitted it did he? So, you got him to sing. How many others has he gone for? I suppose you can't tell me. Probably just as well."

"Did you threaten him in any way sir?"

"No, why would I do that? I didn't know he was trying to tap me for tips until you told me now about what he was up to. I sort of take people at face value you see. I can see now I'll have to be a bit more careful. What else can I help you with today, Detective Sergeant Smith? Would you perhaps like me to knock something up for the police station? Sort of shock the ones you arrest into a life of penitence? I'm sure Sheila could root out some more bits and bobs from the attic. I won't charge of course, you know, do my bit for the local constabulary. What do you say?"

"I'm honestly not sure what to say Mr Johnson."

"Enough said then. Just your smiles when I deliver it will be enough. Don't say another word!"

Ella stood up and slipped her notebook back into her pocket. "Well, thank you Mr Johnson, we'll be in touch. Oh, by the way, how often do you do fast food deliveries?"

"Eh? Oh, I don't do fast food, hate the stuff, full of chemicals and things. Sheila's a good cook and so am I actually. Eat natural stuff, that's what I say. If nature meant you to eat your beans out of tins, it would have made them in tins in the first place, wouldn't it? Do you do fast food Constable Smith?"

"Here's my card Mr Johnson, my name is right there, at the bottom."

"Oh right. In the meantime, I'll get busy with those creative juices and thanks again for nailing that Lane fellow."

Ella walked back to her car without a second glance and drove back to the station.

Ash looked up as Ella walked in. "How did you get on with Pablo, Ella?"

"Who?"

"Pablo… Pablo Escobar, our mobster, Mr Johnson."

"Please, don't do that different name thing. I don't think I could deal with that right now."

"So what did you find out?"

"I'm not sure where to start. I think maybe my powers of communication are not all that they should be. It's difficult to know what to make of it all."

"Was he evasive?"

"No, quite the opposite. Never stopped talking actually."

"And the pizza deliveries?"

"He didn't miss a beat, seemed genuinely to not have a clue what I was talking about."

"Do you think Smith has been spinning us?"

"Something isn't fitting that's for sure. Maybe we should see what Mr Cherry has to say for himself."

"Hmm, let's see if he would like to help us with our enquiries."

CHAPTER 108

"You know what, Jim? You, me and Harry are like the Three Musketeers, and Terence is like D'Artagnan."

"Really, that's good to know, I'm sure."

"Harry here tells me that the police would like him to do another one of his sculptures for them at the station. We are doing all sorts of good for the community aren't we?"

"Apparently." Jim gave Harry a quizzical glance.

"What can I say? I also had some arsehole trying to plagiarise my style. They caught him and have him remanded in custody, or whatever they call it."

"How do you know that, Harry?"

"They came to my house and told me about it. Warned me off eating fast food too. It's nice to see that the cops still have time to care about things like that isn't it?"

"Brings tears to my eyes Harry. I must say, I'm a bit confused about what we are going to do."

"That is why we have contingency planning Jim, what-if analysis and all that."

"So, who's going to do that Harry?"

"I will Jim. I keep saying we need to plan better. There has never been a greater need to plan than with this operation we have laid out here. It makes D Day look like the teddy bears' picnic. I want you all to list everything you can think of that can go wrong, then we can conjure up a contingency plan to deal with each cock up."

Jim ripped off some sheets of paper from his notebook and, after a bit of a rummage, found a pencil for each of them.

"Have you got a pencil sharpener Jim? This pencil is blunt, I can't deal with blunt pencils."

"Yeah, and I need a board to rest on."

"Haven't you got a biro? I prefer using them."

"For fuck's sake! No! I don't have a pencil sharpener. Go use a kitchen knife or something. Whilst you're there, bring in the chopping boards, and you're all welcome to wander around my house looking for biros, fountain pens, quills and ink pots or whatever your delicate needs might require."

"Ooh, sorry. Look I've just made a hole in my paper, see what I mean. We can't do this half-cocked."

Jim looked over towards Terence. "I hope you haven't set your heart on this happening before Christmas."

CHAPTER 109

Ash put his phone down and shook his head. "Hey Ella, guess who's graced us with his presence? None other than Mr Bob Cherry. He's downstairs in interview room No.1. Came wandering in to have a chat after we contacted him. I must say I was hoping he'd do a runner."

"I'm coming boss, I don't want to miss this one."

Bob Cherry looked up as Ella and Ash came into the room.

"Good morning Mr Cherry, this is Detective Sergeant Thompson and I am Detective Inspector Ash Kamau. Thank you for giving up your time to help us with our enquiries."

"It's a pleasure Detective Inspector." Cherry let his eyes roam slowly over Ella from head to foot. "Definitely a pleasure."

"We would like to ask you about the events that took place on the night of the fourteenth at your, er, establishment."

"What about them?"

"Tell us what happened that night when the contaminated pizzas were delivered."

"Well, we was doing some renovations on this social club we was planning to open for the local community."

"How very public spirited of you."

"Yeah. Then this geezer rocks up with a load of pizzas. Says like he has to deliver them, we can take 'em or leave 'em sort of thing. So, we take them in and chow them."

"Did you eat one?"

"No."

"Why not?"

"They were all loaded with mushrooms, I hate bloody mushrooms."

"Did you know they were poisonous?"

"Of course not, how would I know that?"

"Maybe you wanted to poison all your chums?"

"Oi, hang on, is that what this is all about? You trying to land this crap on me?"

"We are just trying to cover every possible scenario," interjected Ella.

Cherry smiled. "Is that right darling? I wouldn't mind covering a couple of scenarios with you either."

Ash glared at Cherry.

"Come on Detective Inspector, I'm just trying to be as accommodating as I can to Detective Sergeant Thompson here." Cherry looked at Ella and winked.

"So, everybody ate the pizzas except for you. That was lucky, wasn't it?"

"Bloody right it was lucky."

"What happened then?"

"Nothing happened, we got on with our stuff and went home. Then the next morning, everyone starts moaning on about being sick and feeling crap. I thought they was all hung over and told them to stop acting like a pack of girls."

"Is that when you hit Arnold Smith?"

"What's that little shit been telling ya?"

"He told us you hit him."

"A bit of an argument between ole mates. He happened to run into my hand, that's all."

"What did you do when you found out they'd been poisoned?"

"I prayed for their swift recovery."

"Really, didn't work, did it?"

"God works in mysterious ways, his wonders to perform, Detective Inspector."

"Indeed. What do you know about Eric Crabbs?"

"My ole mate Eric? Terrible what happened, innit? I went to visit him a couple of times in hospital. Very distressed I was. But I reckon it messed up 'is bonce a bit, cos he got all stroppy. Said it were my fault."

"Really, how do think he came to that conclusion?"

"Not a clue Detective Inspector – maybe he hit his head?"

"So where were you on the night of the fire?"

"What fire?"

"The fire that burnt down Crabbs' place along with most of his gang."

"I dunno. When was it?"

"Exactly three weeks ago."

"What time?"

"Eight in the evening."

Cherry looked at the ceiling and shook his head and smiled. "Dunno, watching telly probably. What about you Detective Sergeant Thompson, what were you doing?"

"Stick to the question Mr Cherry."

"I was just making a point that most people dunno what they was doing three weeks ago."

Ash pulled out the newspaper article showing Harry receiving his prize.

"Do you recognise this person?"

Cherry picked up the paper and looked at Harry's smiling face. He made the connection immediately. The face in the newspaper was the pizza delivery man. "Nah, who's this old geezer?"

"You are sure you've never seen this man before?"

"He looks like every other old bloke."

"Why didn't you come in when I was talking to Eric Crabbs in the hospital that time?"

"Eh? Oh, was that you? I saw he was busy so I decided not to bother. You know, three's a crowd and all that."

"And you never saw the man who delivered the pizzas?"

"Nah, it was dark."

"Well, thank you very much Mr Cherry for giving up your valuable time. I hope we can rely on your cooperation going forwards if necessary."

"Only a pleasure Detective Inspector Kamau. Always happy to help. So might I ask what Detective Sergeant Thompson does on her nights off?"

Cherry looked across at Ella and winked again.

"Good day Mr Cherry."

CHAPTER 110

The scribbled bits of paper were handed to Harry, who carefully transcribed the list of possible "calamities", as he labelled them, onto the board.

Lordship doesn't believe Mervyn and Jim

Snakes won't bite

Snakes bite everybody

They phone police

Harry stepped back and inspected the list. "Right, so how do we meet these, er, challenges?"

There then ensued an intense brainstorming session during which each member of the conspiracy applied their individual skills to address each issue. Eventually Harry stepped back again to look at the results on the board.

Lordship doesn't believe Mervyn and Jim	*Go back home*
Snakes won't bite	*They probably will*
Snakes bite everybody	*They probably won't*
They phone police	*Go into dithery mode*

"So, let me get this right. If our story doesn't work, we do a runner. We keep our fingers crossed about the snakes. Oh, and if the shit hits the fan, we all act stupid."

"I would say that pretty much sums it up Jim," Mervyn replied contentedly.

"Hmm, the only bit I feel any level of confidence about is the last bit. I would say we are woefully ill equipped to deal with the middle bit. As for the runner, I think we can all rest assured it will be more of a toddle, but I suppose that will have to do Harry."

Harry walked back to the board. "No, wait a minute, that can't be job done. There must be more finesse than that. We need to prepare counterarguments in case they are reluctant, that sort of thing."

"Oh, I think we can leave that to you Harry, you're way more adept at that sort of thing than we are."

Everybody got up to get themselves a drink.

"What do mean Jim? Where are you all going? This is a team session, remember – Three Musketeers, all for one and one for the lot of you or something like that."

"I need a cocoa Harry."

"You can't leave me with all this, you sneaky bastards, that's not fair."

"Want a beer, Harry?"

"Yeah, please. No, wait, you can't buy me off with a beer."

"So you don't want one then?"

"Yes, I do, but… Oh what the shit, let's just jump off the cliff like normal!"

"That's the spirit Porthos!"

"Hey, who you calling Porthos? He was the fat bastard, why can't I be Aramis?"

"OK, you can be Aramis, I don't mind being Porthos."

"I'm so glad to see we treat premeditated murder with the respect it deserves gentlemen."

CHAPTER 111

"Cherry's a slippery bugger isn't he Ella?"

"Hmm, very calm and slimy. Almost psychopathically so."

"He admitted everything we could have wound him up about and nothing we have no evidence of. Didn't fall for knowing when Crabbs' place burnt down either."

"He's either innocent or very slick."

"Didn't seem to recognise Johnson, I was watching his face very carefully, not a flicker."

"Do you think Smith made it up about Cherry poisoning them?"

"It was me who put that idea into Smith's head, Ella. I don't think Cherry poisoned them, it's too sophisticated for him. But burning down Crabbs' joint is right up his street I reckon. I would like to find out a bit more about how friendly he and Crabbs were. Maybe that line of bullshit could be dug over a bit more."

"Crabbs insisted he didn't poison them either. Not that that means much, but again, it's too sophisticated for Crabbs. The man has the finesse of a ten-pound hammer."

"True. It's starting to look like we have a third party involved. The only lead we have is this Johnson character. What is he like?"

"He seems to be overloaded with disconnected thoughts, I could hardly get a meaningful answer out of him. Though he didn't seem evasive in the slightest, just wandered down lots of foggy paths."

"Do you think he could be our hit man?"

"I suspect his most dangerous weapons are his wandering thoughts."

"Yeah, we only have Smith's testimony. Maybe I should have a chat to Mr Johnson."

"It would certainly do no harm. Actually, it could be harmful to your mental wellbeing."

"Ha, my mental wellbeing went off the rails long ago, so no worries there."

"Just one thing, before you go. Make some name tags of who you are going to talk about and use them all the time, otherwise you might go nuts."

"OK. I'm just thinking. How did your mate Johnson get hold of Smith? Why did he phone him?"

Ella took out her notes and flicked through them, shaking her head. "What a mess, oh, here we are, he said something about Smith wanting one of Johnson's specials."

"How did he get Smith's number?"

"Hmm, sorry boss, don't know. Things got a bit muddled. I could phone and ask him?" Ella winced as she thought about a phone call to Harry Johnson.

"Please Ella, shouldn't take long, eh?"

Ella found the number, took a deep breath and dialled.

"Hello, Harry Johnson speaking."

"Hello Mr Johnson, its Detective Sergeant Thompson from the Wimbledon branch, we spoke the other day."

"Oh yes, hello Detective Sergeant Thompson, how are you?"

Ella punched the air triumphantly when she heard him get her name right. "Very well, thank you. You remember we spoke about you phoning Mr Arnold Smith?"

"Yes, I remember."

"How did you get his number?"

"Oh, Rebecca gave it to me."

"Who is Rebecca, Mr Johnson?"

"Lady Rebecca one of my fan… er, customers."

"Do you know how she came by it?"

"What?"

"The number of Mr Smith."

"Good lord, I hope you're not suggesting Lady Rebecca is in cahoots with such a scoundrel, are you? She was only trying to help. He phoned the newspaper looking for me but then got cut off or something. She was able to pass the number on to me."

"What is Lady Rebecca's full name Mr Johnson?"

"Now look, I don't want Lady Rebecca getting dragged into… Oh wait a moment. I'm sorry Sergeant, I'm such a fool. You want a second opinion of my work before I get going. I'm sorry, I'm a bit slow. Talking of slow, I have yet to sort through what Sheila found in the attic…"

Ella gripped the phone tightly. "No Mr Johnson, Mr Johnson…" But it was too late.

"Would you believe, there was an old policewoman's hat, eh? What are the chances? I mean if that isn't providence, I don't know what is. And a large china doll with its eyes pushed in, and an enormous set of wind chimes. We could make it bi-sensual, is that the word? Maybe even tri-sensual if we scattered some suitable smells on it. Wouldn't that be something?"

"Mr Johnson I…"

"Yes, a sort of Son e Lumiere with some odours thrown in. I think that would certainly make the wayward sit up and take notice. They don't have to be nice smells, do they?"

"Mr Johnson, could I have Lady Rebecca's contact details?"

"Well, yes, I suppose she wouldn't mind, but maybe I should ask her permission first."

"I will be very polite Mr Johnson."

"Oh, yes, I suppose it will be OK. It's, er, Lady Rebecca Benjamin Grey, let me get her number. You will tell her that it's for a reference for my art, won't you?"

"Yes Mr Johnson, I promise."

Ella wrote down the number and hung up.

She took another deep breath and dialled.

"Hello Rebecca speaking."

"Hello, Lady Benjamin Grey?"

"Please, call me Rebecca. How can I help you?"

"It's Detective Sergeant Ella Thompson here from the Met Police Wimbledon branch. It's about Mr Harold Johnson. He is about to do some work for us."

"Oh, how wonderful, are you the people who phoned the *Gazette* the other day?"

"Phoned the *Gazette*?"

"Yes, were you the people wanting to contact Harry, whose number I passed to him?"

"No, I am not that person."

"Oh, somebody new. That's excellent news, he is so talented isn't he? You must send me a picture of the work when he has completed it. Has he started yet?"

"Er, no, not yet."

"How very exciting. Have you any idea what form it will take?"

"It's to be, er, tri-dimensional."

"Really, how very extraordinary. The man is truly amazing isn't he? What did you want to know from me?"

"Oh, just if you would recommend him?"

"Absolutely my dear, Harry is your man."

"Well thank you your Ladyship, you've been very helpful."

"It's Rebecca, and you are most welcome. Goodbye."

Ella walked over to Ash's desk.

"So, what did Johnson say?"

"He said that a Lady Rebecca Benjamin Grey gave him the number after Smith had tried to contact the *Gazette* looking for Johnson. I just phoned her, and she confirmed his story."

"Aha, did he have anything else to say?"

"Yes, he did unfortunately."

"What was that?"

"We are going to get a doll with a police hat on, that has had its eyes pushed in and smells bad."

CHAPTER 112

Ash was momentarily alarmed to see Smith's bed unoccupied, until he saw the man sitting in a chair by the window. He pulled up a chair and sat down next to him.

"So, 'ave you got that psycho yet?"

Ash looked Smith up and down.

"You think we are all as stupid as you, don't you Smith? You told us this bloke got hold of you, eh?"

"Yeah, that's right."

"I've just heard another story told by people who don't live up to their necks in crap like you. This story goes a bit differently to yours. This story tells how you tried to contact him first."

Smith shifted awkwardly in his chair.

"This other story also suggests that the real nasty individual is some prick called Arnold Smith. Apparently, this shuffling heap of pig shit thinks he can fuck everybody around by talking bollocks and still get away with it."

"I didn't get through."

"And you're not getting through now either. But never mind, we are a forgiving lot. You're free to go. My constable needs to get back to doing something useful and I can confirm that your good mate Bob Cherry can't wait to have his old mate back again. He told us he has been missing you. Although he was saddened when we told him what you had said about him. So you might need to kiss and make up a bit."

"You can't fucking do that, we had a deal, you fucking…"

"Yes, go on. You were saying something about me?"

Smith looked down at his knuckles twitching with rage.

Ash leaned in closely. "Go on Smith, take a shot at me and see how far that gets you."

"He'll fucking kill me."

"Pretty much guaranteed I would say. I gave you a chance Smith. But shit like you never learns, does it?"

"I told you the truth. That fucking psycho brought them pizzas."

"And Johnson phoned you out of the blue, did he?"

"No, I tried to get hold of him. But I didn't want him to know I was on to him."

"I've had enough of this shit Smith. You've been wasting a lot of people's time with your crap. But it ends right here. You're on your own, china."

CHAPTER 113

Jim and Mervyn flopped back into their chairs after saying goodbye to Terence and Harry.

"I'm rather excited about our new operation aren't you, Jim?"

"I think I would be a little more excited if I had any idea of how we are going to pull it off. I suppose we do have shitty Lord Percy's sordid habits to help us along. I doubt whether the disgusting little creep would be able to resist the idea of an endless supply of unattached, unsupervised children to tap into."

"Maybe we should do a role-play. You know, to get in a bit of practice and all that."

"What, now? I was rather hoping we could watch the snooker on telly."

"I'll be Lord Percival. You can be, er, you, I suppose."

"Oh bloody hell. OK, so where do we start?"

"Er, umm, yeah, you make a phone call to introduce yourself."

Jim sighed and lifted his left fist up to his ear.

Mervyn made a ringing sound and then lifted his fist to his ear. "Good evening, you are through to the residence of Lord Percival Bransford-Smythe of Bransford Manor, how may I help you?"

"Er, I'd like to speak to umm, his Lord… um… ship… please."

"Who are you? And what is your enquiry about?"

"I have a proposition to put to his Lordship. It involves lots of children who don't have a home."

"I beg your pardon? What possible interest would his Lordship have in that regard?"

"Wait a minute, who are you? I want to talk to his Lordship, not one of his toe rags."

"Click."

"OK Merv, that was a mistake. Let me try again. Who are you? No. Er… May I enquire as to the identity of the personage I am currently addressing?"

"I, sir, am Lord Percival Branford-Smythe's gentleman's gentleman."

"Gentleman my arse… no I didn't say that. The proposal is for his Lordship's ears alone."

"I am his trusted butler sir. I am not about to trouble my master with a begging call."

"We're not begging, we are giving kids away for free. Er, no… We are looking for suitable foster homes for some beautiful, unattached and very humbly grateful young people."

"How did you get our number?"

"Oh, you come highly recommended by high society, er, very high. We understand that you used to take unfortunate children into your care."

"No, we didn't."

"Yes, you bloody well did."

"Click."

"I don't think I'm up to this Mervyn, he keeps pissing me off."

"Give it another go, at least you're having some practice."

"OK, where were we? You said 'No we didn't.' So I'll say, er, um, right… Oh, I must have heard incorrectly. Most of the guests at your art expo were very impressed with the wonderful work that you do."

"You don't say. So, what do you expect his Lordship to do?"

"We would like to come and explain how we find homes for orphans who have been abandoned by the authorities and society in general."

"No doubt you people will then spend endless hours disturbing our privacy with follow-ups and such."

"Good heavens no. Once we've dumped them, er, settled them in, you can do what you like with them. I mean, we have a very laissez faire approach. We find the children prefer that."

"Very well, you can come and see me, when I find it convenient."

"See you? I need to speak to Lord Pervert… er, Percy, not you, you arrogant piece of snivelling shit!!! Fuck it Mervyn, I can't do this."

"No, I'm beginning to spot a problem, maybe you're right Jim. Let's swap rolls."

Mervyn lifted his hand to his ear. Jim did the same. "Hello, Lord Pervert's grovelling slime blob speaking."

"Keep to the programme Jim, I need to concentrate. Good morning my good man, so pleased to make contact with you at last. My good lady said that I should contact you with regards to our children's homes for the wayward."

"Really? That sounds right up our street, how many are we getting?"

"No, they aren't going to say that are they? Give me a bit of cold shoulder."

"Oh OK. Er… No, fuck off, we don't want any snotty kids. Shove them up your arse."

"Jim no. They aren't going to say that either are they?"

"They might, you need to be able to deal with any contingency."

"Not that one."

"Why not?"

"Because it not a likely contingency."

"Says who? Just because you don't like it doesn't mean it won't happen."

Mervyn put his imaginary phone back on the hook. "I'm going to have a rum and cocoa, why don't you watch your snooker."

CHAPTER 114

Arnold Smith felt his stomach churn as he watched his police guard gather up his stuff and walk off down the corridor. His choices, sparse as they were before, had whittled down to one option. He was as exposed as a flasher without a mac. He would have to do a runner before Cherry and his psycho mate found him. He rummaged in the cabinet beside his bed and found his shoes and socks, slipped his wallet and his mobile phone into his jeans pocket and pulled on his anorak. A quick glance confirmed that the coast was clear as he stepped into the corridor. He thought the retreating policeman saw him as he turned towards the exit, but the cop carried on walking away.

His legs wanted to run but he managed to achieve a semi-relaxed saunter. The hospital doors came ever closer until a rush of crisp air told him he was outside and free. He walked to the bus stop and hopped on the second bus that came past.

Across the road, Ash put down his phone. The police constable had told him that Smith was making his move. Ash started the car and smoothly moved into the traffic as he followed the bus eastwards with Smith inside it.

Ash decided that it was time to move things along a pace and let Smith have his head. As much as Smith deserved everything that was coming to him, Ash still felt bound to protect him, whilst seeing where fate took the man. Ash had a strong suspicion that it might take him, probably unwillingly, to Bob Cherry's tender clutches.

The bus eventually stopped close to a block of grim flats in Clapham. Smith got out and ambled up to one of the ground floor apartments and let himself in through the door. Ash parked across the road and phoned Ella. "Hi Ella, he's back in his flat."

"So, what now?"

"My gut feeling is that he will link up with his lifeline soon. He'll need some resources to keep him going and is probably planning to disappear. I'll just hang around for a while and see what happens."

Diagonally across from Smith's apartment, a hooded individual sat on a park bench with his mobile phone in his hand. He had also watched Smith's arrival. He dialled Smith's number. "Hello Arnie, so good to see ya out and about again."

Smith nearly dropped the phone as he recognised Bob Cherry's voice. "How d'you know I was out?"

"I know everything about you, me old china. Can we have a chat then? About ole times eh?"

"Not now, I'm getting on the tube."

"Really Arnie, I didn't know you got your own tube station in that rat hole of a flat of yours."

"I'm not in my flat."

"Arnie, Arnie. Of course you're in your flat. I told ya, I know everything about you, me ole mate."

"What d'ya want?"

"Just a little chat. You like having chats these days, don't ya?"

"Eh?"

"Yeah. My mate Arnie was very chatty to his rozzer mates the other day, weren't he?"

"I never told them nothing."

"You told them I hit you."

"You did, and I went and done nothing wrong."

"Ahhh, Arnie, you getting me all choked up here. Look, never mind about all that tripe. Did they show you that photo of the bastard who went and delivered them pizzas?"

"I dunno." Smith's mind raced as he tried to work out whether Cherry had sent Johnson or not.

"Don't play the dumb fuck Arnie. I'm on your side. You know you can't get away from me. It's time to confess your sins to Father Bob."

"I showed it to 'em. Said he delivered the pizzas."

"Where'd you get the picture my old mate?"

"It were in a newspaper. Saw it in hospital."

"You should have told Father Bob and not run to the rozzers, shouldn't you?"

"Yeah… sorry."

"Well never mind that now. To err is human, to forgive is divine. And I'm full of forgiveness today, Arnie. It's gonna be my job and yours to find that old bastard."

"OK, Bob."

"Oh, and if I were you, I wouldn't go wandering anywhere too soon. Our mate Detective Inspector Ash Kamau is watching you. Right now."

"What, where?"

"Never you mind Arnie. You've got me to protect you now. Oh, and by the way, there's a couple of quid under ya door mat. Just to keep you going. If you'd been less cooperative, I'd have taken it back and sent some petrol under ya door instead. Cheers me ole mate, and remember, Big Brother Bob is watching. Stay close and do nothing before asking me first, got it?"

"Yeah Bob, got it."

"Speak soon."

Ash saw Smith come to the door and look about, then he bent down and retrieved an envelope from under the door mat before quickly shooting off inside again. A little while later, Ash saw a Deliveroo man arrive at Smith's door and hand him a bag. He saw Smith paying with cash before taking a long look over towards where Ash was parked.

"Bugger," thought Ash, "I think my cover was just blown."

CHAPTER 115

Since their last meeting, Terence had spent much of his spare time researching snake handling techniques. He'd also purchased online a so-called "Snake clamp catcher reptile grabber pick-up handling tool". The snakes he had handled up to this point in his life had all been nonvenomous and reasonably agreeable. The ones he would be dealing with soon would be anything but.

As soon as the handling tool arrived, he laid his vacuum cleaner's pipe out on the lawn and began grabbing it from various positions, making sure that the "venomous" clamp head part, which clicked into the vacuum machine's body, was well but gently secured each time. It took some time before he was proficient at getting it first grab and he was acutely aware that the vacuum hose was considerably more forgiving than anything he would have to deal with in his Lordship's vivarium.

Once mastered on the ground, he began throwing the hose into the air and tried to snatch its head before it hit the ground. The head end, although devoid of venom or teeth, managed to deal out a good measure of pain as it smacked him across the head and shoulders a sufficient number of times to make him realise he had much work to do before quelling the vacuum hose, let alone anything that had a mind of its own.

Harry, on the other hand, had abandoned all thought of his Lordship's extermination after his attempts to drum up any semblance of planning amongst the team seemed destined to fail. Instead, he had thrown himself wholeheartedly into his new art project and was busy salvaging a motor from a broken fan to attach to the wind chimes that Sheila had rescued from the loft. The first attempt to activate the chimes had been unsuccessful. The motor had set the wind chimes off at a speed that caused the tubular bells to swing out alarmingly, cracking Harry across the head before he could switch off the power.

Having decided to call it a day with the Son part of his Son et Lumiere, he decided to apply his mind to the smell that should accompany the work. In line with its theme of stern reprimand, it needed to be pungent but not disgusting. It should cause one to be alarmed but not nauseated. He proceeded to sniff every bottle he could find in the kitchen, but they were either too foody or too perfumed. He even gave Sheila a sneaky sniff, as she often caused him to become alarmed, but disappointingly she just smelt of fabric softener.

The smell needed to be manufactured on site without constant topping up. He didn't want to have to constantly pop down to the police station to spray some kind of Eau De Alarming around. And then, as sometimes happens, circumstances magically provided the answer. The old fan motor, having laboured under the task of churning the wind chimes' bells around like helicopter blades, had arced its geriatric coils tirelessly to produce copious amounts of ozone. The smell was both pungent and sufficiently alarming to fit the bill in Harry's discerning mind. It also had the huge advantage of being produced only when the artwork was activated.

Satisfied in the knowledge of a job well done, Harry took himself off to the bathroom and applied a plaster to the gash on his head before slumping into his armchair with a whisky in hand.

CHAPTER 116

Jim had felt uneasy about his performance in the role-play with Mervyn. He couldn't help feeling that he could have done more, should have concentrated harder and not let his intolerance of arseholes surface so rapidly. A feeling of self-doubt was beginning to pervade his thoughts when the sound of the doorbell brought him back from his reverie.

As he opened the door, he saw the small figure of Doris standing there in a coat and hat, seemingly dressed to go somewhere.

"Hello Doris, how are you?"

"Doing very nicely Jim. I hate to bovver you again, but me sister's taken poorly and she can't be doing for herself anymore. Would it be alright if I asked you to look after ole Archie for a couple a nights, maybe?"

"Absolutely Doris, no problem at all. Are you off now?"

"Yeah, but you won't have to bovver tonight. Here's the keys, thanks ever so much Jim." Doris turned and toddled away, giving a little wave as she did so.

Jim watched from the lounge window as Doris made her way down the street and turned the corner. For some reason he couldn't explain, he didn't believe Doris was telling the truth. He looked at the keys in his hand. "Maybe I should just pop across quickly, just to make sure everything is alright," he thought to himself, and with that, he stepped across to Doris's house.

The cat was in the hallway, sitting looking at the door as Jim entered. "Hello Archie, good to see you, old buddy. I was wondering if I could run something by you?"

The cat turned and made towards the kitchen where it hopped onto a stool. Jim pulled out a stool and sat down. For a while they just stared at each other. Jim coughed nervously. "I'm not sure how to put this, it might come out the wrong way. But I'm sort of having doubts about my ability to pull off this latest project. You know, it's the one with the peado lord. I'm supposed to do this silver-tongued bullshit, but I'm not very good at it."

The cat started kneading the stool whilst purring gently.

"Yeah, I know all that sort of stuff comes quite naturally to you, but I battle with shit like that."

The cat sat up and cocked his head to one side.

"OK, I'm sorry, it's not shit. It's very admirable I suppose. There you see, I just put my foot in it again. It seems I just can't help myself. What do you think I should do?"

The cat remained tight lipped as he stared at Jim.

"You're right, that's it, I must just say nothing! Pretend to be dumb, literally. I can manage that! Just let Mervyn and the rest do all the talking. I can be the handicapped volunteer. How very ingenious you are. I knew you'd come up with a solution. You should think of doing this professionally you know, you really are very good."

The cat turned and looked at the fridge door.

"Oh yeah, that reminds me. I nearly forgot. I brought you some snacks."

Jim reached into his pocket and withdrew a packet of Dreamies. The cat sniffed the bag and then looked up at Jim expectantly. "Hey, let me just tear open the top. I guess that's a bit tricky for you, eh?"

The cat rubbed its body against Jim's leg.

"That's it isn't it? We all have our own skill sets. You give expert advice. I open packs of Dreamies. We work as a team. Mervyn has his skills, I have mine. I'm not sure what they are but I must have some, I suppose." Jim gave the cat a neck scruff as Archie rolled his head around, enjoying the sensation. "All for one and one for all, eh, Archie my old buddy?"

CHAPTER 117

Jim looked from Harry to Terence and back to Harry again. Both sported plasters on their heads. "Have you two been headbutting each other or something?"

Terence looked at Jim sheepishly. "I'd prefer not to discuss it."

"Me neither," said Harry quickly.

Jim shrugged. "Sorry for asking. In fact, I'm going to take a less verbal role going forwards. It's been pointed out to me that I should strive to be the strong silent type."

"Who told you that Jim?"

"Archie did, Mervyn."

"Who's Archie?"

"Doris's cat… er, catastrophist."

"What the hell is that?"

"It's a person who gives good advice."

Terence looked up. "No it's not. Catastrophism is the theory that changes in the earth's crust during geological history have chiefly resulted from sudden violent and unusual events."

"Sounds like the sort of person everybody needs in their life I would say, Jim."

Jim shifted awkwardly in his chair. "Look, can we move on? Has anybody come closer to working out how we are going to bump off Percival Pervert?"

"Maybe we should ask your castrator friend Jim."

"Mervyn, stop it. Sarcasm does not become you."

"I don't know Jim. I'm rather enjoying myself."

Harry stood up and walked up to the door posing as a whiteboard. "Right, I've had enough of this shit. We either do something productive or I'm going home."

"I think I'm going to have a cocoa."

"Well that's more like it, Mervyn. Harry, write that up on the board."

"Now who's being sarcastic Jim? Let's have a ten-minute break."

Harry watched as everybody filed out to the kitchen. "Ten-minute break from what? We've done absolutely bugger all so far."

On their return, primed with assorted beverages, they all took on a stern expression of determination.

"Right Harry, we're ready. Go for it."

"Go for it? Go for what? A walk round the block? A quick piss?"

"No need to get testy. Tell us what we have so far."

"Mervyn, we have this."

Harry turned to the board and drew a circle on the door. "That's what we have. Zero. Nothing. Sweet fuck all."

"We need to script a dialogue that we can use when we phone the manor. A bit like telemarketers do. You know, if they say this, we say that and so on."

"I like that, Terence. A bit of planned blurb. Who's going to do that?"

"I'll have a go at that."

"Great Mervyn, that's a good start."

"I'm going to be dumb."

They all turned to Jim.

"Alright Jim, that should come pretty naturally."

"You really are cranking that old sarcasm thing today aren't you Mervyn?"

"Come on Jim. You wouldn't have been able to resist that response after a comment like that."

"Yeah, but I don't mean dumb like stupid, I mean as in not able to speak. I was advised that it would be the best way to stop me saying something I would regret."

"Who told you that?"

"I told you, Archie did when… umm, never mind."

"Oh, Archie, your castrator. How much does this Archie know about what we are doing? He seems to be giving lots of advice."

"He knows everything."

"Is that wise Jim? How do you know he won't rat on us?"

"Firstly, because I trust him implicitly." Jim closed his eyes and through clenched teeth continued. "And secondly because he's a fucking cat, OK?!"

CHAPTER 118

Harry glanced at his buzzing phone and saw that Rebecca was on the line. His first thought was that the teddy had fallen off its rope. The second was that she had woken up to the fact that she had blown 50K on a complete pile of crap.

"Hello Rebecca, it's Harry here."

"Harry, I have a bone to pick with you."

Harry's heart missed a beat and he swallowed hard. "I can come and take it away Rebecca, I completely understand."

"Oh, stop fooling around Harry. I want to know why you haven't cashed your cheque yet? I hope you're not considering a better offer from someone else, are you?"

"For that piece of cra… er, creative effort, no absolutely not. It's all yours that's for sure."

"Well then, please cash my cheque. Whilst I have you on the line, I would like to ask you something. I hope you don't think I'm being forward or anything, but I was wondering if you would consider accompanying me to Percy's masked ball. There will be many art collectors there and I would just prefer your company to that of the dreadful bores I usually wind up with."

"Er, is that the Percy who did the art expo thing?"

"Yes of course."

Harry's mind raced. This could be an opportunity to get to his Lordship. It also meant he would be on a date with Rebecca, which he wasn't sure he trusted himself with. He felt a disturbing shift in his trousers which only heightened his fear.

"Well, I'm very flattered. I'm not sure that I will be any less boring than they are, mind you," he heard himself reply.

"Silly man. Well, that's done then. I'll send you the invitation so you can prepare. I can't wait to see what mask you are going to create. Maybe you would make me one as well?"

"Oh, I have to make a mask do I, or actually two?"

"Well, you could just buy one, but I know you would never miss a chance to let your creativity go wild."

"Oh yeah, absolutely, wow, when is it?"

"In a week's time."

Harry shut his eyes in panic.

"Right, OK then. Yup, great. Can't wait."

"I think it will do you a lot of good Harry. Goodbye."

He saw that his hand was trembling as he placed the phone back on the table. Firstly, he was going to be on a date with a woman he reluctantly lusted after. Secondly, he had been presented with an opportunity to be close to Percival Pervert which meant they were going to have to do some serious planning to maximise the opportunity. And thirdly, he had to conjure up two masks from heaven knows where.

CHAPTER 119

Mervyn was agonising over how to deal with Jim's apparent obsession with a cat. He seemed normal in every other way that he could determine, but he was not sure what to do with the knowledge that his friend was basing his approach to everything on the opinions of a furry domesticated animal.

He looked up nervously as Jim came into the room.

"Mervyn, we need another meeting urgently. Harry is coming around now, and Terence will be here soon. Harry has been invited round to a party at Brandford Manor, he is going to need all the help he can get."

Mervyn was tempted to ask if the cat was on its way as well but decided to keep off the subject for the time being. "Really, that's interesting."

"Yeah, that must be Harry now."

Jim went to the door and let Harry in. Harry related the story of Rebecca's invitation.

"So Harry, you never told us what happened when you went to set up that creation of yours at Lady Rebecca's. In fact, there was absolutely no feedback at all, come to think of it. That's not like you, you normally can't stop rambling on. And now she wants you to go balling with her. What are you not telling us you crafty bastard? Have you been slipping her ladyship a bit on the side?"

"No Jim, I have not."

"You've been thinking about it though, haven't you?"

"Let's change the subject. We have more important things that need to be discussed."

"So that's a yes then. Ah, here's Terence."

They all settled down and looked at Jim.

"Right, this is the thing. We have a situation wherein Harry here will be trying to manage an out-of-control erection on the dance floor with rampant Rebecca at Percival Pervert's Palace. This gives us an opportunity of some sort that we need to exploit. What that opportunity is and how we should exploit it heaven knows."

"Maybe you should give Archie a call."

"Fuck off, Mervyn."

Silence fell upon the group as each member wrestled with their thoughts. Mervyn was wondering whether Jim received advice from any other animals, Jim was cursing the moment he had let on about the cat, Harry was preoccupied with visions of Rebecca's backside swaying as she climbed the steps at her house and Terence was nursing his sore wrist from too much vacuum cleaner pipe grabbing.

"OK. Who would like to start?" said Jim suddenly.

Mervyn held up his hand. "Is there a possibility that we could get into the ball as well, Jim?"

"Well, we would all be masked up, so I suppose there is a chance."

"To what end?"

"Not sure, but I would imagine whatever Harry could do on his own would be better achieved if there were lots of us there to help him."

"We didn't really have a plan once we got into the art festival either but that went alright, didn't it?"

"Went alright in which way Mervyn?"

"Well, Harry met Lady Rebecca, and we now have another opportunity to get close to Lord P and maybe have a chat."

"Mervyn has a point, Jim. Maybe we should just concentrate on getting in first and then see where that gets us," said Terence.

"Well, another 'wing it and wish' plan takes shape, what a surprise."

"Harry, unless anybody has a better plan, I suggest you concentrate on your mask designs for all of us."

"What? Bugger off. You're not lumbering me with that. I'll do mine and Rebecca's. God knows, that's enough to occupy one week."

"Oh no, not another creative mountain to climb!"

"Come on Jim, I'm sure there must be somebody you know who can provide good advice when the need arrives."

"I'm sure that clipboard man will be creeping around the entrance. They are not going to just let anybody in with a bucket on their heads, are they?"

Jim watched as he saw Mervyn scribble something on his hand.

"What's that Mervyn?"

"Oh nothing. Just a note to self."

"Hmm, we probably need some good copies of the invites, although that bastard will probably have a guest list. I suppose we just wing it and hope."

Harry logged into Jim's laptop and found the invitation from Rebecca. He printed copies and handed one to each of them.

"Ooh, look here Harry. Rebecca has asked that you bring extra condoms and a fresh pair of underpants."

"Very funny Jim. You notice that there are no names or numbers on the invites."

"That's a bit weird. They could have all sorts of people crashing."

"Huh, I doubt that's ever been a problem. Who would want to hang around with Lurch and his mates in the first place?"

"You don't think it's a front for a paedo party do you?"

"Shit, I don't know. Do you think Rebecca's a bit weird like that?"

"Definitely not – judging by her choice of partner, I would say she's more into necrophilia."

"Very funny Jim. You're just jealous that she prefers a sophisticated person like me rather than an individual like yourself who's as rough as a bear's arse."

"Harry, you're right. If I was in your position, she would be getting banged off like a belt-fed mortar."

"Fortunately for her, you are not in my position. I am not banging her as you so politely put it, I am happily married. I am going with her only to further our ambitions."

"Right, and Dolly Parton doesn't have to sleep on her back."

"Excuse me guys, can we get back to the point at hand? Will these invites get us in as long as we have our masks on?"

"On the face of it, I would say so Mervyn, but they might want us to take our masks off before they let us in."

"Oh no, that's very bad form. But just in case, I would suggest that we design masks that don't come off too easily, and maybe have a backup mask painted on underneath."

"They might ask us for our names too Mervyn."

"Then make sure your mask is very well put on and muffles your voice effectively. That's probably our best chance I would say."

CHAPTER 120

Bob Cherry sat at his laptop and did a search for Harold Johnson. He knew it would be a long shot. It was hardly an unusual name, and the name might be false as well. Especially if the guy was a professional hit man. The search yielded a boxer and a game reserve in South Africa. He looked at the images. An assortment of faces appeared, none of which resembled his quarry. He punched Arnold Smith's number into the phone.

"Allo."

"Hello Arnie, me old mate. It's your uncle Bob here. Hope you're keeping well."

"Yeah."

"I'm so pleased to hear it. Warms the cockles of my heart it does. I am very interested in getting hold of Mr Harold bloody Johnson. Where is he?"

"Dunno."

"You sure you don't know Arnie?"

"Honest."

"Hmm, tell ya what. If you wanna make me really happy, you'll go and do a bit of work on finding the bastard. Get it?"

"Yeah, Bob, OK, I'll try."

"Make sure you try bloody hard." Click.

Smith stared at the phone. He wasn't comfortable letting Cherry know about his conversation with Johnson. He still had a sneaking suspicion that the two were working together and that Cherry was just sounding him out to see how much he knew and was willing to blab about. If this was true, any information he divulged would almost certainly invite a visit from psycho Johnson and that would not end well.

If Cherry was on the level, withholding information from him would also not end well. Cherry had an unnerving way of finding things out. He looked at the phone numbers from outside calls. There were only the two from Cherry and the one from Johnson. He made a note of Johnson's number and deleted it from his phone.

It didn't occur to Smith at that point that if Cherry and Johnson were working together, Cherry would know about the phone call anyway.

CHAPTER 121

Ash stared at the graphic he had on his desk linking the various events and characters. He tapped the dotted line between Crabbs and Cherry. Cherry had told Ella and Ash that Crabbs was an old mate. That at least was a statement that could be tested.

"Ella, have you been able to stir the sludge a little and see what the word is out there with regards to Cherry and Crabbs being good mates?"

"Yes, I was busy sending you a note."

"Come, talk to me."

"Word is, out on the street, that they hated each other. With good reason. Both were in the dog fighting game and Cherry was starting to squeeze into Crabbs' sector. Cherry had been way more successful than Crabbs had anticipated. Open warfare was just around the corner when the toadstools arrived."

"Do you think Crabbs might have been trying a double bluff, hiring someone to come up with a weird hit to keep us off the track?"

"I honestly don't think Crabbs has the finesse to try even a single bluff. The man is a thug and would have wanted to have some direct interface with the operation, so he could observe the suffering he was meting out. No, my gut tells me that someone else did the toadstool hit. But Cherry ran to his first conclusion and set Crabbs and his mates alight."

"Have we any other poisonings on record like this?"

"There are a couple of novels out there about it and apparently Emperor Claudius was murdered that way."

"That's helpful Ella. Normally there's a calling card. Some signature from the killer. This doesn't fit the bill."

"It has the mark of a professional assassination in that respect. I still think we need to expand our range of suspects to a possible group or organisation. Maybe one that has members past middle age as well."

CHAPTER 122

Smith looked up at the CCTV camera in the corner shop as he pondered pocketing the two packets of cigarettes he had in his hand. He weighed up the odds and decided sulkily to join the queue and pay. As he did so, he spotted a new issue of the *Gatwick Gazette* going free on the magazine stand. He picked up a copy and shuffled forwards in the queue, flicking through the pages as he did so, wondering whether there might be more about Johnson.

He saw an article announcing the upcoming masked ball at Brandford Manor. He sneered as he looked at the grinning death's-head features of Lord Percival above the caption announcing the "Glittering Annual Event". He remembered that this was the same place that that bastard Johnson had been at. He bit his lower lip in thought. Maybe he would be at this do as well. They seemed to all be pally pally.

He walked quickly back to his flat, slapped the *Gazette* on the kitchen table and grabbed a beer. He ran his finger under the lines of the article as he pondered his options. Should he tell Cherry or keep schtum? If Cherry was in with Johnson, he'd know about it anyway. If not, Cherry would be keen to know. He picked up his phone and dialled the number.

"Hello Arnie, what a lovely surprise, what can I do for you, me old china?"

"That place that bloke Johnson was at. They've got another do going on. I was wondering if maybe he might be there again."

"How do you know about this Arnie?'

"It's in this local paper thing I got from the corner shop."

"OK Arnie, take a photo of it and send it to me. I'll get back to ya."

CHAPTER 123

Jim stared into his bathroom mirror. He shook his head. Now he had to make a mask. When would this insanity ever end? His painting had strained every creative brain cell in his head to the very limit. Now he had to push his luck again. He went to the kitchen and looked around. He tried on the tea cosy, but it was itchy and had a funny smell. He tried on the pressure cooker pot and reluctantly realised he would have to cut two holes in it for his eyes, thus rendering its pressure function useless.

The wicker laundry basket held brief promise but would have to have its sides cut out to fit on his shoulders. He could see vaguely through the cracks, but eye holes would probably work a lot better.

"This is fucking ridiculous!" he mumbled and walked back into the lounge. There he found Mervyn with a galvanised bucket on his head trying to push a ruler up inside it. "Hi Merv, I see you're following a similar line to me."

"I'm trying to mark where my eye holes need to be. Have you got any ideas?"

"I'm sorry Merv but there's something wrong with the sound. It's like you've got your head in a bucket."

"Very droll Jim, very droll."

"I thought so. Maybe we should put the bucket alongside your head and then let me mark off where your eyes would be."

"Yeah, that would be better, eh? I've stuffed a little cushion up inside, so it doesn't hurt my head."

Having duly marked the eye holes, Jim produced his electric drill and drilled a row of holes along the outlines and bashed out the inside piece. They looked at their handiwork. The holes had a jagged edge that resembled a metallic row of eyelashes.

"It looks rather medieval doesn't it Jim? I rather like that," said Mervyn as he tucked the bucket handle under his chin and peered out through the holes.

"Very Sutton Hooish Mervyn. Right, that's you done, now what the shit am I going to do? We can't all go with pots on our heads I suppose. I'm going to do a Harry and have a look in the loft."

A little later, Jim emerged with a dusty cushion with a smiling pig's face on it. He showed it to Mervyn. "I've always hated this thing. It's got such a smug bloody face, hasn't it?"

Mervyn looked up, blinking through the bucket's eye holes.

"Why the hell have you still got that thing on Merv?"

"I need to make sure I can endure it on my head for an extended period without panicking."

"Hmm, good point."

"What are you going to do with the pig cushion?"

"Dunno. Probably pull out the stuffing, cut eye holes out and pull it over my head."

"If I were you, I'd give it a bit of a scrub before you do. You're likely to catch something nasty from breathing in whatever that thing has to offer."

Jim patted it gently.

"Hmm, you're probably right. Let me de-gut piggy first."

Jim stepped into his back garden and disappeared briefly in a cloud of dust as he briskly bashed the cushion. He then set about cutting its lower seam open, allowing its insides to flop onto the ground. Then he cut out two holes where the pig's pupils were. Heeding Mervyn's warning, he gave the cover a good shake before pulling it over his head and stepping back inside to look at himself in the mirror.

It was quite difficult to see much as the eye holes weren't very well aligned to his eyes, but the reflection told him enough to know that much work was still required. The head was sadly deflated and a fold below his head gave him the resemblance of a cod.

Mervyn, now bucket-less, looked at Jim. "You look a bit alien Jim. I think your head needs some padding."

After a few scrunched-up newspapers and several cottonwool pads had been stuffed up inside the cushion and around the sides of Jim's head, they returned to the mirror.

"I now look like the elephant man. Bugger it, that will have to do. I hope Harry and Terence are having more luck."

Terence, despite his artistic talent, had little imagination to call upon with regards to his mask challenge. Remembering a badger cull protest he had taken part in, he found the papier-mâché badger head he had used and placed it on the mantlepiece until needed. The whole process had taken some forty seconds.

Harry, unfortunately, was not so blessed. Not only did his own mask creation loom in front of him, but Rebecca's as well. He was sure his own low standards of expectation were not shared by her Ladyship. Maybe it was time to call in some professional help. He recalled seeing a fancy-dress shop at the quiet end of the local high street and decided to pay it a visit.

A little later that day, he was in front of the shop. He was hesitant to enter, having always judged people who frequented such shops to be introverted, unstable and macabre. He was wary that such places fell into the same category as tattoo parlours, clairvoyants, taxidermists and occult specialists. He took a deep breath and walked in.

The shop doorbell loudly announced his arrival. The assistant looked up as he entered. She was short and swarthy, with pale blue eyes that stared at Harry in a way that made him want to run. She looked him up and down unsmiling.

"You want to be someone else," she said, in an accent that Harry hoped didn't come from Transylvania. Harry couldn't make out if she had issued a question or a statement of fact. Her manner was disturbing his already nervous disposition badly. He looked around anxiously as grotesque rubber masks returned his gaze amongst bizarre harlequin suits. In one corner, a horned goat's head with terrible red eyes stared at him malevolently.

"I just wanted a thing for a masked ball, sort of," he whimpered apologetically.

"Many do." She continued to stare at him.

He suddenly had a feeling that somebody was creeping up behind him. He glanced quickly behind him, trying to supress a shudder. "Wha… what do you suggest?" Harry closed his eyes to shut out her terrible stare and jumped as she gripped his arm with her strong fingers.

"Come this way."

Harry shuffled obediently past the ghastly heads, each one more desperate for demonic gratification than the last, all of them past any hope or desire for salvation. He turned a corner as she let go of his arm and pressed her hands to the side of his head.

Harry realised at that moment that this was how he would meet his end. Not at home watching TV or quietly in his sleep, but by his head being crushed between the icy grip of a gypsy's hands, sending him directly to eternal damnation. He closed his eyes, accepting his fate.

"You have big head. Over there will fit you."

He opened his eyes dizzily and saw her pointing to a shelf on the left. By the time he had realised he wasn't going to die, she had returned to her counter. He stood there breathing deeply, fighting off a wave of nausea as he looked up at his choices. There were various classical Regency masks in pink and blue, some with plague beaks attached. There was a Miss Piggy head alongside a Darth Vader helmet. He searched for a Stormtrooper helmet but was disappointed to see that the only one available was on the other shelf and would not fit his "big head". Hastily, he settled for a donkey's head and returned to the counter with it under his arm.

The assistant looked up at him and smiled. "I see you like my Bottom."

A new panic gripped Harry as he looked with horror into her face. Way more terrible than her stare was her smile, laced with lechery, desire for abnormal sexual practices and obvious lustful intent.

"Your Bottom?" he asked in a quivering whisper.

"Bottom difficult to get these days, you lucky I have one for you."

"I don't think I…"

"Will you be going alone, or do you need something more?"

"More?"

"You want more head?"

"No. No head or the other thing. I'm happily married."

"That's nice. How about giving your wife head? Always good for balls."

"What?"

"It would be nice. A surprise, no?"

"That's no, maybe… Um, I'll just take the donkey, thanks." Harry handed over the money.

"I have idea, for a good price I have nice body. I can show you it in storeroom."

"I told you I'm happily married."

"I know, maybe your wife gets head and you both get inside this body I have for you. It is fun, though sometimes a bit hot and sticky."

"No!"

"Yes! My boyfriend and I did it at party. I told him, he had to go in backside of course and everybody watched as we moved around. It was big success."

"My wife wouldn't…"

"OK. But let me show you my body, I think when you see it you will want to get inside."

The vice grip on his arm returned as she led him into a small room at the back of the shop. Cold beads of sweat ran down his back. She stood back and pointed. There, suspended by a coat hanger, were the shoulders, body and legs of a horse costume.

"It's good yes? Think how you and your wife will enjoy."

Harry stared at the lifeless four-legged creature and gripped his donkey head closer to his body. Had he somehow got the wrong end of the stick? His mind ran back to when he had been at Rebecca's place and how he had nearly made an absolute arse of himself there. Without a further word, he turned and ran out of the shop, taking the head with him.

Harry arrived back at his house and put the donkey head down on the couch. As he did so, Sheila walked in and looked at the head.

"So, who's doing Bottom? Please tell me it's not you!"

"I never did anything. How did you know about that?"

"The head, Harry, Bottom, *Midsummer Night's Dream.* Are you into Am Dram now?"

"I don't want to discuss it."

CHAPTER 124

Upon receiving the article about the ball from Arnie, Cherry made a couple of enquiries through a contact and established a general understanding of the way such occasions were organised and supplied. He figured getting into the affair would be a bit of a laugh, and if they were lucky enough to find that Johnson berk there, it would be worth it big time.

He and Arnie should be able to slip on some overalls and become part of the workforce putting up the marquees and such like. Then they would see what they could get away with. It wasn't as if they were MPs or anything like that, just a bunch of toffee-nosed twats, so security would be lax. His only problem was Arnie. He was bloody thick. Never mind, Cherry wasn't, and maybe Arnie's chronic stupidity would prove useful. He decided it was time to put things into action.

Arnie was surprised and then terrified to see Cherry at his door.

"Hello Arnie, me ole mate. Aren't ya pleased to see me? Look, I brought round a couple a lagers. You and me are gonna have a bit of a natter."

Arnie stepped back nervously as Cherry strolled into his flat. He watched as Cherry looked around the place.

"Very nice Arnie, cosy."

Cherry picked up the remnants of Arnie's fish and chip supper from the previous evening, still in its paper, and threw it onto the table, clearing himself somewhere to sit on the sofa.

"I like the ambiance Arnie, retro squalor, if I'm not mistaken. Very nice. Can you open a couple of windows me ole mate? It's a bit stuffy in here."

Smith did as he was told and managed to rattle some windows open.

Cherry opened a can of beer and took a slug. "Help yourself, Arnie don't be shy. I've been thinking about that toffee-nosed ball you reckon that Johnson geezer might be at. I reckon we bust the party and have a bit of fun. What d'ya think?"

"How we gonna do that?"

"We put on some matching overalls, get a toolbox and a plank or two.

Then we just strut about looking busy."

"What we gonna say when someone asks us who we are?"

"I'll make up some foreign language, and you can just say anything ya like. Trust me Arnie, no one's gonna give a rat's arse as long as we behave."

"What if we see the geezer?"

"Johnson? We nail him. If what you say is right, he can handle himself, so we don't want no Queensbury rules punch-ups. Gently, gently catchy monkey Arnie. And if he ain't there, we just grab what we can and have a bit of fun."

CHAPTER 125

Over at Doris's place, Jim sat quietly watching Archie as he stretched on the stool. "I told them about you, I think I made a mistake. They don't seem to understand our relationship. It's a sign of their stupidity in my opinion. Sod them anyway." He looked down at the pig's head cushion case in his hand, stuffed with newspaper and cottonwool wads.

"I wanted to ask your opinion about this masked ball thing we're going to. I've made this head, but I'm not sure if it's good enough. I'm not sure that I'm capable of doing much better mind."

He put his hands into the cushion and proceeded to lift it gently onto his head. For a while he couldn't see anything. He wiggled it around until the eye holes were aligned. There was a trace of a dusty smell which made Jim sneeze and caused the eye holes to become misaligned again. By the time he could see out once more, the cat was no longer on its stool.

He glanced around the kitchen as the newspaper rustled in his ears. Archie was nowhere to be seen.

"Yeah, I suppose that says it all really." He lifted the head off again. As he did so, he saw Archie's head peep cautiously around the corner of the cupboard.

"That bad, eh? Maybe you're setting the bar a bit high Archie. Mervyn's going with his head in a bucket after all. But I suppose you don't care about him after the sarcastic comments he made about you. I don't blame you. You expect a better standard from me though, don't you?"

Archie walked under Jim's stool whilst giving the cushion head a disdainful glance.

"OK, Elephant Man is out, I get it. I can't say that I'm all that surprised, you're right of course. You got any suggestions?"

Archie jumped back on the stool, sat upright and cocked his head to one side whilst staring at Jim.

"A cat's head! You're right. That would be way more sophisticated, wouldn't it? Here, your chicken is ready."

Whilst Archie munched on his chicken, Jim made a call to Harry. "Hey,

Harry, have you made any progress on that mask thing yet?"

"I'm halfway there. Still haven't done anything for Rebecca yet, why?"

"I'm looking for a cat's head mask. Any idea where I might get one of those?"

"Unfortunately, I do. There is this portal to hell just down the road that has things like that."

"Really! Can I ask a favour? Could you maybe pop down there and get one for me, I'll pay you back when I see you tomorrow."

"You have no idea what you are asking of me. The woman there is a maniac."

"Eh?"

"I'll give you directions, you'll have to go yourself. I'm buggered if I'm going down there again."

"Oh, OK."

Harry continued looking at the phone after Jim had hung up. He had thought over the whole ghastly experience in detail and was convinced that the Gypsy Acid Queen, as he had christened her, was hellbent on dragging him down into the fiery pits of cunnilingus, sodomy and no end of other depraved practices that his overactive imagination had conjured up. And now, he was sending his friend Jim down there as well.

The guilty feeling lingered until it occurred to him that Jim might be able to get something for Rebecca as well. He dialled her number.

"Hello Harry darling, how are you?"

"Er, yeah, hello Rebecca. I was wondering if you had any preferences for the sort of mask you want."

"Oh Harry, I wouldn't dare interfere with that wonderful creativity of yours."

"Yeah, no, but maybe there's something you like particularly? Maybe a favourite animal or something."

"Well, I love dogs, does that help in any way?"

"Um yeah, maybe. Leave it with me."

He decided to call the shop to determine whether the lady had what he wanted in stock. Seeing as he was sending Jim into Hades, it was the least he could do to ensure it wasn't a wasted journey.

"You want to be someone else."

"I was, er, yes, have you a dog head and a cat head there?"

"I have."

"Good." Harry ended the call quickly before she could start talking dirty again. He phoned Jim and told him that they had what he wanted in stock and asked if he would pick up a dog head as well whilst he was there. As he put the phone down, the guilt flowed over him. He couldn't do it. He couldn't let his friend face her alone. He phoned Jim again and told him he would meet him there. It was the least he could do.

Jim arrived early and walked into the shop. The lady was behind the counter and looked up as the bell announced his arrival.

"You want to be someone else."

"No, not really. I was told that you have a cat and dog head available."

"Oh, it was you that phone, yes, I do. They in the back room. You come and try on."

Jim followed her as she walked into the room at the back of the shop. As they went inside, Harry arrived. He opened the door nervously and gazed inside. The lady was nowhere to be seen but he could hear voices coming from the back room. As he moved closer, he could make out her voice.

Inside the room she held up the cat's head and stroked it, pouting as she did so. "You see, such a nice pussy, don't you think? You want to try it, yes?"

"Yes please." Jim held the head up and turned it around to get a good look. "I must say this is great."

Jim pulled it onto his head, "Ooh, it's a bit tight."

"Wait, let me open it up a bit." She took it and adjusted the strap. "There, how's that?"

"Oh, yeah that's perfect," Jim said as he pulled the mask over his head. He walked over to the mirror.

"This is really good."

"Yes, I thought you would like it."

Outside, Harry became increasingly alarmed as he recognised Jim's voice and realised that he was already too late. Jim had fallen for her temptation.

Inside the room she lifted the dog's head. "You want to try doggy now?"

"Why not, it's not really for me but let me give it a go anyway." He put the head on and looked at himself in the mirror. "This is great, look at me." He panted and let out a howl. "It's really fun. I could get addicted to this."

"I so glad you like it, but what about poor pussy, is she not wanted now?"

"Oh, don't worry, That's what I'm really here for. I can't believe I nearly didn't come. My friend can be such an idiot sometimes. This is just what I needed. You wouldn't believe the mess I was getting into trying to do it myself. I tried to knock one up, but the damned thing was all floppy, I'll never try that again. This is way better than anything I could do myself."

"You want more maybe?"

"Hah. I could go on all day. I wonder where my friend has got to? He was supposed to meet me here. Pity, he would enjoy this."

Harry had heard enough. Jim was obviously lapping it up and would rope him in if he had half a chance. He quickly turned and left, closing the shop door quietly behind him.

A little later, Jim paid for his masks and left. On the way home, he texted Harry: *Wow, you missed out on a bit of fun at that shop today. I got some great heads!*

CHAPTER 126

Ash had decided it was time to talk to Cherry again. The man was way too smug; he needed some roughing up and maybe his edgy relationship with Crabbs was the way to do it.

Cherry saw the "invitation" to help with the police enquiries as a red flag waving vigorously. He knew he would have to be careful. Detective Inspector Ash wasn't a dumb cop and that hot Detective Sergeant of his was sharper than she pretended to be. He was shown to the same interview room and sat calmly back in the chair, fully aware that they would be reading his body language through the CCTV.

Ash turned to Ella who was still studying the screen. "Well, there he is – shall we go and rattle his cage a bit?"

"Let's do it!"

Cherry stood as they walked in and smiled. "Detective Inspector Kamau and Detective Sergeant Thompson, how nice to see you both again. Hope you been doing alright?"

"Thank you Mr Cherry, we are doing just fine." Ash slumped into his chair with a sigh. "Mr Cherry, I recall, during our last conversation, that you maintained that Mr Crabbs was a friend of yours."

"Yeah, but he got all stroppy on me. Thought I burnt 'is joint down."

"Are you telling me that before the fire, he was your best mate?"

"You leading the witness Detective Inspector? How should I know what was going on in his nut? I didn't have any problems with him."

"Even though you were competitors?"

"Competitors?"

"You both ran dog fighting rackets."

"Nah, not me. I'd never do that. Is that what Crabbs was up to? Well, I never. Just goes to show how people can surprise ya, eh?"

"So, what were you doing at the establishment where some of your friends were poisoned?"

"Like I told ya last time, we was starting up a social club for the local community. You know, bingo nights, bit of a youth club, that sort of stuff."

"Really? And the sawdust and ring in the middle of this, er, youth club. What purpose was that to serve?"

"We was gonna start with a bit of a circus. You know, give them all a bit of a laugh and all that."

"Of course, what a wonderful idea. And your assistant Arnold Smith would be able to confirm this would he?"

"Probably not, I kept the plans to myself. Wanted it to be a surprise, see."

"Hmm, I see."

Ash glanced at Ella out of the corner of his eye. She stood up and headed to the door.

"Aw, you leaving Detective Sergeant Thompson? Hope it weren't something I said."

Ella went to her desk after giving a written note to the duty officer and dialled Arnold Smith's number.

"Allo."

"Hello, is that Mr Arnold Smith?"

"Who's this?"

"It's Detective Sergeant Ella Thompson, I work with Detective Inspector Kamau."

"What do you want?"

"What were you doing on the night that your friends were poisoned?"

"What do you mean?"

"What were you doing, why were you there?"

"We was getting the place tidied up."

"For what?"

"Can't remember."

"Oh, that's a pity. I tell you what, I've got an idea. Why don't we collect you and help you with your memory down at the station?"

"I've done nuffin' wrong."

"Maybe we can confirm that for you down here Mr Smith."

"Leave me alone."

"You're not refusing to cooperate with a police investigation are you Mr Smith?"

"I need to phone someone."

Ella looked at her phone. The police car had arrived at Arnie's place in accordance with her written note. "I suggest you answer the door Mr Smith. I sent someone around to collect you. We want to inconvenience you as little as possible, so we've provided you with a lift. Isn't that nice?"

Ash watched as the mobile phone Cherry had placed on the table began to vibrate. Before Cherry could reach out to take it, Ash grabbed it and placed it out of his reach.

"Let's leave that for later shall we? I'm sure you don't want any distractions during our little chat."

Cherry watched as his phone continued to buzz.

Arnold Smith bit his lip. Why wasn't Cherry answering? He heard the knocking at his front door. He went to the back door, opened it and ran across to the wall at the end of the small garden. As he landed on the other side of the wall, he looked up to see a policeman waiting for him.

"Hello Arnie, off for a bit of a jog are we?"

Ella walked back into the interview room and gave Ash a slight nod.

Cherry looked from Ella to Ash and back again. He knew he was being played and needed to be extra careful now. "Would it be alright if I used your conveniences?"

"Certainly." Ash watched as Cherry got to his feet and took his mobile phone as he walked to the toilet.

Smith sat in the back of the squad car as the screen on his phone confirmed Cherry was dialling him.

The constable in the back of the car with him looked at Arnie. "Answer the phone Arnie. Don't wanna keep your mate hanging on, do we? Here, let me just put it on speaker so we can all hear, shall we?"

Cherry's voice came on the phone. "Hello Arnie, look me ole mate, if the fuzz come sniffing around, you just say we was cleaning up to start a youth club the night those pizzas got eaten, OK? You got that? You know nothing else, yeah?"

The police constable wrote on a piece of paper and gave it to Smith. He read it out loud and slowly. "What… about… the… dogs?"

"Shut up about the fucking dogs Arnie, you know fuck all, got it?"

"Yeah, alright."

"You alright Arnie? You sound a bit funny."

"Yeah, I'm alright."

Cherry put down the phone.

"Stupid prick," he cursed, and proceeded to relieve himself in the toilet cubicle.

In the police car, the policeman switched off his recording of the call and dialled Ella. He played back the conversation whilst Ash listened in.

They both looked up as Cherry returned.

"So, is there anything else I can help you with today?"

CHAPTER 127

Two days before the masked ball, Jim arranged for them to gather at his place with their costumes for a dress rehearsal. They had all been told to dress in formal wear in accordance with the invitation, along with their chosen masks. He glanced around at the gathered crowd. They all stood there awkwardly with their assorted masks on their heads.

"How long do we have to stand around like this? I fancy a beer."

"They are a bit stuffy, you're right. We need to get practice wearing them for the duration. They are our only protection against being recognised."

"What did you say? I can't hear a thing inside this bucket, it's all echo-ish."

"Sorry Merv, I didn't catch what you said."

"What?"

Harry took his donkey head off. "We've got a bit of a problem haven't we? I can't hear a fucking thing inside this head. It sounds like everybody is talking backwards with their underpants in their mouths."

"Hower ee spoosed to chink?"

"Take the badger head off Terence."

"I said how are we supposed to drink with these on?"

"That's a point. We can't take them off, and I'm buggered if I'm shuffling around at his Lordship's creepy dump without some alcoholic reinforcement."

"I've thought of that, see." Mervyn took a straw from his bucket, bent its flexible bit and proceeded to put it in his mouth whilst sliding his bucket back onto his head, leaving enough straw sticking out below his chin to be dipped into a glass.

"So I have to suck my beer through a bloody straw, do I?"

"You aarf a redder ideee?" mumbled Mervyn through clenched teeth.

Harry looked down. "No, I don't have a better idea, but if I'm going to drink anything through this bloody donkey's head, the straw's going to have to be over two foot long. Damn, I wish I hadn't been so hasty, she made me do a panic purchase."

"The costume lady? I thought she was really accommodating."

"Yeah, I know. Wasted no time getting in there did you Jim?"

"Thanks to your recommendation. If ever I want something a bit, you know, out of the ordinary, that's the place to go, eh?"

"Apparently."

They all took their heads off and made their way to the fridge.

"Where did you get that tux from Mervyn?"

"It belonged to my dad, why?"

"I've never seen lapels that thin before. Very big in the fifties, were they?"

"Very much in now I believe. Is that a soup stain on your right sleeve or a fashion statement of some kind?"

"Eh? Oh shit, I never saw that before, must have been there for years."

Jim leaned against his fridge as he passed out the beers. "Look guys. We all look like shit, but I think it's probably as good as it's going to get. Let's all get used to masking up and getting some beer down at the same time, shall we? Harry, do you think Rebecca would be willing to take us all in her car? It would certainly increase our chances of getting in."

"It would, wouldn't it? I'll ask her. Now how the hell do I get past this bloody donkey nose."

CHAPTER 128

On the day of the ball, they all watched through the windscreen of Mervyn's car as Rebecca's gates opened regally, inviting them up the gravel drive to her house. As they approached, she came out to welcome them, waving as she did so.

"Well, she seems pleased enough to see us all. You must have done a good job of convincing her to put up with us lot as well, Harry."

"Seemingly so. Well, so far so good."

Rebecca walked up to Harry and gave him a kiss on his cheek, then walked over with her hand out to the others as Harry introduced them. "Welcome to my home gentlemen, it's so nice to see you all again. Please come inside, I thought we'd have a nice drink out on the patio before we set off. Bit of Dutch courage and all that. I have to say that Percival's dos can be a tad tedious until one gets warmed up so to speak."

The prospect of a drink certainly cheered up the group and they followed Rebecca through the front entrance to the conservatory at the rear.

"I took the liberty of getting some cider in. I seem to remember that being your tipple of choice at Percival's art thing, but if you'd prefer something else, the bar is over there."

Harry looked around proudly at his friends, eyeing the stone flagon of scrumpy on the table.

"I can assure you that cider will do very nicely Rebecca."

They all settled down and looked out across the garden.

"I must say, you have a delightful place here Reb, er your Ladyship."

Rebecca scowled. "Rebecca, please, Mervyn. And yes, it is nice. I have to say, I'm rather intrigued to see what masks you have. I suspect, they are not all Colombinas or Voltos are they?"

"Oh, no, we didn't do them. Let me show you."

Not having the faintest idea what Rebecca was talking about, Harry got up and made for the car. He returned with a box which he put gently on one of the chairs. "These are what we have."

He lifted out the bucket and gave it to Mervyn, gave the cat's head to Jim, wrestled out the donkey and badger heads and then, with a flourish, held out the dog's head to Rebecca. "Do you like it?"

"Harry, I love it!"

She placed it carefully on her head and went to look at herself in the mirror. "Woof," she barked at her reflection.

By the time she had returned, the rest of the ensemble had suited up. She clapped her hands. "Gentleman, bravo! I knew you would push the boat out. The bucket is absolutely exquisite. I can't wait to see Percival's face when he sees this lot." She lifted her glass of champagne. "Cheers to one and all, this is going to be fun."

Harry watched with growing concern as Rebecca worked her way through the bottle of champagne, mindful of the fact that she was driving them all to the ball in her Range Rover. He piously reached for the flagon of cider and recharged his glass, delightfully unaware that the alcohol content of the cider left the champagne in the dust.

It wasn't until Harry decided to duck to the toilet that he suspected something was amiss. His knees seemed to be suddenly able to bend sideways as well as backwards and forwards. As he returned, he heard Jim begin regaling the story of the lady at the costume shop. Terrified of the ghastly revelations of lust and sodomy that were about to be revealed, he tried to interrupt. Unfortunately, little more than a slur issued forth from his lips. Rebecca turned to look at him briefly, before returning her attention to Jim's story.

Harry felt a trickle of cold sweat run down his back as he slumped back into the chair. Despite his fears, Rebecca was smiling at Jim. By the time Harry had managed to tune in to Jim's story, it was seemingly over. Everybody was nodding in approval. Were they all rampant perverts or had Jim managed to lie his way out of the sordid tale? Harry opened his mouth to speak and then thought better of it and closed his mouth again.

Mervyn, who had remained reasonably silent for a good amount of their time there, started to say something. Harry couldn't be sure whether it was Mervyn's diction or his own hearing that was slurring. He'd never heard of slurry ears before, but he was, nevertheless, struggling to make sense of what Mervyn was saying. Mervyn stopped, seemingly halfway through whatever he was trying to say, and reached for the stone flagon. Instead of pulling out the cork, he seemed to be trying to focus on the label.

"Is swixtin pisent," Mervyn announced swimmingly.

Harry and his friends remained silent, contemplating their situation thoughtfully, until Rebecca stood and, with a determined stance, pointed towards the front door. "Right darlings, I think we should be off. I've a couple more jars of cider in the car to keep us going. Harry, will you be a dear and bring the masks along? I rather think I'll keep mine on whilst we drive there."

"Well, if you're keeping yours on, I think we should all keep you company." And with that, Terence twanged the straps of his badger face as he fastened it onto his head.

Jim, Mervyn and Harry made their way to the toilet, whilst Rebecca went to fetch the car keys.

They then got themselves into Rebecca's car, after a brief interlude of confusion where Mervyn feared he had become a victim of sudden blindness after putting his bucket on backwards. Then, following a rousing cheer initiated by Rebecca, they moved off steadily for the masked ball at Brandford Manor.

CHAPTER 129

Ash hesitated. Should he reveal to Cherry what they now knew about him, or should they hold that as collateral? Ash decided on the latter. "Thank you, Mr Cherry, for your cooperation, but that will be all for now. The constable will show you out."

Cherry stood up and walked out. He'd been rumbled. He was sure of it. Kamau was way too calm. He was being given rope; he needed to be careful not to use it.

"OK, Ella. I presume our old friend Arnie is dying to meet us next door."

"He is indeed. I looked in on him a little while ago. He's looking very ill at ease."

"Is that so? Well, we can't have that now, can we? Let's show him the path to righteousness."

Arnie looked up nervously as Ella and Ash walked in. Unlike Cherry, his ability to control his body language was totally absent. He looked like a trapped rat.

Ash smiled as he sat down. "Mr Arnold Smith, the miracle man who avoided certain death by poison. You're the stuff that legends are made of Arnie, do you know that? Why, I wouldn't be surprised if someone writes a song about you. You must be feeling very lucky."

Smith looked down at the table and sniffed.

"It would be terrible if a man of your fame was to make some tiny error of judgement that would jeopardise his seemingly immortal status, wouldn't it? Imagine, if you can, making one simple mistake like, er, for instance taking me and Detective Sergeant Thompson here for total fucking idiots."

Smith moved in his chair but remained looking down at the table.

"Do you understand where I am going with this Arnie? Let me put it more succinctly – you're fucked. We know it. You know it. And if you don't walk down the path of righteousness, Bob Cherry will know it too. I like you Arnie, I want to help. You've made a couple of mistakes in your life, fair enough, we all have. But you now have a chance to put that all behind you."

"He'll kill me. You want me to rat on Cherry…"

"Hold it right there Arnie – well done! You've nailed it. If you keep schtum, we go straight to Cherry and arrest him for running a dog fighting ring using your recorded phone call as evidence. We then let justice take its course. He'll realise that your evidence is critical, and probably make an executive decision about your future."

"You bastards…"

"Arnie, Arnie, there is another way. A way of sweetness and light. You tell us everything and then go into witness protection. We keep your name out of everything and Mr Cherry goes down on weight of evidence alone. End of story."

"I can't…"

"Oh, but you can Arnie, and you must, because this is one of those limited time offers. It runs out in, let me see…" Ash looked at his watch. "In just under ten minutes. Either way, Cherry goes down. You have to decide whether you want to go with him. As you already acknowledged, if you go down, you'll go six feet under. Well, we'll leave you to decide. When your watch tells you it's half-past, time's up. Have fun."

Ash and Ella stood up and left.

They both went to the screen and watched Smith sitting there. He began to tremble. Bob Cherry was coming to pick him up at his place to go to that manor with all those toffee-nosed twats in just under two hours.

"Now we just watch."

"What do we watch for boss?"

"I want to see if he checks the time."

CHAPTER 130

They were not long into their journey before the second flagon of cider's cork squeaked out with a resounding pop. The mood was upbeat when they arrived at the gate of Brandford Manor. Jim recognised the repulsive butler despite the pinched mealie-mouthed mask he had attached to his head. The butler walked up to car with his clipboard at the ready.

"Name please," he squeaked as he squinted into the car.

"What do you mean name? For goodness' sake, Caruthers, how many people do you know with a dark blue Range Rover who come to your master's gatherings? Get with the programme my good man. Next, you'll be asking us to remove our masks I shouldn't wonder!"

"Well yes ma'am, could you…"

"Rubbish Caruthers, now step back and stop your nonsense. Otherwise, I will have no choice but to have a word with Percy. Now off with you, go. GO!" Rebecca shooed him away dismissively with her hand and drove off as he quickly stepped back to avoid having his foot run over. "I can't stand that man, he's such a snivelling little rat. Pass me that flagon please Harry darling, I need some fortification."

As they drove up to the manor, Harry wondered if his legs would behave. He toyed with the idea of asking if there might be a wheelchair available. Mervyn was wondering if his nose might be bleeding from the action of the bucket on his face during the journey, and Jim was past caring about anything. Only Terence was conscious of why they were there, although even he was finding it difficult to not let the thought slip from his grasp.

Guests were wandering around the grounds as Rebecca and her passengers offloaded themselves. Several children, whose parents were busy enjoying the flowing champagne, were racing around excitedly, weaving between the annoyed guests.

"Really, why do some people insist on bringing their ghastly offspring to a ball, for goodness' sake! I need to powder my nose," Rebecca announced as she set off into the house with some urgency.

Harry held onto the car's bonnet for support as the fresh air coursed through his body. "Bloody hell, I don't know about you lot, but I think I'm a bit pissed."

Jim looked at Harry with amazement.

"I should bloody well hope so. We've polished off three flagons of that scrumpy and I'm ready for some action."

Feeling somewhat bewildered, Harry gazed around and contemplated what form the "action" should take.

"We need to be mindful of our purpose gentlemen," Terence announced, with as much gravity as he could muster.

"Yes, of course," nodded Mervyn, his bucket handle squeaking slightly as he did so.

"Could we have a bit of a heads-up on the purpose thing? You know, just so as to ensure we are all aligned… sort of."

They all turned to Terence and waited.

"Why are you all looking at me?"

"You seem more aligned than we do at the moment Terence."

"Oh, yes, right." Terence cleared his throat and gripped his lapels.

"*We few, we happy few, we band of brothers;*

For he to-day that sheds his blood with me

Shall be my brother;

be he ne'er so vile, this day shall gentle his condition."

There was a long pause whilst each pondered what they had just been told. Mervyn assumed his bucket was filtering out too many words for him to make sense of it. Harry thought his loins had been girded by what Terence had said until he realised it was merely pressure on his bladder. Jim just stared at Terence with his mouth open. "What the fuck does that mean?"

Terence shrugged. "You'd have to ask Shakespeare. I had to learn that whole bloody thing as a kid and have been waiting for an appropriate moment to wedge it into a conversation ever since. This seemed like a suitable moment."

They all looked up as Rebecca came towards them.

"Sorry to leave you so suddenly, nature called you know. Shall we go inside and see what Percy has arranged?"

Harry watched Rebecca's behind swan serenely into the main hall. Rebecca made confident strides towards Sir Percival who was engaged in conversation with somebody in the corner of the room. "Percival, so good of you to invite us. Let me introduce you, er, let me see… Yes… It's Harry the donkey, Jim the English short hair, Terry the badger and my personal favourite, Iron Man Mervyn."

Percival held out his hand limply and shook their hands in turn. Jim had to stop himself from wiping his hand on his trousers. Percival looked from one to the next.

"Er, yes, welcome one and all, where was it again that we met?"

"Oh Percival, don't be such a bore. When have you ever met a badger, donkey, cat or tin-headed man before?! It's a masked ball Percival, everything is a mystery!"

"Er, oh, ha ha, quite so Rebecca. I was just…"

Rebecca had turned her back on Percival to address her companions. "Come, let's have a cocktail. We'll stop disturbing you now, Percival. He's such a busy man you know."

Jim turned to see Percival watching them retreat from his presence.

"Well, thank goodness the pleasantries are over. Now we can all relax and have a good time. I'm so glad you brought your friends along Harry. We can make our own little crowd and don't have to mix with Percival's sycophants. They really are such a sad bunch."

Harry scratched the side of his horse head.

"Can I ask, if you hate it so much, why do you come?"

"Because, dear Harry, there are always one or two people here who are worth knowing and they are as desperate to be rescued from the rest of the crowd as I am. We instantly form a common bond. It makes socialising so much easier."

"Really?"

"Of course. For instance, John Shelby will be here, and he will be very interested in your endeavours."

"Oh, er right."

"Now, what is your tipple? The caipirinhas were delightful last time."

CHAPTER 131

Ash and Ella watched Smith. He wiped his mouth, fidgeted on his chair and kept looking at his watch. Cherry would kill him if he was late.

"Ha, there Ella. Let's see, four minutes to go. So far, so good."

Smith closed his eyes and bit his lower lip.

"I think his brain cell might be booting up. One minute to go."

Smith looked at his watch and then anxiously at the door and then again at his watch. He stood up.

"OK, Ella. Let's go."

Smith stood anxiously watching Ash and Ella come back into the room.

"Time's up Arnie. What a shame. Ella, will you stay with Mr Smith here whilst I arrange to bring Cherry in."

"But you said if I told ya, I'd be alright."

Ash looked at his watch, shaking his head.

"Yeah, what a shame you didn't speak up sooner Arnie. Goodbye."

Ash watched as Smith got unsteadily to his feet and walked quickly out of the interview room.

"Well Ella, I think that's enough police harassment for one day."

CHAPTER 132

As Rebecca and her newly found companions made their way to the bar, Bob Cherry and a very nervous Arnold Smith drove up to the gates.

"Now remember Arnie, you say fuck all. You're dumb, right. You know, not stupid dumb, but dumb like you can't talk."

They came to a halt as the butler came over to speak to Cherry.

"Name please."

"Atkins Plumbing."

"What do you want here?"

"We got a call out. Problem with the caterers' equipment. Emergency."

"What? I know nothing about this."

"Look mate, we came out pronto, sounded serious. If you don't want us 'ere, you'll still get a call-out charge and the problem stays unfixed."

The butler looked at the men; he was about to phone the house, but saw another three cars drawing up behind with guests. "Um, very well, report to the service door at the left of the stables."

"Right you are," smiled Cherry.

As they drove off up the driveway, Cherry turned to Smith. "You see Arnie, you stick with me and you won't go wrong, ole Uncle Bob will see ya right."

They drove up to the house and parked their car as directed. "Right Arnie, you grab that toolbox, I'll grab this wrench and off we go. Just remember, you can't talk, so stay fucking schtum."

They entered the side door and stepped into the main kitchen. The catering staff paid them no attention as they walked past and into the main hall. "Right Arnie, keep yer eyes peeled for that Johnson geezer and look like you're doing plumbing stuff."

Smith looked at the crowd. Everybody was dressed up like an idiot, with a stupid mask on. He made his way over to the bar and crouched down behind some crates. He could see a bunch coming over and heard them talking. One toffee-nosed tart was rambling on.

"...he's absolutely extraordinary John. I have a piece of his work and would dearly love some more. Yes, that's right, Harry Johnson is his name. Just look out for the man with the donkey's head. He'd love to chat to you, I'm sure."

Smith remained where he was until the group had moved on. He then grabbed his toolbox and caught up with Cherry who was making his way towards the toilets. "He's got a donkey's 'ead on. This tart was talking about our bloke."

Cherry was about to remind Smith to shut up, but then made him repeat his story. "Well done, Arnie, you little biscuit. Let's find refuge in the bog and work out what we're gonna do next."

CHAPTER 133

Harry and his three companions propped themselves up in a corner and left Rebecca to socialise.

"You know, maybe, just maybe an opportunity will present itself."

Three young children, all under twelve years old and clearly brothers with shocks of red hair, came up to Harry and smiled at his head. "Hello Mr Horse," giggled one child.

"Hello."

"What's your name Mr Horse?"

"Er, it's Dobbin."

"Can we have a ride, Dobbin?"

"Maybe later."

"OK, we'll come back. I'm Rory, and this is Timmy and Josh." The children skipped off towards the French doors, bumping into a stout elderly man and making him spill his drink. The interchange between the children and Harry had been watched and listened to carefully and covertly by Sir Percival.

Once the children were gone, he strolled over to Harry. "I say, you friends of Rebecca really do have a fine array of masks, I must say."

"Do you think so?" replied Harry, glancing around in a futile attempt to see who was talking to him.

"Absolutely, making me quite envious. Hawa hawa."

"You wouldn't think so if you had your head inside this bloody thing, I can tell you!"

"Oh really? I've got an idea, just for a jolly laugh, why don't we swap heads so to speak – my mask for your head?"

"You've got yourself a deal!" said Harry, as he hurriedly took off the head, blinking blindly as he did so. By the time he had focused, Percival had already placed his head inside the donkey mask and was holding out a classical carnival mask for Harry.

"Ah, thanks, at least my mouth can get to a bottle now." He turned to see who he had been talking to, but Percival had already made off in the direction of the children with a feigned gallop.

Jim came across, holding out a beer for Harry.

"See you're getting chummy with Sir Pervert there. Already swapping masks? Next step, you'll be holding hands."

"What? Was that his Lordship? I couldn't make out who he was. Thanks, I need a beer."

"Why did you give him your donkey head?"

"He said he wanted it, fuck knows why. I was just so bloody glad to be rid of it."

"Hmm, well cheers, here's to opportunity."

Outside in the garden, the brothers looked up at the approaching gallop of Sir Percival.

"Hello Dobbin, can I have a ride now?" said Rory.

"Of course you can. Here we go." Sir Percival lifted him onto his shoulders. "Shall we go for a little ride in the woods?"

"Yes, yippee."

Bob Cherry and Smith watched from the kitchen window as the figure galloped off with the child on his back away from the house.

"There's that bastard! Quick Arnie, grab ya spanner."

They ran out of the back entrance in pursuit. After glancing about, they saw Percival making off into the woods. Nobody was there to see Smith and Cherry as they followed him.

Percival and his rider reached the clearing. "Would you like to see some snakes?"

"Ooh, yes please Dobbin, where are they?"

"Over there in that castle." Percival took Rory off his shoulders and held out his hand.

"Wow!"

Percival opened the doors of the vivarium and stepped inside. "You must cuddle up to me so that they don't bite you."

"OK," said Rory nervously.

"And we must make sure they don't bite you down here. Let me just put my hand there to make sure you're safe. There, that's better, isn't it?"

The child nodded uncertainly as he took in the scene and focused on the reticulated python moving slowly towards the glass.

"Don't worry, he won't bite as long as my hand is down there to protect you."

"No! I don't want to see any more!" Rory wriggled loose and ran out of the door and back towards the mansion.

Percival heard the sound behind him moments before the pipe wrench caved the back of his skull in.

He staggered several steps forwards, bumping into the glass door of the black mambas' cage and releasing the latch with his head as he slid to the floor. Both Cherry and Smith watched the child run back through the clearing. "Don't worry, the kid saw nothing, let's scarper."

Blinded by the light from outside, their eyes failed to notice the dark shadows moving through the open glass door and across the stone floor towards them. As they moved back to check the body of the donkey-headed man, Smith let out a scream. Half a second later, Cherry felt a burning pain in his leg and reached down to grab it. The action excited their aggressors which struck repeatedly at the heads and necks of both Cherry and Smith as they began to writhe on the floor. They both finally managed to stumble out into the woods and fell to the ground in a clearing. Smith turned towards Cherry; his head was pounding and his body tingling. He tried to say something, but the neurotoxin was taking effect and his facial muscles were becoming paralysed. He watched as Cherry lay and quivered, a frothy drool coming out of his mouth. His lungs were starting to fail him as he realised he was going to die in the most horrible way.

Back at the manor, Caruthers the butler and his chauffeur companion discussed their master's sudden departure into the woods with a child in his possession. They assumed correctly that he had planned to amuse himself, and decided to investigate, just in case more amusement could be on offer.

Entering the vivarium, they saw the body of their Lordship lying on the floor, still wearing the donkey head. There was no sign of the child. They stepped cautiously into the gloom. Four black eyes watched their arrival and coldly followed their movements as the men bent down beside their employer.

Their screams went unheard as the mambas set upon them, leaving them to die as well.

Harry was having second thoughts about swapping his donkey head. The deal had caused his Lordship obvious pleasure, something that the man should be denied at all costs.

"I reckon I was a bit hasty. I think I should get my head back. Did you see where he went Jim?"

"He went galloping off towards those kids over there."

Harry went outside and looked around. "Hey, did you kids see someone with a donkey's head?"

"You mean Dobbin? He's taken Rory for a ride in the woods over there."

The thought of a kid being alone with his Lordship sent a panicky shiver through Harry's spine. Without thinking further, he set off rapidly in the direction the children had indicated. In a short while, he recognised the clearing and the folly within which the vivarium was installed. He saw the door was open and cautiously made his way towards it.

He squinted into the dark. "Hello, anybody there?"

He was greeted by a dark silence. He made his way cautiously in and promptly tripped over the body of Caruthers, hit his head on the wall and passed out on the floor.

CHAPTER 134

Mervyn sipped at his drink as he looked around the room.

"Where's Harry?"

"He went to ask those kids if they've seen his Lordship; he wants his head back."

"I hope he doesn't do anything rash. He seemed a bit pissed off when he learnt that it was Percival Pervert who had scored his donkey head."

"Yeah, maybe we should go and see if everything is alright."

Terence, Jim and Mervyn went over to the children.

"Hi, did you see where the man went with the donkey head?"

"Yeah, he went through the trees. Rory here said the man with the donkey head showed him his snake."

"Bloody hell, the dirty bastard's up to his tricks already, let's get over to the vivarium."

The three made their way to the clearing. They peered into the vivarium, letting their eyes grow used to the darkened interior. There on the floor lay three bodies. Alongside was Harry, sitting with his back against the wall nursing his head.

"Bloody hell Harry, what happened?"

Harry gazed vaguely in their direction. "What? Where am I? My head hurts!"

Terence looked at the butler's neck. "Oh my God, he's been bitten!" He glanced quickly at the vivarium door which was lying ominously open. "For God's sake, don't move! The mambas have got out!"

They all froze except for Harry who was getting unsteadily to his feet.

"Stand still Harry!" whispered Terence as he glanced around the room, switching his phone's torch on as he did so. He cautiously shone it around the fallen bodies. "They seem to have gone. Come slowly over here Harry." Harry did as he was told, still rubbing his head.

The three backed out, cautiously pulling Harry with them. Terence glanced around the clearing whilst Mervyn looked at Harry's head. "You've got quite a nasty gash there."

"What the fuck happened Harry? You've nailed the lot of them! How did you do it?"

"Can't remember. I was coming to get my head back after one of the kids said his Lordship was taking Rory for a ride."

"We heard he flashed his dick at one of them."

"Really? I should have known, fucking bastard!"

"Bloody hell Harry, you certainly nailed the bastards!"

"Did I? I don't remember anything after I walked in."

"I've heard of this before," nodded Mervyn. "Blind rage can cause amnesia."

"What do we do now? We need to cover your tracks!"

Jim took off his cat head and gave it to Harry.

"Quick! Put this cat head on to cover that bash on your head and give me that mask. I think our best bet is to just back off and get back to the party. The sooner we get away from here the better."

With no other options being proposed for consideration, they split up and all arrived from different directions.

As soon as they gathered together, Rebecca came over to them. "Come on you guys, you can't just lurk in the corner all day like this. Come and meet my art collector friend. I've told him all about your work, Harry, he's dying to meet you."

In the meantime, Timmy and Josh had convinced their younger brother to show them where the snakes were. Upon arriving at the vivarium, they found the dead bodies and ran back to tell their parents.

"What do you call your movement again Harry?" said Rebecca.

"Er, it's Pessi…"

A voice called out from across the room. "Can I please have your attention. There seems to have been a terrible accident at the folly. I am afraid Lord Percival has been found dead."

CHAPTER 135

Ash read the report as it came in. Some lord had been murdered at his home, and four other people had been found dead. What had drawn his attention to the report was that two of the deceased were none other than Bob Cherry and Arnie Smith. The latter was found still holding a pipe wrench with traces of Lord Percival's blood and hair on it.

The initial investigation found that a further two deceased persons had been found in addition to the lord, Cherry and Smith. Four of them had seemingly succumbed to snake bites. The snake, a black mamba, had not been found.

Ash looked at the pictures. The lord was face down wearing a donkey's head. The other two deceased, both employees, lay beside him with ball masks on their faces. Smith's and Cherry's bodies had only been found some time later in the surrounding wood as a search for the snake took place.

The report also made mention of a blood stain found against the wall. The blood matched none of the deceased.

Ash tapped his pencil on his desk. The whole affair was extremely weird. No apparent motive. Why only one murder? Did the lord try to defend himself by letting the snake out?

A random idea entered Ash's thoughts. "Ella, have a look at this lord's background, will you?"

"OK boss, anything in particular?"

"Yeah, see if he had any sleaze attached."

Within half an hour, Ella had found that there were rumours of paedophilia attached to this member of the aristocracy and to the two employees found dead by his side. Charges had been made several times but had not been brought to court.

Ash swallowed. "Ella, can I please have a list of everybody at that party. Somebody else was there in that room."

They poured over the list.

"Any little old ladies?"

"None so far Ella."

Then Ella's eyes fell upon one name that she recognised. She sifted through the various statements made by the guests and staff. Eventually, there was the one she was looking for.

Statement by Harold Johnson:

I was a guest at Brandford Manor on the night in question. I was accompanied by Lady Rebecca Benjamin Grey, Terence McGrath, Mervyn Pearce and Jim Spoonwall. Lady Rebecca drove us to and from the party. Whilst at the party, his Lordship approached me and told me how much he admired the donkey head I was wearing. I told him that the thing irritated me immensely, so he suggested a swap. We did so and Lord Percival then galloped off wearing the head to speak to a group of children. It was the last time I saw him.

Ella flicked through several more statements and picked up on one by a minor named Rory Branstone.

Statement by Rory Branstone:

The man that looked like a horse took me for a ride through the trees to a castle where he said there were snakes. He put his hand in my trousers to stop them biting me, but I wanted to be back with my brothers and left.

CHAPTER 136

Sheila called out to her husband. "Harry, it's Detective Sergeant Thompson to see you."

Harry stood up as Ella entered his study. "Hello Detective Sergeant Thompson, how nice to see you. I haven't forgotten about you. I have made a start, but it was a bit dangerous, so I've had to make some adjustments. Would you like to see?"

"Could I ask you some questions first?"

"Oh, very well. What can I tell you about it?"

"You were at Brandford Manor the other night."

"Yes, that's right."

"Did you know Lord Percival well?"

"No, hardly at all really. Terrible thing though, I was talking to him a little earlier, just before he died actually. Good heavens, I might have been the last one to see him alive. Is that what this is all about?"

"What makes you say that?"

"Well, in detective stories, the last person to see someone alive always has some significance. They're usually the murderer I suppose."

"Did you murder Lord Percival?"

"No, we exchanged masks. He made off for the vivarium as far as I could determine. I've told the police this but I suppose you know that."

"Did you speak to the children when you had the donkey head on?"

"Actually yes, I did. It was just before his Lordship came to talk to me actually. They asked me my name, and I said it was Dobbin. They wanted a ride. I said maybe later."

"Why later?"

"I wasn't in the mood, that bloody donkey head was making me sweat like a pig and I needed a drink."

"And then what did you do?"

"That's when his Lordship came up to ask me about the donkey head. But I couldn't see who was asking, I was just pleased to get rid of that uncomfortable thing."

"Did you know that Arnold Smith was there?"

"Who?"

"Arnold Smith, the one you keep calling Arnold Lane."

"Eh? Oh, that bastard who wanted to plagiarise my work? He was there? I didn't know that. Everybody had masks on. Not that that would have mattered I suppose, I've no idea what he looks like, we only spoke on the phone. How did he escape?"

"Escape?"

"He must have escaped, otherwise he wouldn't have been at the party, would he? You had him locked up."

"We didn't have him in custody."

"You assured me you had him. I must say I'm rather disappointed Sergeant. Now he's probably going to carry on copying my stuff and no end of other poor buggers' stuff as well no doubt."

"Why do you say he will continue?"

"Well, he's hardly likely to just stop being a creepy little shit, is he? He was probably sniffing around for more ideas at the party. There were quite a few artistic people there according to Lady Rebecca."

"You don't like Arnold Smith do you?"

"You mean Arnold Lane. No, I don't."

"Would you like to see him dead?"

"Hah! Not half… No, I suppose death is probably a bit harsh wouldn't you say?"

"Yes, I would Mr Johnson. I would."

"Do you want to see how far I've got with my sculpture? I've got the smell thing about right I think."

"No, not right now Mr Johnson."

"Oh, I get it. Want it to be a bit of a surprise. Anything else can I help you with Sergeant?"

"Nothing for the moment Mr Johnson, unless there's something else you want to tell me?"

"No, I can't think of anything. I'll let you know if anything pops into my head."

"Yes, you do that Mr Johnson." Ella handed Harry her card.

"No, you can keep it Sergeant. See, I still have your card on the mantlepiece here."

Harry showed Ella out and waved goodbye. Having closed the door, he ran to the toilet and promptly threw up.

CHAPTER 137

Jim, Mervyn and Terence listened as Harry regaled his story of the police sergeant's visit.

"Probably just routine Harry. They are probably interviewing everybody."

"Hmm, they haven't interviewed any of you, have they?"

"Well, not yet. We must make sure that we all keep to the same story. Remember, we just tell the truth about what we did up to the time we went to the vivarium. That bit never happened. Keep telling yourselves it was just a nightmare we had later."

"Do you think she was suspicious?"

"I think she is probably always suspicious, that's her bloody job, isn't it?"

"What was all that business about that other bloke, Arnold somebody or other?"

"Oh, Arnold bloody Lane or whatever he calls himself now, Smith or something. Don't know, she seems a bit fixated on him for some reason."

"Wait a minute." Terence walked over to his coat and pulled out the evening paper. "Look, there's a bit in the paper about it tonight. Nothing new really, but they released the names of those who died of snake bites. Let me look... here they are, er, Caruthers Carmichael, Benjamin Drought, Arnold Smith and Robert Cherry. Could that be the Arnold Lane you were talking about?"

There was a silence around the room. Jim's mind churned as he heard Cherry's name.

"Robert Bob Cherry?!"

"Yes Jim, why, do you know him?"

"Shit gentlemen, I think we might be in over our head. I don't believe in coincidences. First Arnold Lane and then Bob Cherry!"

"Who's Bob Cherry?"

"Another of our, er, let's say people we preferred to see dead, Terence."

"Really? Seems you got your wish. Did you want to bump off Arnold whatshisname as well Harry?"

"No, I only knew him by reputation. Funny though, the Detective Sergeant asked me the same question."

"Really?"

"Yes, I told her that death was probably a bit much, even for him. I didn't know he was dead. She didn't tell me."

"She wanted to see if you knew. Good job you didn't."

"I'm not sure my nerves can take all this tap dancing with the police. I can't help thinking I've already dropped us all in the shit somehow."

"You're doing fine Harry. Remember, we know nothing about the vivarium."

CHAPTER 138

"He mentioned that Lord Percival made off to the vivarium."

"Did he now? What did he say exactly Ella?"

Ella looked at her notes and read them out. "We exchanged masks. He made off for the vivarium as far as I could determine. I've told the police this, but I suppose you know that."

"He didn't mention the vivarium in his statement."

"No, he didn't."

"Do you think he's lying Ella?"

"I don't know, he seems a bit dithery. I can't make out whether it's an act or not. The child's testimony is certainly damning. I think we can rest assured that his Lordship was up to his old tricks again. The fact that the chauffeur and butler were also milling around the vivarium looks pretty suspicious as well, although the child never mentioned anything about them."

"The whole thing stinks Ella. There are layers upon layers of stuff going on here. What the hell Cherry and Smith were doing there, heaven knows. It was certainly away from their normal stomping ground. Why the hell they'd bump off Lord Percy is beyond me, and to do it at his party is asking for shit. It all seems a bit desperate."

"The only person Smith knew there as far as we can determine is Harold Johnson. Remember, he fingered him as a cold-hearted killer. He seemed really scared of him too. It would have made more sense if they had bumped him off."

"Wait a minute, what if they *were* going after Johnson? Maybe they didn't know they'd swapped heads? Maybe, just maybe, they thought his Lordship was Johnson?"

"I must say that makes a bit more sense. But what about all the snake bites, what was that all about?"

"Whoa, Ella, let's not get ahead of ourselves, I'm trying to eat the elephant one bite at a time. The only player still standing in all this is Harold Johnson. Bugger it, let's get him in here and make him fidget a bit."

CHAPTER 139

Harry looked up at the police station entrance with dread. His stomach churned and his knees were not working too well. The night before, the four had gathered to discuss the police interview Harry had been invited to attend.

"Why didn't the Detective Sergeant just pop round again? Why must I go to the police station?"

"I don't know Harry, but just stick to the story. They have no evidence that you were anywhere near the vivarium."

"You don't know that, maybe somebody saw me."

"Harry, remember, you don't remember."

"I know I don't, but that worries me even more. I don't know if I saw the bastard doing something bad with that kid and just lost it and bashed him. Maybe I opened the snakes' door and whistled to them. Shouted out *come and get it,* before banging my head against the wall and knocking myself out. Maybe they've figured all this out and I'm going down for multiple murder."

"Harry, just listen to me, calm down and think clearly. You were nowhere near the bloody vivarium, you don't know about any vivarium, you don't even know what a bloody vivarium is, OK?"

"It's all very well and good for you to tell me to be calm – you're not going before the bloody firing squad, are you?"

Harry was shown to the interview room. There was a mirror that he was sure was two-way, so that they could observe him, coldly analyse his every move. See the lies oozing out of him, watch the guilt leak out of every pore. He looked up with a start as he recognised Ella coming into the room with a tall black policeman behind her. He reminded Harry of an older version of the detective in that TV series, oh what was it – Lucien… Lucifer… LUTHER!

Detective Sergeant Thompson smiled. "Thank you for coming in Mr Johnson. This is Detective Inspector Kamau. He is working on the Branford Manor case with me."

"Hello sir," Harry ventured, very aware that his mouth could dig him into an endless prison sentence, with horrible people who would deliver torment, anguish and buggery in unbearable quantities.

"We'd like to ask you about the events following the swapping of masks between you and the deceased, Lord Percival Brandford-Smythe."

Harry nodded, looking at each of his inquisitors. His nodding made him feel slightly dizzy.

"What can you tell us about the vivarium?"

"The what?" he asked, remembering Jim's advice from the night before.

"The vivarium."

"What's that?"

"The place you told me you saw Lord Percival going towards when I spoke to you at your house the other day. The bit of information you didn't mention in your statement."

Harry felt a warm movement in his bowel and realised that he should have made sure he had gone to the toilet before the interview. He considered passing out, he considered running for the door, he considered soiling himself and realised that the only option really open to him was the last one.

"Could I please go to the toilet sir?" he heard himself say, in a voice that reminded him of being back at school.

"Eh? Sure, it's down the corridor on the left."

Ash watched as Harry rose very carefully to his feet and shuffled slowly to the door, clenching his buttocks as tightly as he could.

"I'm not sure Ella, but I think he might have just shat himself. I wonder if it's just his condition or whether our question caused him some anguish."

"I suppose we will only learn that on his return."

Harry shuffled with care to the toilet. He was very relieved to see that the cubicle was unoccupied. He didn't have a lot of time.

He sat pondering his situation and came to the conclusion that the only tool he had at his disposal was dithery confusion. An aid he was finding available in large quantities of late. He returned to the interview room at a normal pace.

"Thank you, Inspector, that was very kind of you."

"Don't mention it Mr Johnson. Now, where were we? Oh yes. The vivarium you mentioned to Detective Sergeant Thompson the other day. How did you know Lord Percival was going there?"

"I didn't. I just assumed he would. Why wouldn't he? He owns it you know."

"How do you know about the vivarium?"

"Everybody knows about it don't they? It's famous for the, er, vivarium things it has in it."

"Really, like what?"

Harry closed his eyes tightly. Should he know that there were snakes in it or not?

"Rare reptile things of all kinds."

"Why did you say earlier on that you didn't know what a vivarium was?"

"Did I? I don't remember."

"Did you like Lord Percival?"

"Didn't really know him. Knew of him a bit, of course."

"What did you know about him?"

"Er, um, oh his charity, stuff, fondling with kids. Er, I mean fond of kid… er, children."

"Are you suggesting that Lord Percival abused children?"

"Why would I say that about Lord Perv… Per… cival?"

"I thought you just did. Did I hear you wrong?"

"Oh yeah, absolutely, I would never say that about that ba… bard of a man. Wonderful person our Lord Percival is. He would never fondle children, never, perish the thought. And neither would his toe rags, I mean two regal… servants."

"Do you know Bob Cherry?"

"No, never heard of him or Arnold Lane."

"Who?"

"Arnold Lane, the bastard you let go so he could come sniffing around. He was at the party, wasn't he? The Detective Sergeant here said so."

"Why do you think Arnold Smith and Bob Cherry are associated Mr Johnson?"

"Both are pieces of shit."

"How do you know Bob Cherry?"

"Never heard of him."

"Then why do you call him a piece of shit?"

"Well, he must be if he knows Arnold Lane."

"Did you kill them, Mr Johnson?"

"No, don't think so."

"Aren't you sure?"

"Not really sure of anything really. I mean, is this reality? Are you really here or is this just my imagination working overtime?"

Harry sat back and felt the hammering of his heart starting to subside. He was wandering into more familiar territory now. "I mean, everything is relative, or so Einstein tells us."

"Did you kill Lord Percival because he was a child molester?"

"Oh, I thought it was Arnold Lane and Bob Cherry I was supposed to have killed. Did I take out the lord and his sidekicks as well? Probably, I don't know. It's amazing what one can accomplish after a couple of flagons of cider at a party. Any other buggers I've bumped off maybe? I must have been on a bit of a roll, I must say."

"How did you get that gash on your head Mr Johnson?"

"Eh?"

"The gash on your head, how did you get it?"

"Your wind chimes hit me."

"I'm sorry?"

"And so you should be. I was doing it for free. Ask the Detective Sergeant here, she knows. I was going to show her but she wanted it to be a surprise. They need gearing down. I haven't done that, but the smell is just right."

"Can we keep to the subject of the party Mr Johnson?"

"I was quite happy to, but you brought up my sculpture, so I presumed you wanted to know how it's coming along."

"We were talking about the gash on your head."

"So was I. It was very sore at the time I can tell you. I have to admit I cursed you people a little, actually a lot. I want to apologise for that. It wasn't right, it wasn't your fault any more than everybody's deaths at the party was mine."

"Could you excuse us for a minute Mr Johnson."

Ash stood up and indicated for Ella to follow him out of the interview room.

"Bloody hell, is he always like this? I can't work out whether he's fucking us around or whether he really is a dithery old fart."

"I told you didn't I boss? He is a bit of a handful."

"My bloody head hurts. Bugger this, let's get a DNA sample from him. I need some solid evidence."

CHAPTER 140

"You mentioned the vivarium?!"

"I'm sorry guys it just slipped out. I'm not very good at this."

"Do you think they are on to you, Harry?"

"They asked me if I killed Lord Percival. They even reckon I killed Bob Cherry and that bloody Arnold Lane arsehole."

"This is ridiculous, we can't let Harry take the rap like this, we must get them off his back."

"Are we going to start rubbing out the fuzz now?"

"Don't be an arse, Mervyn. We merely provide Harry here with a cast iron alibi. We tell them that he was with us the whole time in the manor. With a bit of luck, we might even get Rebecca to confirm that."

"Maybe we should just leave you guys out of it."

"Rubbish Harry. Remember, we are the musketeers. One for everybody and, er, all for somebody or something like that. The next time you get a call from them, we all go in together."

"Why wait for them to call? We must move onto the offensive. Attack is the best form of defence!"

"You're right Mervyn, but we're going in together. I think you should do most of the talking. You're the calmest amongst us and the least likely to lose your temper."

"Guys, I'm still not sure this is a good idea."

"Shut up Harry."

Ella walked up to Ash's desk. "Johnson is here and he's brought along a posse."

"A what?"

"There are four of them down there. They say they were all at the mansion and have important evidence to present."

"Really? Well, let's go and see what we have. Get some more chairs in there Ella."

Harry and his friends sat in a row on one side of the table. All except Harry had adopted a stern expression. This was where the nonsense would end.

As Ella walked in, they all stood to attention, with a couple of groans accompanying the action.

"Please sit gentlemen. I am Detective Sergeant Thompson and this is Detective Inspector Kamau."

"We understand that you have certain information in regard to the Brandford Manor case."

Mervyn rose slowly to his feet, cleared his throat and tucked his thumbs behind the lapels of his jacket. "Indeed, we do. I know that I speak for all here today when I express the sincere gratitude and admiration we all have for the police force. Their undying dedication is to be applauded. I would like to think that each of us would willingly give whatever assistance one could to support their sterling efforts to bring crime to book."

"Thank you, so why…" interjected Ash, but Mervyn was on a roll.

"Why, only the other day, I observed one of your fine constables going about his duties in a firm but measured manner, and I thought what a credit to the force this fine young man is and how lucky and indeed privileged we are to know that we can sleep soundly in the knowledge that all is well in our community, thanks to that fine gentlemen and his colleagues.

"It is therefore in this spirit of willing cooperation that I would like to point out that my companion, Mr Harold Thompson here, had nothing to do with the death of Lord Percival Brandford-Smythe. I know this to be a fact because I killed him myself."

There was a brief silence as everyone looked at Mervyn.

"You sneaky bastard, I see what you're doing. He's trying to take the blame because he hasn't got long to live Inspector." Terence groaned to his feet. "I killed him not Mervyn."

"Crap, it was me. I did it like this," said Jim wrapping his hands round Mervyn's neck as he did so.

"The inspector knows that it was me. Stop making arses of yourselves," said Harry, as he resigned himself to his fate.

"How did you kill him?" asked Ash quietly.

Everybody fell silent as Harry looked at Ash.

"What? Well, you know. I gave him the old one two and then put the boot in, sort of thing."

"And you three, did you kick him to death as well?"

"Yeah, all of them."

"Why are you doing this Mr Johnson?"

"They're bad people."

"No. Why are you lying?"

"You don't know that. I don't know it either. I could be telling the truth."

"I beg your pardon?"

"I can't remember what I did because I hit my head when I fell over something in the vivarium."

"Why were you in the vivarium?"

"He wasn't, I was."

Ash turned to Mervyn. "Could you please be quiet for a moment."

"I was worried what his Lordship was doing with that little kid."

"Why would you be worried?"

"Because the bastard was a sick fucking pervert. That's why."

Ash leaned back in his chair.

"Thank you, gentlemen. Now we're getting somewhere."

CHAPTER 141

"There is a DNA match between Johnson and the blood stain on the wall of the vivarium."

"Thank God for that Ella. At least something supports what Johnson has told us. Let's look at what we've got. Johnson says he tripped over something in the vivarium, possibly Lord Percival's dead body. It looks like he was killed by Smith and Cherry, possibly because they thought he was Johnson. The snake door was opened either accidentally or on purpose. It was almost certainly done before or during the assault on Lord Percival. I can't imagine Cherry and Smith hanging around inside there for long after they crushed his skull with the pipe wrench, and the snake had to have had time to bite both of them before they left.

"The child saw nobody but Lord Percival in the vivarium before he left. So the butler and chauffeur probably arrived later. Almost certainly after Cherry and Smith had finished with his Lordship, otherwise there would have been a scuffle. They probably found Lord Percival's body and were attacked by the snake whilst there.

"Whether Johnson arrived before or after they did, heaven knows. The fact that Johnson was not bitten could have been because he arrived after the snake had left or because, having hit his head and passed out, the snake ignored him, much as it ignored Percival's body."

"OK, so what did Johnson do when he came round? Just stumble back to the party? He must have seen the bodies lying everywhere. You'd have thought that he would have raised the alarm, wouldn't you?"

"Hmm. There are definitely still a few layers to be peeled back. That bunch of Johnson's friends are certainly no lifelong buddies of Percival that's for sure. I wonder what they were really doing at that party?"

"Maybe a visit individually to them might yield something."

"OK, no harm in trying. I'll go this time."

CHAPTER 142

Jim was taken aback to see Ash at his doorstep. He led him into the lounge. "Hello Inspector, have you come to arrest us?"

"Why do you ask Mr Spoonwall, have you done something wrong?"

"Well, we did all confess to a murder at your offices the other day."

"Yes, indeed you did."

"Would you like a cup of coffee Inspector?"

"Yes, thank you, no sugar."

Whilst Jim was in the kitchen, Ash glanced casually around the lounge; something caught his eye. He went over and gently took the object from the mantlepiece, turning it over as he did so.

Jim came back into the lounge holding two cups of coffee. He nearly dropped them when he saw the Inspector holding the three-legged platypus in his hands.

CHAPTER 143

When Mervyn returned from the shops, he found Jim in a state of crisis. The Inspector had left a few minutes earlier.

"I told you to get rid of it didn't I? What did he say?"

"He said something about it being a very nice platypus and how it was such a pity one of its feet was missing. I told him that that was why I was able to pick it up so cheaply from a car boot sale a couple of days ago."

"That was quick thinking Jim."

"Hmm, I'm not so sure he bought it though. He seemed to be in deep thought."

"What about the zapper thing in the shed? You need to get rid of it. I don't think the *picked it up in a car boot sale* story is going to wash so well with that thing of yours unless you're planning to explain that's how you cook your steaks these days."

"Shit, you're right. I'd forgotten about that. Chucking it into the river is a bit risky. Maybe I should dismantle it into little bits and bury it somewhere. Maybe take it to the tip."

"Did he say he was coming back or what?"

"He didn't say very much at all. Didn't ask me any questions either, just drank his coffee and then upped and buggered off."

"You should dump the platypus as well."

"That's going to look a bit suspicious now. I think we have to just play dumb for a bit longer. Let me get the zapper dismantled. I reckon once it is back in its component parts, it will be fairly innocent. You want to help Merv?"

"Not really, I am still trying to get the sight of that burning head rolling towards me out of my mind."

"That was a very brave but very stupid thing you did at the police station, Merv. I don't really know what to say. You fell on your sword for Harry."

Mervyn shrugged. "It was a bit of a spur of the moment thing really. I conjured up the speech pretty much as I sat there and it just seemed like such a logical thing to do."

"Have you had any more check-ups, Merv?"

"Whoa, what's the date?"

"Er, it's the 17th today."

"Gee, Harry, I completely forgot, time has been flying past. I have an appointment tomorrow!"

CHAPTER 144

"Front right foot Inspector," said the lab technician.

Ash put down the phone slowly. It had to belong to the platypus in Spoonwall's flat. No coincidence was that stretched. He could well have bought it at a garage sale, but Ash's spider sense was telling him loud and clear that that was a load of bullshit. Why would Spoonwall lie about it unless there was something to cover up?

He was also sure Johnson knew more about Bob Cherry than he was letting on. The problem was that trying to get to the truth was so very difficult when your subject and his mates were all hellbent on confessing to a murder they almost certainly hadn't committed. Why would they be more than willing to take the rap for that, and yet be so evasive about the other connections? Maybe they were just a bunch of dithery old farts.

He decided that another chat with Johnson was necessary. He also decided that a meeting at Johnson's home was likely to yield more than a chat at the station. Ash looked up as he saw Ella approaching with a docket in her hands.

"Hi boss, not sure if this has any bearing on things, but I've been making some cross-reference searches. One of Johnson's buddies, Jim Spoonwall, his name popped up as a witness to some guy dying when he was run over by a truck outside his house. The guy was part of a gang trying the old loose tile racket apparently."

"Hmm, another scumbag bites the dust. Ella, I think I should pay Mr Spoonwall a visit. Want to come along?"

CHAPTER 145

Jim peeped through the curtains as he heard the doorbell ring. His heart jumped as he recognised Ash and Ella. "Hey Merv, those two bloody cops are at the door, what should we do?"

"Pretend we aren't here. Sit tight."

The doorbell rang again.

"There's definitely somebody there boss, I saw the curtains shifting."

Ash pounded on the door. "Come on Mr Spoonwall, we know you are in there."

"Shit Merv, they must have seen me peeping."

Ash smiled as Jim opened the door with a pre-prepared clenched grin on his face. "Ah, there you are Mr Spoonwall, hope we aren't popping by at an awkward moment. Can we come in?"

"Er, yes, no. I was just out the back."

"Of course you were." As Ash stepped into the lounge, he saw Mervyn sitting rigidly in a chair looking as if he had seen a ghost.

"Ah, Mr Pearce isn't it?"

"Yes Inspector," squeaked Mervyn as he jumped to his feet, rubbing his hands together as he did so. "I, er, um, am staying over for a while. I'm having some work done on my house."

Ella watched as Jim scowled at Mervyn, shaking his head slightly.

"Really Mr Pearce. What are you having done?"

"Eh? Oh, er, I'm having a new fireplace put in, yes, that's it, sort of thing."

"I need a new fireplace at my house, who is doing it for you?"

"Um, er, can't remember."

"Do me a favour and find out for me. I would love to see the finished job if I may. You get so many chancers these days. I presume you would recommend the ones you are using?"

"Er, yes, I mean no. They're terrible."

"Oh, why not?"

"Expensive and making a mess sort of thing, yes messy, that's why I'm here."

"Dearie me, that's terrible. They should be ashamed of themselves. I tell you what. Why don't you let us pop round there and give them a scare, off the record of course. It's terrible how some of these outfits take advantage of our senior citizens."

"No, you can't do that, they haven't started yet."

"They haven't started and yet they've made a mess already?!"

"You can't talk to them."

"Whyever not?"

"He's my friend. Brother. He's my brother."

"And you don't know his name?"

"I'm dying you know."

Jim stepped between Mervyn and Ash. "Would you like a coffee Inspector? Sergeant?"

"Thank you Mr Spoonwall, that would be very nice."

Ash made towards Mervyn but Jim sidestepped to block him. "Could you both come with me to the kitchen please?" Jim held out his hand and waved Ash and Ella into the kitchen. "He's delusional. He's staying with me for his own sake so I can keep an eye on him."

"That's very nice of you."

"What can I do for you Inspector?"

"I'd like to know how you and Bob Cherry were connected."

"Who?"

"Bob Cherry. Mr Johnson didn't like him very much."

"Never heard of him."

"Why did you guys go to Lord Brandford-Smythe's place?"

"We were invited."

"Oh, I see, who invited you?"

"Rebecca got us in."

"Rebecca?"

"Er, Lady Rebecca, er, um, whatshername."

"Big friend of yours is she?"

"Harry's friend really. You want milk?"

"Yes please. Why did you want to go along?"

"Eh? To keep Harry company."

"But surely he had Lady Rebecca to do that? Why the four of you?"

"We don't get out much, it seemed like a chance to have some fun."

"At a place owned by somebody you hated?"

"Hated?"

"Yes. Mr Johnson told us he was a, let me see, *a sick fucking pervert.*"

"Oh right, we were desperate. Mervyn's dying you know."

"So I gather. Everyone keeps telling me that. How did the man get run over outside your house?"

"What, the one trying to steal my tiles? How do you know about him?"

"How do you know he was stealing tiles?"

"I saw the bastard up his ladder in my driveway."

"So what did you do when you saw him?"

"What, I, er, dunno. Can't remember."

Ella looked at her notes. "You told the investigating officer that you heard the lorry's brakes and only then came out to investigate."

"I was a bit confused. It was very disturbing. But Doris, the little old lady from across the road, can confirm what really happened."

"And if we asked this Doris what happened, what would she say, Mr Spoonwall?"

"I don't know. It's all a blur now. I was very distressed."

"What distressed you? The man stealing your tiles, or the fact that he died?"

"Bastard deserved it," said Jim through gritted teeth.

"He deserved death because he stole some tiles?"

"No Inspector. He deserved a bloody medal for being such a fine, upstanding citizen. How the hell do you put up with all this lowlife getting away with murder – literally in some cases? Smugly smiling into the cameras, waffling on about how abused their fucking rights have been. There is so much scum floating around in society, and they all seem to thrive. In the meantime, we have to pussyfoot around, stoically accepting our fate whilst we hear about prisoners' bloody rights and fifth amendment bullshit. They should all fucking die, slowly and painfully."

"Are you by any chance helping that happen, Mr Spoonwall?"

"If only I could, Inspector. If only I could."

Ash turned to look at Ella, but she had walked back into the lounge to engage with Mervyn.

"And if you could Mr Spoonwall, would you?"

"Yes Inspector, I fucking would… But we both know that I can't, don't we?"

Ash looked into Jim's eyes as he sipped his coffee. In the lounge, he could hear another conversation taking place.

"I used to be a pharmacist at the hospital before I retired. Now I live alone. Well, when I'm not here with my friend Jim, that is."

"That must have been an interesting career."

"It was as boring as hell, counting tablets here, counting tablets there. Occasionally, someone would appear with an ailment that needed my skills, but most of the time it was about as exciting as a wool shop."

"Really. Can I ask your advice? I sometimes suddenly get a loss of appetite."

"Tricky, we'd need to ascertain the underlying reasons for it. A natural remedy would be garlic strangely enough, boiled in water, which stimulates the digestive system. It would also have the benefit of keeping other people at a distance whilst you tuck in."

"I bet, and recurring migraines?"

"Again, try to remove the cause. Migraine is often triggered by certain foods or dehydration. Triptan is usually prescribed for the pain associated with them."

"What if somebody had ingested *amanita virosa*, what would you prescribe?"

"*Amanita virosa*? I would suggest an intravenous drip of benzyl penicillin be given."

"What is *amvnita virosa* anyway?"

"*Amanita virosa*? It's a toadstool, its common name is destroying an…"

"Sorry, destroying what?"

"Er, don't know, forgot. It happens a lot now, I'm dying you know."

"We all die eventually Mr Pearce, just like that poor old platypus."

"I know nothing about the platypus, nothing at all."

Ash walked back into the lounge with Jim close behind him.

"Can I ask why your friend seems hellbent on trying to be found guilty of murdering Brandford-Smythe?"

"Harry's innocent, he didn't do anything," said Jim.

Ash turned to Jim. "I know that he is innocent of murdering Brandford-Smythe. Have you ever heard of Charlie Kerns, Barry Brumpton, Derrick Dunston…?"

Ash had been watching Mervyn's face, and the mention of Derrick Dunston caused him to twitch.

"Do you know any of them, Mr Pearce?"

Mervyn shook his head violently. "No, never heard of him. Derrick Dunston, never heard of him."

"And the other names, do you remember their names?"

"Er, no."

"Do you ever take the stairs at Covent Garden station?"

"I'm sorry Inspector, stairs?"

"Don't worry. It was a long shot. We have to be going, thanks for your time and the coffee. Goodbye."

As they walked out, Ella turned to Jim. "What number did you say your neighbour Doris lives at?"

"No.12, over there." Jim pointed across the road.

Jim watched Ash and Ella as they climbed into their car and drove away.

"I don't think I can stand Jim. My knees are shaking so much."

"They are onto us Mervyn. It's only a matter of time now."

CHAPTER 146

Jim couldn't relax. Mervyn had gone for his check-up, or "final curtain rehearsal" as he'd called it. The meeting with the cops the previous day had rattled Jim and now he was pacing up and down, agonising over how to deal with a sad Mervyn. He wondered why they insisted on him having check-ups when he had already been condemned to death. It was a bit like dragging a prisoner on death row back for another trial every so often. It was actually cruel.

His heart missed a beat as he heard the key turn in the lock of the front door. Mervyn was back. He stood in the middle of the lounge and waited, drawing in his breath as he did so. Mervyn walked in unsteadily.

"Hello Jim," he wheezed. "I need to sit down."

Mervyn lowered himself very slowly into the chair and stared across the room. Jim sat down and, finding nothing to say that seemed appropriate, remained silent.

Eventually, Mervyn looked up with tears in his eyes. "It's gone."

Jim looked at Mervyn. "I'm sorry Merv?"

"The cancer. It's gone. There's no trace of it. The oncologist said that it is rare but does happen. They don't really know why."

"Merv, that is… unbelievable… I'm sorry, I mean, of course I believe it – but, wow! You're gonna live!"

"It's a funny feeling Jim. I should be overjoyed, but I am actually battling to come to terms with the fact that I am not going to die. At least not yet, with a bit of luck."

"Do the guys know? Have you told them?"

"No, I've told nobody but you."

"Fuck that Merv, this calls for a celebration." Jim picked up his phone and began dialling.

"Maybe tomorrow, Jim. I just need to sit it out today I think."

"Sure Merv, but I need to tell Harry and Terence, they'll be over the moon!"

"Yes, I suppose so," said Mervyn, lost in thought.

CHAPTER 147

Ash and Ella stood back from the investigation board that showed the names of all the deceased. The blurry picture of the old lady in the stairwell at Covent Garden station was pinned up along with the names of Harry and his three friends. Three features were newly added: destroying angels had a new line to Mervyn's name; there was a line from Jim's name to the tile gang member; and a line from Jim, via a platypus, to Derrick Dunston. A line also connected Mervyn's name to Derrick Dunston's.

"They are terrible liars," said Ella, shaking her head. "Mervyn clearly knew about Derrick Dunston."

"They are… or are they? I can't help thinking we are being played. That outburst from Spoonwall about how all criminal scum should die hardly seems useful if you are trying to cover your tracks."

"I had a message from Johnson today informing me that his latest creation is ready for installation at the station as soon as we are ready to receive it."

"What did you say?"

"I've said nothing boss. I don't know how to reply."

"Have you told the Chief?"

"No, I haven't – wouldn't you like to bring it up? You're my senior after all."

"Ha, nice try. He already thinks I'm as useful as a one-legged man at an arse kicking party. If I told him I'd organised a pile of whirling things that stink for the foyer, I'd be binned forever. You're bright and on the up. You have a way better chance of getting away with that than me."

"Shall we go and visit Auntie Doris at No.12?"

"Maybe you should go alone Ella. She might be more comfortable with just you there."

When Doris eventually opened the door, she was dressed in a pinnie with her hair in curlers and a pair of woolly slippers on her feet.

"Sorry, I was out the back me darling. What can I do ya for?"

Ella held up her ID. "I'd like to ask you some questions with regards to the incident involving a pedestrian who was run over outside."

"Ooooh, it were horrible. 'Is head was all squashed. You wanna come in Sergeant?"

"Yes, thank you, I won't take up much of your time."

"No worries me dear, time is what I got a lot of. Can I make ya a cuppa?"

"Yes, thank you. Milk no sugar." As Doris disappeared into the kitchen, Ella looked around the lounge. As she did so, she became aware of a large white cat watching her.

"Hello there. Is Auntie Doris a nice mummy?" Ella watched as the cat appeared to shrug before purposely going to the front window and gazing longingly across the road towards Jim's house.

Doris returned with a tray of tea and biscuits. "That's Archie, me cat."

"He's lovely." Ella watched Doris bend, put the tray down on the table and glance round at Archie behind her. As she did so, Ella had a moment of déjà vu.

"Do you have cats Sergeant?"

"No, spend too much time at work to make it fair. Can I ask you what happened the day the man got run over?"

"Well, I was over at me neighbour's place across the road dropping off the keys so he could look after me cat whilst I was away. We 'eard this noise outside and came out to see what was going on and saw the bloke all squashed. The fuz… er, police, arrived very quickly, just before the ambulance took him away."

"Do you know what the man was doing there?"

"What, on the ground? Dying I suspect."

"No, I mean before that."

"The lady at No.18 said they was ripping off people with the old loose tiles scam."

"Did you, or anybody else, see them up a ladder doing anything, maybe?"

"Dunno, don't think so."

"Which neighbour were you at when you heard the accident?"

"I was at Jim's place at number seven. He looks after me cat when I'm away."

"That's nice of him, do you have to go away a lot?"

"Now and then."

"Well, thanks for the tea. I must say you have a lovely home. Do you get help in?"

"What, ya mean cleaners? Nah, do it all meself. Don't like strangers going through me stuff."

"Well thanks, that's about all. Thanks for the tea. It was lovely. Bye bye Archie." The cat looked up at Ella, sporting a disapproving look as it did so.

As Ella drove back to the station, she pondered the déjà vu episode she had as Doris bent down in front of her. What was it? Why did it seem familiar? Try as she may, she could not place it.

CHAPTER 148

Despite Mervyn's preferences for solitude, Harry and Terence were at Jim's house within minutes.

Mervyn felt bewildered by his reprieve but gave in to their desperation to celebrate. He allowed himself to be dragged, not exactly screaming, off to the pub. Pints were ordered and whisky chasers were lined up, thus ensuring that everybody would suffer to the same depths the following day.

"Well, here's to Mervyn, the Lazarus of the hour. A man who stood at the edge of the abyss, gazed into its fiery depths and then stepped back saying *not today thank you.*"

"That's all a bit dramatic Jim."

"Coming from you, that's rich. I've still got your confession speech at the police station in my head."

"Oh hell. I was gambling on a sure horse that I wouldn't make it to prison, but now I probably will."

"Bollocks Merv. That detective guy doesn't believe that you, me or any of us did anything."

"Well, speak for yourself there Jim. I still don't remember what happened in that bloody vivarium."

"Water under the bridge Harry. It's a new dawn for Merv here. I suppose you'll be stepping back from our vigilante variety show now, won't you Merv?"

"No, I won't. I've felt more alive since we first caught sight of Bob Cherry than I have for most of my previously boring life. I think we should step on the go-faster pedal and never look back."

"Well let's drink to that. Mervyn the Formula One Vigilante, carving them up at every corner."

CHAPTER 149

"So, Ella, what did Auntie Doris have to say?"

"She corroborated Jim's original statement almost to the word. I'm not sure if I am becoming paranoid but something didn't sit right."

"Like what?"

"She gives the visual impression of being a shuffling old granny but underneath, there is a strength that belies her appearance."

"How so?"

"I don't know, it's small things. I flashed my ID at her. She looked at it very briefly, no squinting, no glasses but she addressed me by my rank straightaway. When she bent to place the tea tray down, she did so like a weightlifter, no groans, no slow rise up and, I know this sounds funny, but there was no musty smell in the place or on her. She smelled of Joy, subtly applied."

"Joy? You mean she smelled happy?"

"No, Joy. The perfume by Jean Patou. It was my mum's favourite perfume, over six hundred quid a bottle the last time I looked."

"So, she saves up her pension and treats herself."

"Yeah maybe. I guess I'm just seeing something that isn't there."

They walked into the ops room and Ella glanced at the investigation board. She grabbed Ash's arm.

"That's it, the déjà vu!" said Ella, pointing at the picture of the old lady coming up the stairs at the tube station.

"What?"

"As I watched Doris bend and place the tea tray in front of me, she glanced quickly around at her cat. It reminded me of the CCTV footage of the old lady coming up the stairs and turning suddenly to watch Brumpton run down past her. The movement was very quick for an old person. It looked out of place."

"Are you saying that Auntie Doris is our assassin?!"

Ella shook her head. "I don't know what I'm saying, but just like

Johnson's mates, Doris doesn't quite fit the bill. Maybe I just need to get away from it all. I think I might be hallucinating."

"Rubbish, my spider senses are tingling as well. Every time we pop in to see any of this crowd, something weird happens. Maybe we should pop around again."

CHAPTER 150

Jim stood at the bench in his shed. He looked proudly at his zapping device, nodding contentedly at the professional looking grommets he had inserted to prevent the cables from fraying. It had been built to last and stand the test of time. If the thing had been getting ragged or had a battered look about it, it would have been easy to terminate its existence, but it truly was a work of art, a piece of engineering excellence.

He looked at the angle grinder in his hand and switched it on. The tool twitched in his hands as it reached full speed. He moved the spinning disk towards the zapper, but he couldn't do it. It was sacrilegious. He switched the angle grinder off and stood in deep thought as the disk came to a halt again. "Fuck it," he muttered under his breath. There had to be another way, another place. A place where this beautiful thing could be preserved for his private pleasure, a place where nobody else would ever think to look.

Mervyn was at the shops, so he would have time to place the device in the loft whilst he formulated his plan. He lifted it onto his shoulder and marched back towards the house. As he did so, he saw Mervyn walking down the garden path towards him.

"Hi Jim, I forgot my shopping list and, just as I arrived back, the Inspector appeared and asked if he could have a word."

Jim looked beyond Mervyn just in time to see Ash walk out of the back door and into the sunlight, squinting slightly as he did so. "Hello Mr Spoonwall, I hope I haven't come at an inconvenient time," smiled Ash, as he focused on the zapper machine in Jim's hands.

Jim looked from Ash to Mervyn; both were looking intently at the zapper, the former with a look of curiosity, the latter with a look of undisguised horror.

"What's that Mr Spoonwall?" asked Ash in an attempt to start with some small talk.

"What's what?"

"That thing you're carrying. Is it some kind of hedge trimmer or something?"

"Yes, hedge trimmer, that's it. Nothing to…" But before Jim could finish, he heard Mervyn squeaking out in a falsetto that it was "a steak flamer, makes beautiful rare..." They both fell silent and looked at the floor.

Ash looked from Jim to Mervyn and then back to the zapper. He made a step towards it, holding his hand out as he did so.

Jim clutched the thing to his chest. "No, don't touch it," he stammered.

"Why?" asked Ash innocently.

"It's mine... er minding its own business... er, I mean, umm..."

Mervyn stepped between the two men. "He made it Inspector, he's very possessive of it. He won't let anyone touch it. Not even me. Look." Mervyn held his hand out towards the zapper.

"No, er, go away," mumbled Jim with less conviction than he would have liked, but his nerves were failing him.

"You made it?" asked Ash as he cocked his head at the device to get a better look.

Jim pulled instinctively away, wrapping his hand tightly around the device and trying to shield it from the Inspector's enquiring gaze.

"Yes, he did," ventured Mervyn, now regaining some courage. "But he still has to patent it, so he has to keep it very hush-hush you see."

"Hush-hush you say?"

"Yes, Inspector, top secret. There are terrible people out there. Why, only the other day poor Harry discovered somebody was trying to steal his artistic ideas. Your Detective Sergeant told him all about it and how you had him in custody and everything."

"We did?"

"Yes, absolutely, very impressive I must say." Mervyn turned to go back into the house. Ash began to follow him after gazing over his shoulder just in time to see Jim running back towards the shed with his device clutched tightly to his chest.

"Did I hear you say that the hedge trimmer also cooks steaks?"

"What? Oh, er, yes, that's what makes it so sought after, sort of thing."

"But why would anybody want to...?"

"Wonderful concept, isn't it?"

"No, not really. I don't get it."

"Well, ours is not to reason why Inspector. Cup of tea?"

"Coffee if I may. I was rather hoping I could have a word with both of you." Ash glanced back towards the shed.

"Yes, of course. I don't think Jim will be long. He just needs to put the zapper away."

"Zapper?"

"What?"

"Is that what you call it?"

"No, I don't really. How did you… I'm not dying anymore you know."

"Really? I'm very relieved to hear that. Ah, here comes Mr Spoonwall. Managed to hide your 'zapper' did you?"

Jim gave Mervyn a filthy look. "It's just a prototype, we've never used it on anybody's body. It's just for self-defence. We are old and need protection from all the filthy scum out there…"

Mervyn was shaking his head at Jim but it was too late. The man had panicked.

"You want to use a hedge trimmer/steak cooker for self-defence?"

"What?"

"I was telling the Inspector that I'm not dying anymore."

"What?"

Ash took a deep breath. "I was wondering if we could have a chat and clear up a couple of loose threads from our talk the other day?"

The three of them walked inside and Jim went off to make the coffee and try to get his hands to stop shaking. Mervyn walked into the lounge and took a seat, smiling weakly at the Inspector who was now opening his notebook.

"Derrick Dunston, how did you come to know him?"

Before he could stop himself, Mervyn was on his feet. "Er, um, yes, Mr Dunston, er, old Derrick Duh…"

Jim had entered with a cup of coffee and placed it on the table.

Mervyn pointed at the Inspector. "The Inspector was asking us how long we had known old Derrick."

"Derrick who?"

"You know, our mate, Derrick Dunston."

"What do you mean, mate? I would never be mates with a crawling chunk of dog shit like that."

Ash looked from one man to the other. "So, you do know him then?"

"Derrick fucking Dunston was the sort of lowlife none of us should have to share this planet with Inspector. Sub-human bloody pond slime."

Mervyn's jaw had dropped down further and further as his friend let his hatred run away with him. It was too late to go back now, so he joined in with Jim's theme in the hope that Jim knew what he was doing.

"Ha, yes, of course, I was being cynical when I said he was our mate. He was a horrible creature and we hated him, didn't we Jim? He deserved the zapping that what was coming to him, foul oxygen breather that he was."

Jim and Ash both turned to look at Mervyn.

"Zapping?" said Ash as he wrote something in his notes. "And how did this zapping take place Mr Pearce?"

"What? Er, um, I, er, it's good news about me not going to die, isn't it?"

"Absolutely made my day Mr Pearce. Now, how did this zapping take place exactly?"

"Can't remember."

"Hmm I see, and what about you Mr Spoonwall? How's your memory doing on the subject of zapping?"

"Don't know."

Ash bent down and picked up his coffee. "Look gentlemen, do you really think I believe this bullshit? You're up to something. And it isn't his Lordship's death, so don't feed me that line of crap. I'm going to be crawling all over you like a bunch of crabs on a dead fish until you fess up to what is really going on. Do I make myself clear?"

Mervyn and Jim looked at each other.

"Right gentlemen, I'm going to leave you now with this thought. The next time we meet, and we will be meeting soon, I want the truth. I don't want to hear any more about Mr Pearce's health, as wonderful as that news might be. I want to hear the truth and nothing but the truth. Does that sound familiar?"

"I will see myself out gentlemen and this time, the platypus is coming with me." Ash went to the shelf, carefully slid the platypus into a plastic bag, turned and let himself out.

Mervyn looked down at the cup as he heard the front door shut behind Ash.

"I should have burnt it, Merv."

CHAPTER 151

Ash sat opposite Ella in the coffee shop.

"So that's what happened Ella. I have no idea what my little ultimatum might produce. I had the platypus checked against the leg we have. They match perfectly. It ties those guys to that place where Dunston was fried. To be perfectly honest, I'm not sure I'm ready for any of it, true or not. I have this gutfeel that there is some real sick shit floating about out there."

"Actually boss, I have to agree."

"Hmm, I'd rather take a good old psychotic murder scene steeped in gore than what I suspect lies in wait for me with this lot. Any more news on the deaths at the manor?"

"We've been invited to an inspection of Mr Cherry's house."

"Really? That's the first I've heard of that, when did that come through?"

"I overheard the Sergeant telling the Chief earlier this morning."

"Bloody hell, why wasn't I told? Is everything on the fucking secrets list?"

"Sorry boss, I thought you knew."

"Come on Ella, drink up. I want to get there before everybody stomps all over the place."

When Ash and Ella arrived at Cherry's place, they were stopped by a policeman at the door after they flashed their IDs. "Sorry Detective Inspector, the Chief gave strict instructions for nobody to enter the house until he arrived."

"The bloody Chief has obviously got fuck all to do these days," Ash said quietly to Ella. "So, what are we supposed to do in the meantime Constable?"

"There's Mr Cherry's car over there, Sir, maybe you could start there? Here's the keys."

Ash glanced over his shoulder and saw the Jaguar parked in the garage. He shrugged. "OK, what the hell. Come on Ella, let's see what it feels like to sit in a Jag."

The car smelt of fine leather. It didn't smell like a felon's car; it smelt of the finer things in life.

Ash instinctively started looking under the seats, opening the boot and lifting the carpet. He was running his hands down the side of the spare wheel when he heard Ella's voice.

He went round to where she was sitting in the passenger seat. There in the cubby hole was a mobile phone. She held it up with gloved hands and slipped it into a ziplock bag before putting it into her handbag.

A further search yielded nothing other than a betting card from several days ago. "Pop that in there Ella."

They sat inside the car as they waited. Eventually, Ash went back to the Constable. "Sorry Sir, the Chief said he will be delayed by a couple of hours."

"Did you tell him we were waiting here?"

"No Sir, he didn't ask. Sounded like he was a bit rushed Sir."

Ash walked back to Ella. "He won't be here for another couple of hours for fuck's sake."

"Don't worry boss, you go back to the station, I'll wait."

"Thanks Ella, I owe you one, probably many."

Ella held out the plastic bags with the mobile phone and betting slip.

"I'll keep you to that. Here you go."

Ash took the bags and walked off back to the car.

By the time Ash had arrived back at the station, the Chief had already left. He sat and looked at the mobile phone in the plastic bag; he put on a pair of gloves and switched it on. He made a list of all the calls. All outward calls were made to the same number. There were two incoming calls, the first was a pin marking a place in Mile End. The second was a voice message.

"*Our friend is available after 10 tonight.*"

Ash replayed the message several times, the voice was unmistakable.

CHAPTER 152

"What the hell were you thinking Jim? Please tell me the zapper is history now."

"I can't just make it disappear now Merv. The Inspector's going to be very suspicious if I suddenly dump it when it's ready to be patented and everything."

"Not half as suspicious as he is going to be when he finds out your hedge trimmer doesn't have a blade in sight but can deliver a million volts in any direction."

"What are we going to say?"

"Say it blew up on its subsequent trials so you have scrapped it and gone back to the drawing board or something. But whatever you do, get rid of it."

"It's such a nice piece of engineering, the case fits so nicely and everything."

"Right, that's it. It's still in the shed, isn't it?" said Mervyn as he strutted out into the back garden.

"What are you going to do?"

"I'm going to kill it."

"Look Mervyn, you must be careful, it might fight back."

"Just let it try."

Jim stopped and slumped onto the garden bench. He felt a lump grow in his throat as he heard the angle grinder start up and heard the sickening sound of it munching its way through the hapless zapper. The grinding continued for some time until there was a large flash.

"Shit!" Jim, wrenched suddenly back from his deep mourning, ran towards the shed.

Inside was Mervyn with the angle grinder now silent and trails of smoke rising from where his shirt had been singed.

"It fought back," mumbled Mervyn, in a state of shock.

Jim looked down at the badly mauled zapper, fizzing sulkily on the bench, and realised he would have to put it out of its misery. He gently prised the angle grinder from Mervyn and, with tears in his eyes, gently said, "It's OK, Mervyn, I can take it from here. It's only right that I carry out the coup de grace."

CHAPTER 153

Ella closed the car door and returned to sit on the wall outside Cherry's house and wait for the Chief. She looked up towards the Constable at the door. "I wonder why the Chief wants to be here."

"Dunno. Just between you and me, it's a bit of a pain. We could have been done and gone ages ago. We know what we're doing, it's not like the forensics are needed or anything, he didn't die here."

"Yeah, I know. When were you told to hold off?"

"We got the word before we even left the station to not let anyone in before he got here."

Ella's phone began to buzz, it was Ash. "Hi boss, I'm still waiting."

"Have you told anybody what we found in the car?"

"Not yet, why?"

"Good, let's keep it to ourselves for now. Don't wait any longer, get out of there now before the Chief arrives. I'll meet you at the coffee shop, OK?"

"OK boss, if you say so."

Ella saw Ash with two cups of coffee at the table and went straight there after a side look at the tempting pastries. "Hi boss, I must say this is way better than sitting on a wall outside Cherry's house."

Ash waited as Ella took a sip of her coffee. "I want you to listen to something." He pulled out Cherry's phone and gave it to Ella. "Listen to that message."

Ella put the phone to her ear and listened. Ash saw her expression change. "Do you recognise that voice?"

"Yes of course, but I don't under…"

Ash took the phone back and brought up the map with the pin on it, then gave it back to Ella.

"This came from the same caller."

Ella stared at the pin locating a place in Mile End. "Where's that?"

"I'm not sure yet, but I'm willing to bet it's where Crabbs' safe house was.

I know it was somewhere in Mile End. Bit of a coincidence, eh?"

"Ash, you're not suggesting he told Cherry where Crabbs was hiding?"

"I didn't suggest anything. You just came to that conclusion on your own."

"There must be some other explanation."

"I'd be pleased to hear it. Explains the other weird things going on lately though, doesn't it?"

"FUCK! Sorry. What are we going to do?"

"First, we forget all about the phone. We'll just hand in the betting ticket. I need to think very carefully about our next move. I don't want to put you in any danger."

"Danger, what do you mean?"

"Just keep it to yourself, OK? Let me deal with any fallout that occurs. I told you nothing about any phone, the only thing that you are aware of is the betting slip, OK?"

"OK boss, got it."

CHAPTER 154

"So, what do we do when the Inspector comes to call again?" The four companions sat in deep thought around the fire burning in Jim's grate.

"I think we are out of our depth. He knows we are talking bollocks."

"Maybe, but can he prove it?"

"Well, the zapper got stripped down to its component parts and its bits sent to various different dumps around town. Sort of hung, drawn and quartered really."

"Yes, but now he has that bloody stupid platypus. They will certainly match that to the foot. That is what is going to sink us in the end."

"I'm sorry guys, it's my fault."

"What about the answers to the other questions?"

"Like what?"

"Did we kill Pervy Percy?"

"We all say yes, that seems to drive him mad."

"OK. But I'm not sure we want to make him angry."

They all nodded thoughtfully.

CHAPTER 155

Ash sat in Chief Superintendent Riley's office watching his boss's back as he stared out of the window.

"So, nothing new on the Crabbs case yet?"

"No boss, not yet."

"I hear you were sniffing around at Cherry's place yesterday, why?"

"Crabbs and Cherry had history, I thought I might pick something up."

"And what exactly were you planning to pick up Ash? A couple more dead badgers that had been used as deadly assault weapons? I left strict instructions for Cherry's place to be uncontaminated until I arrived, but I see you chose to ignore that. You and Detective Sergeant Thompson decided to go stomping around despite my orders."

"The car wasn't included in the off bounds instruction boss."

"Neither were you given clear instructions not to shit at the entrance to the station, but that doesn't mean you should pull your pants down at the first opportunity, does it?"

Ash watched the back of his chief's head as he continued to look out of the window.

"What did you find Ash?"

The question was loaded. It gave no room for a negative answer.

"Just a betting ticket."

"Nothing else, eh?"

"Nothing else."

"OK, you can go."

Ash walked out, aware that he had been clenching his teeth so hard that his jaw ached. As he went back to his desk, Ella came up to him. "Boss, we need to talk."

"Not here."

The coffee shop was full of young people. Ash glanced around. "What sort of jobs do all these people have?"

"They probably ask the same question about us."

"What is it, Ella?"

"Have you thought about where we go from here?"

"I have, but no conclusions yet."

"I think we have to go to the Independent Office for Police Conduct."

"I know. I just have a gut feeling that I am exposing you to danger."

"Hey Ash, if we can't trust the IOPC, who can we trust?"

"Yeah, I suppose you are right. Let me deal with it. The less you are involved the better."

Ash waited until he was back at his house before he made the call.

CHAPTER 156

Ash glanced up into the air as he came out of the Canary Wharf tube station. The tall buildings shone brightly against the clear blue sky. It seemed to Ash that the scene so belied the slimy situation that brought him there.

He was shown into an interview room and was brought some coffee. A man came in and introduced himself as Chief Inspector Willis. Ash sat down and, after a brief explanation of how he came upon it, handed over the phone. There was no going back now. He had pushed the boat out to sea and would now have to keep rowing.

In the next few days, he became increasingly anxious that no feedback had been received from the IOPC. Had it just been brushed under the carpet, left on the back burner or was his input just no longer required? They had made it clear that they would only make contact if they required additional information from him. But still, he felt he had lost control of the steering wheel of a heavy truck travelling at high speed.

He and Ella kept off the subject completely and in his statement to the IOPC, he had made no mention of her at all. It therefore came as an unpleasant surprise when Ella mentioned that she had just been contacted by the IOPC and invited to go in for an interview.

Ash's senses were immediately on high alert – why Ella specifically? How had they made a connection? Who had they spoken to who had provided them with that link? "Remember Ella, when we both searched the car, you found the betting slip and I told you to put it in the evidence bag, just as it happened. Just remove all thoughts about that bloody phone. I actually wish you had never found the damned thing."

"Don't worry boss. I have it covered."

On the day of her interview with the IOPC, she was shown into the room by a young officer who introduced himself as Inspector Tony Routh. He questioned her about the search that took place and she answered accordingly with regards to the betting slip.

"And the phone, where was that found?"

"I'm sorry, what phone?"

"The phone that DI Ash Kamau discovered and handed to me in this office."

"I'm sorry, I don't know anything about any phone."

"OK, Sergeant, thank you for your cooperation."

Ash had just finished the phone call from Ella during which she updated him about the interview when he received an invitation to return to the IOPC "at his convenience".

On arrival, Ash was introduced to Inspector Routh by Chief Inspector Willis. Willis wasted no time with pleasantries. Ash had hardly sat down before he began speaking. "How long have you and Detective Sergeant Thompson been working together DI Kamau?"

"About four years now." Ash gripped his leg with anticipation under the table, he knew what was coming. How could he have been so stupid? Too late now.

"Why did you fail to mention that Detective Sergeant Thompson accompanied you when you searched Mr Cherry's car?"

"I found the phone, not her."

"Why didn't you tell Detective Sergeant Thompson about the phone that you discovered in Cherry's car?"

"I felt that discretion was required, seeing that the Chief Inspector had given instructions that the house should not be searched."

"Really? Discretion you say? Don't you trust Detective Sergeant Thompson?. Did you think that she was somehow complicit?"

"Complicit in what?"

"Complicit in the complaint that you have levelled against one of your senior officers, DI Kamau."

"No, of course not. At the time of the phone's discovery, I had no idea what evidence existed on the phone."

"Indeed, which leads me to wonder why you would have been so 'discreet', as you put it, about said phone when you had no idea what information it contained – or did you?"

"I had absolutely no idea what information it contained."

"And yet you decided to dig around in its memory instead of handing it in as would have been normal procedure. Why was that?"

"I am currently investigating a breakdown in witness protection security and judged that my investigation warranted accessing the phone."

"Is that right DI Kamau?"

"Yes, that is right Chief Inspector Willis."

"Does my line of enquiry irritate you DI Kamau?"

"No sir, it does not."

"I am very glad to hear that DI Kamau, very glad. When did you access the phone?"

"Immediately upon returning to the station."

"In a bit of a hurry were you?"

"I saw no point in delaying the investigation."

"And you say that you recognised the voice straightaway?"

"Yes."

"And yet you then took… let me see, two days before contacting us. Why so long?"

"I wasn't sure how to proceed."

"Really DI Kamau? I would have thought a man of your experience in the force would have known exactly what path to follow. What were you afraid of?"

"I was shocked to discover that my superior was involved and needed time to work out the best plan of action."

"In my humble opinion, very little has ever shocked you DI Kamau, and I don't believe for one minute that you were uncertain of the proper procedure going forwards. I suggest to you that you are covering somebody's tracks. I don't know whose or why but I hope for your sake that the person you are covering for is on the right side of the law."

Ash just stopped himself in time before assuring his interviewer that she was.

"Thank you DI Kamau, that will be all for now."

Once Ash had left, Willis turned to Tony Routh and nodded.

"You're right, he is probably covering for her. Probably just trying to protect her, but let's do a little background research on DI Kamau, just to be sure. It is not beyond the realms of possibility that he conjured this whole phone thing up. I did some research of my own and there is certainly no love lost between Kamau and Riley."

CHAPTER 157

"Did you sleep alright last night, Merv?"

"No Jim, I kept dreaming that the Inspector was hiding in the bedroom cupboard trying to read my thoughts."

"Yeah, I didn't sleep well either. All this shit is way beyond my pay grade. I'm going to contact Jeremy. We need to be strapped into our chairs and given one-word instructions."

Jim closed his eyes and breathed in before he read the reply from Jeremy telling him where to meet.

"Please, don't let it be somewhere shitty," he whispered in pious desperation.

He read the message: *The Meat Co. a South African Restaurant in White City.* He breathed a sigh of relief as he had read the reviews. It was a while since he had munched a good steak. South Africans were generally intolerant of ropey meat so he made sure that he was subsequently ravenous when he saw Jeremy waving at him from the table.

"We are getting smothered in police sergeants and inspectors crawling through every orifice of our lives at the moment," Jim related, as he shook his head in resignation.

Jim related the situation in some detail.

"I really fancy a nice juicy steak. The last time I sank my teeth into a nice chunk of meat was after we'd let loose with the Zapper. I think I mentioned it last time maybe."

"Yes, you did. Do the police have any tangible evidence or witnesses that you are aware of?" asked Jeremy.

"Not really, don't think so. He just keeps saying that he knows we are lying, and we must start telling the truth."

"Hmm, I took the trouble of making some enquiries, and, unless I am very mistaken, Detective Inspector Kamau and Detective Sergeant Thompson are going to be occupied with more pressing matters for a while to come. My advice would be to lie low for a while."

CHAPTER 158

"Have you come up with anything on our DI Kamau yet Inspector Routh?"

"No sir, he looks clean, definitely old school though. A bit rough around the edges. Subtlety and finesse are definitely missing from his tool bag. Has had some run-ins with his superiors for going beyond the call of duty shall we say."

"How so?"

"There were rumours that some punks in the nineties were hung by their feet over a tall building until they would divulge where they had some girl holed up as their sex slave."

"Really? I'm beginning to like him more and more. Is his boss here yet?"

"Yes sir, he has just arrived."

"Good, inform Superintendent White and let's see where this takes us, shall we?"

They stood up as Superintendent White walked in.

"Good morning, Chief Inspector Riley, very kind of you to take time out to help us with our enquiries."

"No problem at all. I have a lot to do as I'm sure you can appreciate."

"Of course, Chief Inspector, please take a seat. You have no objections to us recording this interview I presume?"

"I was not aware that this was to take the form of a formal procedure."

"Is that so Chief Inspector?"

Superintendent White nodded to Inspector Routh who switched the recorder on and recorded the date, time and those in attendance.

"Do you know Robert Cherry?"

"I know of him of course."

"You arranged a search of his property."

"Yes, it was a routine search following his demise under suspicious circumstances."

"Would you classify this case as one of high priority?"

"No not really. He was a local gangster."

"Would you mind explaining why you sealed the property from your own people until your arrival?"

"We have had some sloppy work performed with searches of late and I wanted to make sure there was not a repeat of this."

"Could you tell us which cases in particular were below standard?"

"I would prefer to deal with such matters within the station. I do not want this to become an IOPC matter."

"When did you last speak to Mr Bob Cherry?"

"I have never spoken to Cherry."

"Are you sure?"

"Of course."

"Not even unintentionally?"

"I have never spoken to Cherry."

"Did you find anything at Mr Cherry's house?"

"No."

"Nothing at all?"

"Nothing of importance."

"What were you looking for?"

"Anything that could place him at the scene of the crime."

"I would have thought that his body being at the scene of the crime was pretty damning evidence, wouldn't you?"

"There might have been evidence linking him to a motive."

"Really, so which was it? Placing or motive, you seem a little confused."

"I'm not confused. It was both."

"Well, thank you Chief Inspector, that will be all for now."

Riley was shown out by Tony Routh.

Superintendent White turned to Willis and winked.

"I think we struck a bit of a nerve there, what do you think? Do me a favour and see what you can find out about sloppy searches conducted from his station. I think we should have a bit of a chat with our DI Kamau again."

CHAPTER 159

Harry stepped back and admired his work. The wind chimes had been calmed by the introduction of a rheostat to control their speed. He had thought about fixing the speed at dead slow, but a bubble of adventurous devil-may-care spirit had taken hold of him. So now, should it be desired, the speed could be increased by means of a lever.

The smell of the ancient arcing motor filled the spare bedroom where the masterpiece had been born. The time had come for it to be placed in its final resting place at the police station. He could only imagine the sense of anticipation that it would generate amongst the staff as it was placed in the entrance hall.

Ella looked down at her phone and recognised Harry Johnson's number. She answered the phone immediately, hoping that he and his friends had considered Ash's ultimatum about the truth and were ready to come clean.

"Hello Mr Johnson."

"Hello Detective Sergeant Thompson, I am about to make your day. I'm ready."

"I'm so glad to hear that. Detective Inspector Kamau will be very relieved to hear that too. Can one of us come round or would you prefer to come to the station?"

"Good heavens no, I will come to you."

Ella called Ash over. "That was Harry Johnson, he's decided to come clean."

"Well saints preserve us, let me know when he arrives. Book the interview room and make sure the recorder is up and active. Progress at last."

Harry drove up with his creation carefully separated into its component parts in the boot and on the back seat. He parked across the road and went into the station. Ella saw him approaching and called Ash to the interview room.

"Would you like a cup of coffee before you begin, Mr Johnson?"

"Yes, thank you, that would be very nice."

Ash walked in and sat down.

"Good morning, Inspector. I understand you are also looking forward to what I have for you."

"Yes indeed Mr Johnson. It is going to make my day, I can assure you."

"I have broken it down into its component parts, otherwise it becomes too complicated to deal with."

"That's fine. You can just tell us about it in whichever way you wish."

"Thank you. I have to say, just between you and me, I'll be glad to let go of it. It has been a bit of a burden."

"Well, all of that is about to change. I'm sure that you never planned for things to turn out the way they did," said Ash, hoping he was easing the way towards Johnson's confession.

"No, you are right. I had no idea that I would be capable of such things. Even now, looking back, it's hard to believe that I actually managed it."

Ash looked up as Ella brought in the coffee for Johnson. "Why don't you just tell us how it all started?"

"Oh really? OK. Where should I begin?"

"At the beginning."

"When I first heard what we were going to do, I wasn't sure I could go through with it. I had no previous, er, what do you call it…?"

"Convictions?"

"Confidence I suppose. The others were far more willing to just pile in and have a go so to speak."

"By others you mean Mr Spoonwall, Pearce and McGrath."

"Well, Jim and Mervyn anyway. Terence had been at it for yonks."

"Go on."

"Well, the first thing was to work out how to carry out the job itself. I knew that being a bit of an amateur at it, the chances were it would be a bit messy. As it turned out, it was way more of a horror show than I could ever have imagined." Harry shook his head and gave a little chuckle.

Ash felt a shudder run down his back. "How did you select your target?"

"Didn't really have a target or end goal. It was all a bit random really. We made it up as we went along. We all had our own special approach. Old Merv with that woman with a knife sticking out of her back, Jim with those little dead bodies all over the place and me with that hairy little bugger with his arms and legs ripped off. It's quite hilarious when you think about it isn't it?"

"What did you do with them after you were finished?"

"I think Merv's and Jim's wound up in the dustbin. I was lucky, I made a killing. It made me feel great. That's what made me realise I might as well have another go." Harry lifted his thumb and smiled.

Despite herself, Ella was starting to feel a bit queasy.

"So, there have been more?"

"Jim and Merv haven't had any more goes that I know of. I think I'm the only one who's still going strong so to speak."

"When was the last time you…?"

"Knocked one out?"

"Yes."

"Well, that's why I'm here, isn't it? It's my little contribution to society."

"What is?"

"My latest job. I took the same approach as before, you know, identified some piece of rubbish and became creative. Actually, my wife helped in the selection of the subject matter. She has more of an eye for it really, bless her."

"Your wife helps select your victims?"

"Ha, my 'victims'. Yeah, she spots garbage long before I do."

"How did you execute the latest one?" Ash winced; as hard as he was, Johnson's manner was getting to him. He recalled how Arnold Smith had referred to Johnson as a "fucking psycho".

"Didn't really have to do much, you know. The eyes were pushed into the head. I just had to apply some electrical current. This one actually fought back, would you believe – look, I've still got the scar." Harry enthusiastically pointed to his forehead. "Personally, I think it was the smell I liked the most. It was quite unexpected – that smell of arcing electricity just rounded the whole thing off nicely."

Ella wasn't sure she could remain in the room, and asked if she could leave for a moment.

"Could you hold on for one moment Mr Johnson?" Ash got up and followed Ella onto the steps of the station after making sure the interview room was locked.

Ella was retching.

Ash felt like joining her. "Bloody hell, this is worse than I expected. You going to be OK to come back in?"

Ella nodded her head. "I'm alright now boss. Let's go back and finish this."

They both looked through the window to where Johnson was sitting. He was tapping his fingers on the table whilst pom-pomming out a little tune to himself.

"I've read about pure psychopaths. He fits the profile precisely."

They entered and sat down quietly as Johnson smiled at them both. "Well, do you want to see it?"

"See what Mr Johnson?"

"My latest job. I brought it along of course."

"You mean you have it here!"

"Yup, exciting isn't it?"

"Where is it?"

"It's in my car just across the road. But you might be a bit disappointed at first because it wouldn't fit, so I had to put some bits in the boot and the rest on the back seat."

CHAPTER 160

Chief Inspector Riley tapped his fingers on his desk nervously. Those bastards at IOPC had managed to rattle him. Why were they so interested in some botched forensic searches, especially when there hadn't been any? He had not been expecting to be hauled over the coals about sealing off the Cherry house. He cursed himself for being so ill prepared.

"Fucking interfering bastards with nothing better to do," he growled to himself as he looked out of the window. There was a tap at the door; he turned to see Ash letting himself in.

"Chief, we have a suspect in custody who has admitted to a murder and has the body chopped up in a car across the road."

"What?"

Ash repeated the story and added that the suspect was mentally unstable and could possibly have booby trapped the car.

"For fuck's sake, get the bomb squad here and clear the bloody street!"

"They are putting up the cordons as we speak, boss. I've cleared everybody from the offices overlooking the street. The bomb guys said they will be here in ten minutes. That was, er, let me see, three minutes ago."

"OK, right."

A small crowd had gathered at the end of the street where the cordon had been placed. The policemen on guard waved through the bomb squad van as it approached. Ash met them as they deployed from the back of the truck.

"OK, gentlemen. This is what we have so far. The suspect we have in custody has parked his navy blue Polo across the road over there, and told us he has the dismembered body of his latest victim packed in the car. We have reason to believe he is mentally unstable and extremely dangerous. We took the precaution of calling you guys in case the car was booby trapped."

"Does he know we are on to him?"

"I would guess so, he admitted everything I've told you except for the booby trap. That's my theory."

"OK, let's test your theory. Could we possibly ask him to open the car himself?"

Ash looked around. "Let's see where that gets us. We have the road sealed off so he can't do a runner."

Ash went back to the interview room where Harry was still sitting and wondering why things were taking so long.

He looked up as Ash and Ella entered. "I don't suppose I could bother you for another coffee could I Inspector?"

Ash turned to Ella and nodded. As Ella went out, Ash sank slowly into his chair. "Mr Johnson, could I ask if you would be prepared to bring what you have in your car into the station yourself?"

"Of course, Inspector, you guys just get on with the sterling work you do. Why, you have already extended me every courtesy, it is the least I could do. Don't you worry about a thing."

Harry smiled again and slurped the coffee Ella had brought him.

"You guys, go attend to your work and leave everything to me. I'll just finish my coffee if I may, and then I'll bring it in."

Ash and Ella stepped out of the interview room, leaving the door ajar. The station entrance had been cleared. All staff had been evacuated from the building and were now standing at a distance down the road. Ash and Ella went to join them.

Harry finished the last dregs of his coffee and walked out of the interview room. The place seemed deserted. He looked up and down, there was nobody to be seen anywhere. Slightly confused, he walked to the front entrance and stepped out into the sun. To his amazement, the street in front had been cleared and everybody from the police station was standing some way back.

"There he is!" somebody shouted.

In that moment, Harry realised what was going on. The whole station had come out to witness the arrival of his masterpiece. He felt a huge lump in his throat, and with tearful eyes, approached his audience. As he did so, the bomb squad guys moved to form a barrier between him and the crowd.

Harry was stunned. The guards were moving forwards to prevent him being mobbed by his fans. It was unbelievable.

Unprepared as he was, he felt duty bound to address them. "Dear friends, I had no idea. I am beyond words. I can only hope that what I bring to you today brings joy into your life and is a warning to all wrongdoers that their sins will find them out and they will be brought to book."

He bowed and was a little disappointed to hear no applause, no roar of approval. "They must be spellbound by the magnitude of the event," he concluded.

He turned sharply and marched, with as much spring in his step as his arthritic heals could muster, towards his car, getting his keys out as he did so. Everybody winced as he opened the boot and bent inside to retrieve something. He proceeded to place everything beside the car in preparation to take it inside.

The bomb squad commander watched the scene through his field glasses.

"Items are not organic, repeat not organic. Object has wiring attached, probable explosive device. Prepare to neutralise. Drone is go."

Harry heard a sound and, to his amazement, saw a large heavy sheet of some kind fall from the sky to cover his sculpture. As he was standing there perplexed, strong arms lifted him from the ground whilst his body was frisked.

"No triggers detected, suspect is clean, repeat clean." Harry was carried back into the police station and locked in the interview room again. He felt his heart racing and, staggering to a chair, slumped into it.

Outside, a detonation device had been put in place.

Harry jumped as he heard the dull thump of a controlled explosion.

CHAPTER 161

Riley looked down at the notes he had in front of him. "Let's see. A policeman's helmet, what appears to be a doll's head, a set of wind chimes and some kind of electric motor." He looked up.

Ash and Ella sat hunched at the other side of his desk.

"Is this your idea of a fucking joke? Have you any idea of the ridicule I am getting from every bloody direction? You two are going all the way down for this."

"It was my call, Detective Sergeant Thompson had nothing to…"

"Did I give you leave to speak Kamau? Did I request information from the biggest dumb fuck on the force? Did I?"

"No Chief."

"Precisely, so why are noises coming out of that clueless fucking head of yours. Shut the fuck up!"

"Yes Chief."

"Detective Sergeant Thompson. Have you any explanation for why I have been made to look like a complete cunt?"

"It was a sculpture, Chief, a work of art."

"The only works of art around here are you two morons. Get out of my office and don't go anywhere or do anything, I'm not even close to having finished with you. OUT!"

As they walked out, they saw Johnson being carried out on a stretcher with a drip attached. The paramedic leaned towards his patient.

"Just relax Mr Johnson, you've had a big shock. We are just taking precautions."

They just heard a weak voice from Johnson as they lifted him into the back of the ambulance.

"They blew it up. Why did they blow it up?"

Ash watched as the ambulance drove away. "How the hell could I have got it so wrong Ella?"

"Not you boss, we. Remember, he had me retching."

"Where do we go from here? If I so much as go near Johnson or his cronies for that matter after this, I'll be hung, drawn and quartered."

"Maybe he planned it that way."

Ash shook his head. "If he did, it was brilliant, and he actually deserves to get away with it."

"So where to now boss?"

"Well, the only case I'm not getting ridiculed for is the leak that led to the Crabbs killing. The only problem with that is that the Chief is the prime suspect. I think you could say that one way or another, my career is well and truly fucked."

CHAPTER 162

Victor Bokov stretched lazily as he stood on his penthouse balcony looking out across the London skyline. He loved Rome, Amsterdam, New York and of course Moscow, but London had something special about it. London provided him with the biggest demand for his Russian "beauties".

Girls from rural areas had all the right qualities: pretty, simple, poor and easily removed from their families. His hunting parties always returned with a rich harvest, and the latest delivery was no exception. He had sampled at least ten of them in the past week. The sweetest was only thirteen years old. By the time he had finished with her, she had a carnal knowledge way beyond her years, forced into her by being repeatedly raped.

The system worked well. His customers were much less severe than he was, so the girls would remain with their owners, knowing that the alternative was to be returned to the pool gang, where his special attentions were guaranteed.

He glanced at the cleaner in the hope that she may be worth his attention but saw a stooped woman in the later years of her life. She mumbled that she had finished and let herself out through the front door.

He stretched again and went into the toilet for a pee. As he flushed the toilet, the two bottles of ammonia and bleach placed upside down in the half-full cistern began to mix, dumping a toxic gas into the toilet. He tried to open the door, only to find the doorknob coming off in his hand. He tried desperately to re-attach it, but the effort demanded more air, air that was no longer available. As he gasped, the merciless gas tore and burned into his lungs, leaving him to curl into an agonised ball on the floor. It provided a sufficiently slow and agonising death to atone for a portion of his sins.

CHAPTER 163

Ella read the report and walked over to Ash. She found him staring into the middle distance.

"Penny for them boss!"

"Don't waste your money." He shook his head in frustration.

"Boss, there's been another accidental death of a shit bag. Victor Bokov, suspected people trafficker and personal friend of Vladimir Putin. But wait for it – it seems that an 'oldish' cleaning lady was seen entering his penthouse earlier in the day. She signed into the daily register as Gladys Emmy Laughton. When they tried to contact her at the agency, nobody had ever heard of her. Does that sound familiar?"

Ash leaned back in his chair and looked at Ella for a long time.

"You know what Ella, I'm starting to wonder if we are on the right side. Here we are trying to stop somebody taking out the trash. Maybe we should get her email address and send her a list to work on."

"What she is doing is against the law, boss."

"Don't give me that line, Detective Sergeant Thompson. Do you think I don't know all the reasons I bother dragging myself out of bed in the morning?"

"Ha, yeah. I wonder where she conjures up the names from?"

"Out of the air? Humphrey Blognose, there you go. Or, er, Esmeralda Poppencoop, easy. We still have no proof that any of these are connected. It's all circumstantial."

"Hmm." Ella returned to her desk and brought up the list of names of the old ladies who were associated with the murders. They were listed in the chronological order of the incidents. Anne Vickers, Emily Nolan, Gladys Ingrams, Nancy Graham, Ania Novak, Gladys Emmy Laughton. She stared at them, there had to be something there.

Suddenly, she saw it. Her heart began to race. She let out a yelp. "Boss! Come here. How could I be so dumb? It's right in front of my eyes, dammit!"

Ash came to her desk and leaned over, looking at Ella's screen. "They're linked Ash, the names are linked. There's nothing random about those cases!"

Ash stared at the screen shaking his head.

Ella took her pen and pointed to the capitals.

Ash read them out in turn. "A,V,E,N,G,I,N,G,A,N,G,E,L."

"Bloody hell Ella. Avenging Angel – you are brilliant!"

CHAPTER 164

Still a little perplexed, Harry told the story of his visit to the police station from his armchair. Jim, Mervyn and Terence listened in stunned silence until he had finished his tale.

"And then I was taken to the local hospital for the night. They had to call Sheila."

Mervyn held up the morning newspaper. "There's a bit about it in here: *Prank bomb threat averted by quick action from local police.* It doesn't mention anything about your sculpture being blown up Harry. There's just a photo of some Chief Inspector telling everybody that the threat was neutralised, and that the investigation is ongoing."

"Just shows what a prize bunch of lying sods they are, doesn't it?"

"Why would they blow it up? I didn't threaten them with anything, other than a job well done."

"They can all go and get fucked. We have to tell the truth, but they can lie through their teeth. Old Harry here could have had a heart attack. Bunch of bastards." Jim was just about to fetch another beer for everybody when the doorbell rang.

He opened the door to see Ash and Ella looking up at him. "Hello Mr Spoonwall, could we come in for a minute?"

Jim turned his head towards the hall. "Hey Harry, it's Inspector Kamau and Sergeant Thompson. They've come to blow us all up and finish the job." He turned and walked into the lounge followed by Ash and Ella.

Ash and Ella stood awkwardly at the doorway to the lounge whilst everybody looked on and said nothing. Ash cleared his throat. "Detective Sergeant Ella and I are here unofficially to offer our sincere apologies about the incident that occurred yesterday. We completely misunderstood the situation, and I am to blame for that…"

"The Inspector was not alone in his assumptions. I too got it terribly wrong."

"Nevertheless, I as senior officer must take the blame and would like to tell you that the case against all of you has been dropped."

The silence continued for some moments before Mervyn broke out into applause, but then, realising he was alone, became silent again.

"I will leave you to enjoy your evening. Good night gentlemen."

When they were back in their car, Ella turned to Ash. 'Do you think they are innocent boss?"

"Ella, I don't know and quite frankly I don't care."

Jim watched from the window as they drove off.

"Well, that was unexpected I must say. Harry, you have probably just saved us from a remaining lifetime of penal servitude."

"Well, if that is true Jim, the sacrifice of the whirling wind chimes was definitely worth it."

Jim phoned Jeremy to report the good news, but Jeremy had already been brought up to date. "I have to say Jim that you and your team have some of the most ingenious methods of operation that I have ever seen. Getting the cops to take the bait and make themselves out to look like complete fools was pure genius."

CHAPTER 165

Ash sat at his desk and opened a drawer. He pulled out each case involving their newly discovered Avenging Angel and returned the others to the drawer. Then he hesitated, and pulled out the Crabbs execution as well.

He sighed a sigh of relief. Dealing with Johnson and his mates had been more of a burden than he had realised. The whole process had been like trudging in circles through thick mud. That was behind him now. Rightly or wrongly, Johnson had presented Ash with the perfect excuse to back off.

He stepped up with his files and beckoned to Ella as he walked into the meeting room. He let her in and closed the door behind her.

"Right, Detective Sergeant, let's get back our sanity. What have we got on our Angel?"

"Well, the only visual of any kind is the one on the steps at the tube station."

"Get on to it Ella, I am going to rummage around a little more with the Crabbs leak."

"Isn't the IOPC running with that one?"

"Running might be a bit optimistic, more like limping along I suspect."

Ash looked down at his phone. "Bloody hell, speak of the devil!"

Ash gave Ella a meaningful look as he answered the phone. "Good day Chief Inspector Willis."

"Good day DI Kamau, I was wondering if we could have another chat."

Ash looked at his watch. "Give me an hour."

Ash stood up and gave his files to Ella. "I'm off to IOPC, see if you can dig up any other treasures from this lot."

"Will do boss. What do I say if anyone needs you?"

"Hmm, tell them to phone me. You don't know where I am."

The train journey from Wimbledon to Canary Wharf took a little over three quarters of an hour and gave Ash time to ponder his career. Ratting on your boss was not generally looked upon with favour, whatever the circumstances. He was probably sealing his fate one way or another, he just didn't want to drag Ella down with him.

Chief Inspector Willis and Inspector Tony Routh were waiting for Ash as he walked in.

"Right, let's go." Ash was shown into the interview room.

"DI Kamau, thank you for coming in at such short notice. I am not going to waste your time dancing around the maypole. I and my assistant have concluded that you are trying to protect Detective Sergeant Thompson from this affair. I believe your intentions are sincere and, for the time being, I am willing to conduct the investigation with you alone. I hope my decision in this regard is not wrong."

"Thank you."

"Don't bother, I'm not doing you a favour. I'm using it as a threat that if at any time I believe you are being less than candid, she will be in here quicker than you could wipe a drip of snot off your nose. Do I make myself clear?"

"Yes Chief Inspector."

"Good, let's proceed. Apart from the phone call that you have identified coming from Chief Inspector Riley, have you had any other cause to suspect that he is corrupt?"

Ash moved back in his seat. Willis's direct manner needed some getting used to.

"Well, I only have my own opinion on this, it is not concrete evidence…"

"Just get to the point DI Kamau, I don't need any caveats. We will make our own minds up about whether it is evidence or not."

"He mentioned the location of the safe house within which Crabbs was executed. He let it drop in conversation a couple of days after the event. I confirmed with the witness protection crew that that information was not available to him."

"Did you ask him how he got it?"

"Yes, he said that I must have told him. I pointed out that I didn't know about it until he mentioned it to me. Then he said that he had probably read it in some report that had come past his desk. I asked if there were some reports on the case that I had not been shown. He said maybe but he had some important work to complete for the Commissioner and had no further time to discuss it."

"Did you follow up with him at a later time?"

"No, it didn't seem that important at the time and I have a way of annoying him, which doesn't help my career."

"Did you drop it then?"

"I did ask Detective Sergeant Thompson to try and find out where the safe house was in which Crabbs had been killed."

"And did she find it?"

"No."

"When exactly did you have this conversation with CI Riley?"

"It was last Friday afternoon."

"What else do you have on CI Riley?"

"Nothing that I am aware of."

"Very well, thank you DI Kamau. That will be all for now. Does Detective Sergeant Thompson know that you are here?"

"Yes, she does."

"May I suggest that in future, you tell nobody about these meetings."

"Yes, of course."

CHAPTER 166

Jim sat in Doris's kitchen chatting with Archie whilst the chicken fillets boiled away.

"So that's what happened. Through endless confusion and copious amounts of stumble and bumble, we seem to have slipped off the hook so to speak. I suppose we should be grateful and just call it a day. What do you think?"

Archie shook his head and shivered before settling down on the stool again.

"Really, you think so? Maybe you're right. You've always been right. So, you're saying we should keep on going? You are right! They wouldn't expect anybody in their right mind to engage in any skulduggery after the scrutiny we've been under. If we do start up again, they would probably be only too happy to ignore us and hope we don't bog them down with the sort of mist and bollocks that seems to occupy everything we do."

Jim started chopping up the chicken and poured the specially prepared gravy he had bought from Waitrose over the pieces. "There, that should be a bit tastier." He placed it on the floor and watched Archie tuck in.

"Right, well that's it then. Back in the saddle we get. Thanks Archie, see you this evening." Jim walked back to his house and helped his companions to reduce his beer stocks even further.

"I reckon we need to keep going. There is no better place to hide than out in the open. The cops would never suspect that we were busy again, would they?"

"I must say Jim, I've been quite depressed at the thought of sitting around with nothing to do."

"Me too, Merv, so what do we say? Do we open up for business again?"

The vote was carried unanimously.

"Right, let's get hold of Jeremy." Jim picked up his phone theatrically as they all gazed on approvingly.

"Hi Jeremy, it's Jim. We've had a discussion and decided to keep on going. We need another list."

"Any preferences Jim? The list continues to grow."

"Somebody a bit more challenging maybe. Let's go for broke."

"I'll be in contact soon."

CHAPTER 167

Chief Inspector Riley saw the missed call on his phone from Superintendent White. He picked up his phone and contacted the IOPC.

Riley tried not to grit his teeth as he was led into the interview room. Superintendent White and Chief Inspector Willis watched as he sat down.

CI Willis opened the dialogue after he had announced for the recorder the time, date and attendees. "Chief Inspector Riley, thank you for coming today. As before, Superintendent White will be conducting the interview."

White looked directly at Riley. "Good morning CI Riley. I would like to refer you to the execution of Mr Eric Crabbs that took place on the 27th of last month. Do you recall the incident?"

"Yes, I do."

"We understand that you knew the whereabouts of the safe house, is that correct?"

"No, I had no idea where it was."

"Do you know where it is now?"

"No, why should I?"

"In the previous interview in this office on the 3rd of this month, you stated that you have never spoken to Mr Robert Cherry, is that so?"

"Yes, that is so."

"You do know who Mr Bob Cherry was do you?"

"Yes."

"So, you would definitely know if you had made contact with him, would you?"

"Yes of course."

"Of course, indeed. Would you then mind explaining how the following message was found on Mr Cherry's mobile phone? CI Willis, please."

Willis picked up the phone with a glove and pressed the play button.

Riley felt the blood drain from his face as he listened to the message. "I'm being framed, I wish to reserve my right to remain silent and request the assistance of a lawyer."

Superintendent White nodded to CI Willis. "Chief Inspector Riley, I recommend that you recuse yourself from your duties forthwith until such time as this matter is resolved. Interview terminated."

CHAPTER 168

Riley cleared his desk in accordance with the instruction from the IOCP. He put the last two files in his case and looked out of the glass door of his office to where Thompson and Kamau were huddling over a screen.

"What Punch and Judy show are you two conjuring up this time?" he mumbled to himself as he walked off down the corridor. "Surplus to requirements for sure."

Ash looked up to see the Chief sauntering off down the corridor.

CHAPTER 169

Jim looked at the letter that plopped through the front door. It was like the other one he had received from Jeremy, a single piece of paper with a printed message on it lay inside the envelope.

"Bloody hell!" he mumbled as he read the contents.

Jim decided a meeting was called for at his house despite pressure from the others for a pub session.

"Sorry guys, we really need to keep this one under wraps." Later in the day, another letter arrived with a similar piece of printed paper. Only this time it contained just one line.

Once everybody had settled down into his lounge with their beverages in hand, Jim cleared his throat and picked up the first note. "Er, you remember we decided to ask Jeremy for a more challenging project? Well, I think we've got one. Let me read out the note that arrived this morning."

Your subject goes by the name of the Bluebottle in the underworld. This person has been the reason for as many as twenty serious criminals being released due to evidence going missing. Every investigation into the operations of this individual, and there have been several, has been thrown out due to a similar loss of evidence. There is almost certainly a connection between this person and a very senior member of the police force, but this has never been substantiated.

In addition to the above, your subject has caused the death of at least ten people in the criminal world who have strived to expose him and at least two members of the police force who have come too close to the truth.

Your mission is to eliminate this individual. Attempts to bring this person to justice by conventional means are deemed to be highly likely to fail and would most probably result in the death of his accusers. The Bluebottle's identity will follow.

Jim then held up the other sheet of paper. "This note arrived just before you lot got here. It just has a name on it. He's a cop!!"

CHAPTER 170

Chief Inspector Willis looked at the evidence in front of him. It was not beyond the realms of possibility that Kamau had somehow cobbled the message together to nail his boss. It would have been more convincing had he 'discovered' the phone in Cherry's car and made sure that Detective Sergeant Thompson was a witness to that. Instead, he had gone out of his way to avoid that, which made his case more friable.

Knowledge of the safe house was not independently verifiable. It was Kamau's word against his boss.

Kamau was no fool. If he had wanted to stitch his boss, he would have come to light with a way tighter case of well-crafted bullshit. The evidence available was tatty at best and for that reason Willis tended to believe it to be genuine.

The case stood or fell on whether the voice on the phone was Riley's or not. He dialled his assistant.

"Inspector Routh, get a voice recognition expert to work on the alleged message from Riley please. Without that, we have nothing to move forwards with."

An hour later, Routh phoned back. "Sir, there is a problem with the phone. They can't get into it."

"What do you mean?"

"The phone is demanding a password."

"Well get them to bypass the bloody password."

"They've tried that. They reckon an encryption app has recently been downloaded onto the phone. They can't access it."

"What? How could that happen?"

"I don't know sir."

Willis put down the phone. That encryption app's appearance was all he needed to convince him that Kamau was on the level. But now he was powerless to act upon it.

CHAPTER 171

"I don't think I'm up to bumping off a cop, Jim."

"I agree with Merv, it seems wrong, even though he sounds like a right bastard."

"So, what do we do?"

"I think we have to ask for somebody a bit lower on the list Jim. Maybe an estate agent, somebody we can really hate!"

"Hmm, OK, let me get back to Jeremy and see what he says." Jim walked out into the garden and phoned.

"Hello Jim. Bit rich for the blood, was it?"

"Yes, how did you know?"

"You are phoning me so soon after receiving the name. Just do me a favour and destroy those notes I sent. We don't want those floating off in the wind."

"No certainly, will do. We sort of wanted somebody we could hate more."

"Ha, like an estate agent I suppose. Sorry, we don't have any local ones on the list at the moment, surprising as that may sound. I'll tell you what, seeing as killing cops is a bit abhorrent to you, how about a cop killer? Could you handle that?"

"Yes, I think so, that sounds a bit more our style."

"Good, I'll send you a name."

"Does this mean the other bloke goes free?"

"Don't worry about that Jim. It will be taken care of."

As Jim returned to the lounge, he took the two pages from his pocket and tore them up before placing them reverently into the fire. "We have a cop killer on the way."

Mervyn sat back in his chair. "Ah, now that sounds way better Jim. We can get stuck into that."

"Bugger, I wish the Inspector and Detective Sergeant had let us off the hook a bit earlier, we could still have had the zapper to help us with this new project."

"Yeah, not to mention our three-footed friend. How will we ever survive without him to swell our ranks?"

The name subsequently arrived: Hakal Khan. Jim wrote the name up on the door board for all to see.

"This Hakal Khan lives in Wandsworth, so that's nice and close."

"Definitely sounds like a nasty piece of work, doesn't he? Anybody with a name like that must be bad."

CHAPTER 172

Hakal Khan looked at the message that appeared on his phone. His dark eyes narrowed as he savoured the prospect of a well-priced job. Not one, but two targets. He could take both out at the same time and receive double the rate for a single execution.

His modus operandi was simple and effective. He never stalked his victims. They always came to him. The hunters became the hunted. Just like in the wild, he would let them track him and then double back and take them out when they least expected it. The British were so vain – at their weakest and most vulnerable when they believed they were invincible. When they thought they were in control, on top of their game. That's when they toppled so easily.

There was no time limit placed on the job. He preferred that, he liked to pace his work carefully. There should be nothing to lift his heart rate above normal, no surprises. There would be contingencies in place for every eventuality that he could envisage, and his imagination allowed him to envisage many.

The sun was still to rise as he performed Fajr, the first of his daily prayer rituals.

CHAPTER 173

The phone has been hacked. We can no longer access it. An encryption app has been loaded that we cannot bypass. It may as well have been crushed by a steam roller. Ash listened to the message from CI Willis and swallowed hard. They had been out manoeuvred and he had done nothing but expose himself and Ella to danger for no reason whatsoever.

Later that day, he saw the Chief return to his office with the files he had gathered the previous day, and lay them back on his desk. He looked up and saw Ash watching him. He smiled and waved his hand. Ash awkwardly nodded and lifted his hand to acknowledge the greeting. That was the first time the Chief had ever smiled at him, and it made his flesh crawl.

He looked down at his notes. The Angel investigation had again arrived at a brick wall. Ella had contacted the witnesses in each case to see if there was anything more they could remember about the old lady. All but one of them could recall less than they did at the time of their statements. The one who remembered the scene just kept repeating that she was an elderly lady who looked like every other elderly lady. It would probably mean that they had to wait until she slipped up.

The Crabbs case was doing little better. With the phone dead in the water, there was little to go on. The forensics had found nothing at the safe house that pointed to anything other than the fact that it had all the makings of a professional assassination.

Ash put his head in his hands. Maybe he should just do everyone a favour and walk out forever. He realised that the only thing that kept him there now was Ella. He had put her in danger for nothing, the least he could do was protect her in whatever way he could.

CHAPTER 174

The dossier on Khan arrived at Jim's place later that day. As always, it was a detailed study of his life and misdemeanours.

Born in Hackney, he had rebelled against his parents' moderate Muslim beliefs at an early age. By the age of fourteen he had become an avid fundamentalist. He was crafted by his masters in the arts of sabotage and terror and was soon recognised to be a treasure that could not be sacrificed. His future lay not in martyrdom, but in training others to give their lives for their faith. In this he excelled, stirring up a hatred in his students for all who did not align themselves to his beliefs.

He had, in later years, extended his skills to include that of an assassin for hire. It mattered little to him what his target had done to deserve his special attentions. The only qualification needed was that they were not one of his own creed. Devoutly Muslim, he attended the local mosque four times every day.

"So how do we handle this one Jim?"

"Well, er, um, we, er… I know, let's make a list!"

"Yeah, that always gets things going nicely."

The list appeared on the door:

Nasty terrorist type

Hired assassin

Sneaky looking

Clever

Muslim

37 years old

Certainly armed

The most dangerous piece of work we've had to deal with

They contemplated their options. "None of that appears to be good news Jim."

"There's no maybe. So what do we do now?"

"What did we do last time?"

"Buggered if I know, I struggle to remember what happened yesterday."

"I reckon we should come up with a positive aspect for each of those points there. That will at least make us feel better."

"Good idea Merv, I like it."

After several minutes of deep thought, they nodded with satisfaction at their new additions:

Nasty terrorist type – Certainly no loss to anybody

Hired assassin – Won't be expecting to be assassinated himself

Sneaky looking – Helps you not to feel guilty when you bump him off

Clever – Thinks he's invincible

Muslim – scared of pork

37 years old – May have a few aches and pains already

Certainly armed – Makes us more alert

They considered their new list. "Right, I'm not sure I feel any better though."

"We should track his movements, put a tail on him."

"Oh really, why?"

"So we know what he does."

"We know what he does. He's very regular, it says he goes to church a few times each day."

"Ah, but what does he do when he's being sneaky?"

"Hmm, it could be tricky. They all dress in similar clothes, don't they? It'll be a bit like picking my grandkid up at school, they all look the same in those uniforms."

"You're right."

"Sod it, let's go hang around the church and see if we can spot him."

"Mosque."

"What?"

"It's called a mosque not a church," said Terence.

"Technically maybe, but they still pray and say thanks to God and everything, just like we do, and ring the bells."

"They say God is most great, *Allahu Akbar*. No bells, they call the faithful to prayer, the muezzin recites the Adhan at certain times of the day."

"I say Terence, you seem to know a lot about it, how come?"

"I was at a progressive school, Jim."

"At my school, it was '*And did those feet in ancient times*' or nothing at all. There was Protestant or pagan, that was the choice and woe betide anyone who should wander from the true path over to the dark side. So, when is mosque time Terence?"

"Fajr, quarter to five in the morning, asr normally seven fifteen in the evening, magrib normally quarter to nine in the evening and isha at ten forty-five."

"Whoa, four times a day, that certainly eats into pub time. Not surprised that alcohol is off the list. Not worth having a TV either really, is it?"

"A Muslim is required to pray five times a day."

"I can't imagine us Christians putting up with that, can you? Once a week on Sundays is pushing it for most of us."

"True, Muslims tend to be way closer to their faith."

"Right, let's hang around the mosque in Wandsworth and see if we can spot him."

"I reckon Mervyn and Jim are best at that. They cased out old Bob Cherry and managed to get us an invite to the dog fight and everything."

"Oh yeah, you're right, Harry. Merv and I were the epitome of calmness and composure. We both agreed that if we ever tried that stunt again, we would make sure that along with the pork pies and croissants there were adult nappies included in the action pack."

"Come on Jim, you got us an invite, that was brilliant tactics."

"Tactics my arse, how we got out alive is still one of life's great mysteries. But OK, sitting around outside a mosque can't be too life threatening, I suppose."

Mervyn was writing a note. "Jim, I'm just making a bit of a shopping list."

CHAPTER 175

Ash looked up to see the Chief coming over to him with a smile. Once again Ash felt a shudder go down his back.

"Ash, I have a new job for you. I think we can both agree that the Crabbs case is going nowhere fast, and this has just come in. I would like you and Detective Sergeant Thompson to follow up on this one. It requires those special skills that you two have."

"What skills are those, Chief?"

"Eh? Oh, I'm sure you know Ash."

Ash watched the Chief turn and march back into his office, closing the door behind him. He looked down at the file and cautiously opened it. There was a photograph of a man scowling towards the camera. The face projected a cold menace. Ash flicked through the case file. The man had no form and had recently been identified on CCTV at an armed robbery of an all-night convenience store in the area.

He called Ella across. "OK Sergeant, the Chief has given us this case because you and I have special skills apparently."

"Oh really, what are those?"

"Your guess is as good as mine. It looks like a straightforward case of armed robbery. Let's see what the surrounding CCTVs picked up in the area – maybe we can trace his escape route. And can you find out what you can about what was stolen?"

CHAPTER 176

It soon became apparent to Jim and Mervyn that their stake-out was presenting some challenges.

"Jim, like we suspected, they all look the same in those uniforms or smocks or whatever they call them. Most of them are Eastern-looking like our mate. I've seen at least forty people who look identical. My eyesight is not great at the best of times."

As time went on, the worshippers started to arrive in ever-increasing numbers.

"Bloody hell Mervyn, there must be well over a thousand so far. Certainly knocks the shit out of the Sunday congregation at our local church."

"Didn't know you went to church Jim."

"Christenings, weddings and funerals, Merv. Mainly the latter of late as is the way of things I suppose. Pass me another pork pie will you?"

"Jim, it might be just me, but we seem to be getting some funny looks."

"You're right, I noticed that too. Maybe it's the pork pies. Maybe we should duck our heads down when we take a bite."

"Hmm, can't be too careful, eh?"

They were unaware of two men watching them from the upper window of the mosque. The younger man turned towards the elder man. "There they are my Imam. It's probably nothing, but they have been parked there for over half an hour and seem to be ducking down every so often as if they don't want to be seen."

"Hmm, I see that. I am reluctant to call the police. I don't want to waste their time or appear paranoid. But I also do not forget what happened in Christchurch. Let's approach them and see what they do."

"No Imam. With respect, I will not permit that. I will find two close friends and see what those two men are doing in that car."

"Take caution with you my friend, we are searching for peace, not conflict."

"As you say Imam."

Jim was the first to catch the eyes of the three men approaching them in traditional prayer dress. "Don't look now Merv, but I think we've been spotted."

Merv ducked down and placed his pork pie under his seat.

"For fuck's sake Merv, sit still. We've done nothing wrong, remember."

"Nothing wrong, right, absolutely. Oh my God, they are coming for us."

The three men stopped by Mervyn's window. One man made a gentle gesture indicating that Merv should wind down his window.

Déjà vu flooded through Mervyn's brain as the terrible memories of their encounter with Bob Cherry came raging back. With trembling hands, he wound down the window of his car.

The man bent down and smiled. "Good day sir. May I ask what you are doing outside our Masjid? Maybe we can help you, are you lost?"

Mervyn looked down, saw the pork pie wrapper on his lap and panicked. "I haven't eaten any pork! I don't like pigs, hate them… like you. I mean I don't hate you and you're not like pigs but what I mean is that I hate pigs like you… I mean like you, I hate pigs, er, mmm…"

Jim watched the darkening expression on the man's face.

"We are just parking up to eat our croissants. Totally vegetarian, they are, like you. I am also a vegetable… a vegetable, er, um, vegetable eater, er, thing."

The man leaned closer to Mervyn and spoke quietly so that his friends could not hear. "How dare you insult me, you infidel piece of shit. I will slit your flabby neck from ear to ear. I have the number of your car, I have your stupid face in my memory, you are a dead dog."

In that instant, as Jim stared past Mervyn into the man's face, twisted full of hatred, he realised that they had found their man. They had found Hakal Khan.

CHAPTER 177

Ash and Ella looked at the CCTV material covering the possible exits from the shop. Despite them covering every possible angle, there was no sign of anybody leaving over the period concerned.

Ash shook his head – it didn't make sense, the man had simply vanished.

Ella had paid a visit to the shop which specialised in Halal goods. The owner explained how the man had held a gun on him and demanded cash from the till, which, according to the shop owner, amounted to just over two thousand pounds. Once he had been given the cash, the man left the way he had come in – through the front entrance.

"How could he just disappear?"

"Doesn't make sense unless the shop CCTV has the wrong time or something, but the shop owner confirmed the time. Let's look at the shop CCTV again."

They ran the clip again. "You can't actually see him leaving through the entrance, just walking away from the counter, but the shop owner said he left through the front door."

Ella picked up the photograph. "Where did this mug shot in the file come from?"

"Don't know, it was in the file when the chief dropped it off. It looks like the guy in the clip, but it's far from conclusive that it's him. The name given here is Hakal Khan."

"Maybe he was short of cash?"

"Hmm, but he's a devout Muslim, why would he hit a Halal shop? Nothing sits right here."

"I suppose we have no idea where this character operates from?"

"Quite the opposite Ella, there is an address in this file. He apparently lives in Wandsworth."

CHAPTER 178

Mervyn didn't trust himself to say anything as he started the car and ground the gears, before setting off with a jolt. He looked in his rear-view mirror and saw a sickening grin on Khan's face as he watched them drive away.

When they were no longer in sight of the mosque, Mervyn pulled over. "I don't think I can do this anymore Jim. I think I'm close to cardiac arrest. I suppose I am going to die now anyway. He certainly seemed to confirm that."

"You have to dump this car somewhere Mervyn, that's the only way he can trace us."

"Hell, you're right, let's leave it somewhere and we'll catch a bus. Good thinking. I'm afraid I can't think very clearly at the moment."

"Don't feel lonely, I'm on the edge of soiling myself."

"He knows what I look like, he said he knows my face and he could trace my car number!"

"Crap Merv. You look like every other old fart. It's not like you're on TV or anything is it? Just as they all looked the same to us today, we all look the same to them. And, er, maybe we borrowed the car."

"He could get my address from the authorities Jim."

"All the more reason why you must stay at my place until he has been dealt with."

"Why do I have the feeling that the end of the line is just around the corner for me Jim? I can't get rid of the look on his face as he sneered out all that hatred."

They drove to the large shopping centre in Wandsworth and parked in the multi-storey car park. Wimbledon was a short bus ride away.

Once back at Jim's, Mervyn made himself a large rum and cocoa and waited for the others to arrive. Jim had told everybody he needed a meeting – "bloody chop-chop".

When everybody had settled down, Jim stood and walked up to the door where Khan's details were still displayed. "Er, Merv and I have made contact with Hakal Khan."

There was a mumble of awestruck approval from Harry and Terence. Harry patted Mervyn on the arm. "Way to go guys, how the hell did you do it? But why do I get the feeling this is not good news?" As Jim told his story, the mood went from elation, through unease and finally arrived at abject terror.

"So, what do we do now?"

"I reckon we are out of our depth, Harry."

They fell silent.

"We must phone Jeremy. He'll know what to do won't he?"

Jim picked up his phone. "Let's find out."

Jeremy listened in silence whilst Jim related his story. "Now listen very carefully Jim. You must back off and lie low. Don't do anything until you hear from me again, OK?"

CHAPTER 179

Khan looked at the note he had made of Mervyn's car registration. He dialled his contact at the licensing department. "My friend, I have a need. Tell me to whom this car belongs and where this good man lives."

"Very well effendi, I will message you back."

Within half an hour, Khan had Mervyn's address on his phone. A local man in Wimbledon. He contacted one of the youths from the mosque. "Mustafa, I want you to go see a man for me in Wimbledon. I want you to give him my greetings."

Khan gave the youth the message he must give to Mervyn. He squinted as he remembered the fat little pink man and his companion, telling him that they hate Muslim pigs. He would die slowly for that, and Khan would watch him do so. It almost seemed too easy.

Khan was frustrated when the youth contacted him only an hour later to report that the man was not there. The house had several circulars laying inside and had all the looks of having been deserted for several weeks. There were cobwebs in the keyhole. He thanked the youth and returned to his thoughts. It was time for those he helped to help him.

He waited until a familiar voice came onto the phone.

"Yes?"

"I need to know the whereabouts of a Mervyn Pearce. He is not at his residence."

The phone went dead.

In a little under fifteen minutes, a message came through on his phone. "He was recently under investigation by two of my detectives and is currently lodging with James Spoonwall, who was also under investigation." Jim's address then followed.

Khan redialled the contact.

He heard Riley's voice. "Yes?"

"I will be paying the Spoonwall residence a visit at six tonight. I think maybe our friends Kamau and Thompson should be informed of my whereabouts." Khan smiled and prepared for prayer.

CHAPTER 180

"Ash could you come here for a moment please."

Ash cursed under his breath as he saw that the Chief had a smile painted onto his face again. He lifted himself from the chair and walked into his office.

The Chief looked down at a file in front of him. "You and Ella have been in contact with a mister, er, Mervyn Pearce, is that right?"

Ash winced as he remembered the debacle with the bomb squad. "Yes, he was one of the people helping us with our enquiries."

"Well, it has come to our attention that he currently keeps company with none other than our friend Mr Khan. Isn't that interesting? What enquiries was he helping you with?"

"A couple of suspicious deaths."

"Sounds like you were right on the money. One of our informants reckons there is going to be a bit of a meeting at a Jim Spoonwall's house tonight at 6pm. Do you know him?"

"He's one of the others helping us with our enquiries, yes."

"Maybe worth a visit, what do you think?"

"I might be going in a bit light sir."

"Make sure you take Thompson along. Anyway, there it is Ash, let me know what goes down."

Ella listened as Ash repeated his conversation with the Chief. "That sounds completely off-kilter. Pearce and his mates are definitely up to something weird, but I don't see the likes of Khan fitting in with them, do you?"

"No, I don't. But then very little makes sense about any of that crew. Does this Khan guy have any form?"

"Nothing, there is no file on him at all, which also beggars where the information we have in this file came from."

"The pieces are not fitting. There is no certainty that the guy robbing the store is the guy in the picture, and no evidence that either of these is this

Khan individual."

"Let me have a chat with my long-lost cousin in Central. Maybe he can do a bit of a rummaging around on this lot."

"Worth a try Ella, let me know if anything comes up."

Within the hour, Ella heard back from her contact. He remembered the name Hakal Khan being on the terrorist watch list, but when he accessed the file, he found it missing.

"A bloody terrorist?!"

"Well, at least on the terrorist watch list."

"Sod this. I need another chat with the Chief."

The Chief waited until Ash had finished relating the Khan connection to the terrorist watch list.

"So Kamau, let me get this right, despite there being no evidence other than your friend's memory about who is on a list some twenty thousand long, you've now decided we are dealing with a terrorist cell? Do you want me to get out the fucking bomb squad again? Maybe we should get a few helicopters circling the sky whilst you pay your geriatric friends a visit? Fuck, let's go the whole hog and get the SWAT teams mobilised as well. They can smash down the doors of everyone in the neighbourhood and drag any shifty looking grannies off for interrogation.

"Look Kamau, you are out on a very long limb, but seem to be completely unaware of it. I gave you this case to bring some normality back into your operation, but as usual, you have to load the whole case with a load of bollocks fired up by your own paranoia. I strongly suggest that you get off your arse, get down to that bloody house and do your fucking job!"

Ella looked up as Ash returned to his desk. "What does the Chief think?"

"As usual, I'm top of the arsehole pile again. Just keep digging around for me Ella."

CHAPTER 181

Ash walked up to Jim's front door.

"What the hell am I doing here?" he thought to himself. A pack of fog-mongering old farts dancing around the maypole with a terrorist? What was he supposed to do? Arrest them all? For what? Being in possession of an unsavoury attitude? Displaying a dithery disposition during the hours of darkness? He sighed and pushed the doorbell.

He watched the look of disappointment wash over Jim's face as the man recognised his guest. "Detective Inspector Kamau, what have we done wrong now?"

"Mr Spoonwall, please excuse the intrusion. I know it's late, but I have been instructed to pay you a visit. May I come in?"

Jim stood back and beckoned Ash into the hall. As he closed the door, he failed to see the dark shape of Hakal Khan sitting in a delivery van across the road.

"Good," Kahn thought to himself. The crows were almost all gathered in their roost. Only Thompson was missing. She was supposed to have arrived with Kamau. His contact was letting him down. Too late now. He would make his move.

The decision caused his body to rapture in the warmth that always came with a kill. He savoured the feeling, closing his eyes as he did so. This execution would be so easy, like slaughtering crippled sheep; none of his skills, honed over the years, would be called upon. He offered up a silent prayer to Allah, took his blade, held it to his lips and then slipped it beneath his tunic. "Tonight, it will be a prince of a night, Inshallah," he thought to himself as he slipped out of the van and let his feet carry him confidently towards the house like a wraith.

Inside the house, he could hear three voices in hesitant conversation. He could smell the foul stench of beer coming from within. He slipped his pick into the Yale lock and, with the third stroke, felt the tumblers fall into place as he opened the door. Closing the door silently behind him, he made his way to the staircase which was shrouded in darkness. That evening, he had bathed as normal, but had been careful to use a bland soap that would give off very little odour. His stealth needed to be precise should it become required.

The voices continued from the lounge. "Our Chief Inspector asked me to pay you a visit to clear up a couple of queries we had."

"I thought we were off the hook Inspector."

Ash looked at Mervyn. "You are. This is about another matter."

They waited for Ash to continue.

"Do you happen to know somebody named Hakal Khan?"

Ash saw the effect the name had on his audience. He watched as Mervyn almost spilt his cocoa before grabbing his cup. The look on Jim's face was one of pure horror.

"I'll take that as a yes. Can I ask you how you come to know him?"

In the darkness, Khan heard his name spoken by Kamau. That, in itself, was of no concern to him. But the fact that the fat white infidels knew his name was not to his liking. Their meeting at the Masjid was not by chance – they knew who he was.

He reasoned quickly that their instant deaths would be ill advised, and that extended interrogation would yield both valuable information and extended pleasure. He felt his mouth water as he savoured the thought.

Ash remained silent as Jim and Mervyn exchanged looks of panic. It was Mervyn who first burst into a blustering reply. "Er, we were passing by the local mosque in, er, Wandsworth and, er, thought we'd stop for bite to eat, sort of."

"You stopped for a bite to eat at the mosque?"

"What? No, we took a packed lunch along."

"As one does."

"Yes, well. We were minding our own business, watching the church, er, mosque goers arriving and everything, whilst we had our pork pies and beer."

"You were outside a mosque eating pork pies and consuming alcohol whilst the faithful were gathering for prayer? Was this as a bet or a dare or something? I don't understand why anyone would…"

"No, no dare. We just felt peckish."

"Really? Carry on."

"Well, we were doing no harm, when out of nowhere these three Muslim men came across and asked us what we were doing."

"What a surprise."

"Yes, it was. It was quite a shock. I tried to hide my pork pie and told him I don't like pigs but I think he got the wrong end of the stick and thought I was calling him a pig and that I didn't like him."

"I can imagine why that would piss him off. Go on."

"Well, from there on, things went from bad to worse."

"I would never have believed it."

"Yes, they did. He became very nasty and called me a citadel."

"Pardon?"

"He called you an infidel Merv."

"Oh, yeah, that was it, Jim. Very nasty."

"So, what happened after that?"

"We drove away very fast."

"So that was how you met Hakal Khan?"

"Yes Inspector."

"So, no introduction, no exchange of names and addresses, no swapping of business cards?"

"Of course not, it was no laughing matter, Inspector, we were very distressed."

"I wasn't making a joke Mr Pearce. I was merely trying to establish how you knew that this person you met was Hakal Khan?"

"That is what I would like to know too," thought Hakal Khan in the darkness.

Mervyn stared at Ash.

"What?"

"How did you know, Mr Pearce, that the man who came to speak to you was Hakal Khan?"

"I, er…" Mervyn looked at Jim.

"Yes?"

"I, um recognised him from a newspaper report about what an evil terrorist man he was and everything."

"So, you knew he was a terrorist?"

"Yes, certain of it, horrible man. Did terrible things."

"Like what?"

"Eh?"

"What terrible things did he do?"

"He um blew up a pub because of the alcohol, and children too, and that sort of thing, um..."

"The children were in the pub were they?"

Mervyn nodded vaguely, exhausted beyond measure.

"I suppose I shouldn't be surprised any longer when dealing with you lot. I have never in my whole career had to listen to quite as much extended bullshit as I have in the past couple of weeks from you men. You seriously don't expect me to believe that you would purposefully go and eat pork pies and chug a couple of beers outside a mosque, do you?"

"We did Inspector, that bit is absolutely true."

"So which bit isn't?"

"Eh?"

"So which bit of that cockamamie story was pulled out of your arse?"

"I can't remember."

In the darkness, Kahn closed his eyes in an attempt to control his patience. How the policeman had not wrenched the little fat man's liver out and fed it to him was beyond comprehension. He decided he would have to act soon.

"Mr Spoonwall, I don't suppose you have any light to throw on the heap of steaming shit that has just been delivered by your friend?"

"No Inspector."

"I thought not. Seeing as you are aware of so many things with regards to Mr Khan, you will no doubt be aware that he is about to pop around here any moment now?"

This time, Mervyn really did drop his cup on the floor and Jim made a nervous move towards the window, peeping through the curtains as he did so.

"Here? But how could he know we are here?"

"Maybe you should tell me that."

"How the hell would we know? We were told to keep a low profile."

"Told to? By whom?"

"Er, don't know, can't remember."

"Very well. You seem to have everything under control. Memory loss, confusion, I'd say my work is done here. I'll let myself out."

Kahn readied himself to meet Ash as he appeared in the hall, but stood back when he heard Jim's voice. "OK, we are out of options Inspector, you win. I will explain."

Mervyn stared at the table in front of him whilst Jim took a deep breath.

"We were given the job of taking Khan out. He was our mark. We were at the mosque to try and put a tail on him, but he spotted us first. We didn't even know it was him until he came up close and started getting nasty. We got a scare and were told to stand down and wait further orders. That is the status we find ourselves in now. I can only assume he found our address through Mervyn's car that we ditched in Wandsworth after the visit."

Ash just stared at Jim with his mouth open.

"You guys just never fail to…"

Jim saw a shadow move behind Ash. The shadow turned into a dark hand which pressed itself into the side of Ash's neck. He fell like a rag doll to the floor. In the lounge doorway stood Hakal Khan.

CHAPTER 182

"What the hell are you doing here Thompson?" Ella looked up to see the Chief glaring down at her.

"Following up on some leads on the armed robbery sir."

"Why aren't you with Kamau for fuck's sake? You were supposed to be at the Spoonwall house."

"News to me sir."

"Bloody Kamau is going to fry for this."

The Chief looked as if he was going to explode, but then became very suddenly withdrawn. Of course, Kamau was going to fry anyway. It was just that Thompson was supposed to be in that pan as well. He had to be careful, he had to think fast. Let things take their course. There was little else that could be done now, too many wheels had been set in motion. Way too many.

He turned and walked slowly back to his office, closing the door behind him.

CHAPTER 183

Khan smiled as Mervyn tried to crawl backwards over his couch.

"Hello my friends. Do me a service and place our Inspector friend into this chair please."

"Wh… Why should we?" stammered Jim. "You are going to kill us anyway."

"True, but you still have a choice in the way in which you will die. There is the quick way. Or there is the other way, which you will discover if you disobey me."

With much wheezing and shaking of knees, Jim and Mervyn slouched the police inspector into the chair.

"Good, now stand over there, away from everything."

Khan watched them do as they were told, their breath coming in rasps.

Khan smiled. "Maybe too many pork pies and beers, my friends?"

When satisfied that they were where he wanted them to be, he took out four cable ties and bound Ash's hands and feet to the chair. Jim and Mervyn then had their legs and hands tied to chairs in a similar way.

Khan went to the kitchen and poured himself a glass of water, turning away in disgust from the empty beer cans left on the table. As he walked back into the lounge, he noticed that Ash was starting to come round. "Ah good, our Inspector friend is joining us at last."

Khan sat in a chair and sipped at his glass of water whilst looking from one captive to the next.

Ash took in his surroundings and, recognising Khan, tried to free himself.

"You are wasting your energy Detective Inspector Ash Kamau. Yes, don't look so surprised. I know exactly who you are. You and your assistant, Detective Sergeant Ella Thompson. Such a pity she isn't here tonight. I was supposed to be entertaining both of you here, but your esteemed Chief Inspector Riley has made a mess of it. He has nobody to blame but himself if this endeavour costs him a little more than the agreed fee. I have decided to render Thompson a little additional service before she is despatched. I have noted that she is comely and worthy of my special attention for a few hours. I had intended to give you all ringside seats, but she has spoilt your fun by not being here. I will have to have a private moment of romance with her later, such a pity."

Ash glared at Khan as his mind raced.

"Be calm my friend. Your boss wants both you and Thompson dead. You should not have passed in that telephone. So silly now, wasn't it? It has cost both your lives – one silly little phone, and it achieved absolutely nothing."

"OK Khan, you've got me. But you don't need to kill these silly old sods. They're not worth the trouble, they are below you. Take me and finish this but leave them alone. They are nothing to you."

"You are right, they are below me, and they are old and silly. But they are slime that needs to be washed away. It is part of the ongoing Jihad, Inspector. I would be turning my back on my holy duty if I were to suffer them to live."

"How are you going to kill us?" squeaked Mervyn.

"Ah, the fat one has found his voice. I will keep my promise to you. Remember in your car I told you how you will die. I will slit your fat neck from ear to ear and let you bleed to death. I will do the same to your friend. The Inspector has not insulted me as you have done, for him there will be a merciful garrotting.

"I think my mercy will extend to despatching the Inspector first, that way he will not have to witness the rather distressing sight of watching the two of you dying in agony over an extended period."

Khan turned towards Ash. "Time to die Inspector." Khan drew the scarf from his neck.

Very gently, a quivery little voice was heard calling from the hallway. "'Allo Jim, are you there? It's me. I was wondering if I could 'ave a word."

Khan put his finger to his mouth. They sat there in silence.

"'Allo, is anyone there? Jim?"

To Jim's horror, he saw the hunched form of an old lady come shuffling into the lounge.

"I can't see so well, I left me glasses in the sink. I 'ope you don't mind me using the spare key…"

She squinted around the room. "'Ave you got guests Jim?"

Jim looked at her; she seemed vaguely familiar.

She shuffled painfully over to Hakal Khan. He stood up as she approached.

"'Allo, I'm pleased to meet you deary."

She held out her hand shakily; Khan held out his hand cautiously.

As he did so, she grabbed his hand and, pulling him towards her, smashed a karate punch into his head just below his ear, dealing a crushing blow to the nerve endings there. The shockwave shot through his brain as he collapsed to the floor like a wet pile of washing.

She stood up straight. The little old lady had gone and Harry's wife Sheila, with a grey wig on, stood in her place, albeit with a pinnie still wrapped around her body. She pulled a knife from her sleeve and used it to cut the cable ties binding Ash to the chair.

"Sheila, what the…?"

She shook her head and glanced at Ash.

"Is everybody OK, no injuries?" she said in a clear calm voice. She looked over to where Jim and Mervyn were sitting with their mouths open, unable to speak.

"Here, let me untie you."

"I'd better call this in," said Ash vaguely.

"I think that may be a bad idea DI Kamau. You will not wish to alert Chief Inspector Riley to the failed attempt on your life just yet. You need to think of Detective Sergeant Thompson's safety. Get her and yourself to a place where he can't find you."

Ash shook his head in disbelief. "Who the hell are you?"

"Let's just say for now that I am your Avenging Angel."

She watched Ash's face carefully and saw the reaction – he knew. What he did with that information would seal his fate going forwards.

"You were dealing with a very nasty piece of work in Hakal Khan there."

"How did you get in?" asked Jim in a weak quivery voice.

"I picked your lock, just like Khan did. I watched him do it. Then I waited until he made his move. It was risky but I figured he would want to savour his victim's terror before the kill and in that he didn't disappoint, did he?"

Ash pulled himself to his feet. "I'm going to make contact with Ella. I have no idea what just happened here other than to know that you saved our lives and for that I am in your debt. I trust that between you, this issue will be made to disappear and that I can erase everything that happened here tonight from my memory."

Sheila nodded. "You can indeed DI Kamau, thank you for your understanding."

"No, Madam, thank you." Ash turned and let himself out without a backward glance.

Sheila waited until Ash had left and then turned to Jim and Mervyn.

"Hi guys, bit of a surprise eh?"

"Sheila, what the hell…?"

"Jeremy contacted me shortly after telling you to go to ground. He was very concerned about your safety and rightly so. I saw Khan arrive in his truck just before Inspector Kamau arrived. We were unsure whether Khan was intent on killing Kamau and his Detective Sergeant but suspected he had been hired by their Chief to assassinate them both."

"You work for Jeremy?!"

"Yes Jim, you, your friends, I and many others belong to the same organisation."

"Harry never told us!"

"Harry doesn't know, well, not yet anyway. I hope you'll let me explain it to him first. It might come as a bit of a shock."

"There's no maybe! What a coincidence!"

"Coincidence had nothing to do with it Jim. I happened to catch sight of the letter you were sending to the local paper after you sent a copy to Harry. I thought you might have the right temperament to join the team, so I tipped Jeremy off with regards to your letter. That's why he sent his 'Disgusted from Skegness' letter and the rest, as they say, is history."

"You've been playing me along ever since."

"No, I had my own job to do. I handed over to Jeremy and literally forgot all about you until he contacted me about Khan threatening you. Only then did I know that you had been recruited. And I only knew Mervyn was part of everything when I walked into your lounge. Up until then he was just A.N. Other. Remember, we run on a need-to-know basis. That's what keeps us secure."

Sheila stopped and turned. Khan had started to move, letting out a groan as he did so.

"Please excuse me for a minute, I just need to truss up our little chicken here." She took the remaining cable ties that had fallen from Khan's grasp as he fell and tied his arms and legs to the chair, tightening them hard as she did so.

"I am going to need some plastic sheeting to lay on the floor. Have you got something like that Jim?"

"What? Yeah, I'll just go to the shed and get some."

"Thank you. Then maybe you should get yourselves a drink whilst I prep him up a little."

Sheila laid the plastic sheet out on the floor and between them they lifted Khan and the chair onto the sheet.

"Right, I think you might want to miss the next bit gentlemen. I need him to assist me with a little research."

"What are you going to do?"

"I'm going to ask him certain questions. If, as I suspect, he is initially unwilling to be cooperative, I will apply some persuasion."

"Are you going to hurt him?"

"Most probably more than he could ever imagine was possible Mervyn."

"Good."

Mervyn stood up and made off to the kitchen as he saw Sheila place a gag into Khan's mouth.

"Bloody hell, Sheila of all people! She makes sheep look vicious. I mean, I've never really noticed her when I'm round at Harry's, she sort of blends into the furniture. I couldn't imagine her doing anything more dangerous than trying a new way of boiling a cabbage."

"I think you had better start imagining it. You might want to stay in here for a bit Jim. Sheila is about to work on our friend back there."

"Bloody hell, why here? Don't they normally go to some deserted warehouse with just one chair in the middle and hooks and chains hanging from the roof or something? And what's with the plastic sheet? Do you think he's going to ooze a bit?"

Jim cracked a beer whilst Mervyn warmed some cocoa and threw in a triple rum.

"Look at that Jim, my hands are as steady as a rock. How could that be?"

"Don't know Merv. It's funny how delivering retribution to those in need has a calming effect."

They heard muffled sounds of agony coming from the lounge as they sipped their drinks at the kitchen table.

"Who would have said old Sheila was one of us eh?"

"I'm not sure we match up to Sheila's skills Merv. I still haven't the faintest idea how she took him out like that and the little Dance Macabre going on in there now is a bit beyond anything I could conjure up."

"Hey Jim, you created the Zapper. That was a work of genius."

"I suppose it was actually, eh?"

Sheila popped her head around the kitchen door. "All done," she said brightly.

She came into the kitchen taking off her wig to reveal her normal pixie cut hairstyle.

"Could I maybe join you boys in a drink now?"

CHAPTER 184

Ash had contacted Ella and they had agreed to meet at a pub on the other side of town.

"The Chief wants us dead Ella."

"To what end?"

"He knows that we are on to him – someone at the IOPC grassed on us, probably the same bastard who loaded the encryption app onto the phone. I know I sound paranoid, but the force seems to be rife with bloody corruption. We can trust nobody."

"Suggestions?"

"For now, we lie low. Hopefully he will think that Khan has eliminated both of us."

"There must be somebody we can trust, we are the Metropolitan Police Force after all."

"Yeah, and a great deal of good it's done us so far eh?"

"How do you know all this?"

"Khan is an assassin. We were sent on his trail with that bullshit case of a shop heist to lure us both into his trap. Then by chance another scenario presented itself to Khan wherein he could take us out and a few others as well. He wanted you there."

"At the Spoonwall house yes – the Chief was furious when he found out that I wasn't there with you."

"As far as the Chief knows, the plan has succeeded. I know this is a difficult thing to do but you can't contact anybody until we sort this out, not family, not friends, nobody."

"Hmm, not a big problem there. My friends gave up on me long ago and my family couldn't give a shit."

"Sounds like we are both well suited to solitude."

CHAPTER 185

Mervyn and Jim were having problems coming to terms with the situation in which they now found themselves. The revelation that Sheila was not Sheila was making their heads spin.

"So what is your real name or mustn't we know?"

"Sheila Johnson is my real name. I didn't make it up. Next, you'll be asking if I'm really Harry's wife."

"Are you?"

"Yes, of course. OK, back in the day, I worked with Jeremy and before that I was a terribly unsuccessful actress."

"I would have said you are an incredibly talented actress!"

"Aaav only ever 'ad to play one part dearie," smiled Sheila as she curled into her old lady role.

"But the way you wiped out that Khan bloke in there – that wasn't acting."

"Aah, that used to be my daytime job Jim. I'm sorry to change the subject but I have the pressing matter of Mr Khan in your lounge there."

"Is he OK Sheila?"

"Oh yes, he is perfectly OK. I wouldn't be in here having a chat if he wasn't. He's as dead as a door nail."

"Did you find out what you wanted to know?"

"He sang like a nightingale. Trouble with zealots like him. They always try to kill themselves when they realise you're trying to get them to squeal. Cowards, they cannot stand up to too much pain, but are only too happy to deal it out."

"Not much time for the Muslim faith Sheila?"

"I have all the time in the world for Muslims. People like Khan hide behind the pillars of Islam to sanctify their vile actions. They are the bane of every faithful, righteous Muslim's life. Anyway, suffice to say that he gave the information I needed in return for me ending his pain and his life along with it."

"How do you know he didn't lie?"

"I knew the answers already, I just needed a bit of confirmation. Anyway, getting back to that pressing matter, I need to process him. Can I borrow your wheelie bin?"

"Are you going to make him into pies?"

"Hah, there's an idea, I wonder if they would classify as Halal? No, I've ordered a home delivery – wonderful service, they drop off an M&S chicken tikka with a garlic naan and I give them a corpse."

"I hope they don't recycle," said Jim, mostly to himself, as he watched Mervyn pinch himself.

"Just checking Jim, just checking."

Sheila stood upright. "I'd better get a move on, he's probably beginning to ooze a bit."

"I knew it, I told you there would be some oozing didn't I Merv? Come on, we'll give you a hand. I must say, I'd love to see old Harry's face when you tell him all this."

They watched as Sheila carefully wound the plastic sheeting round Khan's body, fastening the ends with some masking tape where necessary. They then dragged him on a small rug to the back door and tipped him headfirst into the wheelie bin.

Mervyn stepped back panting as he checked out the result. "His legs are still poking out Jim."

"Yeah, I see that, I'll go and get a black dustbin bag."

The bag was duly pulled over his legs and fastened with some more masking tape.

"That looks better eh?"

"Much better Jim. Now what do we do Sheila?"

"We wait for the takeaway which should be here any moment, check that the coast is clear, and off he goes."

"Do you do lots of body dumping Sheila?"

"No, very little. I usually leave the bodies where they are."

Jim and Mervyn exchanged looks.

CHAPTER 186

Chief Inspector Riley tapped his hands on his desk. Where was bloody Khan? Bloody radicals. He didn't have an enormous choice in the matter. There were alternatives, but he could hardly spread his business too far and wide. He did have his reputation to consider. He did his bit in ridding the world of criminal scum. Admittedly they were all about to shop him but that was just a detail. The fact that he kept the best and most ruthless criminals in the South protected was just good business. If he hadn't done it, somebody else would have stepped up to the plate that was for sure. He maintained some semblance of order in the ranks and upheld the status quo.

The police officers he occasionally had to take out of the equation were collateral damage, an omelette and eggs situation. Kamau and Thompson were particularly expendable. He thought of the message that he would soon receive that they were history.

He smiled and looked towards their desks, now empty.

CHAPTER 187

"You know what Ella? I'm starting to realise that whatever happens from here on spells the end of the force for me. I don't have the stomach for it any longer. I can't help feeling I'm fighting for the wrong team. Forever backing off when the accused's rights are threatened, always having to do things by the book. Who wrote that bloody book anyway? The criminal's lawyers most likely."

"With Riley out of the way, things will be different."

"Do you think so? I hope so. I fear it might still be the same bloody book, just somebody else smacking you over the head with it. Yes, Riley is a total chunk of shit, but he exists and flourishes because the system allows him to. We are both very lucky to be having this conversation. If he and his system had not had a spanner thrown in the works, we'd be long gone."

"What will you do Ash?"

"I've got enough money stashed away for a lifetime. I battle to spend a tenth of my salary living the lifestyle I'm used to. Maybe I should just drift for a while. You still love the force don't you Ella?"

"I do, what's the matter with me?"

"Nothing, the force needs people like you to root out worms like Riley. You've got everything it takes to go all the way to the top. Especially now you know not to trust anybody too much on the way."

CHAPTER 188

"You guys don't have to be out here. I can handle the body when the delivery truck arrives."

"No way Sheila, it's the least we can do to help after you saved our lives. We insist, don't we Merv?"

"We do? Oh yes, we do."

The delivery truck arrived, and a short stocky man stepped out with the takeaway in a bag.

Mervyn, in an attempt to show willing, started to move the wheelie bin a bit closer but lost his balance and dropped the bin on its side. As it fell, Khan's body flopped out onto the pavement and his legs popped through the plastic bag Jim had placed there.

"Bloody hell Merv! He's popped out of his wrapping."

As all four looked down at the newly exposed body of Khan, a voice came from behind them.

"I see yer got anuver deadun Jim."

They turned and watched as Doris waddled up and prodded Khan's body with her umbrella.

"Was 'e nicking tiles like the uver one?"

Jim shook his head in a vague way.

"Yer better get rid of 'im Jim before someone phones the fuzz."

Jim and Mervyn watched in a detached way as Sheila and the truck driver rolled Khan's body into the truck, helped along by Doris as she continued to prod his body with her umbrella.

They watched as the truck drove away.

Doris pointed with her umbrella at the receding truck.

"Good to see yer doin' God's work Jim, goodnight."

They watched as Doris gave a little wave and trotted off to her house.

"Do you think our secret's safe gentlemen?"

"Safe as houses Sheila. I think."

"Good," said Sheila as she carried the takeaway into Jim's house.

Jim and Mervyn followed.

"Here's our tikka and naans guys."

Jim looked at the box. "Was he doing a bit of a round trip, gathering a few other stiffs as well?"

"No, I don't think so Jim, why?"

"I'm just wondering what that box has been rubbing up against along the way."

"Oh, don't be silly now. This is one of life's little luxuries, a nice takeaway after a successful assignment. Where do you keep your bowls?"

Sheila didn't seem to notice that, despite her assurances, Jim and Mervyn abstained from any nourishment with the result that there was enough left to take home to Harry.

She pondered on how to break the news to him that he was not married to the person he thought he was. She wondered how he would deal with it. She wondered how she would deal with such information herself.

By the time she had arrived home, she had made up her mind. The direct approach was the way to go, no swerving about, no tangents, just the necessary truth delivered full in the face. She only hoped his body could take the shock.

She waited until Harry had dipped his naan into the gravy before she began. By the time she had revealed all that she had to about her role, his tikka had gone cold and his gravy-soaked naan had flopped onto his trousers.

"You bumped off this assassin who was going to kill Jim and Mervyn?"

"Jim, Mervyn and the police officer, correct."

"With your bare hands?"

"Yes."

"Do you do this a lot?"

"You don't need to know that."

"Oh, so what do I need to know?"

"Everything I have told you."

"And you work for the same bloke as we, er, Jim and Mervyn do?"

"Yes."

"And it was because of you that Jim was contacted by this Jeremy guy?"

"Correct!"

Despite the rather alarming news that his sweet wife was a cold-blooded killer, he couldn't deny the dark thrill that accompanied it. Never again would she just be his dear wife who cleared out attics, slept beside him at night (unless he was snoring a lot) and made the best Yorkshire puddings in the world. She had transcended onto another plane. He briefly wondered how many she had slaughtered. But he let the thought drift away in the fresh new breeze of wonder that he now felt for her.

It thus came as a bit of a shock when his thoughts turned in on themselves and his situation. Did she know he was part of the gang? She hadn't made any reference to it. Maybe she didn't need to know, but inwardly he yearned to tell her. His soul wanted to scream out that, despite his endemic cowardice, he had shown some courage on the battlefield as well. He too was doing his bit for the cause, however quivery.

"You've messed your trousers."

"Eh?" Harry's mind started to search within his underpants for incontinence brought on by the startling news.

"There, you've dropped gravy all over them."

He looked down at the stain.

"Oh thank goodness for that." He sighed, closing his eyes and offering up a quick prayer of gratitude.

CHAPTER 189

The way Doris had disturbed them loading Khan's body was nagging at Jim. He needed to find out how she was taking the whole ghastly affair. He knocked gently on her door.

"'Allo Jim, need 'elp wiv another stiff? Just joking, come in."

Jim walked in and saw Archie trotting towards him. He knelt down painfully and scruffed Archie's neck. "Hello Archie my old buddy, how you doing eh?"

"Wanna cuppa Jim or can I get yer sunnink stronger?"

"A scotch would be nice Doris."

"Yeh, I think I'll join yer."

Jim sat in the lounge and watched Doris pour two very generous shots of Chivas.

"There yer go. Cheers."

Doris took a generous slug and sat down opposite Jim.

"First of all, just let me say Jim, you don't 'ave to worry about that body you was getting rid of. If I'd wanted to rat on yer, the fuzz would 'ave been all over you by now. So that's water, and probably that body too, under the bridge."

Jim watched as Doris chuckled at her own joke.

"The second fing is, I 'aven't been completely 'onest wiv yer Jim. But I sort of figure that we both 'ave a couple of secrets we need to keep close to our chests, so here's mine. The times when you've looked after Archie, I wasn't really at me sister's or in 'ospital and all that. I was 'aving it off with this bloke I met some time ago. He's a bit younger than me but I look after meself, do me gym, me eyesight's alright and you need a bit of the uver now and agin don't you? You know 'ow it is?"

Jim wasn't sure whether he was being asked if he knew how it was or not, so he ventured a sort of nod come shake of the head and took a long slug of his scotch.

"You got someone special Jim?"

Jim looked up and saw Archie looking at him expectantly.

"Only old Archie here Doris."

"Aaargh, that's nice eh Archie? You like yer Uncle Jim too don't yer? Me boyfriend is away for a couple a weeks but if yer wanna keep looking after old Archie when 'e gets back, that would 'elp me out with me love life a lot."

"Absolutely no problem Doris, that would be great actually."

"And Jim, if you need any more 'elp wiv stiffs, I'm always here." Jim watched as Doris gave him a wink.

CHAPTER 190

"You know what Jim? I need a bit of a break. I think I need a holiday."

"So do I Mervyn. I wonder if Harry, Sheila and Terence are game, shall I ask them?"

"Why not, we all deserve one I reckon."

Jim phoned Harry and informed them of their plan. He was careful not to mention about Sheila until Harry brought the subject up.

"So, what do you think of Lara Croft, my wife?"

"Yeh, who would have thought it, Harry? I'll tell you this, that Inspector bloke, Merv and I would all have been history if it wasn't for Sheila. She was amazing, like really amazing. One thump and that Khan bloke was history. She was so calm and in control too. Not like us lot. Have you convinced her to join our team yet?"

"Umm, not exactly. I haven't told her. I'm not sure I'm supposed to with all this 'need to know' business floating about."

"Bollocks man, you can't keep schtum. What if you got taken out and she wasn't there to help us, I mean you?"

"I see where this is going – we let old Sheila know just enough to worry about us stumbling into shit, so she can come riding over the hill to save us every time."

"Er, yeh, something like that."

"Hmm, I need to give that some thought. Where are you thinking of going?"

"Well, I don't know about you but I'm not up to marching all over the place. I was thinking maybe we could park up and let the sites come to us, sort of thing."

"So what do we do? Sit in your lounge, get pissed and watch the bloody Travel Show on telly?"

"No, you silly arse, I'm talking about taking a cruise somewhere."

"Oh right, that could be fun. Are there still places available?"

"Don't know. Not sure of the prices, got to be a bit careful these days."

Suddenly a thought came to Harry. "Hey, I've got a brilliant idea. Why don't we use the money Rebecca gave us for that pile of crap I cobbled together?"

"That's your money Harry, we can't take that."

"What absolute bollocks, we all came up with the art scheme. That money would never have floated in without us all participating, it could have gone to any of us, we were all as useless as one another. It would make me feel way better about accepting it if it was going to a good cause."

"Well maybe…"

"Good Jim, that's settled then. Sheila and I are in. Well, I think she's in, better check."

"I'll give Terence a call and I suppose we had better let Jeremy know we are taking a break."

CHAPTER 191

Harry was slightly hesitant about suggesting a holiday again after the Paris fiasco. He had messed that up royally thanks to his own faint heartedness. He knew that keeping his involvement with Jim and Mervyn secret would never last. Sheila was obviously far more in tune than he had ever given her credit for. It was only a matter of time before he was rumbled.

"Er, Sheila, I, er, need to have a bit of a word."

Sheila looked up as he came into the kitchen. "Are you having an affair?"

"What? No, nothing like that. It's about Jim and Mervyn's team. I'm sort of part of it as well. I delivered poisoned pizzas to a load of rotten people and fried this cat killer bloke and…"

Sheila came over to Harry and put her finger to his lips and then kissed him on the cheek.

"No need for me to know. Just know that I am intensely proud of you and love you dearly."

Harry looked down shyly. "We're like that Mr and Mrs Smith film. We've both found out that we are assassins kind of."

"Yes, it's quite romantic isn't it?"

"Jim has suggested we all go on holiday together. What do you think?"

"Oh no, not another camping outing to Margate."

"No, nothing like that. We were thinking of maybe going on a cruise."

Sheila put down her dish towel. "Really?"

"Yeh thought it would be nice."

"You're right, it would be."

"Any idea where we should go?"

"Leave it to me Harry, I'll get back to you in an hour, OK?"

CHAPTER 192

The failure of Khan to eradicate both Ash and Ella had posed a serious problem for Riley. He had decided the day previously to put through a promotion for Ella as an additional smoke screen to protect himself from suspicion. He fully expected her demise before the promotion could come into effect.

When he received the news that a body matching Khan's description had been discovered close to the police station, he knew things could rapidly unravel – if they searched Khan's body, they might find something leading back to him. He immediately took sole command of the case and was on the scene in less than five minutes.

The body had been found down an alleyway by an old homeless person. When he arrived on the scene, he immediately dismissed the constable on duty after having the homeless person pointed out to him. She was sitting on a wall not far from the body, looking very down.

Riley walked up to her. If there was anything on Khan's body, she might have already stolen it.

He looked down at the body and could see that the inside pocket of the jacket lay open and empty.

"What did you take from him?"

"Nuffink."

After looking to see the coast was clear, Riley grabbed her by the arm and lifted her closer to his face. "Don't lie to me you old bitch. I'll shake the living shit out of you."

"You're 'urtin' me," she whimpered.

"Good. Where is it?"

"Here!"

He felt a sudden pain in his temple milliseconds before the lights went out. The Bluebottle would fly no more.

CHAPTER 193

Ash sat in his study and stretched. The old body was not as fresh as it used to be. There was a tender patch on his neck where Khan had put a sleeper hold on him. If he'd been twenty years younger he could have taken Khan… maybe. He pondered the odds of his survival that night and decided that they were very long indeed.

Saved by the Avenging Angel, the very being he had been hunting down. How many people get to be saved by their prey? Not many, those were long odds too. He was about to go to bed when he heard somebody knocking at his door. He cursed and went to open it. A woman of about his age stood on the doorstep. He screwed his eyes up, using the light in the passage to try and identify her.

"Detective Inspector Kamau?"

"Yes."

"I trust you have recovered from your encounter with Mr Khan the other night?"

It hit him like a train. There in front of him stood his Avenging Angel, albeit with different hair.

He instinctively went on the defensive and then, just as quickly, realised how ineffective he would be against this person. He let his shoulders relax and stood back from the door.

"Come in ma'am."

"I hope I'm not arriving at an inconvenient moment, but I feel there is unfinished business between us."

Again, Ash tensed for a moment before the inevitability of the situation took hold of him again.

Ash showed her to the lounge.

"What do you want with me?"

"Let me paint a scenario if I may. You have been investigating several suspicious deaths that you believe are connected. These deaths have occurred in all cases to people who, in a just world, would have been incarcerated. It has been your duty to prevent any more of these people dying. You and another member of your team have also been subject to an attempt to murder you both by a senior member of the very police force you are part of. All this has left you somewhat jaundiced towards the system that you have given your life to support. Would I be correct?"

"Go on."

"I suspect that you are preparing to step back from all this and to turn your back on everything your career is supposed to stand for."

"What if I am?"

"I am here to offer an alternative. One that would allow you to fulfil your ambitions in a way that is not impeded by inefficient systems."

"You want me to kill people?"

"It's not about what I want but what you want. If you don't want to kill people, as you put it, then don't. Use your skills in other ways."

"Like what?"

"Bring people to justice."

"Kill people."

"Detective Inspector. You know what I am talking about. If you wish to be obtuse that is your choice. You only have to say go and you will never see me again."

"What if I try to arrest you?"

"Do you want to?"

"No, I don't."

"Here is a number you can contact any time day or night. You can keep it or flush it down the toilet. The choice is yours. I will leave you now and hope that you have a pleasant evening. Goodbye Detective Inspector."

Ash watched as she stood and turned, went to the front door and let herself out onto the street, closing the door quietly behind her.

He went to the drawer and opened it. He looked at the platypus lying there. He picked it up and walked to the fireplace and threw it into the flames.

CHAPTER 194

It was a bright fresh morning in Southampton. Jim and his friends leaned on the deck railing of the ship and looked out across the harbour.

"Well, I must say Sheila, your choice of cruise seems very nice. I've never been to the Far East before. It sounds very intriguing. What made you choose this one?"

"Oh, this and that Mervyn. There is one passenger travelling with us who I have always wanted to meet."

"Really?"

Jim was about to ask who it was when he saw somebody he recognised on the deck and walked over to him.

"Hi Jeremy, what are you doing here?"

"I could ask you the same question Jim, but I actually know the answer. I hope you don't mind me being around?"

"Not at all, the more the merrier – unless the need-to-know thing is still in force of course."

"What the hell, Jim. Let's get together. Just because we shouldn't compare notes all the time doesn't mean we can't have a good time."

"Great, let me introduce you to the gang. You already know Sheila over there of course. This is Harry, her husband, Mervyn and Terence. Are you here on your own Jeremy?"

"Not entirely, I'm meeting somebody who I am told could be a worthy addition to our team. You'll meet him yourself later."

Jim held out his hands and looked around. "Wow, he gets a way better reception than bloody McDonald's – he must be good!"

"Hah, yeh, well there is an ulterior motive, but we don't need to discuss that just yet."

"Well, it's great to have you here Jeremy. Here, help yourselves to some champagne."

"It's all rather grand I must say, I've never been on a cruise before."

"I'm sure you are going to love it Mervyn."

"Yes, I rather think I am. Oh Lord, no, not him. This can't be happening!"

"What's up Merv?" Jim followed Mervyn's gaze and dropped his glass.

There, walking purposefully across the deck in their direction, was Detective Inspector Ash Kamau.

CHAPTER 195

The news of Chief Inspector Riley's tragic death rippled through the station. Everybody had been celebrating Detective Sergeant Thompson's promotion to Detective Inspector when the news came in and dampened everybody's spirits. The only person in the station who did not share the same amount of shock was Ella. She had been informed by Ash that Riley was history the night before and that it was safe to return to work.

"Congratulations Sarg, oops, I mean Inspector, well done."

Ella smiled and nodded graciously. The promotion had caught her completely by surprise and whilst she knew Riley's motives were nefarious, she took Ash's advice and grabbed the opportunity with both hands.

"You deserve it, Ella," Ash had told her on the phone when she told him the news. "At least some good came out of that burst arsehole after all."

CHAPTER 196

Jeremy turned to see what Jim and Mervyn were so concerned about. He saw Ash one step away from them and turned back towards the group.

"Gentlemen, I understand that you have all had the pleasure of Ash Kamau's company previously. But what you probably did not know is that Ash has decided to relinquish his previous title and retire from the police force. He is now Mr Kamau, the newest member of our organisation."

Ash looked from one member to the next with raised eyebrows, waiting for their comments.

Jim shook his head. "This is a bit weird, I'm going to need a bit of time to sort this out in my brain. Whenever I see you, I sort of get anxious, I can't help it."

Ash looked directly at Jim. "I understand those feelings entirely Mr Spoonwall. Between you, Mr Pearce and Mr Johnson over there, you have given me more grey hairs, sleepless nights and indigestion than I thought was possible."

"What made you decide to come over to our side so to speak?"

"That lady there." Ash nodded towards Sheila. "She just laid my thoughts out in a straight line. I could either do something with the rest of my life or just walk away from everything. The latter just became too depressing to contemplate."

"It's going to be way more comforting having you batting on our side Inspector, I mean Mr Kamau."

"Likewise, I can tell you. There are so many questions I would like to ask but have been told to let them rest. There is one that I just have to know the answer to. May I?"

Jim looked at Jeremy.

"It's up to you Jim, it's up to you."

"OK, fire away, one question."

"That bloody hedge trimmer – could it really cook steaks?"

"Yes, it could and it did, they were very juicy too, ask Mervyn."

Mervyn nodded vaguely.

"OK and the platypus…"

"Sorry, one question, that was it."

"Damn!"

Mervyn looked down at his glass, now half empty. "I'm just a little scared that I might miss the thrill of the chase a bit on this cruise."

Sheila came over and put her arms around him. "Don't worry Mervyn, do you see that oriental gentleman over there? He is Mr Lac Long Bao, the largest dealer of rhino horn in the world. I especially picked this cruise so that we can get acquainted. We want to give him a good time, don't we?"

Mervyn looked up at Sheila and nodded.

Jeremy charged all their glasses.

"Well, here's thanks to the providence that finds us all safe and that will hopefully look over us on this cruise and beyond."

Their cheers were drowned out by the ship's horn as it announced its departure.

THE END

BREAKING NEWS:

The body of a man found washed up today on a Spanish beach north of Vigo has been identified as Mr Lac Long Bao, a Vietnamese businessman. The body, dressed in women's clothing, was found tied to an inflatable toy rhinoceros. Mr Bao went missing after last being seen on a luxury cruise ship bound for Singapore. The investigation is ongoing.

ABOUT THE AUTHOR

Paul was born in Hackney, London, in 1948. He studied as a Mining Engineer at Nottingham University and went off to work on the South African Gold Mines for several years. In 1996 he started a software house developing programs for the mining industry based in Johannesburg.

After handing over the reins of the business to his son, he decided to try his hand at writing.

This book is one of the results.

Printed in Great Britain
by Amazon